ON THUNDER ROAD

Michael Alan Shapiro

Stone Street Publishing
Orlando, Florida

Acknowledgements and Dedication

I would like to thank my editor, Alexander Braddell, for his insightful commentary and patient line edit.

I would like to dedicate this work to all the men and women who served in Vietnam and to the families that waited for them to come home.

Michael Alan Shapiro
March, 2020

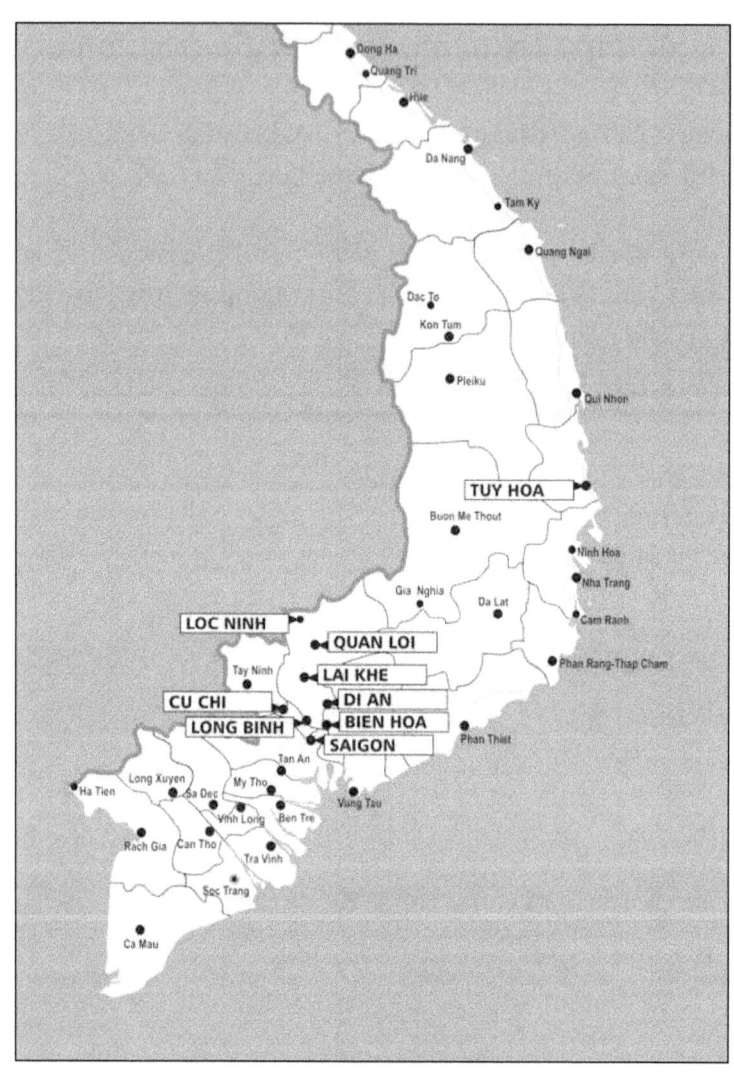

SOUTH VIETNAM

iv

Chapter One
The Wind Cries, Mary

July 1967

We marched up the hill in the dark, six hundred soldiers carrying heavy duffel bags over our shoulders. The sound of our stomping boots on the asphalt road in rhythm with the cadence called out by the drill sergeants. The road grew steeper and I stumbled, still half asleep. I had to grunt as we made the top of the hill and stopped alongside railroad tracks to wait for the troop train. The landscape lit by countless stars, all I could see of the men around me were their cigarettes in the dark. As we waited the first light of dawn broke the night's hold over the land. Color slowly returned to the Colorado landscape. Pike's Peak and the snow-capped Rocky Mountains towered above us. To the east the Great Plains stretched wide and flat to the horizon. Sunlight struck a column of cumulus clouds and they flamed red, faded to gold and now were as white as cotton.

Overhead an Air Force jet ran a white vapor trail across the sky. I looked up to follow it but the sunlight made me blink. My head throbbed from the tequila we had finished in the dark as we waited in chow line before the march up to the mesa. I needed my sunglasses but there was no use in pulling them out of my duffel bag; one of the Sergeants would only confiscate them.

My gut hurt too, not from the tequila but from boredom. Only the majesty of the Rocky Mountains helped ease the impatience that gnawed inside me.

Next to me, Kirshner rocked from one foot to the other.

"Can we sit down, Sarge?" he suddenly called out.

"Hell no," Platoon Sergeant Mumford hollered back.

"They got us up at three in the morning so we could come out here and stand around," Kirshner grimaced. Dimples in his cheeks matched the cleft in his chin. "Hurry up and wait. Hurry up and wait. God damn them!"

"I feel like shit," I said. "The air's so dry I can't swallow."

"Want to eat the worm now?" he asked me.

I looked up at him. "Shut up, Kirshner. You'll make me puke. Besides, you don't look so hot either."

"That tequila got me good too," he said. "How'd they come up with that in the first place anyway? Those two guys must have been really fucked up. 'Hey, put that worm in the tequila bottle and then we'll eat it, okay?'"

"What makes you think it was two guys?" I asked.

"It had to be," Kirshner said. "One thought it up but somebody else had to agree it was a good idea."

"I see, and how did the worm feel about it?"

Kirshner crossed his eyes, sucked in his cheeks, and belched.

I laughed. "I bet the worm didn't look half as bad as you."

"Sure," Kirshner laughed, "he'd been laying around in hundred proof longer than me."

"What do you think, two-thirty before they get us out of here?" George O'Donnell asked.

"We'll probably stand here all day," I said, "until they realize no one requisitioned the train."

"Smoke 'em if you got 'em," Sergeant Mumford called out.

"We've been smoking since we got here," Kirshner mumbled, then louder, "Get your head out of your ass, Mumford." I poked him with my elbow. "Ooof," Kirshner groaned. "Now I'm gonna puke."

The men around us laughed, and Sergeant Mumford put his hands on his hips and stared us down. He wore a drill instructor's "Smokey the Bear" hat, his boots had a mirror spit-shine and his shirt was starched and pleated. When he turned away O'Donnell jumped in front of the company and put his hands on his hips. He made a face that looked remarkably like the sarge's and walked back and forth in front of us in Mumford's strutting style.

"What? What are you doing there?" Mumford yelled. "You boys are the goddamn worst I ever did see."

O'Donnell bent over and searched the ground. "What is it you're looking for, O'Don'ee?" Sergeant Mumford asked as he walked up.

"My mind. My mind," O'Donnell said. "I think I've lost my mind." He imitated Groucho Marx's voice; bent over at the waist and with his bushy eyebrows he looked convincing to me. I laughed, then winced from the sharp throb of a headache.

"Goddamn it," Mumford barked, "get back in formation!" He was a coffee-colored man from Mississippi with a manicured pencil mustache. In his early thirties he was a typical lifer; in it for the retirement pay and three sure meals a day. He had twelve years in the army; Korea, Germany and stateside but not a day in combat. We were draftees, in for two years and we didn't give a damn about promotions or retirement.

"Hey, what's that?" I pointed down the tracks.

"Why, it's the morning commuter," O'Donnell said.

"Train's a-coming. Train's a-coming," Sergeant Mumford sang out.

When it stopped the drill sergeants hustled the six hundred soldiers of the Brigade into the old passenger cars. They hurried us along but once on board we waited in the airless train in the high plains heat for another hour and a half. The smell in our car was nearly lethal with body odor and farts when the wheels finally creaked and the train began to roll. We cheered sarcastically.

I looked out the window. "This is goodbye to Fort Carson."

3

"Home of the brave and depraved," O'Donnell said from the seat next to mine.

"Home to us since they shipped us out from Fort Dix," I said. "I remember the first time I saw you, Kirshner." I leaned over his seat back in front of me. "You were scrubbing a urinal with a toothbrush but acting cool, like you were Elvis Presley."

"Yeah, that's right." Kirshner's deep dimples lit up his face. "Scrubbing urinals with toothbrushes. That's got to be good training for later on in life, right? Don't you think?"

"In your case, yes," O'Donnell said.

Kirshner threw a paper cup, O'Donnell threw it back and the trash fight was on.

I fell asleep after lunch. When I woke up my khaki dress uniform had a million wrinkles and my mouth felt glued shut. I looked out the window. It was evening and the moonless night was cold and remote. I had to get some water. I looked under and around my seat but couldn't find my upside-down rowboat hat. Kirshner and O'Donnell both were decoying me into thinking they were asleep. Okay, right. I nodded my head and smiled. Their plan I surmised was for me to be the only soldier with no hat on when we got off the train in Kansas. The sergeants would have a ball with that. I could see it now; "Where's your hat, Gee-bart?" Sergeant Mumford would ask. "You can't find it? First Sergeant Horn, First Sergeant!" he'd call and over would saunter First Sergeant Horn. Horn was a short, stocky man. He was bowlegged and leaned forward when he walked. His ramrod-straight back made his butt stick out. "Is it Gelbart again?" he'd ask Mumford, then put his face into mine so that I'd smell his stale breath. "You've misplaced government property, son. I should send you to the colonel to explain your carelessness with the taxpayer's money."

"Do colonels pay tax, First Sergeant?"

"You wise ass son of a bitch. Get down and give me fifty, NOW!" "Not bad, not bad," I said as I stepped past O'Donnell into the aisle.

In the tiny closet of a bathroom I splashed water on my face and used cupped hands to rinse my mouth. On the way back I saw that Kirshner really was asleep. I took his hat and went to my seat by the window behind him. Outside the train the endless Kansas night streaked by. I could see O'Donnell's reflection in the black glass. At 26, he was six years older than the rest of us. Our first week in basic training I told him that I had volunteered for the draft and he laughed. "You're an idiot, Gebhart." The squad laughed at his John Wayne impression as he mocked me. "You bought into all the bullshit, son. Okay then, over the hill, Gebhart. Kill 'em in hand-to-hand!"

He was right; I was an idiot. I had volunteered for the draft to prove my manhood to the guys in the neighborhood. It was a stupid thing to do, but I couldn't help it. I was raised on war movies; God, Glory and Victory at Sea. My friends warned me I was headed for trouble. They told me that the army was a miserable place and that I should stay in college. They were right. I should have.

I looked out the window. The lights of an isolated farmhouse pierced the darkness of the Kansas prairie. There wasn't anything I could do about it now. I laid my head back and fell asleep.

About midnight, the train rolled through the gates of Fort Riley and the lights went on in the car. A commotion of coughing and complaining woke me up. The soldier next to Kirshner yelled, "Give me my hat, asshole."

"This is my hat, McDermitt," Kirshner said.
"Your hat? Yeah, right." McDermitt grabbed at the hat. Kirshner was six inches taller and twenty pounds heavier but

McDermitt never took shit from anybody. I watched as they wrestled each other to the floor.

"What the hell are you two doing?" Sergeant Mumford yelled as he came into the car from the far doorway. I laughed as I stepped around them. They were the last two off the train, Sergeant Mumford behind them. He made them shout out pushups in front of the formation. "ONE, TWO," Kirshner yelled. "One, Two," McDermott echoed the count. I straightened my hat and smiled.

It was a humid summer night. Heat lightning flashed across the evening sky. The brigade divided up into companies and a fleet of two-and-a-half-ton trucks came and we loaded up. I stood along the rail in back of one of the trucks as it slowly pulled away from the train depot. Bright spotlights lit the roadway and buildings but that late at night the base was deserted and the trucks roared down empty miles of asphalt until they pulled onto a dirt road that led to compound at the edge of a woods. The company poured off the trucks and fell into formation. We were assigned to barracks and I carried my duffel bag into one of the old wooden buildings. Through the screened windows, the humid night air smelled of rain. I picked out a bunk, undressed and fell asleep as distant thunder echoed in the forest.

In the morning after breakfast I stood between Kirshner and O'Donnell in formation.

"What kind of training do they put us through now?" Kirshner asked.

"As long as it keeps us out of Vietnam," O'Donnell said, "they can teach me to knit."

"Atten-hut!" First Sergeant Horn called from the steps of the headquarters building. "Every two weeks this summer," he bellowed, "Rot-cees will be coming in. We've been given the honor of putting those rich smart asses through basic training."

"Now we're the bastards," Kirshner said under his breath.

"Sure are," I said. "What we need is some grass. I'm going to get my girlfriend to send me some so we can have some fun out here."

We were assigned positions as instructors. Some of us would teach parade and close order drills others would lead the three mile hikes. I had qualified as expert in marksmanship and they made me an instructor on the rifle range.

On a rainy afternoon a few weeks later I walked into the barracks and flopped down on my bunk.

"I may only be a private with one stripe," I said to O'Donnell, "but that's one stripe more than these Rot-cees have. I had them doing push-ups in the rain and mud until they hated my guts."

"You may have found your calling," O'Donnell said.
"Some of those guys are all right though," I said. "Potheads just like us."

I noticed a package on my bunk. "Hey, what's this?" I asked O'Donnell.

"It's yours. It came with mail call this morning," he said.
I tore off the brown paper wrapping and took out a bottle of baby powder from a cardboard box. When I pried the lid off, marijuana leaves fell out. The bottle was stuffed with grass. "She sent it! Chicago Green," I said. I smelled the strong, sweet aroma and passed the bottle to O'Donnell. His eyes lit up.

"Hey, what's that?" A skinny, redheaded kid walked up behind O'Donnell.

"It's parsley," I said. I took the bottle back. "My girlfriend sent it to spice up the meals."

"Yeah, right. Let me smell that." He reached for it.

"Easy, Owslee," I said pulling it away. "You'll spill it."

"Aren't you going to share it?"

"No, I'm going to smoke it all myself."

"Come on, man don't be a shithead."

"You idiot. Of course I'm going to share it. Look, why don't we go to the USO tonight? We can smoke some on the way."

"We can take Kyle's Oldsmobile," Owslee said. "He just drove it in today from Fort Carson."

That evening O'Donnell and I met Owslee and Kyle on the blacktop road a quarter mile from the barracks. Ron Kyle was a tall, gangling twenty-two-year-old from the Bay Area.

"Come on, get in," Owslee called to us from the shotgun seat. We jumped into the back of the 1958 Oldsmobile and Kyle drove off.

I lit a joint, took a hit and held it in as long as I could. I reached over the seat and handed it to Kyle. "Hey, Kyle, roll up your window," I said.

He took the joint. "It's too hot. We need the air."

"Yeah, but to save the smoke," I explained.

"We'll be sticking to the seats," Kyle said.

"With this stuff you'll be melting, not sticking."

We finished the joint just as Kyle pulled into the USO parking lot. The club was a faded gray building in the middle of a gravel lot bordered by clipped hedges. We sat for a few minutes inhaling the thick, sweet smoke that filled the hothouse interior of the car. It was a moonless night with a pitch-black sky but the parking lot was lit up bright as day with spotlights. On some unseen signal we opened the four doors in unison and walked into the USO. It was one large room with thirty tables and a bar. Soldiers packed the place. I led the way to a half-empty table in front of the jukebox. Cigarette butts lying in puddles of spilled beer littered the floor. The Beatles song "Norwegian Wood" began to play as we sat down. Each chord flowed through my brain. I saw everyone in the room moving in slow motion and in perfect rhythm to the beat. I could see the vibrations of the notes float out of the jukebox and across the room like fish swimming in water. The lights from the jukebox vibrated with the music.

"I can see sounds and *hear* colors," I said. "Listen... The pink and blue neon lights sound... they sound... pink and blue."

My friends just nodded. I couldn't speak for a while either. When the song ended I said, "Was it me or did that record last a long time?"

"I aged two years," Owslee said.

"You know, this *is* good stuff," O'Donnell laughed.

"Listen, Gebhart," Kyle broke in, "we met a nymphomaniac last night. We're going to go see her again and thought you guys would want to come along."

"Yeah, right," I said.

"No, really," Kyle said. "It's true."

"Honest," Owslee added.

"What's she look like?" I asked.

"Who cares?" O'Donnell said. "When do we leave?"

We listened to a few more records and drank our beers before going back to the car.

Kyle threw the keys to Owslee. "I think you should drive, Sam. I'm tripping. I could hardly figure out how to open the door."

"Sure," Owslee said. "This big Olds is a bad-ass car." Owslee turned to smile at me and O'Donnell. He put it in gear and rolled the big Ninety-Eight out of the lot.

I took another joint from my pocket and lit it.
The speedometer never rose above twenty miles an hour but it felt like we were zooming along. Owslee went over a bump and we all went up together, and down together.

"Nice bump," I said.

"Yeah, find another one," Kyle said. Owslee turned and smiled at me from the front seat.

"You know Owslee," I said, "with your freckles and red hair you look just like Alfred E. Newman."

They laughed, hard. Kyle held his sides; tears rolled down his cheeks. A few minutes later, he was the only one still laughing.

"Hey, Kyle," I said. "Are you laughing because you want to or because you can't stop? You know one time I smoked this stuff and I think I laughed for an hour. I wanted to stop and even forgot what it was that I was laughing about but I couldn't." Kyle's face was twisted in silent laughter. I leaned over the front seat. "So are you laughing because you remember what was so funny or because you can't stop?"

Kyle pounded his leg in agony. I turned to look into O'Donnell's bloodshot eyes. "I think I heard once that a person could actually die from laughing."

"What a way to go," O'Donnell said.

Owslee drove into the little town of Manhattan, Kansas, and parked the Oldsmobile in front of a small, single-story house with a white picket fence and an oak tree in the front yard. Kyle reached over and honked the horn and in a minute a woman in her early thirties came out. She had brown hair and a plain face and was twenty pounds overweight. She wore a yellow chiffon nightgown and I could see her breasts through the thin material.

Kyle got out of the car and let her sit between them in the front seat. Owslee kissed her on the mouth while Kyle felt her up.

O'Donnell and I looked at each other in amazement.

"Ahem," O'Donnell cleared his throat.

"Oh, yeah," Owslee said. "Shirley, meet Paul and George."

Shirley half turned so she could look at us. "Hi guys," she said.

Owslee and Kyle kept feeling her up.

"Hi, Shirley," O'Donnell said.

I nodded to her.

"I'm going in first," Kyle said. He opened the door and took Shirley by the hand and walked her to the house.

"Wow, man. This is great," O'Donnell said.

"She sure gets right to it," I said. "You guys were all over her and she didn't say a thing."

"She loves it," Owslee said. "She's a real pig."

"I love real pigs," O'Donnell said.

"Oh yeah?" I said. "Maybe she'll marry you."

"Yeah, and we could all come over and visit," Owslee added.

O'Donnell slapped him on the top of his head.

"Hey, man, watch my hair," Owslee said.

"Hair?" I said. "Owslee, you don't have hair. You have stubble."

When Kyle came back he looked at me through the car's open window.

"She wants you next, Paul."

"Me? Yeah?"

"Yeah, so are you going or not?"

I looked at O'Donnell and laughed, "Yeah, I'm going."

Shirley waited for me at the front door. "You're cute," she said. "Come on, let's go into my room."

We stopped to kiss in the doorway. She stuck her tongue deep into my mouth and I played with her breasts.

"Should I put on a rubber?" I asked her when we got to her room.

"No, I've taken my pill. It's more fun without it." We sat on her bed.

"Okay, turn over," I said.

"Mmn mmn, no," she said. "I want to see your face."

"From the back is more fun." I didn't want to see her face. But she didn't turn over. "Okay," I said. I took my pants off and she lay back on the pillows and spread her legs. She wasn't pretty, but she wasn't ugly and she was very available.

We climaxed together.

"Send in that other new guy," Shirley said before I had gotten out of her.

"George?"

"Yeah, him. Tell him to come in."

I got up and she threw me a towel. "Okay, sure," I said.

I washed up in her bathroom then walked to the car shaking off a sense of guilt. I saw my girlfriend's face. "It was just for fun, Mary." I rationalized to her spirit within me.

My three friends stared at me from the car.

"Well?" Owslee asked as I got in.

"Well what?"

"Did you do it?"

"Yeah, man. She likes it."

"I told you," Owslee said. "Who did she ask for next?"

"She said George should come in but she was saving her best for you."

"Bless that woman," Owslee said.

"Yeah," Kyle laughed, "it may be sloppy fourths but she won't be dry."

"I'm going in," O'Donnell said.

After O'Donnell, Owslee had his turn, then he and Shirley came out together. She sat between Owslee and Kyle in the front seat.

"Hew," she moaned as they felt her up. "How many men are there in your barracks?" she asked.

"What, where we sleep?" Kyle asked her.

"Yeah, how many men sleep in the same barracks?"

"I guess about fifty," he said.

"Fifty men in the same room?" she asked with interest.

"Well, it's a big room," I said from the back seat.

"I want to go to the barracks with you," Shirley said.

"You can't," Owslee said. "We can't get you on the base."

"You can sneak me in," Shirley said.

"No, we can't," Owslee insisted.

"Sure we can," I said.

"Yeah, in the trunk," O'Donnell agreed.

"No way, man," Owslee argued. "If they found her we'd be court-martialed."

"Yeah," Kyle agreed.

"I'll be quiet," Shirley said.

"She'll be quiet," I repeated.

"She might be," Owslee said, "but fifty guys will be screaming their heads off as she does her rounds."

We all laughed and Shirley went back into the house.

"Man, Owslee," I said as we pulled away, "wait 'til they hear that a nymphomaniac wanted to come to the barracks but you wouldn't let her. They're going to kick your ass."

"It wasn't me," Owslee said, "I wanted her to; it was Kyle."

"What?" Kyle screamed and hit him on the arm. Owslee threw his head back and laughed.

The summer of 1967 broiled with civil unrest and in late August our brigade began riot training. On a smoldering, humid afternoon after a riot training session Sergeant Mumford walked through the barracks. I sat on my footlocker polishing my boots as he passed me.

"From the looks of it," he stopped to say to me, "they'll be calling us up any day now. You'd better take this training a lot more seriously than y'all did today."

"I'm not going to Detroit or anywhere else to fight black Americans," I said. "We should be going down south to kill the Ku Klux Klan and the evil sons of bitches down there. Don't you think, Sarge?"

"You'll go where you're ordered to," Mumford said.

"Is that how it is, Sarge? You'll do whatever they tell you to whether you believe in it or not?"

"Damn right. I'm a soldier and I follow orders."

"Yeah, well, I'm not going to follow those orders," I said.

"Yes, you will or y'all go to jail." Sergeant Mumford raised his voice and nodded his head to emphasize his words.

"Well, jail it is then." I looked up at him. "That's not what I came into the army to do."

A couple of others echoed my objection. Mumford cursed us but gave up and went to the NCO's quarters on the second floor.

The brigade wasn't called in for the riots but a few weeks later there was a special evening formation held and while frogs and crickets sang an orgasmic mad chorus under a half moon, First Sergeant Horn stood on the steps of the headquarters' building with a typed list of names in his hand. We joked around until Horn called us to attention.

"The following people are granted thirty days leave," he shouted, "after which they'll report to Oakland and will ship out to Viet-naam."

A buzz of excitement spread among the men.

"Hold it down," he yelled. "You're at attention, goddamn it!

"Okay. Now then, when your name's called, I want to hear from you. Abel, Joseph."

"Yo!" I heard PFC Abel yell from the next platoon.

"Alonzo, Tony,"

"Yo!"

"Aronson, George..."

I recognized each of my friends' names and heard their voices in the dark.

"Gebhart, Paul."

I felt my face flush. "Yo!" I called out.

As soon as the formation was dismissed there was a wild dash for the pay phones. When it was my turn I made plane reservations then called, Mary.

"Hi, hon, it's me," I said when she answered. "Listen, I've got some bad news."

"I've got some news too," she said. "But you go first."

"I'm coming home for thirty days then I have to report to Oakland on my way to Vietnam."

"Paul, I'm pregnant," Mary cried. I felt her hurt and fear go through me as if it were my own.

"Everything will be all right," I said. "We've talked about getting married. I think we should. Will you marry me?"

"We don't have to," Mary said as she caught her breath. "My parents said I could keep the baby and live at home with them. They said I shouldn't marry you."

"Is that what you want to do?"

"No. Paul, I love you."

"I love you too, Mary. So, will you marry me?"

"Okay," she said.

"Feel better?"

"Yes. Hurry home to me."

"I will, hon. I'm leaving here in three days. I just booked a flight out of Kansas City. It's United 2150. It lands at JFK at 6:30."

"I'll pick you up."

"Great, I can't wait to see you."

"I love you, Paul."

"I love you too, Mary."

I called my parents next. It wasn't easy explaining to them that I was on my way to Vietnam but I was going to marry Mary before I shipped out. And oh yeah, she was pregnant with our first child. I guess by now they had given up trying to talk sense into me but I could tell they were worried about me. I was worried about me too but mostly I felt happy. I was going to see Mary. The baby must have been conceived when I was home on leave for two weeks in July. I had a warm feeling about becoming a father. I didn't have any reservations about marrying Mary either. We had dated since high school and was the first girl I ever went all the way with. It was true love between us and I knew she felt that way too.

Arriving at night into JFK three nights later; metropolitan New York laid out like a vibrating carpet of lights below, I knew I was home. Mary was at the gate. She was wearing a knee-length yellow summer dress. Her shoulders and freshly-shaved legs were a smooth, olive tone. She wore her brown hair shoulder length. The color highlighted her hazel eyes. She was tan and wore a little makeup; dark eye shadow and red lipstick. Her smile reflected her good nature. She was 5 foot 2 with straight-up breasts and a butt that gave me a hard-on every time I saw it. I held her and we rubbed together as we kissed. I loved her and was a lucky man to have her love me.

We drove to my parents' place and made love all night.

We were married in a civil ceremony two days later. Mary wore a white dress and carried a bouquet of flowers into the judge's chambers. Her parents and mine left the courthouse afterwards and we all drove to Short Hills for a nice dinner.

Mary had rented us a bungalow in Bradley Beach and after dinner we drove to the New Jersey seashore and unpacked our bags.

The next morning I lit a fat joint and laid on the couch and listened to Sergeant Pepper, the Rascals, Dylan and Hendrix and some of my favorite jazz artists like Josef Lateef and Thelonious Monk. Mary stopped smoking marijuana because of the baby but she didn't ask me to. She wanted me to do whatever I wanted.

We took long walks in the afternoons. The shops on the boardwalk were closed and the summertime aroma of French fries and suntan oil had given way to the crisp, salt-air breezes of autumn. I took black-and-white photographs of the seagulls and sandpipers on the deserted beach and we collected pieces of driftwood and seashells to make mobiles.

I held one shell up to the sunlight and showed it to Mary.

"These are works of art," I said. "Each one is so beautifully shaped and colored. Nature is perfect."

Mary touched the shell and I put my arm around her and we walked farther down the beach as the waves crashed rhythmically against the shore. I noticed her staring at me.

"What's the matter?" I asked.

"We're having a baby but you won't be here. I may never see you again."

"I'm sorry things turned out this way," I said.

"I wanted you to stay in school. Why couldn't you stay out of it?"

I turned to face her. "I told you. I wanted to know what combat was like. It was a mistake, okay?"

"Now we're all paying for it." A single teardrop welled up in her eye. It ran down her cheek to the corner of her mouth. I stopped her and kissed the salty tear.

"I'm sorry," I said. We walked across the board walk and down the street towards the bungalow.

"What about the baby?" Mary's voice was restrained. "I may have to raise him never knowing his father."

"I'm coming back, let's get that straight."

The ground was covered with fallen leaves. Their sweet, fermenting odor and the damp, chill autumn air sobered me. We stopped at the corner of the house and I hugged her.

"I checked into it," I said. "If anything happens to me there's ten thousand in life insurance. You'll get that right off. As a widow you'll get VA benefits until you remarry. The baby would get VA benefits until he's eighteen."

"I would never remarry," Mary said. She blew her nose into a hanky. Her cheeks were flushed. "I'll always love you, Paul." She reached up and kissed me.

I looked into her almond eyes and held her close. I kissed her hair. "I know you do."

"My parents would help me out," she said as I held her.

"That's right. So would mine. You'll be okay."

"I want you home with us, Paul."

I pulled back and looked her in the eye. "I'm coming home to you. It'll be a long year but I promise I'll be back. Right now neither of us can do anything about it. Let's just stop talking about it."

The Friday before my leave was up I drove Mary's '65 Chevy Impala from the beach to visit our families. My brother Stephen, just a year younger than me and home from college, was at my parents' house. We played poker, drank beer and kibitzed with my father, Harold. On Saturday night Mary and I went to Jersey City to see her family. Her parents and aunts lived near each other in brick duplexes. They were a tight-knit Sicilian family. Aunt Rosemary cooked an Italian dinner and we sat around the Formica kitchen table drinking homemade red wine with my in-laws, aunts, uncles, and cousins. All of her family wished me good luck and Godspeed home. On Sunday evening Mary and I drove back to the beach.

The next week my thirty-day leave was up but I stayed with her. In bed at night, her eyes red from crying, she'd ask, "Won't you get in trouble?"

"Nah, it'll be okay," I said. I ran my fingertips along her belly and over her breasts. She was nineteen and had a knockout little body.

"Won't they come looking for you?"

"I probably have three or four weeks before they send someone to my parent's house," I said. "Right now the MPs are tracking down guys that are two months late. It'll be all right."

"What are you going to do?" she asked me again.

"I don't know. Maybe I'll stay a couple of days more."

"That would be nice." She kissed my face and shoulders and cuddled into my arms.

October 22nd, two weeks later, I packed my duffel bag, locked up the bungalow and drove to my parents' place. We had a quiet lunch with my mother and father. I felt a sad heaviness in the air but the importance of the moment; the last meal at home also brought a peaceful light into the kitchen. We ate slowly. My father had purchased a riding mower years ago so I would cut the lawn and I joked, "You be careful not to wreck the mower while I'm gone."

He laughed and the atmosphere changed. My mother and Mary recalled with fondness trips we had taken together. My mother was in her forties. She had been a beautiful woman, dark brunette with a trim figure. Her hair was just beginning to turn gray. My father was going bald and had a paunch. A photograph of him in his World War Two army uniform sat on the dining room sideboard. In his twenties he had been athletic and handsome. In the photo he looked into the camera without smiling.

After lunch I left Mary and my mother weeping at the front door as I walked down to the car. As I looked back I saw that my mother had her arm around Mary's shoulders; tears came to my eyes but I smiled and waved goodbye.

My father waited with me at Newark Airport. We sat in silence as the other travelers moved about the gate area. Memories from my childhood came to mind. I knew my father loved me but I couldn't remember ever having been hugged or kissed by him.

"You're 20 years old and have a wife and child on the way," my father said. "I was against you getting married. You're too young." He stopped, unable to find the words to sum up his feelings for his oldest son.

"Be smart over there," he said. "Make it home..." His chest heaved a sigh and tears welled up in his eyes.

They announced my flight for boarding. "Well, I guess this is it," I said.

"Please be careful," he said. "And write your mother."

"I will."

We shook hands. Neither of us could find anything else to say and I felt uncomfortable so I turned and walked through the open gateway toward the plane.

I was homesick before the plane even landed at San Francisco. Standing in line with the other soldiers waiting for the bus to Treasure Island, I felt isolated from the civilian world around me. Those people hurrying to their cars were all free. I was trapped.

At Treasure Island the bus parked in front of ivy-covered brick buildings. I went into headquarters and a young clerk with a crew cut took my papers and read my orders.

"You're two weeks late," he said looking up.

"I got sick," I said. "The flu or something."

"You should have called."

"I didn't have your number."

The clerk shook his head. "You're in barracks number seventeen. Take this door here, go to the right and follow the green line." I set off for building number seventeen surprised at his reaction. I had been prepared to serve a week on KP duty but I guess they were so busy processing 15,000 men each month, they were happy if you just showed up.

The green line led into a quadrangle of large brick buildings. I hoisted my duffel bag and climbed the steep flight of stairs up to the second floor. The smell of urine wafted across the barracks room. I picked out a lower bunk and unpacked. Jimi Hendrix's *The Wind Cries, Mary* played loud on a radio.

"This place sucks," a blond kid with a little beer belly and round face said as he unpacked his duffel bag on the bunk next to mine.

Every other item rolled off onto the floor.

"Got any ideas?" I said.

"Yeah, we should go into San Francisco and check out Haight-Ashbury and the flower children."

"I like the sound of it," I said. "Do you know how to get there?"

"Don't worry, I know where it is," he said.

"So how do you get there?" I asked.

"From here?"

I stopped to look at him. "No, from New Jersey."

"Don't worry, I know," he said.

I turned away and finished unpacking my bag.

"You take the bus over the Oakland Bay Bridge," he said.

"Which bus?" I asked without turning around.

"I don't know the number; whatever bus comes by. If it's headed into Oakland and not San Francisco, we'll change downtown then get another one into the city."

"Okay, then what?"

"No sweat. We take the bus that goes to Market Street, get off on Divisidero then change buses for Haight Street."

"Say, what's your name anyway?" I asked.

"Jimmy McLoud," he said with a handshake.

"Nice to meet ya. I'm Paul Gebhart. Why don't we sneak out of here tonight, Jimmy?"

"You'll get arrested if they catch you," the man in the bunk above Jimmy's answered. He had a thin, pockmarked face.

"The hardest part will be the MPs at the front gate," Jimmy agreed.

"We'll just say we didn't know we couldn't leave," I said.

"They'll court-martial you and put you in jail," the other soldier warned.

"Well, I'm for giving it a try," I said.

"Me, too." Jimmy looked at me and laughed. "What the hell."

"What can they do," I said, "send us to Vietnam?"

We waited until everyone left for dinner before putting on our Khaki dress uniforms. We walked out of the quadrangle and boarded the first bus to come by. It did stop at the front gate but the MPs waved us through.

"Man," I said, "sure beats sitting around those barracks."

"Yeah, we lucked out," Jimmy agreed.

As we crossed the Oakland Bay Bridge the San Francisco skyline sparkled in the night. "It will be a year before we see the States again," I said. Neither of us voiced the rest of my thought—if we ever do.

On the other side of the bridge we rode through rush hour traffic to the terminal where we found the cross-town bus.

"Come on, this is our stop." Jimmy nudged me when we got to Divisidero.

"It's just a few blocks." He pointed up the steep hill and we started to climb. We had to lean forward as we walked to fight the force of gravity. Halfway up I had to stop to catch my breath.

"We've humped for ten blocks already," I said. "Are you sure you know where you're going?"

"Absolutely. It's right up there at the next corner. Look, Haight Street."

"Okay, good," I said. "Now left or right?"

"I think right."

"You think?"

"It's right. Yeah. It's right. Ashbury is just a couple of blocks."

We went right on Haight and walked five more blocks before I pulled up again. There were winos crashed in doorways and some pretty tough dudes hanging out on the street corner. "These people don't look like no flower children to me," I said. "This can't be the Haight. I'm going to ask somebody."

I went into a liquor store. When I came out I shook my head. "Say, Jimmy numb-nuts, the guy said that Haight-Ashbury is fourteen blocks back *that* way." I pointed to the way we had come.

"I must have missed a turn," Jimmy said.

"Yeah, your turn when they handed out brains."

Jimmy laughed and caught up to me. After a mile hike we went by a small park; the aroma of incense and marijuana filled the street. A crowd of men with long hair and young women dressed in colorful gypsy clothing loitered on the sidewalks and sat on the stoops in front of old Victorian houses. Psychedelic music blared out of apartment windows.

We stood in front of The Drog Store checking it out.

"Got any joints?" Jimmy asked a tall guy wearing a bright tie-dyed shirt, jeans, and a formal top hat.

The young man stopped, looked over our heads, and whispered. "I got super stuff but it's at the apartment."

"How far?" I asked.

"Just up the block," he said. He looked down at me, "Want to get some?"

"Sure," I said.

"They call me Top Hat," he said. "What do they call you?"

"They call me Moe," I said. "This here is Curly."

Jimmy looked confused but Top Hat nodded. "Okay, Moe, Curly. Follow me."

He led the way to the corner and up the stairs of a four-story apartment house. The place had been nice once but it was beat up now and needed paint and repairs. The wooden steps creaked under our feet. A Bob Dylan album played inside an apartment on the third floor. Top Hat knocked twice then opened the door. Black lights in the living room gave everything an otherworldly appearance. Jimmy smiled and I laughed at his green teeth.

"Take a seat. Relax, man, I'll be right back," Top Hat said.

I sat on the old sofa and Jimmy plopped down on a beanbag. The front door opened and a middle-aged woman came in. She was dressed in loose pants and tee shirt. "You here for the acid?" she asked.

"No, we wanted some weed," Jimmy answered.

"Oh, grass, huh-huh," she nodded and sat down on the sofa by me and waited with us. Top Hat came back into the room with a young woman. She was in her early twenties and pretty, with a turned-up button nose and blue eyes. She wore a tie-dyed sack dress and I could see the outline of her perky tits. Top Hat laid four fat joints on the coffee table.

"They're five bucks apiece," he said. "Good stuff, man. You're gonna trip."

I took out a twenty and handed it to him.

"Where do we smoke it?" I asked Jimmy.

"Well, hey, right here seems fine." He looked at Top Hat and the girl.

"Sure, you can smoke here. No sweat, man," Top Hat said.

I lit one of the joints and handed it to Jimmy then lit another one for myself. I passed mine to the young girl but the old woman intercepted it.

"Thanks," she said.

"Don't mention it," I said.

"You in the army?" the girl asked.

"Yeah," I said.

"Bad vibes," she said.

"What, us?" Jimmy said as he exhaled. "No, not us."

"You're not cops or anything?" she asked.

"God no," I said. "We're in the army is all. This is our last night in the States before we ship out to Vietnam."

"Bad vibes," she said again.

"Quit saying that," Top Hat said.

"They shouldn't go to Vietnam to kill people," she said. "Stay here in the Haight with us and make love not war."

"I'd love to make love," I said. "Really, I'd much prefer it..." I could tell I was stoned now because it all seemed like a movie. "But we can't stay," I said. "We've got to go 'cause we've come this far."

"Why not just leave the army?" she asked.

"They have rules," I said.

"Fool's rules, Fool's rules." She said it a few times then began to sing it. Over and over. "The Fool's rule and make Fool's Rules. Fool's Rules-Fool's Rules." She danced around the room to the heavy Dylan music. The black light and the marijuana had all taken effect and I was slightly unsure of where I was, how I had gotten here and who the hell these people were. In the middle of our lady's "Fool's Rules" song, two teenage girls dressed in flowing silk skirts of purple and orange came into the room from a bedroom off the hallway. They danced and sang with her. The three women whirled round and round, waved their arms in the air and jumped on the coffee table.

"This is crazy here," I said to Jimmy.

"It's cool," he said with green teeth.

It was fun. I wanted all three of the girls but then the old woman, who had pretty much hogged my joint, got up and turned on the ceiling light.

"Whoa!" we all said at once. The harsh bright light put a bitter reality on what had been the black light's magical curvature of space and time.

"Turn it off, turn it off," the girls yelled. Top Hat left the room. I looked at Jimmy.

"We got to go," I said.

"You don't like it?"

"Sure," I said, "but she's right, these uniforms don't go here. We're the freaks, not them."

"Yeah," he agreed. "Say, why don't we go down to Fisherman's Wharf?"

"Cool." I patted him on the shoulder. "Do you know how to get there?" He nodded assuredly.

"Do you?" I asked looking into his bloodshot eyes.

"No," he shook his head, "but we can ask them." He asked the middle-aged woman about the bus and we went outside and waited.

I was stoned and on the ride over the steep hills of San Francisco I had the strange feeling that I was in a book and when it ended I would be sitting by a lake in another time and place and I would close the book and laugh because it never really happened. The night air soon sobered me and as we walked from the bus stop to Fisherman's Wharf it all became very real. Life was as hard and as cold a reality as the cement sidewalk we were on. And like cement once you set something in motion it hardens and there is no turning back. I was in the army and headed to Vietnam in the morning. Those were the cold hard facts.

I heard the sound of congas and bongos from an amphitheater at the end of Meigg's Wharf. We walked towards the music and from the top step of the open-air theater looked down over the scene below us. Several groups of young men and women played guitars and flutes to the rhythm of the drums.

The different jam sessions clashed but to me they sounded like an overture to a modern opera. The lights on Alcatraz reflected off the bay and the evening stars shone overhead. We sat down on the stone steps of the amphitheater and I lit another joint.

"What's it like growing up in New Jersey?" Jimmy asked.

"You learn everything you need to know on the school playground," I said as I passed him the joint.

"Pretty tough, huh?"

"When I was eight years old," I said, "I was playing softball at lunch time when four big kids came over and circled around me. 'You dirty Jew, you Jew, you kike son of a bitch,' they said. They knocked me to the ground and beat me up pretty bad. I was just in third grade and didn't even try to fight back. I lay on the ground and covered my face as they punched and kicked me. A kid named Billy Rostock came over and pushed them away and sat with me until I stopped crying."

Jimmy passed me back the joint. "Sounds too tough for me. I'm glad I didn't grow up there."

"Nah, it wasn't always like that." I took a long toke and passed it back to him and he put it on a roach clip.

"I had a lot of fun as a kid," I said. "I went to school with all kinds of people. They were all my friends: Italians, Polish, Black guys, Puerto Ricans too. I played baseball and wrestled. On a team it didn't matter what color you were or your religion. You were teammates. You know what I mean? I'd fight for them and they'd fight for me."

Jimmy leaned back against the stone steps and followed my gesturing hands.

"We always had a good time," I said. "We hung out at the playground and the big kids showed us the ropes. My dad gave my brother and me a dollar a week allowance. If we couldn't hustle at pool or cards, we were dead broke in a day. I learned to play cards when I was six years old; Acey-Deucy."

Jimmy looked like he was tripping and no longer listening.

"You know that game?" I asked him.

"Acey-Deucy? Yeah, I've played it." He took a hit off the roach like he was sucking milk from a cow, sneaking up on it from underneath. "Shit!" he hollered and flipped it to the ground. He looked at me for sympathy. "I got burnt."

I laughed at him. He picked the roach clip up and put it in his pocket. "I could tell when I first saw you that you were tough."

"Nah, man," I shook my head. "I'm not tough."

"Yeah, you are. You walk tough."

"I'm too small to be really tough but what I am is willing to fight. If you let people know you'll fight if you have to, usually it's them that will back down. Besides, a fight is good for you once in a while. It keeps things interesting."

"How did you get drafted?" Jimmy asked.

"Me and four buddies from high school went to the draft board and upped our draft number."

"You wanted to go to into the army?" He looked incredulous.

"Yeah, well, at the time I did," I said. "I had gotten a wrestling scholarship to Penn State but after my freshman year I didn't want any more school. I was tired of it. And, yeah, this was our war. I was raised that you fought for your country, just like you fought for your friends or for your school and I wanted to know what combat was really like. Now I'm not so sure. I keep going back and forth. Sometimes I feel like I want to go then again I think I'll probably get killed and I should poke my eye out with scissors or something. But I can't do it. Then those thoughts pass and I want to go again."

"Yeah," Jimmy nodded. "I've thought about that too."

"Really?"

"Yeah, of course," he said. "I know going to Vietnam will change me. I'm not sure in what ways, or even if they'll be good changes. I just know my life will be different. But what if I get killed? That would change things a little too much."

"Yeah, right. Well, nothing we can do about it now," I said.

"I don't know. I'm thinking of going back to the Haight and staying there," Jimmy said. "I'll just drop out. That's what I really want to do. I feel like I'm at a crossroads."

We looked out at the black bay waters.

"You're right about that, Jimmy," I said. "We are at a crossroads. Whatever way we chose, it's going to change our lives forever."

It was after midnight when we caught the bus to the base. At a stop near Filmore Jimmy got up and shook my hand.

"I'm going for it, Paul."

"What do you mean?" I asked. He smiled and I understood. "You can't, man." I shook my head. "The MPs will come after you. They'll catch you easy."

"Maybe not," Jimmy said. "I'll get clothes at Goodwill and find a job."

"What about your stuff in the barracks?"

"There's nothing there I need. I'm staying here and dropping out. "

"Man, Jimmy, think about it. You'll be on the run."

"It's the crossroads, Paul. Just like you said and this is the way I should go. I feel it. I can see where it leads me. My hair grows long and I join a band and drop acid. This is where I'm suppose to be, not in Vietnam."

I didn't know what else to say. A part of me wanted to join him. I could send for Mary and we could be hippies having a good time in the Haight but I knew I couldn't do it. If I was still walking after a year in 'Nam, I'd head out to the coast and join them but right now my road led to the jungles. Jimmy pulled the cord and got off the bus. A noisy street sweeper came by and the smell of water and the night air came through the open window.

He waved to me as the bus pulled away and I held my hand up in a half-wave goodbye.

Back on Treasure Island someone called to me as I walked across the darkened barracks.

"Hey, Gebhart! They called your name in the evening formation. You're in trouble."

"Yeah?" I said. "I'm not worried about them disciplining me for a night out."

"They're going to put you in jail," the soldier who had warned me not to go put his two cents in. I hung up my khaki shirt and sat down on the bunk.

"I don't think so," I said. "No, they'll probably put me on the first flight out."

"Where's Jimmy?" he asked.

"Who?"

"The one in the bunk next to yours. Didn't he go with you?"

"No, not with me," I said.

"Where is he then?"

"I have no idea," I said.

In the morning I went to chow with the other men. After breakfast we fell into formation. The quadrangle in the middle of the brick buildings was packed tight with soldiers but the lieutenant in charge called my name right off.

"Yo!" I shouted and the lieutenant with a sergeant by his side, walked over to me.

"Attention!" the sergeant yelled into my face. I snapped to and stared straight ahead.

"Gebhart, you were AWOL last night," the lieutenant said. His voice was high pitched.

"No, Sir!" I shouted.

"No?" the lieutenant said.

I had to smile his voice sounded like an eight-year-old.

"We called your name," he squeaked. "You had a flight out this morning, Gebhart."

"Sorry, Sir."

"Sorry doesn't get it. You were A-W-O-L and missed your flight." He shouted into my face.

I shrugged. "Well, I guess I'll go home then," I said.

I heard the boys laugh behind me. The lieutenant glared. I knew what he was thinking. He could have me court-martialed then I'd spend thirty days in the brig. I also knew it would mean a lot of paperwork for him and one less recruit they could stamp "Shipped to Vietnam."

"Yeah, you're going home okay," the lieutenant said. "Get your goddamn gear. You're on bus 211 at oh-nine hundred. Be on it!"

After the formation I packed my duffel bag and found a seat halfway down the aisle on bus 211. When the buses were all loaded we drove in a caravan to Travis Air Force Base. Drill sergeants waited for us outside an airplane hanger near the runway. We poured out of the buses and they marched us into the hanger.

There must have been seven hundred men inside. Hundreds of bunk beds stacked not two or three, but four high. They had ladders to reach the upper bunks and they stretched in aisles the length of the hanger. It was a sea of beds and a sea of activity; all of it under the hanger's massive high ceiling. Shouts from card games and loud radios reverberated back from the ceiling and walls as if we were in a big cave. I had to walk down several aisles before I found an empty bunk. I lay down but between the never-ending flow of people around me and the thought of leaving, my nerves were on edge and I couldn't sleep.

It wasn't until evening that I realized I hadn't spoken to anyone all day. I stood in the long chow line for a few minutes before I gave up on the thought of food and went outside to smoke the last of the super-dupers.

Except for the bright spotlights around the buildings the night was pitch black. I stepped around to the back of the hanger and lit up. I saw payphones and after I finished the joint I went to call Mary.

"I'm on the first plane in the morning," I told her after the hellos.

"I love you, Paul and I'm scared," she said.
I was stoned and had the giggles. I tried to joke with her to cheer her up but it didn't go over too well. She cried as we said goodbye.

I called my parents next. My mother cried and I heard my father's voice break with emotion. I promised them that I would be careful.

Going back into the hanger after the calls I realized how messed up I must have sounded to them. My family was hurting because of me; what could I have said to make it easier for them? How could I change anything now?

That night as I lay in my bunk the marijuana wore off and I felt miserable. I realized I might have spoken to Mary and my parents for the last time. I wanted to sleep but the bright glare of the lights kept me awake. "They don't even turn out the lights in here!" I said to no one. I felt like grist for the mill, a lamb in the belly of the beast. I tossed and turned and didn't fall asleep until just minutes before the 5 a.m. reveille startled me awake. The trumpet's blare echoed among the high beams and rafters and I joined seven hundred men in the scramble to shower, shave, and eat breakfast.

I couldn't swallow the cold shit-on-a-shingle they featured as the morning special so I boarded one of the buses and waited. Once everyone had loaded the buses drove onto the runway and parked next to four American Airlines commercial jets.

I found a window seat on one of the planes and distracted my own thoughts by studying the faces of the young soldiers as they came aboard. The fooling around had stopped. I think we all felt the same way. As the plane lifted off a clock began to tick inside our minds; one year, a tour of duty or the end of life and an eternity of what?

Chapter Two
The Pungee Pit and
Other Obstacles to Fun

November 1967

We were an hour out when a stewardess rolled the food cart down the aisle. I waved her off. "I'd rather sleep," I said.

"You better eat now while you can." She motioned with her eyes that I should let my tray table down. She was in her forties and used too much hair spray.

"These are the oldest stewardesses I've ever seen," I said when she was gone.

"They get bonus pay for the flights to Vietnam," the soldier in the middle seat said as he opened his utensils and prepared to eat. "The women with the most seniority take them to make extra money."

A black soldier in the aisle seat nodded. "They'll look a whole lot better on the flight home. That is if you're flying up here and not in baggage."

"Very funny," I said.

I picked at my food and looked out the window. Line after line of white-capped waves rose and were absorbed again by the endless Pacific. I hadn't slept for three nights and it didn't take much to put me into a trance. Before the food trays were picked up, I was out.

When the plane landed in Oahu to refuel we disembarked into the modern terminal building. I wanted to call Mary but two dozen sergeants formed a ring around the gate area blocking the exits and the phones. We were kept separated from the flow of civilians.

We smoked and walked around the gate area, escorted by the sergeants to and from the lavatories and snack bars. An hour later they herded us back on board.

On the flight to Guam and no longer able to sleep, I walked the aisles to relieve the tedium. Up and down the plane, soldiers played cards, talked and wrote letters. I spoke to a few of them then finally returned to my seat an hour later. By then half the men on board were up and walking the aisles.

After seven hours the plane landed in Guam. From the top of the gangplank stairs I saw the soldiers ahead of me walk to the shade of the single-story, grey Air Force terminal. The island was flat and despite some palm trees it looked desolate. I took my place in the shade against the wall and lit a cigarette. A light sea breeze blew in from the beach. The smell of the South Pacific and the humidity made me realize that we had traveled into another hemisphere.

We smoked, drank sodas and took turns using the latrines. An hour and a half later we boarded the refueled jet and took off on the last leg of our journey—Guam to the Republic of South Vietnam.

Five hours later, after eighteen hours of flying my muscles ached and I was bleary-eyed. I got up to stretch just as someone behind me yelled; "There it is, 'Nam!"

The plane came alive with conversation. Those not in window seats leaned across to catch a glimpse of their destination. Low green hills ran down to a coastline of narrow white sand beaches. I noticed that the beaches were empty. A red clay dirt road wound inland from the shoreline through green jungle forests. I caught a glimpse of a small village on a hill. A few minutes later, a soldier called out; "It's Bien Hoa."

The base below us was laid out in a rectangular grid, with row after row of metal Quonset huts. Personnel carriers, Jeeps and trucks drove around the base. Fighter jets and rows of helicopters lined the runways on the airfield.

I felt a ball of foreboding and excitement stir in my stomach as we saw two fighter jets take off from the strip of narrow asphalt runway. "Hey! Check them out!" someone shouted. I watched as the planes banked sharply to the left and streaked out over the jungle.

A moment later the wheels of our own plane screeched onto the tarmac. The men fell silent as the jetliner taxied to a row of Quonset huts and stopped. Still silent, we all rose and stood in the aisle as the pilot's voice came on the intercom. "Move away from the airplane as soon as you are on the ground. Move away from the airplane."

My turn came and I stepped out onto the top of the stairs, out of the air-conditioned plane and into a wall of heat and humidity. The sun beat down with such force that I felt as if weights had been placed on my head and shoulders. I walked down the stairway immersed in the pungent odor of damp raw earth and cattle manure. I smelled charcoal being made close by. I was in Vietnam and it didn't feel like home.

"Hustle up, hustle up!" the sergeants shouted to us. "We need to get off the runway. Hustle up!"

I climbed into one of the waiting green army buses and looked through the window. I felt I was seeing a piece of history, South Vietnam in 1967. Unlike the movies this history had dirt and smells and disorganization.

The sweltering hot buses took us to the processing center at the far corner of Bien Hoa where once accounted for we were told to fall out and take a bunk inside any of the nearby barracks. I carried with my duffel bag into one of the prefabricated buildings and found an empty cot and flipped the mattress. I put my duffel bag underneath and went back outside to the shower shed where I washed and changed into fresh fatigues. In the two minutes it took me to walk back to the barracks my new fatigues were soaked in perspiration. It was only slightly cooler inside the barracks. Men played cards or read, napped or wrote letters. I wondered what Jimmy was up to in San Francisco. Did the MPs catch up with him or was he safe in Haight-Ashbury? I lay down on my cot and dozed off dreaming of how it would have been if I had stayed in San Francisco.

The sound of the men going off to dinner woke me. I dressed and walked alone to the mess hut. Going past the headquarters building I stopped and saluted as two soldiers brought down the flag. A circle of white rocks at the base of the flagpole matched the white rocks that lined the red dirt path to the headquarters building. Next to it was the mess hut which unlike the other buildings, metal Quonset huts, was a wooden building. It was a long building with large screened windows. Outside, several hundred men stood in line to get in.

I waited twenty minutes for my turn. The evening trade winds carried a light breeze through the screen windows and made the inside of the mess hut a welcome relief from the blazing sun outside. I passed on the dinner menu, put several pieces of fruit on my tray and found an empty seat. I bit into a plum and suddenly saw my grandmother's face. I remembered swimming with my brother off the end of the wooden dock at her lakeside house in New Jersey. We'd sit on the porch afterwards and she would bring out a bowl of fresh fruit. The red plums were sweet and juicy and we ate them as the sound of cicadas filled the humid summer afternoon.

After sundown, I lay in my bunk and wrote a letter to Mary.

I feel closer to you, even 12,000 miles away, then I do to the men around me. It's like you're inside me and can see what I see. But since you can't, I'll try to describe it. Vietnam feels strange and it's hard to explain why. It's the same old army way of doing things. This processing

37

center could be in Texas. It's alive with activity. Men
and vehicles are constantly coming and going, yet
with all these people around me I still haven't made
any friends. Everyone seems to be in their own world.
The men going home just want to get out. The new men
seem to be in a daze like me, wondering what our fate
will be. Still, it's more than that. Vietnam itself is
strange. It's humid like New Jersey in August but
the smells are more tropical. I can feel I'm near
the equator. Maybe it's not even the weather maybe
it's the fact that I'm in transit. I don't know where
I'm going or what it will be like. I've always lived my
life believing that having fun was the most
important thing but there isn't any fun in this. I'm
as alone and as lost as I've ever been. Maybe it's the
jet lag catching up with me. I hope tomorrow will be
better."

Before I put the pen and paper away I was asleep on
the cot.

The pink light of dawn woke me with a gentle breeze
through the open windows. In the distance a truck motor
labored through gear changes then faded into the chirping of
birds. I got up and dressed and went outside. The morning
air was fresh and cool. I stood and watched as the sky turned
from pink to gold and the barracks' walls brightened with
color. Eight wooden latrine sheds stood in an open
area behind the barracks and as I came closer to them the
odor of ammonia jolted me awake. I went into one of the
sheds. It stunk from feces and urine. Large black flies
hovered over and inside the can. I balanced myself above
the hole, refusing to let my buttocks touch the wooden seat.

The sun rose above the horizon as I set off to the mess hall
for breakfast. Only a few soldiers were in line so I got right in
and put a bowl of cereal and a cup of coffee on my tray. I carried
it to a table by a window where I sat across from two soldiers,
one with dark hair and a scar on his upper lip, the other blond

with a mustache. Both men had dark tans. "Just coming in?" the one with the scar asked me as I sat down.

"Yeah, my second day," I said. "You going home?"

"That's right. Going home. It sounds sweet".

"You been assigned out yet?" the blond soldier with the mustache asked me.

"No, I suppose today though."

"Just hope you stay down here with the First Division," he said.

"Why is that?" I asked.

"The farther north you go the worse it gets. Anything from the central highlands on up is not the place you want to be." The one with the scar nodded his head in agreement.

"I heard that they started filling up openings in the 503rd," he said after he swallowed a mouthful of cereal.

"That's the worst unit," the blond said, "the 503rd Infantry Brigade up in Tuy Hoa. It's bad up there, man. The 503rd arrived in country only a month ago and they don't have it together."

"What do you mean?" I asked.

"They're going out without artillery support," he said.

"No use telling him all of this," the other soldier said. "You've got no choice in the matter anyway."

"How do they decide who goes where?" I asked.

"Who knows?" They both looked at me and shrugged.

Back in the barracks, I opened a book but a commotion of new soldiers arriving from the airfield took my attention. Could that be? Yes, it was the unmistakable laughter of George O'Donnell. I looked at the men coming in the barracks door.

"O'Donnell!" I called out. "Hey, O'Donnell!"

"Hey, Gebhart!" His eyes widened in recognition and he walked to my bunk. "Well, your boyhood dream's come true," he said. "You are now in a war zone."

"Yeah, right." I shook his hand.

39

"So, have you volunteered for any suicide missions yet?" he asked.

"I'm just doing my best to stay off latrine duty," I said.

He unpacked his gear on the bunk next to mine and we went out to explore the base. When we got to the mess hut the line was already forming, 45 minutes before the doors opened. Vietnamese music from a radio drifted through the screened windows. A woman's high-pitched whining voice was accompanied by rhythm-less music.

"It's out of tune or something," I said as we leaned against the shady side of the building.

"I give it a 90," O'Donnell said. "Good melody, pretty hard to dance to."

I noticed a red blotch on his chin. "What happened to your face?" I asked.

"I don't know. I'm getting some kind of rash. I think it was from a mosquito bite."

"Great, there aren't too many of them over here."
"You don't suppose they'd give me a medical discharge, do you?"

"Sure, you just have to ask nice." I said.

Inside the mess hall I passed by the meat and potatoes and put two biscuits on my tray. "Is that all you're having?" a black cook in a white apron asked me from behind the steel gray counter.

"No," I said. "That green apple there will be desert."

"Don't mind him," O'Donnell said. "He grew up on peanut butter and jelly sandwiches. All of this is a bit greasy for him."

The cook laughed, "Yeah, well wait till you live on C rations for a few months. You'll remember this mess hall and wished you'd have loaded up."

"You're probably right," I said.

"Not probably, I am right," he said.

"Let's go find the USO and get a drink after this," O'Donnell said as we found a table and sat down.

"Sounds good to me," I said.

After breakfast we walked to the green Quonset hut with a USO banner hanging above its front doors. We heard loud thumping music coming from Inside. We opened the door and saw the place packed with soldiers standing shoulder to shoulder. The smell of vomit, urine, body odor, cigarettes, and spilled beer were all mixed together in the close humid air. There was a din of noise from the shouting soldiers and thumping soul music. I sipped my beer at the bar and recalled how I first met O'Donnell. We were in the barracks the first week of basic training. The platoon was getting ready for lights-out when a tall, thin white guy from Milwaukee called out; "Hey, O'Donnell, is it true that you acted in some soap opera?"

"'All My Children, that's right," O'Donnell told him.

"Shit, that ain't acting," he said. "No real actor I ever heard of does that junk. Like, Marlon Brando in 'General Hospital,' right?"

In response, O'Donnell, dressed only in his underwear, his face burnt red from the Colorado wind and sun the rest of his body lily white, stood on his footlocker and launched into the soliloquy from Hamlet. "'To be or not to be,'" he declaimed, "'that is the question: whether 'tis nobler in the mind to suffer the slings and arrows of outrageous fortune...'"

There had been the usual commotion going on and at first not everyone was listening. The men who did notice laughed at him but as O'Donnell continued the barracks fell silent.

"To grunt and sweat under a weary life but that the dread of something after death, the undiscovered country from whose bourn no traveler returns.'"

To me it sccmcd hc was bathed in a special light as he explained to each of us our blight.

41

"'Thus conscience does make cowards of us all.'" O'Donnell hung his head and we all cheered him wildly.

"Cowards of us all," I said out loud.

"What's that?" he asked. He had to shout—half the men in the bar were singing at the top of their lungs along to Johnny Cash's *Ring of Fire.*

"Nothing," I said. "Think we can get another pitcher?" I shouted into his ear.

Our talk soon became a reminiscing; telling Kirshner stories and recalling the antics of the other crazies from basic training. I told O'Donnell what I had heard about staying with the 1st Division and not going up north, especially not to the 503rd.

After a day of drinking and laughing we left the USO and walked back to the barracks.

"Remember those Vietnamese women we saw today by the mess?" O'Donnell asked. "They reminded me of little birds."

"Yeah, right," I said.

"No, they do. They chatter to each other and walk with little, close steps." He took small, mincing steps and sashayed like a Geisha girl.

I laughed at him. "You're drunk."

We made our way through the black night to the barracks and I lay down on my cot and was asleep before I had my second boot off. I woke that way early the next morning, one boot on and one off. I needed coffee so I got up and stumbled to the mess hut feeling hungover.

After breakfast O'Donnell and I stood in a formation with several hundred new recruits. O'Donnell was quietly mimicking the officer's southern drawl as he called out the names of the people who had been given assignments: "Jones, Theodore, Second Engineers; Wallace, Herman, First Cavalry." Then, "O'Donnell, George, Five Hundred and

"Third Infantry." O'Donnell was shocked into silence.

"Sorry, George," I said under my breath.

"Gebhart, Paul, First Infantry Division."

"Yo!" I yelled, happy with my good luck.

I felt lucky but disappointed. I wanted O'Donnell and me to be in the same unit.

After formation, O'Donnell and I walked back to the barracks to pick up our gear.

"Well, this is it," I said as we shook hands on the barracks' steps.

"Yeah, take care of yourself," O'Donnell said.

"You, too, man."

"Well, soldier..." O'Donnell took small steps and leaned forward as he walked. Holding his elbows out he was moving and sounding remarkably like John Wayne. "I'm gonna go up there and kick some butt."

I laughed. He was making fun of me but of himself as well. He stopped and turned to look at me. "That's right, men," he said, reproducing John Wayne's broken, deep-voiced staccato. "You follow me to glory, to glory I'm telling you."

We laughed, picked up our duffel bags and headed off in opposite directions.

Behind the headquarters building I climbed into a deuce-and-a-half open truck with about forty other soldiers and found myself a place on the rail. The truck rattled out of Bien Hoa and onto a two-lane dirt road where it joined a stream of local traffic. Vietnamese civilians on bicycles and mopeds jostled for room with ragged men and women traveling on foot. Many of them were weighed down with packages and bundles, fruit and vegetables, even caged birds.

The truck turned right at a crossroads where a sign read "First Infantry Division, Di An." I read it out loud, pronouncing it with a Dee, like Dee-ann.

"It's Zee-On," a soldier a few places down from me said.

"A Dee is a Zee?" I asked.

"It is here," he smiled.

Some miles later I saw the insignia of the First Infantry Division hung over a wooden gate that stretched across the dusty road. The truck drove through the gate and onto the base and stopped in front of division headquarters. We jumped down and formed a line. When it was my turn I entered the office and waited until one of the eight clerks in the room called my name. He went to get a drink at the water cooler while I stood in front of his desk. He was young guy with a crew cut, blonde hair. He thumbed through a pile of papers and typed my name on a list. "You're assigned to Bravo Company, First Battalion, Tenth Infantry." He looked up at me. "Your company's outside of Long Binh, on Highway 13." His tone was formal. He waited to see my reaction but I simply looked back at him. "The First Battalion was just in a big fight in a place called Loc Ninh," he said. "They ran into a regiment of North Vietnamese regulars. It was pretty tough. We heard the body count was over eight hundred."

"That's a lot of dead people," I said. The clerk smiled.

"Yeah, it is."

"Is the battle over yet?" I asked.

"Yeah, it's over, but you're going to see some action with this unit. You catch your ride right outside the door there. They'll be by to pick you up in about twenty minutes. Any questions?"

"Yeah," I said.

"What's that?"

"How do I get your job?"

"Sheer luck," he said. "The day I came in was the day a clerk was leaving. I could type, so here I am."

"I can type," I said.

"Yeah, but I'm not leaving." He laughed and handed me my papers. "Good luck, Gebhart."

I left the air-conditioned office to wait for the truck to Bravo Company. Sitting on the steps in the shade I realized that if I hadn't taken the two extra weeks on leave I would have been in the battle at Loc Ninh my first week in the field. I felt lucky; twice in the same day.

An army pickup with a camouflage canvas spread over its roll bars stopped in front of the headquarters office. From the passenger seat a soldier with a two-day old beard and bloodshot eyes called out, "Bravo Company, First of the Tenth?"

"Yeah, that's me," I shouted. I jumped aboard and sat on my duffel bag in the open truck bed as they drove around the base on the perimeter road. There were no paved roads or brick buildings in Di An. It was a big base though and all the way around the perimeter road other dirt roads intersected it; each road leading to a different unit. The streets were empty. In the heat of the day only the men who had to be were outside. The First Battalion was set up on the northernmost part of the base. The pickup truck pulled into a dirt quadrangle half the size of a football field. There were six wooden barracks and two Quonset huts around it. The soldier with the bloodshot eyes pointed to the nearest Quonset hut.

"That's headquarters. Report in," he said in a quiet voice.

I jumped out of the truck bed and walked over to the headquarters' hut. I left my duffel bag on the wooden steps outside and opened the screen door. A tall floor fan turned slowly behind one of the two desks in the front office. It had no effect on the temperature but did manage to give the office an air of comfort, almost a feeling of luxury. A blond clerk logged me in and said, "Go next door to supply to pick up your gear, then find a bunk in one of the barracks across the way."

My duffel bag had only been in the heat a few minutes but I burned my hand on the canvas strap when I picked it up. I heaved it onto my back and the heat penetrated my khaki shirt. At the second Quonset hut I brought the bag inside with me. The lights were off and I stopped for a moment to let my eyes adjust to the darkness. A supply sergeant sat in the corner on a pile of folded mattresses. He smoked a cigarette and stared down into the pages of a *Playboy*. I waited at the grey steel counter that kept unauthorized personnel out of the long aisles of equipment. After a few minutes he looked up, put his cigarette out on the concrete floor and came over. He looked to be in his late twenties but he moved like an old man. Without saying a word to me he took my papers, initialed them and filed them in a drawer. He walked up and down the aisles and pulled equipment off the shelves and laid everything on the metal counter. He brought an M-16 rifle, six ammo magazines, two boxes of cartridges, a rifle cleaning kit, a steel helmet, a plastic helmet liner and a camouflage helmet cover. He walked down another aisle and brought back a green web belt with suspenders, two green plastic canteens, a rucksack frame with a backpack attached, a green plastic poncho, a thin camouflage poncho liner, a pair of jungle boots, two sets of green fatigues, four pair of green boxer shorts, two green towels, a gray rubber air mattress and an aluminum mess kit. While I put all of these in order, he handed me a shoelace.

"Here," he said, "take your dog tags off of their chain and tie them to this instead."

I looked at the shoelace.

"Tie a couple of knots so the tags can't clank together," he said.

Since I didn't understand what he meant he took the shoelace back and tied two knots three inches apart. He motioned for me to hand him my dog tags. I pulled the chain over my head and handed it to him and he took the two tags off the chain; put the shoe lace through each one, on either side of the knots and handed it back to me. "Okay, now you won't be jiggling around out in the jungle."

"Thanks," I said as I tied the shoelace around my neck.

"Sure. Now, when you go out to the field you have to come back over here to get two hand grenades. Don't forget."

"I won't."

"Good. Now around Zee-On you can load one magazine with shells but you have to keep the magazine out of your rifle while on the base. Unless you're out at the perimeter. Do you understand me?"

"Yes, sergeant."

"Good, because if you are caught with a chambered round, you'll do 30 days hard time. I don't want to hear that no one told you."

"Gotcha," I said.

"Good. Now go find an empty bunk in one of the barracks across the yard."

I hoisted the rucksack filled with my new equipment onto my back and carried my duffel bag and rifle outside and crossed the dusty quadrangle to the row of barracks. My dress uniform was sticking to my body and beads of sweat rolled down my forehead. A Vietnamese woman dressed in black silk pajamas shined boots on the steps of one of the barracks. I smiled to her as I looked through the open door. There were a couple of dozen cots on either side of the rectangular room. The wooden aisle down the middle was five feet wide and led to the door at the other end of the barracks. A group of soldiers sat on bunks in the middle of the room.

"Hey, man, how you doing?" a Puerto Rican soldier called out to me.

I went in, feeling shy and out of place.

"You just coming into country?" another soldier asked me.

"Yeah," I said.

"Well, hey, man, welcome to Bravo Company, First of the Tenth."

"Thanks," I said and shook hands with everyone. They introduced themselves but I didn't get their names.

One of the soldiers pointed out an empty bunk and I dragged my gear to it and began to put my things into a green wooden footlocker at the foot of the bunk. A few of the men followed me.

"Say, is it true they had tanks in the streets in Newark?" a Puerto Rican soldier who looked like Smokey Robinson asked.

"Yeah it's true," I said. "They had my outfit training for riot duty. We told them we'd go to jail before we'd shoot at Americans. That's when they shipped us to 'Nam."

"Shit, man, same as me. I'm Rafael Santos, by the way."

"Paul Gebhart."

"I'm from Bedford Stuyvesant," he said. "Where are you from?"

"New Jersey," I said. "I've never been to Bedford Stuyvesant, but I've heard of it. Isn't it one of those quaint places in New York City where you come out of a store and find your car on crates and all four wheels missing?"

"That's if we can't get it started," Santos laughed. "Listen, I was doing time in the Tombs for burglary but a judge gave me a choice: enlist in the army or go to prison. Man, I think I'd of been better off in prison. This place, it's bad, man." He spoke with a Spanish accent but at a smooth, unhurried pace.

"Hey, you want some grass?" He pulled a joint from his fatigue shirt pocket and looked around the barracks. "It's okay, everyone here is cool."

He lit it and passed it to me. I pulled the sweet, harsh smoke into my lungs and felt it choke me. While I was coughing

Santos casually took the joint out of my hand and took another drag.

"Hey, man, your eyes," he said. "They're bloodshot bad. Are you fucked up or what?"

I had to concentrate to form my words, "I'm what," I nodded.

Santos laughed. "Pretty good shit, huh?"

I thought I said, "Yeah, great," but I may have just thought it because he seemed to be waiting for my answer.

"This the first Vietnamese consa you've smoked?" he asked.

"Yeah." I smiled.

"It fucked me up good the first couple of times too, man. Don't worry, it's okay here. No problems." He turned and yelled down the aisle, "Hey, let's have some music, man." He popped his right-hand fingers as he spoke to emphasize his words.

Do You Like Good Music began to play on the eight-track tape player. They turned the music up loud and Santos and the other men danced in the aisle. I watched them get down. The music made me feel good but when I stood up to dance my feet seemed very far away. I looked down at my boots and swayed. I felt twelve feet tall. Not used to the height, I stumbled off balance, caught myself and held my arms out like I was on a tight rope. Santos pointed at me and laughed.

"I'm a short timer," he yelled over the music as we danced. Well, they danced; I still had my arms out to my sides to keep my balance but I was bouncing in rhythm to the heavy bass line.

"You can't even see me, I'm so short," he yelled. "I'm gone, this is my shadow you see here. I got just eleven days left in country. Can you dig it?"

A black soldier came over after the song finished. His helmet was cocked off to one side and he walked with a cool shuffle; one hand in his pocket, his shoulders bopped up and down in rhythm. He was my height and weight. His skin was dark black and dark sunglasses hid his eyes.

"This is Marion but we call him 'Cool,'" Santos introduced us.

"Hey, man, how ya doing? Que pasa, bro?" Cool said as we shook hands.

I was surprised at how slowly he spoke.

"Nice to meet you," I said.

"Where you from?" Cool asked.

"New Jersey. How about you?"

"Detroit, the Motor City. Yeah, Motown."

I laughed. He *really* talked slow, enjoying each of his own words. "You headed home too?" I asked.

"Nah, shit. I got six motherfucking months left. I got the clap, pretty bad too. They sent me back to Di An for medical."

"Hey, man," Santos interrupted and shook his finger at me, "you watch your dick over here. These Vietnamese women don't *ever* see no doctors."

"Yeah, okay, sure," I said. "I'll be careful."

Santos turned to Cool and said, "Listen, you wanna go over to Charlie with me? There's a brother there I think we can get some morphine syrettes from."

"Yeah," Cool said. "That mutha owes me too."

"You stayin' here?" Santos asked me.

"Yeah," I said, "I think I'm going to write a couple of letters home."

"Okay, see you later," Cool said.

"Be groovy, brother." Santos held up the peace sign and smiled.

"I'm going home, muthafucker," Santos said to Cool as they walked away. "I'm going home!" He put his arm around Cool's shoulders and spoke into his ear. "I'm clean like a muthafucker and I'm going home."

"Yeah, shit man." Cool pushed him away and Santos laughed.

I watched them disappear down the barracks steps as I changed out of my dress uniform.

The barracks here are prefabricated, I wrote Mary. *One story, unfinished clapboard construction. The 2 by 4 wall studs aren't covered with wallboard. The roof framing is exposed too. There are four unscreened windows on either side of the long room. On one side, the windows look out across the dirt field to the two Quonset huts of headquarters and supply. The windows on the other side look to the perimeter dirt road and large bunkers out by the barbed wire on the other side of the road. The jungle begins just fifty yards from there.*

I stopped writing when another soldier came over to say hello. He was tall, over six four but he was skinny, hardly carrying 160 pounds. He had light brown skin and a narrow but handsome face.

He smiled and said, "Hey, man, how you doing? I'm Earl Emery."

"Paul Gebhart."

"You just coming in?" Emery asked.

"Yeah. How about you?"

"I'm just coming back from my R 'n R."

"Oh yeah? Where did you go?"

He smiled, "Bangkok."

"Oh yeah? What's it like there?"

"Oh, man, it's great!" His eyes lit up. "Best place I've ever been. The women are beautiful and man I fucked day and night until my money ran out. I had to hitchhike back to the airport." He sat down on the bunk next to mine. "You've got to go there when you get your R 'n R."

"Yeah, well, that would be nice but I'm not due for R and R until I have six months in country."

"Yeah but when you get it, go there. It's crazy I'm telling you."

"I guess they don't call it bang-cock for nothing, huh?" I said and Emery laughed.

"You've met Santos and Cool?" he asked.

"Yeah, they're okay," I said.

"You bet. That Santos, man he's tough."

"Oh yeah?"

"Oh, shit, yeah. Real fun guy but when the music starts he's right there. He was the machine gunner for Lima platoon."

"Oh yeah?"

"Yeah, and he was the best too. Now that he's going home, they're gonna have a hard time replacing him." Emery's voice got serious. "Sweet Jesus! That man could shoot that gun."

"How come he's still just a PFC?" I asked. "I thought machine gunners were sergeants."

"He should be a sergeant." Emery nodded. "They keep busting him for dope and stuff. He doesn't care and they can't take the gun away from him 'cause he's earned it in action."

I figured I knew just what Emery meant.

We listened to the radio for a while then walked to chow with four other men from the barracks.

"Damn, I wish I was home," Emery said as we went across the dirt field and out to the road that led to the battalion mess hall. "If I was home, I'd be getting me a hamburger, shake and fries right now."

"I miss my woman," I said.

A broad-shouldered soldier named Wizard overheard me. "You?" he said. "Shit, I haven't been with my girl for seven months! That's all I dream about, her in her panties."

"Oohh wee!" the guys hollered.

"That's the same dream I'm having too," Emery said. "Your girl in panties."

Wizard slapped at him and they pretended to fight, circling around each other while we walked down the road, neither of them throwing a real punch.

At the mess hut I took a few bites of the tasteless food then lit a cigarette and listened to the table talk.

Breakfast the next morning was the same; I threw my half-eaten meal into the garbage, lit a cigarette and went back to the barracks. Outside on the steps the mamasan was shining more boots. Vietnamese music played on her radio and I sat down next to her. "How are you?" I said slowly. "My name is Paul."

"I, Yu Chi," she said smiling at me.

Instead of sitting on the steps like I did she squatted down on her haunches like a baseball catcher behind the plate. As I caught glimpses of her crotch Yu Chi showed me photographs of her kids and her husband. He was in the South Vietnamese Army and she was worried about him.

I looked up as a black soldier in khaki dress uniform, laden with duffel bag, rucksack and rifle, walked over from the supply hut. He had a little bouncing shuffle to his step and was wearing dark Wayfarer sunglasses. He was about the same height and weight as me but with smooth, jet-dark black skin and fine features including a thin nose and high cheekbones. At the barracks steps he dropped his duffel bag and pulled the rucksack off his back. "Hey, man, how ya doing?" he asked. His teeth were perfectly white and straight.

"I'm good," I said, holding out my hand. We shook the brothers' handshake: first a regular handshake then a shake with hands clasped around the base of the thumbs, then one more regular shake, all in rhythm: one, two, three.

"I'm Mack Moore," he said. He put one foot up on the first step and balanced his weight with his forearms resting on his leg.

"Where you from, Mack?"

"Phillie, and you?"

"I'm from Union, New Jersey," I said. "But I was born in Newark."

"No shit?" Mack Moore gave the word "shit" a high inflection.

"Hey, you know why they call it New Ark, don't you?" I asked.

"No, why?"

"Because you've got to walk around in twos to be safe there." Moore nodded and laughed.

"Yeah, it's a pretty tough town."

"You just coming into country?" I asked.

"Yeah, just got here today. How 'bout you?"

"Yeah, me too," I said. "I got here yesterday."

I moved over so he could sit on the steps next to me and Yu Chi.

"You married, Mack?" I asked.

"Nah, no way. I got a girlfriend and she's raising our daughter but I ain't getting married or nothing. How 'bout you?"

"Yeah, I got married just before I came over. Mary's pregnant, four months now." I took my wallet out and showed him a couple of photographs.

"Here's some of my girl, Sarah and my little girl Anna." He handed me two pictures from his wallet.

"They're beautiful," I said.

"Your wife too," Mack said. "She looks Italian."

"Yeah, that's right."

I handed him back the photos. "Where did you go for basic training?" I asked.

"Fort Polk, Louisiana," he said.

I pulled back and shook my head. "Oh man, real shit hole. I met a couple of guys who were there. They spoke very highly of the place: hot, humid, in the deep South. A real fun spot they said."

"Yeah, shit, I hated it," Moore said. "I'd hate the fucking army anywhere but to be around them redneck motherfuckers is too much."

Santos came out of the barracks.

"Hey, Santos," I said. "I want you to meet Mack Moore. This is Santos, Mack."

They shook the brothers' hand shake; sliding palms together then slapping the front and back of their palms together.

"Santos is going home in a week," I said.

"Yeah, yeah, man," Santos sang out. "I'll be seeing them beautiful round-eyed women soon. I'm gonna make 'em happy too. They be ready for some action when they see me, Jack. Oh, yeah!" He popped his fingers on both hands.

"Hey, you boys wanna smoke some stuff?" he asked.

"Yeah, sure," I said.

"Hell, yes," Moore said in a falsetto voice and I laughed.

"Let's go out to the showers." Santos motioned toward a freestanding wooden building behind the barracks; four fifty-gallon drums lay on top of the open beams of the roof. We sat on benches in the toweling-off room and Santos lit a joint. I took a long pull and handed it to Moore then leaned back and watched the smoke drift up through the open beams. I felt a buzz from my toes to the tips of my ears and it made me laugh.

There weren't any doors on the toweling-off room. The morning air was cool. Out beyond the perimeter leafy bushes and low trees intertwined with smaller plants to make the jungle look as impenetrable as a fence. A few miles away the ground turned into rolling hills. Floating above the low hills cumulus clouds spread out across the sky. I felt myself on the ground; on the planet earth. I could feel the distance between myself and the people who must be out there under the under the clouds at the horizon.

"Vietnam is beautiful," I said.

"It is," Moore agreed.

"I never heard anyone describe it that way," I said, "but I can see that it's true and it's a pleasant surprise."

"Yes, it is." Moore agreed again.

"It's beautiful alright," Santos said. "but you'll get to hate it and everything about it."

We looked at him, not understanding.

"Every time we go out on a mission we lose men," Santos explained. "After that Vietnam loses its beauty and you get to hate it."

That night when I came back to the barracks the room was filled with soldiers. I passed by men I hadn't met yet and they eyed me suspiciously. I was a raised in a middle class neighborhood, Jewish to boot so being in a room filled with men who looked fresh out of Sing-Sing unnerved me. I felt my stomach tighten.

Electric light bulbs burned from exposed wires hanging from the ceiling. The light from the bare bulbs put a cold impersonal color on everything. It was a warm humid night and we opened both the doors and all of the windows to get some ventilation but the air was dead still and what came in were bugs and mosquitoes. As they talked the soldiers' conversations were punctuated with slaps. I had covered myself in insect repellent only to find that although *I* couldn't stand the smell of it, the mosquitoes didn't mind it at all.

Santos called me over and I sat on a bunk in the middle of the barracks with the other men. We passed a pipe around and the strong sweet aroma of the marijuana mixed with the heavy bug repellent fumes. The smell of the weed and repellent became a part of my high so that I was very aware that I was in Vietnam on a humid jungle night. I took another hit when the pipe came by again. I pulled in the marijuana and held my breath but smoke shot back up out of my lungs and I began to cough.

"They say you get higher if you cough like that." Emery said, as if I were doing something very bright.

"Yeah, right," I coughed. "It's a trick I learned from a hippie in,"—cough—"Haight-Ashbury."

I found my breath and asked Santos, "What was the battle at Loc Ninh like?"

"The North Vietnamese soldiers just walked right out of the jungle in broad daylight," a Mexican named Gonzales answered instead. He had brown skin and a wide, flat nose. "I started shooting at them but the lieutenant couldn't believe it was North Vietnamese." Gonzales shook his head. "He thought it must be a South Vietnamese unit. 'Cease fire, cease fire,' he was yelling to us. 'Cease fire shit,' I yelled back at him. 'That's not an R-VIN unit, that's fucking VC!' And before he could say anything else, they were running up the hill at us. You could tell by their weapons they weren't South Vietnamese. They all had AK-47s.

"The strange thing was—well, one of the strange things," Santos said. "It had been a quiet el-zee. The choppers dropped us off without a shot being fired about two clicks from the village. The battalion patrol moved down a trail from the landing zone towards Loc Ninh but only Recon, Bravo and half of Charlie Company had come into the clearing on the hill across from the hill the village was on. The captain sent Lima and November platoons out to cloverleaf the far tree line..."

"Cloverleaf?" I asked.

"Yeah, the patrol goes into the tree line five to ten yards, then out again into the clearing, then back into the jungle farther down. It looks like a cloverleaf pattern. There were hundreds of North Vietnamese in the woods that lay in the valley between the two hills. Lima walked into an ambush. A company of Vietnamese were in a drainage ditch alongside a grove of rubber trees. Anyway, the shooting started and we were pinned down and the rest of the battalion was stuck in the jungle behind us not even in the clearing yet. The platoons that were in the clearing hardly had time to set up a perimeter before all hell broke loose. We had no idea it was a North Vietnamese Regiment. If it hadn't been for their confusion we would have been overrun that first hour."

"How big is a Vietnamese regiment?" I asked.

"About 3,500 men," he said. Our battalion had about 600 men on the patrol."

"Bad numbers," I said. "I can understand your concern."

"Yeah, it was scary as hell," another soldier said. "There were so many of them and at night they mounted machine guns up in the trees. We were taking fire from all over the place."

"That's no lie either." Santos nodded. "The gun ships and artillery fired all night then at daybreak the fighter jets came in. They flew sortie after sortie all day the second day. That turned the fight around. That and the fact they finally ordered artillery to level the village. They had been trying not to destroy it but there was so much fire coming from Loc Ninh that finally the battalion commander convinced division to take it out."

"Yeah, it was a slaughter," Cool said, popping his fingers for emphasis. "Man, after three days it smelled like you can't believe. All them bodies and body parts rotting in the sun."

"They sent us out on a detail to bury them," Gonzales said. "We pushed them into big holes but we had to wear towels over our noses as we were digging; it smelled bad, man, so we soaked our towels in beer and soda, anything to cover over that death stink."

"Look, I got one of their wallets." A Puerto Rican soldier pulled out a cheap black vinyl wallet and opened it up. "It's got pictures of the guy's wife and kids."

"Here, man, let me see that," Moore said. He looked through it and passed it to me.

I felt a morbid curiosity as I opened it. There was a black and white photograph of a young Vietnamese woman, another of a Vietnamese soldier with the same woman and a third of the woman with two children. The pictures gave me a cold feeling. We were strangers killing strangers but the photos made me see that each of us had a history. Each of us traveled a path of circumstances; circumstances that would bring our paths to cross and fight.

A soldier named Hernandez unbuttoned his fatigue shirt. "Look," he said, "I got hit. It might have been that VC bastard right there that shot me." He pointed to the wallet and shook his head in disgust. He lifted his fatigue shirt and removed the gauze bandage on his chest and showed us a bullet wound.

"You're a lucky mutha," Santos said.

"Yeah, the bullet went through my flack jacket and only scratched the skin," Hernandez said. "Then I got this one too." He held up his right arm to expose another bandage. "I got hit twice at the same, exact time. Damn, those rounds were coming in on us."

"Jesus," I said.

"Yeah, lucky, but unlucky," Santos said. "He don't even get to go to Japan. They just let him recoup here in Di An then they'll send his Latin ass back out to the field."

"No way, man," Hernandez said. "They told me I can work for supply. I don't have to go back out no more."

"Well, that's okay then." Santos slapped palms with him.

"You're getting too short to give them any more chances at you."

"I'm not as short as you though, man," Hernandez laughed.

"Hell, ain't nobody as short as me, muthafucka." Santos danced a samba down the aisle with an imaginary woman. His hips swayed in a slow, sensuous rhythm. He was smooth and I laughed along with the others at his style.

"Look what they gave me." Hernandez opened up a small case and showed us the medal inside.

"It's the Purple Heart," Moore said.

"Yeah. It's pretty nice-looking, huh?" Hernandez passed it around for everyone to get a better look. It was finely made silver medallion hanging from a dark, purple ribbon.

Hernandez took it back and sat on the edge of his cot and stared at it for a long time.

The next morning Mack Moore and I started jungle school at division headquarters. We sat with 60 other new recruits in covered bleachers while the sergeants addressed us from a small stage. It was boring and the heat made me drowsy but I woke up when they demonstrated VC booby traps. The instructor showed us how each one worked and how to identify them while on patrol. There were foot snares and grenades with trip wires but the one that made me cringe was the pungee pit.

"The VC will dig a shallow hole and place sharpened bamboo sticks at the bottom." The sergeant used a pointer to bring our attention to a hole dug next to the stage. "They camouflage the top with foliage and if you step on it, your feet and legs are punctured by needle-sharp bamboo sticks." He pointed to dozens of whittled bamboo blades anchored into the bottom of the pit. The sergeant paused to let it sink in, then with a gleeful smile added, "Because the VC dip the points of the sticks into human feces the victim is guaranteed to get gangrene."

As the troops groaned, I leaned over to Moore. "Nice guys, huh?"

"Yeah, serious, ain't they."

After Booby Trap 101 we went to the firing range and were shown how to set up claymore mines. Each of us detonated one.

After the claymores, on lunch break Mack and I smoked cigarettes and drank sodas in the shade of a building.

"Yeah, there are some bad dudes over here," Mack agreed with my description of some of the soldiers we had met.

"I tell you what, Mack," I said. "I'll cover your back if you'll cover mine."

"Sounds good to me," he said and we shook on it.

"Besides," I said, "together we're three hundred pounds with four fists and feet."

"That's right," Moore laughed as he exhaled the smoke from the joint I had just handed him.

"Hey, Mack," I asked. "What does your father do?"

"I haven't seen him in, I don't know, seven or eight years" he said. "Me and my four brothers were raised by my mother and grandmother. My Dad left us when I was about six."

"I'm sorry." I felt bad I had asked.

"Nah, don't be sorry. I didn't know too many kids in the projects who had fathers staying with them." He looked at me and smiled. "It's different with black folk, Paul. Being on welfare, you can't have a man in the house. They cut you back." Moore's voice was peaceful. I would have been bitter but he didn't appear to be.

"That's just the way it is," he said.

"I wish I had been born rich," I said.

"Nah, that's dreaming." Mack waved me off. "Can't change how you're born or who you are. Life just is the way it is, that's all... I wouldn't want to be no rich motherfucker anyway," he said after a moment's thought. "I like my life just like it is. 'Cept maybe this here Vietnam shit. Hope we get enough pussy. You think there'll be enough pussy, don't you?"

"Pussy?" I said. "There's guys going home with no legs, no arms, some in goddamn body bags and you're worried about getting laid?"

"Hell, yes!" Moore answered in falsetto. "Especially with guys going home with no arms, legs or dicks and some in body bags. I might be one of them too before this here tour is up. I'm gonna make sure I have me some fun first."

After lunch break we returned to the bleachers and as I made my way to a seat a bigger soldier pushed me aside. "Hey!" I said as I grabbed the rail to keep from falling.

"You got a problem?" The soldier turned on me. He was over two hundred pounds and had hair pouring out of the top of his fatigue shirt. I noticed his plump, thick hands.

Moore stood up next to me, tilted his head to one side and smiled. "He got no problem at all," he said. "How 'bout you?"

A sergeant hollered at us and the soldier, still pissed, turned away.

Moore had been as good as his word. "Thanks, Mack," I said. "I owe you one." He laughed but I swore I'd back him if he ever needed it.

Jungle school lasted three days. By the second day I was bored with the war stories and could hardly stay awake. Moore and I leaned into each other to stay erect as we both dozed off. Every once in a while one of us would wake the other with a jerk as our head popped up out of a dream. The lead NCO woke me for good when he yelled out, "Not so fast, I haven't told you about your graduation party yet. Tonight, you're going out on an ambush." I looked at Moore and he raised an eyebrow.

"Y'all will reassemble at the bleachers with your gear at seventeen-hundred hours. Last man here walks point."

Just before 4 o'clock, we put our gear together and walked from Bravo Company across the compound to get a ride over to division headquarters. Santos watched us from the barracks' steps. "Hey, no sweat," he called to me. "There hasn't been an attack on Di An for over a year."

I gave him a casual wave but even with his assurance, I was nervous. When our group reached the bleachers we heard the sergeant call out, "Okay listen up. Hey! Listen up, goddamn it. Okay. Now it's lucky for you I'm short because instead of taking you out three or four hundred yards for this night ambush, I'm going to park us just thirty yards outside the barbed wire."

The troops started to buzz but the sergeant shouted over them, "Hold it down, hold it down, goddamn it!" He waited for quiet. "Now, there's sixty of you greenies with automatic weapons. Y'all are by far the most dangerous thing they'll be out there. Just a couple of weeks ago we took a group out like this for their first ambush. There was movement during the night and ended up two men were killed Both of them were shot by their own people; so for Christ's sake I want all weapons on safety and kept on safety. I don't want *any* shooting. You are not to fire your weapon unless a gook has got his dick stuck up your butt. Any questions?"

"Yeah, Sarge. Just how short are you?" A recruit asked.

"Six months," he answered without blinking an eye. The troops hooted and the other instructors laughed. The sergeant smiled, laughed, then with a wave of his arm yelled, "Okay, move 'em out."

We went past the barbed wire in single file. As we approached the thick brush and trees, less than a hundred feet outside the barbed wire they stopped us and we laid out our gear and sat in the short grass. I could see the lights from the headquarters' barracks and could hear men talking as they walked to and from the latrine sheds inside the perimeter.

"This isn't so bad," I said to Mack.

"Yeah," he said. "Any VC this close to Di An better come with a whole lot of friends."

I realized it was just a maneuver and that the sergeant was right; the danger was the nervous recruits around me armed with M-16s. I lay on my poncho liner looking up at heaven. The night, however peaceful, held danger and uncertainty. I might be safe this close to Di An, but a few miles away it was no-man's land. I heard my stomach gurgle from nerves as I thought of what lay ahead in the next eleven-and-a-half months.

In the morning, soaked with dew, we walked back inside the barbed wire. Moore and I made our way to Bravo Company barracks. The sun had come up and it was already hot. We dropped their gear at the barracks and went to breakfast.

In formation later my name was called for perimeter duty. That night, with Emery and another new recruit named Toby, I walked across the road to a large foxhole. Emery brought a radio with him and we sat on the sandbag roof of the bunker and listened to soul music. I took a joint from my pocket, lit it, and handed it to Toby.

"I don't smoke dope," he said disdainfully. He was six foot tall and built solid with blond hair and blue eyes. He was a good-looking guy but he didn't act like a pretty boy.

"Gebhart you're crazy for getting high," Toby said seriously. "My life may depend on you and I don't appreciate you getting messed up around me."

"Don't worry about me, Toby. I'll carry my part of the load." I looked at Emery. He shrugged his shoulders and I passed the joint to him. Toby sat without saying another word.

About ten o'clock we all went inside the foxhole and set up our air mattresses. I had the third watch so I lay down and tried to sleep. Minutes later I felt something biting my balls. "I-YA!" I yelled.

"What?" Emery sat straight up, scared we were under attack.

"Man, something's biting my nuts," I said. I pulled my pants down and looked at myself with a flashlight. I saw three bugs walking across my pubic hair.

"Yiii!" I yelled again and knocked them off.

"Termites," Emery said, looking at the bugs with his flashlight.

"SHIT!" I yelled and squashed the suckers.

"You'd better go back to the barracks and find some powder," Emery said. "Just ask around, somebody will have some."

I went across the road and saw that was Santos up.

"You got any insect powder, man?" I asked.

"What's up?" Hernandez asked from his bunk.

"I got termites. Cheez, it itches me just to think of 'em."

"Here." Santos threw me a small green can.

I dusted myself with white powder and went back out to finish the watch. The termites were gone but I couldn't sleep the rest of the night.

The next day the new recruits got our orders to join Bravo Company in the field. I brought my duffel bag to the supply hut to be stored and was in the barracks packing my rucksack when Santos came over to say goodbye.

"Hey, man, you take care of yourself," he said. "You too, Moore." He sounded sad to see us go.

"You too, man," I said. We shook hands. "Good luck to you."

"Yeah, good luck to you too," Santos said.

I put on my backpack and walked with Moore to the pickup zone. "He stayed stoned," I said on the way across the quadrangle.

Moore stopped and shifted the weight of his pack. "If there's more like him it won't be so bad."

Chapter Three
May I Have Some Purple Haze, Please?

November 1967

The morning Chinook waited at the airfield to take us out to Bravo Company. I walked up the back ramp with the other men and sat on a metal bench in the dim light. We were shoulder to shoulder with our backpacks on and holding our M-16s between our knees. The noise from the engines was too loud to talk over so we sat in silence; each of us in our own world. The Chinook's engines revved and our shoulders rocked together as it lifted off. Flashes of sky and green jungle showed through the small round windows. After a half hour flight the Chinook landed inside the perimeter of Bravo Company. As we touched down and the tailgate lowered we could see purple smoke from smoke grenades that they had popped to guide the Chinook in. I walked down the ramp into a dust storm thrown up by the rotor blades. Soldiers with their heads down, bent over against the tornado of the prop wash ran by me into the hold and carried out supplies. I was barely clear of the Chinook before it lifted off again. I had to turn my back and half bend at the waist to brace myself and keep from being blown over. I felt sand and dirt being driven into my skin and clothes. The deep, thumping, WHUP WHUP WHUP sound of the blades was deafening. The Chinook flew off and I straightened up and looked around. Heat waves shimmered up from the red clay earth.

Jimi Hendrix's *Purple Haze* played on a radio. I paused for a moment to look around. We had landed inside a camp fifty yards wide. It was encircled by barbed wire and ran alongside a two-lane dirt road. The flat roadbed ran for miles in either direction. On both sides of the road a clearing one hundred to two hundred feet wide had been cut out of the thick jungle. Inside the camp smoke from a burning pile of trash wafted up into the still air. Sandbagged foxholes ten yards back from the barbed wire and five to ten yards apart formed a circular perimeter. There were more sandbagged foxholes in the interior of the camp but these were less symmetrically laid out. There was a group of six, a space, then a group of five, another space and another group of five.

Some soldiers sat outside their foxholes playing cards others cleaned their weapons. Men walked to and from the latrines or hauled things across camp. A dozen soldiers worked outside the barbed wire in the clearing that ringed the camp. They were cutting logs and brush and dragging them to a fire to burn. It was hot and very humid and most of the men had their shirts off.

Two tents in the middle of the camp were centers of activity. The large mess tent, big enough to seat fifty people had soldiers on KP duty washing pots and pans. The smaller tent was the company commander's. Several clerks worked at a table outside the open flaps. The grunts at the foxholes didn't have tents but sheltered themselves from the sun by constructing lean-tos with their green, plastic ponchos. I saw soldiers smoking dope and others cigarettes.

I was finally in a combat zone and I was scared. I hadn't counted on that.

"Welcome to Thunder Road," a soldier called out. "New recruits report over to the captain." He pointed us to the smaller of the two tents. Mack, me, Toby, and four other new recruits picked up our gear and walked to where the captain waited for us in front of his tent.

"Welcome to Bravo Company. I'm Captain Allen," he said. He shook our hands and looked each of us straight in the eye.

"He's pretty young for a company commander," I said to Moore when the captain went into his tent to get his clipboard. I put him at about twenty-three years old.

"You are now on Highway 13," Captain Allen said as he came out of the tent. "This is our Ho Chi Minh trail. Whatever goes by vehicle west out of Saigon, goes on Highway 13. We'll be guarding the engineers as they repair it with their earth movers and from our night defensive position here we'll walk patrols into the jungle and sweep for road mines. You are not in the rear when you're on Thunder Road so I expect you to act accordingly." No one said anything.

"Okay, here are your assignments." The captain read from his clipboard. "Mack Moore, Toby Pearce and Paul Gebhart are assigned to Oscar, that's the mortar platoon."

Captain Allen assigned the other four new recruits to rifle platoons, pointed all of us in the right direction and wished us good luck.

I heard James Brown's *I Feel Good* playing at one of the foxholes as we walked through the middle of the camp.

"Hey, what's happening back in the world, bro?" one brother said as he stopped work to look at us. He was muscular and his black skin shined from the sweat of his labor.

"Hey, man! When was the last time you saw a round-eye's pussy?" another black man called out. His gold tooth flashed in the sunlight.

"Hell, these guys are so green they're still pissing water from the States," A skinny white guy yelled from the front of his lean-to.

I dropped my gear next to the mortar pit as the E-7 platoon sergeant came over to meet us. He was a lifer with five stripes and older than the other men, in his thirties. He was a big man, six foot four, two hundred fifty pounds with light brown skin.

"Welcome, men, to Oscar platoon," he said in a southern drawl. He smiled and shook our hands. "I'm Sergeant Bell."

I could tell by his manner that he was happy with the army. He reminded me of my old drill sergeant, Mumford. "This guy would be in heaven back in the States having us police up cigarette butts," I whispered to Moore. Sergeant Bell read from the roster.

"Let's see here, Gee-bart?"

"Geb-hart," I corrected him.

"Ja-bart," the sergeant tried again. He smiled at me and I let it go.

"Anyway," Sergeant Bell went on, "you'll be in Sergeant Delino's squad." He pointed to a Hispanic man sitting by a foxhole. Delino looked over, smiled and gave us a casual, half salute.

"Mack Moore," Bell continued.

"Yo," Moore answered.

The sergeant looked up at him and said, "You'll be with Sergeant Delino too."

Bell looked back at his list. "Toby Pearce?"

"Here," Toby answered.

"You'll be in Gardner's squad." Sergeant Bell motioned to the second mortar where a group of black soldiers sat on the sandbag wall of the pit. They all had their shirts off. Everyone was trim and muscular; only Sergeant Bell carried a few extra pounds. Mack and I shouldered our rucksacks and walked to the mortar pit.

"How you doing, guy? I'm Tony Delino." Delino greeted us and shook our hands. He had a big smile, ruddy complexion and eyes that studied your face when he talked to you.

He introduced us to the rest of the squad.

"You can bunk together in that foxhole near mine." He pointed behind us. Sandbags laid out in the shape of a rectangle made a protected box to place our air mattresses in. We made ourselves at home. It was hot and we took our shirts off. Of all the men Mack Moore had the best build. He was pure muscle, chiseled with definition like a boxer. I was in shape too. I had been a wrestler since third grade and had lifted weights since I was twelve; although my legs were short, my upper body was that of a man forty pounds heavier.

Later that afternoon Sergeant Bell called us back to the mortar pit and asked us about our training.

"I want you to try the fire direction position. Gee-bart," he said when he learned that I had been to college. "Hey, Charles! Charles," he called to a tall, lanky black soldier with a long, thin face. "Come over here a minute and take this man aside." Sergeant Bell pointed to me. "Teach him how to compute. Let me know if you think he can do it."

I followed Charles to one of the mortar pits and sat down next to him on the sandbag wall.

"Have you ever been on a mortar team?" Charles asked me.

"No," I said.

"Okay. Well, it's a little complicated but I'll try to explain what we're doing. We get a map of each area that we go into." He unfolded a map and showed it to me. "Sometimes the lieutenant will fly the area in a recon helicopter and then brief us on the topography. He'll make pencil notes on the map of what he saw." Charles took out a large, round plastic board two-and-a-half feet in diameter which had preprinted compass points on it and a movable straight line that rotated from its center. "We write on the computer board the details of the map." Charles wrote a couple of numbers on the plastic board with a grease pencil to demonstrate.

"Using a compass to align ourselves to north, we now have the board and map set to the ground around us." He demonstrated this by lining the board up with the north on a compass.

He pointed to the five-foot long mortar tube in the center of the pit. "There's a fixed firing pin at the bottom of the tube. When the mortar round is dropped down the tube its primer strikes the firing pin and ignites the internal charge."

He picked up a live mortar round from a stack of them neatly piled along the inside of the mortar pit wall. Pointing to the primer cap on the bottom of the mortar round, he said, "The flash from the primer ignites the internal charge and shoots the mortar back out of the tube. If we want it to travel farther, we attach bags of gunpowder." He showed me several thin, white canvas bags tied around the mortar round.

"Okay." I nodded.

"The distance the mortar travels will depend on the number of charges attached to the round and the angle or elevation of the tube. Theoretically if the round is shot straight up, ninety degrees elevation, it will come right back down the tube, bullet end first." Charles held the mortar round in both hands and pretended that it had just come out of the tube, rolled over at its zenith and fell back down, into the tube.

"That a live round you're playing with?" I asked nervously.

Charles laughed. "Yeah. It's safe. It takes a firing pin to set them off." He put the mortar round down and took out a pencil and notebook.

"So, at forty-five degrees the round shoots farther out. He demonstrated by drawing an arch with his pencil. "We have a mortar manual with tables that tell us the number of charges needed at each elevation for any given distance. For example…" He thumbed through the paperback manual and found a table to show me. "A charge one, at forty-five degrees elevation will land the round 100 yards out. A charge two at the same forty-five degrees will land 110 yards. But a charge two at sixty-five degrees will land at 100 yards, it just travels higher."

He drew a higher arch on the paper and I nodded.

"We want to use the lowest charge possible whenever we can. That's important because you don't want to hit the helicopters or fighter jets. "The only other computation is the direction. Like I said, we use our compasses to get our maps aligned with the real ground around us. Those red and white striped poles with the flashlights attached to them are aligned to due north. We can see them at night and help us line up the compass points. We set up the mortar tube so that we're shooting where we want to. Understand?"

"Yeah," I said.

"We go over the maps with the lieutenant and Sergeant Bell at each firebase. They'll point out the trails that they think the VC will use at night and the open areas where they'll be firing their mortars from. A mortar can't be shot from under trees, so we know they're firing at us from clearings. We also compute our tree lines the entire way around the perimeter," he pointed to the tree line with his pencil.

"The reason infantry companies set up in clearings is so the enemy will have to come at us across an open area. If the rifle platoons have to chop down trees to make a clearing than that's what they should do. Having this open area means that there is a tree line around the camp from which the attack will be launched." He paused and sat down next to me. "We wire in the shots to the tree lines so we can kill them there, before they charge us."

"Let's try to compute some targets." Charles pointed to different locations on the map. I calculated the azimuth, direction that is, from the numbers on the board and I used the manual to set the charge and the elevation needed to hit it. "Good, that's right," Charles said as he checked my numbers on the second problem. "The worst situation for a mortar squad is a dud round. The gunner and assistant gunner have to take the mortar tube off of its base plate, turn it almost upside down and slide the round back out. The gunner then has to catch it with his hands and pull it the rest of the way out."

Charles walked to the mortar tube and took it off of its base and swung it upside down. "If the internal charge is late igniting and suddenly goes off, the round will explode and the entire crew would be killed."

"Who has to do that?" I asked.

"It's the gunner's responsibility."

"Wow," I said.

"Yeah, right? Not fun. I've seen them remove a dud round while we were in the in the middle of a firefight, in the rain, at night, with bullets zinging in over our heads and the gunner had to get up on his feet to turn the tube upside down and remove the round."

"Bummer," I said and Charles laughed. It was the first time I had seen him smile.

"We have two first gunners in the platoon." He went on, "As first gunners they have certain rights, like they're exempt from lone patrol. They have reputations, too. Guys say, 'Oh, that's Gardner. He's the gunner in Bravo Company.' You know, there's some respect in being the gunner, just like there is for machine gunners. The two best guys in the platoon are varsity and each has his gun unless someone comes along who can do it better or is steadier under fire."

Charles had relaxed and he studied the features on my face as he spoke. I listened without interrupting or joking. He was telling me how it was on the line and I appreciated it.

He had me mark the computer board with the location of the night's ambush.

"We need to know where our own people are so we don't end up hitting them during the heat of a firefight," he explained.

"I understand," I said.

When I had finished with Charles I walked to a foxhole where the men from Oscar platoon were hanging out. There were two games of Bid Whist being played. One of the men handed me a pipe and I took a toke. I smoked it and drank a beer from the platoon's beer allotment. Some of the men preferred milk, which they drank straight from orange and white milk cartons. An old tape player was blaring out Junior Walker and the All Stars' *Shotgun*. I listened to the table talk. A soldier named Rojas, a tall man who looked like an Apache warrior, smiled and said hi. His jet-black hair had blue highlights in it. He spoke with a slight stutter but his voice had a relaxed pace. Rojas wore his green towel like a serape, keeping the sun off of his shoulders. I liked that idea and decided I would cut a slit in the middle of mine when I went back to my foxhole. Rojas asked me questions about home. What was going on? What was new?

"They're burning down the cities," I said. "There's tanks in Detroit and Newark and..." I stopped short when I noticed Delino had his shirt buttoned up, both sleeves and collar. Rojas saw me stare and said,

"Tony's sick of the sun."

"It's too damn hot to be wearing your shirt buttoned up," I said.

"I'm not here for a tan like you pretty boys," Delino said. He grinned, ear to ear and I shook my head in disbelief.

I watched them play a couple of hands.

"Can you play Bid Whist?" Rojas asked me.

"I know a little bridge," I said.

"I'll explain the rules and after this game, you'll be my partner."

The team we played against was the gunner Gardner and a soldier named Jesse. Rojas sat across from me. Gardner was to my left and Jesse to my right. Jesse was a couple of inches taller than me. He had a muscular build, and dark black skin with a flat, wide nose. He said he was from Georgia. His head bopped up and down as he spoke and I laughed at him when I first noticed it. Jesse stared me down, putting me on edge. My stomach tightened and my hands started to perspire.

"How many brothers and sisters do you have?" Rojas asked me as we played a hand.

"One sister and one brother in college," I said, "and a younger brother still at home. How about you?"

"I have three sisters," Rojas said.

"Where you from?" the gunner Gardner asked me. He was a big man and well built, like a linebacker. I noticed that he had perfectly formed ears and a small nose. His face looked like the ones on classical Greek urns.

"New Jersey," I said.

"I hear only faggots come from New Jersey," Jesse said.

"You heard wrong," I said.

"What college does your brother go to?" Rojas asked.

"He a cock sucker too?" Jesse said.

"Nah," I said. "He saw your brother licking dick and it made him sick."

A big OOH went up from the gallery.

"Don't you be talking 'bout my brother, motherfucker," Jesse said.

"Then stop talking about mine," I answered.

"Knock it off, Jesse," Rojas said.

Jesse ignored him. "You get your white ass beat bad you talk 'bout my family."

"That right?" I said.

"Yeah, that's right, muthafucka."

"Fuck you, man."

Jesse jumped up and knocked over the card table. The drinks and cards went flying. He pushed me hard in the chest with both hands and I stumbled backward then caught my balance. Rojas jumped in between us and wrestled Jesse to the ground.

"You want to fight him?" Rojas growled as he held Jesse's throat with his left hand and cocked his right fist. "You got to fight me first."

The men jumped in to separate them. I grabbed a man who had grabbed Rojas, Gardner held me.

"Okay, Rojas, okay." Jesse looked away, avoiding his eyes. The fight went out of him and Rojas relaxed his grip.

"I was just testing him," Jesse said as we picked up the cards and put the card table back together. Gardner mixed and dealt out a new hand.

"I was just checking him out." Jesse repeated.

"This is our platoon," Rojas said. "You make a new guy feel at home here. You don't start jiving with them."

"I was just foolin' with him," Jesse said.

"You do it all the time," Rojas said, "I'm tired of it." We played in silence. My hands trembled as I sorted my cards. To break the mood I said, "I think he knocked over the table just to get rid of his lousy hand."

"Yeah, that's right," Jesse said to Rojas. "I fooled ya. Ha-ha." His head bobbed up and down and I laughed at him again but the atmosphere had changed and it wasn't long before Jesse and I were laughing at each other's jokes.

"Hey, how come my joker doesn't win the book?" I asked as Gardner pulled in a book I thought I had won.

"Man, that's the Big Boy right there," Jesse said.
"One joker's the Little Boy one's the Big Boy," Rojas said.
"The Little Boy beats everything except the Big Boy."

"How do I know which is which?" I asked.

"Look here," Gardner said. He turned the two joker cards face up for me to see. "You see there? It's got the trademark on it."

I picked them up. The Big Boy had the Bicycle trademark and the word "Guaranteed" printed on it. We mixed the cards and started a new hand.

"You sure do get excited when you win," I said to Gardner as he slammed his card hard on the table and pulled in the next trick.

"You got to play with style, my man," Gardner said. "Style is what it's all about."

"Any style will do as long as it's your own," Rojas added.

In the next game, Jesse slapped down the little joker and howled, thinking he had won the trick. I looked him dead in the eye, turned the Big Boy over slowly and tapped on the trademark. "Guaranteed," I said.

"Oh, man, shit!" Jesse laughed.

After the card game the entire squad went to chow together. When we came back, Sergeant Bell assigned me to perimeter night watch with November platoon. I took my M-16, ammo, and grenades and walked to November's foxholes out on the perimeter.

"You the new man from Oscar?" November's platoon leader asked as I approached their row of sandbag bunkers.

"That's me," I said, paying more attention to the soldiers staring at me then to the lieutenant.

"That's Carter's foxhole there." The lieutenant pointed to a foxhole at the perimeter. "You'll be on watch with him."

I had heard about Carter. In Di An the men had mentioned him and again this afternoon while we were playing cards. He was the machine gunner in November platoon, and they said the toughest man in Bravo Company. Carter watched me approach from atop his foxhole. He was tall and carried over two hundred twenty pounds, all of it muscle. He had a large head with a square jaw. "I'm from Oscar platoon," I said with a wave of hello. "They sent me out for night watch."

"You're one of the new guys. Where you from?" Carter asked.

"Newark," I said as I put my gear down.

"Shit," Carter said in a southern drawl. "Down home, we eat guys from Newark for lunch."

"Oh yeah? You eat 'em raw or with ketchup?"

Carter looked at me a moment then laughed. "What's your name, boy?" he asked.

"The name's Paul Gebhart, and I'd appreciate you not calling me boy."

"Hah!" Carter laughed. "You would, huh?"

"Yes, Sir, I'd appreciate it." I kept my hands tight on my M-16 so he wouldn't see them trembling.

"Man, I'd take you easy," Carter scoffed.

"Maybe," I said, "but being just five foot seven, I've always had to live my life by Colt's rule."

Carter turned, "What the hell you talking about, boy?"

"It's simple, really," I said. "You see, it was God that created man but it was Mr. Colt that made us equal." Carter broke up laughing.

"You got balls, boy."

"Yeah, and an M-16." I looked at him without smiling.

"Okay, Gebhart don't *shoot* me." He put his hands up in mock surrender. "I won't call you boy no more."

"Thanks, I appreciate it."

He took a joint from his shirt pocket and offered it to me, "You want some?"

"Sure, thanks," I said. I took the joint, lit it and pulled in. The smoke blinded me and I passed it back to Carter with my eyes shut. Carter laughed.

"You sure do make some funny faces, Gebhart."

"I didn't know we were on camera," I said. "I'm just being myself. You play sports in high school?"

"Of course. I played halfback in football, forward in basketball and batted cleanup in baseball. I had scholarship offers from some good colleges too."

"How come you didn't go?" I asked.

"Couldn't," he said softly. "I needed to go to work to help my momma support my seven brothers and sisters." Carter paused. "I got drafted into the army just a year out of high school."

"Well, maybe you can go to school on the GI bill when you get home."

"Yeah, I plan to."

We listened to music on Carter's radio and talked about sports and the civil rights problems. The other men in Carter's squad came over and sat with us. We sang along to Otis Redding's *Try a Little Tenderness* and continued with Aretha Franklin and Wilson Pickett tunes. It started to rain, but when Arthur Conley's *Sweet Soul Music* came on, our voices joined together in a loud, joyous chorus.

Some of the men danced on top of the foxhole, singing and shouting even as the rained poured down. The party was interrupted when we saw one of the headquarters people walking over. He stopped and stood in the rain by our foxhole. The raindrops dripped from his helmet and rolled down his plastic poncho. I could see he was not happy at being sent out as the messenger. I turned the radio off so we could hear what he was saying over the sound of the rain hitting the ground.

"The word is if the captain has to send me back, all of you will go on latrine duty for a week."

People cleared out after that.

"I'll take first watch, Jeb-heart," Carter said.

"Gebhart," I said. "Okay. Well, then I'll take second watch."

Carter laughed, "Okay Jump-start, two hours on, two off, until 6 a.m. then you can go back to Oscar platoon."

"Aye aye, Admiral," I saluted Carter sarcastically and wrapped myself into my camouflage poncho liner and tried to sleep. About an hour later Carter woke me up.

"I hear movement, man." Carter shook my leg, "I hear movement, man. They're coming, they're coming!"

I scrambled to find my M-16. I locked and loaded and jumped to the front of the foxhole and looked out the firing window. "Where? Where?" I shouted, not seeing anything in the dark.

Carter laughed. I turned around and saw him cover his mouth as he belly laughed at me.

"Geez, man," I said, "you got me good." I took a deep breath.

Carter, still laughing at me said, "You're okay, Jeb-fart."

"So are you, Far-ter." I punched him on the arm.

The next morning, I went to breakfast with the men in November platoon. We stood in line outside of the large mess tent and the men joked with their young medic named Stevens. He was slightly built with blond hair, blue eyes, and a fair complexion.

"Hey, Whitebread," one of the men called out. "How come you don't carry a weapon?" Another black soldier with a bandanna on his forehead asked. "You crazy or something, Stevens?"

Stevens chuckled. "Don't care to."

"What's the matter with you, boy?" another brother asked. "Everyone carries a weapon in Vietnam."

"The guys in the rear have weapons, even the damn generals carry pistols," a skinny white kid with a heavy peace metal around his neck said.

"The other medics carry M-16s just like the grunts," Carter said.

"I just don't want to shoot anyone," Stevens answered. He said it without emotion.

"Yeah, but they'll be shooting at you!" one black rifleman said.

"I expect they will. They're shooting at everyone," Stevens concurred.

"Yeah but the VC like killing medics, radiomen and officers," Carter put in. "I think they get extra rice for killing you guys."

"Well I won't shoot back," Stevens said, "so why should I carry a gun around?"

"Why you here then?" someone asked him. "You volunteered for Vietnam, didn't you?"

"My religion won't allow me to fight in a war but I wanted to help out if I could." Stevens spoke in an easy, matter of fact manner. I didn't agree with his philosophy but he had guts and I found it easy to like his style.

That afternoon I was lying on my air mattresses under a leanto. I had just lit up a joint when Delino walked by. He was wearing his shirt buttoned to the collar as usual.

"No thanks, guy." He waved off my offer.

"No?" I said.

"No, uh uh," he said. "I don't smoke that funny weed."

"Suit yourself," I said and took another hit.

"Why do you want to get high anyway?" he asked me.

"It's fun. You see those clouds there?"

"Yeah." Delino looked up at the clouds drifting above us.

"Before I smoked this joint, I hardly noticed them, now I really see them. They're beautiful. Do you see how they break apart and then reform? See the sunlight melting them. Exquisite, don't you think?"

"You're a head okay," he laughed.

"Head and a half," I said.

"King of the heads. Okay, then I'm going to call you Cloud Six."

"Huh? You mean Cloud Nine?"

"No, uh-uh. The Captain is Bravo Six, the Lieutenant is Oscar Six. So, you're Cloud Six."

"Okay, I get it. Cloud Six it is then." I went into my rucksack and pulled out a black felt pen and wrote "Cloud 6" in fat balloon letters on the side of my camouflage helmet cover.

Later that afternoon Sergeant Bell called for a platoon meeting. "Okay, listen up," he said in a loud voice from the center of the mortar pit. "The following people are on LP duty tonight. Emery, you and Gee-bart will be out in front of November platoon. Jesse, you and Cool will take the LP in front of Lima."

"Oh man, shit," Jesse said.

"You got a problem?" Bell asked.

"I just had LP duty," Jesse complained.

"Well, you've got it again and if you give me any more bitching you'll have it again tomorrow. You hear me?"

Jesse just mumbled and the sarge ignored him.

"LPs will go out at seventeen-thirty so eat early and have all of your gear ready. Cool, if you're late I'm gonna send you out there every goddamn night so get your head out of your ass. You hear me?"

Cool didn't say anything but after Bell walked away from the mortar pit he began to rag him. "That farm boy thinks these white people will treat him like their equal 'cause they let him order us around. That dumb-shit, Uncle Tom."

"What's el-pee duty?" I asked Delino while Cool was complaining.

"Listening Post, but we call it the Lone Patrol. It's guard duty outside of the perimeter, an early warning system. If the VC try and sneak up, the listening posts will be able to hear them. They'll report the movement to the company commander and request permission to blow the LP. If permission is granted, the men can detonate their claymores, throw all their grenades and under cover from that barrage, they run their asses off trying to get back inside the perimeter."

Delino walked with me to the mess tent. He told the cook we had LP duty and they let us in to eat early. "The sarge didn't call your name," I said as we filled our trays.

"Yeah, well I'm going out with you," he said. "I want to show you the right way to pull an LP."

"Thanks, Tony," I said.
He patted me on the shoulder and said; "Let's chow up before we go out there."

After supper Delino and I sat together at the mortar pit and prepared our gear.

"There's nothing worse than having to try and find your way back through the small opening in the barbed wire," he explained. "It's dark and there's fire coming from both the Vietnamese behind you and your own company in front of you. It's a lone patrol. If you see what I mean."

Yeah, I do. But how do you get back then?"

"You just go for it, man. You're either right or dead."

He meticulously packed the rucksack with claymores, detonators, extra ammo clips, grenades and ammo for the thump gun. "There are other listening posts sent out by the rifle platoons, too," Delino said. "So when we speak over the radio we have to identify ourselves. Each platoon has its own call sign. We'll be Oscar LP One." Delino kissed his Virgin Mary medal and crossed himself.

About 5:30, just before sundown we met up with Emery, the soldier I had pulled perimeter watch with in Di An. Emery flipped the joint he was smoking and said, "Either of you bring any rations? I've got the munchies."

"I've got a T-bone steak in my pack," Delino said, "follow me to Chez LP."

"Yeah, right," Emery laughed.

We walked to the perimeter, Delino with a radio strapped on his back and me carrying the rucksack. We each had M-16s and I had the short thump gun too. We went single file through the small opening in the barbed wire in front of November's foxholes. There was a tree stump sticking up about forty yards out, sixty yards from the tree line. We set up our LP there. While Emery covered us Delino and I walked out to the tree line and set up trip flares. We came back fifteen yards and put three claymore mines down, inserted the blasting caps and carefully unrolled the wires back to our post. Delino connected hand detonators to the wires and made a little shelf on the tree stump where the detonators would be within easy reach.

While we cleared the ground around us November platoon came out of the barbed wire in single file. "They'll be out on ambush a couple of hundred yards beyond the tree line," Delino explained.

The men in November were going out light, without their rucksacks. They each carried a canteen, ammo clips and grenades; all of it attached to their web belts. Their poncho liners were draped like sashes, hanging from their left shoulders down to their right hips. Each of them had his M-16 except Carter. He carried the 30caliber machine gun. He flashed me the peace sign as he walked by. Two of the men in his squad walked behind him with M-16s and carrying cans of 30caliber ammo. One of the ammo bearers shouted to Delino, "Hey, man. Make sure you don't shoot if we blow the ambush and come back in."

"No problem, guy," Delino called back, "just come back the same way you're going out."

"We'll try, bro."

"Yeah, well don't come back out through there." Delino pointed to the tree line directly in front of our position. The men in November knew we had just set out trip flares and claymores.

"In the confusion of a blown ambush," Delino explained to me, "trying to make it back in the dark, it's easy to go off course. We'll hear it if the ambush blows. If it does we have to be sure it isn't them setting off our trip flares."

"If we wait too long," I said, "VC could get past the claymores."

"We'll know it's them," Emery said. "For one thing they'll be yelling to us. For another, headquarters will be telling us what's happening on the raidio."

I watched the November ambush patrol disappear into the night as I helped clear the ground for our bedrolls. A steady drizzle started to fall. I hoped I'd be able to keep some parts of myself dry but then it really came down. I couldn't see three feet. Enormous raindrops pelted the ground; the jungle turned into a noisy sea of mud.

"How the hell are we going to see or hear anything?" I shouted into Delino's ear.

"Nothing we can do. Just keep watch as best we can."

Emery leaned into me. "This is fucked," he shouted in my ear. I looked closely into his face. Rainwater dripped down his coffee colored forehead onto his high cheekbones.

"My thoughts, exactly." I agreed.

"Write your Congressman," Delino said.

We laughed and Delino gave us his ear-to-ear grin, breaking the sour mood we had fallen into.

For hours we sat huddled together, shoulder to shoulder in the dark. The rain hammered down on our helmets and ponchos. We couldn't see or hear anything more than an arm's length away. I lost track of time. I was tired and the monotonous rain made me drowsy. Under my poncho, where my sides touched Emery and Delino the wet cloth of my fatigues held my body heat. That warmth lolled me towards sleep and only the cold rain hitting me in the face kept me awake.

When the rain subsided I took the first watch. Delino and Emery crawled under their ponchos and covered themselves. My uniform was soaked through to my socks. Now that we weren't huddled together for body heat I felt cold and frightened. Emery from deep inside his poncho liner peeked out at me. "You start to fall asleep; you wake me up, hear?"

"I won't fall asleep on my watch."

"Yeah but if you get sleepy get me up. It doesn't matter if you need help. It's okay to say, 'I'm falling asleep.' What's important is that we make it out of here alive even if it takes all three of us staying up all night to do it. You understand me?"

"Okay, sure," I said.

"Hey," Emery added, "and if I snore just touch me with your foot."

"Yeah, me too," Delino said from underneath his poncho.

It was still raining. I had my back to the tree stump and peered out into the black night. Thirty yards in front of us was a little fort made from a large tree trunk and a pile of logs. I heard what sounded like a twig breaking near there. It could be a deer or just the rain. I heard what sounded like the snapping of branches from another spot by the tree line. I leaned forward and peered intently into the dark. Delino heard me stirring.

"You got something?" he asked without taking the poncho off of his face.

"I'm not sure," I whispered.

"Shit, Paul, you heard movement?" Emery sat up.

"Well I've got branches cracking and twigs snapping," I said.

"I'm not sure from what. Hey, Delino, let me thump that pile of trees out there."

"Okay, go for it," he said from underneath his poncho. "We got tons of ammo, shoot the shit out of it." Then he sat up.

"Wait a minute." He put the radio's handset to his mouth and whispered. "Oscar LP One to Oscar Watch, over."

There was static over the radio then, "Oscar Watch, over."

"Permission to thump in h and i, over."

"Do you have movement? Over."

"Negative, some noises, over."

"Roger, hold, will need to advise Bravo Six, over."

"Roger, out," Delino said.

"What's h and i?" I asked him.

"Harassment and interdiction."

"I see."

We listened as Oscar watch contacted Headquarters watch. The headquarters people had already heard our conversation as had everyone else on that band. Headquarters watch came back on the radio. "Oscar LP One, this is Bravo Five, over."

"It's the First Sergeant," Delino said to me. "I'll tell him it's Cloud Six calling."

I laughed, grateful he was with us and making jokes.

"Oscar LP One, over," Delino said.

"Permission granted," the First Sergeant said. "We'll advise ambush and line platoons, over and out."

"Roger, Bravo Five, over and out." Delino hung up the handset, looked at me, and said, "Shoot'em up, guy."

"Okay, I'm gonna harass and inter-dick'em."

Delino and Emery laughed. I broke open the muzzle of the thump gun and put in a grenade round that looked like a giant green bullet then snapped the barrel closed. When I fired the grenade launcher it made a quiet "thump" without showing a muzzle flash. Shooting it wouldn't give away our position. A few seconds after I fired a quick orange flash and a puff of white-gray smoke marked the site of the explosion. I thumped every sound I heard, shooting a round or two each minute. I shot twenty something rounds—thump, thump, thump—before

Delino laughed at me from underneath his poncho. "If I was the VC I'd find another place to try and come in. This guy's blown up everything out there."

"That's right," I said in hushed voice. "In fact I'm for setting off one or two of those claymores."

"No!" Delino laughed again. "Don't do that. The Captain would have a bird."

"Huh? The Captain would give birth to a colonel?"

Delino laughed, pulled the poncho down to his chin and looked at me, "You're crazy, Gebhart. You know that, right?"

They fell back to sleep and I kept watch. The jungle quieted down and I stopped thumping it. The cold night seeped into my clothes. Mosquitoes buzzed around my face and in my ears. I slapped at them quietly. My hands and neck soon were lumpy with bites. I looked at my watch every few minutes, mostly to have something to do but also because the lighted green dial relieved the monotony of the dark night. At 2a.m. I nudged Delino's leg with my foot. He pulled himself slowly out of his poncho. When he crawled over to the tree stump I crawled away to lie down. The rain had stopped but I was cold and wet and branches poked me through the poncho. I was still awake when I heard Emery take the last watch of the night. I heard them changing places and whispered from underneath my poncho. "Hey, Emery."

"Yeah?"

"You start to get sleepy, you wake me up, you hear?"

"You know I will, bro. You know I will."

In time, without realizing it I dozed off. Just before dawn in my dream, Emery leaned over and shook me. I saw that very clearly and at the exact moment that I was dreaming it Emery really did lean over and shook my calf. "Hey, Paul, come on," he said, "let's get out of here."

I pulled the poncho down off my face and the dawn's light made me blink. Emery started to gather up his gear. Delino reached for the radio and said in a normal voice, "Oscar LP One to Oscar Watch, over." The sound of his voice surprised me awake. I heard the response clearly too because Delino had turned up the radio's volume.

"Oscar Watch, over."

"We're coming in, over."

"Roger, that's affirmative, over and out."

I sat up and stretched. I was sore from the hard ground and wet to the skin. I looked into the camp. It was light enough for the men on the perimeter to see us through a low-lying fog. The air was clean and flush with the smell of wet earth. I saw small fires start inside the camp. All the sounds of the rising men were quiet yet each one floated distinctly over the campground before being absorbed by the fog and jungle brush.

We disconnected the three detonators and rolled up the wires as we walked out to the tree line. At the end of the wires we took the blasting caps out of the back of the claymores and gathered them up. Emery pulled up the trip flares and we packed all of this into the rucksack.

Delino swung the radio onto his back and we walked through the ground fog. I pulled my poncho liner tighter around my shoulders. Thin and as wet as it was, the camouflage liner kept me warm.

As we approached the barbed wire I had a flash of déjà vu of soldiers in the Civil War on a morning with the same low-lying ground fog hovering above the damp earth. We were wet, cold soldiers as soldiers had been a hundred years before.

"Roman soldiers must have had mornings just like this too," I said, "after a rainy night two thousand years ago."

"Yeah, and they must have been just as sick of it as we are," Emery said in a tired voice.

We found the opening in the wire and walked past the perimeter foxholes towards Oscar platoon. It was with a sense of homecoming that Emery and I went to the mess tent to get coffee.

"Hey, Paul," Moore said as I got in the chow line behind him. "You look like you been sleeping on sticks."

"Sticks and stones as a matter of fact," I said. "It's a bitch out there, man."

We took our coffee back to Oscar. Delino had started a small fire and had changed into dry fatigues. I put on dry fatigues too and brought a five-gallon can of water from the water trailer. I filled my steel helmet and put it over the fire. When the water was hot I brushed my teeth with it then heated another pot full and washed my face in that water, then shaved. Delino and Emery did the same in their steel pots. No one spoke. We warmed ourselves by the fire as the fog slowly lifted. I knew Emery and Delino were both my friends. We didn't have to talk about it either. I would go with these two anywhere they were sent. I knew I could trust them and I knew they felt the same about me.

The LPs had the day off while the rest of the platoon had a regular day of work. I lay out in the sun and slept. In the afternoon I went under a lean-to and smoked grass. We had a couple of pipes going while *Crimson and Clover* by the Shondells, *Expressway to Your Heart* by the Soul Survivors, and *I Can See for Miles* by the Who played on the radio. When they could men in other platoons stopped over to smoke and listen to the radio.

In the weeks that followed, my days became a routine of joining in the patrols that swept the road for mines in the morning. Went on patrols through the woods in the afternoon, practiced with the mortars for an hour or two each day and ended with perimeter or LP duty at night. The cooks made us one hot meal a day either breakfast or dinner and every day the Chinook flew in with supplies and the mail. Mail call was the highlight of my day and I saw it was the same for everyone.

They flew out special turkey dinners for us on Thanksgiving and we ate them under lean-tos to get out of the tropical sun. I longed to be in the chill autumn air, watching football games and putting on a sweater and heavy coat to go outdoors. I wrote a long letter to Mary and one to my parents. I told them that Thanksgiving had been quiet and like everyone else I missed being home for the holidays.

Several weeks after Thanksgiving Sergeant Bell brought us the word that Bravo Company was to meet up with the rest of the battalion in the village of Quon Loi. After breakfast everyone in the camp began to tear it down. When we were ready to go I hoisted my fifty-pound rucksack and went across the mortar pit where Delino handed me a pick and hung the round computer board around my neck. Yoakum, a small, dark haired man from Oklahoma and Langford from Kentucky, grabbed the mortar tube and base plate. Astorga,, an Hispanic soldier from Corpus Cristi picked up a box of mortar rounds. Delino handed everything out until the pit was empty. We walked away leaving only the sandbags and empty foxholes as a sign that we had been there.

My M-16 weighed about twelve pounds; the ammo pouches around my waist another five pounds. On my webbing the two grenades weighed a pound each, my two water canteens filled to the brim a couple of pounds more. In the heat and humidity my body was awash in sweat. All around me men were struggling with their loads. "Now I know why they call us grunts," I said.

A Chinook landed and the water trailer was attached to its underbelly with long cables. It flew off with the water trailer swinging underneath it like a pendulum. The men of Bravo Company went into the shallow ditches on either side of the road. I leaned against the dirt embankment to take the weight off of my shoulders. We kept our eyes on the tree line and waited. Twenty minutes later I saw the Huey helicopters approach. They flew in a "V" formation but half a mile out the pilots folded into a single file.

"It takes guts to fly in and out of these landing zones," Rojas said. "The airmen are strict army—polished boots and starched shirts—so we call them 'Slicks.' But we get along with them fine."

"See that door gunner?" Jesse pointed to a chopper landing. "You can volunteer for that but it'll cost you another year."

"You'd get a clean bunk and a shower every night," Charles added, "but door gunners and point dog handlers are the most dangerous jobs out here."

As the Hueys touched down soldiers on both sides of the road struggled to their feet. Oscar platoon covered the men from Lima and Mike as they loaded. When they were in the helicopters took off in a roar of jet engines and whirling dust. Another flight of choppers arrived and loaded the balance of Mike platoon and Headquarters. November and Oscar platoons waited in the ditch for a half-hour until the helicopters returned.

When they approached Sergeant Bell called out, "Okay, let's go. Let's go!"

His orders were echoed along the ditch as we helped each other up and waddled onto the road as fast as we could. A gust of dirt kicked up from the rotor wash and stung my face.

"Let's go! Let's go! Hustle up!" I heard the chopper crew yelling to us.

I threw the pick in. Emery and Rojas climbed in from the other side and were already in the middle. I didn't see how all of us were going to fit.

"You sit there." Delino pointed to the doorway. "Moore, you're on the other side."

Delino and Charles held the frame of the chopper and I sat in between them and hung onto their arms. Our legs dangled out of the open door. The Huey took off and immediately banked sharply to the left. I looked down at my feet; beneath me the jungle treetops flashed by at a hundred miles an hour. I felt my butt sliding out.

"Hey! Pull me in!" I screamed.

"Don't worry, Gebhart, no one's ever fallen out." Delino laughed.

"Yiii! I'm not kidding. Pull me IN!" I screamed again. I held them in a death lock. "If I go down," I shouted over the roar of the engines, "you're both going with me!"

The chopper pilot straightened, then banked to the right. "Whoa! Hey, motherfucker!" I heard Moore yell from the other door. "Pull me in. PULL ME IN! GOD DAMN IT!"

I laughed along with the rest at his pleading.

Ten minutes airborne, the helicopters flew over a remote Montagnard village in the lower central highlands. "I can see tit, I'm telling ya," Emery hollered out. "Look right there." He pointed to the top of a hill where small figures walked along a dirt path.

We stretched our necks and the guys in the middle leaned over our shoulders; everyone wanted to glimpse the half-naked women. I didn't see any tits but the beauty of the landscape transfixed me. The lush green hills and valleys were cut through with streams and waterfalls. "It's beautiful," I shouted into Delino's ear.

"I didn't see her," he shouted back.

A twenty-minute ride brought the village of Quon Loi into sight. Below us acres of rubber trees grew in straight rows and an old mansion house on a hill in the middle of the plantation shone brilliant white in the morning sunlight.

"Quon Loi was a French rubber plantation," Toby yelled into my ear.

"It looks like it," I said. We hadn't spoken two words since the night out at the perimeter in Di An but I had kept my eye on him these past weeks. I liked how he handled himself. He was quiet but had a fresh sense of humor and worked hard. I was glad he was speaking to me again. "Except they've built a base around it." I pointed to the rows of barbed wire and tall watchtowers out on the perimeter.

Our choppers landed on a paved runway and we piled out and walked alongside the tarmac to Bravo Company's new camp. Foxholes left behind by previous grunts were already dug and sandbagged. All we had to do was unload and set up the mortars.

We were off duty that night; no LPs, no ambushes. The men in the other platoons came over to the mortar pits. Radios played; beer, whiskey and weed were in abundant supply. Four gas lanterns lit up the two mortar pits. Outside of this ring of light it was pitch black. The night air was balmy and the men from November platoon began to sing as the radio played. Carter did his best Smokey Robinson *Tracks of My Tears* imitation while his crew danced and sang the Miracles' part. It was our turn next. The men from Oscar stood in the center of the pit and sang along with Aretha Franklin's *Respect*. Gardner sang the lead part with Aretha while the rest of us did a funky line dance and sang the background: "Just a little bit, just a little bit."

We sounded pretty good too except that Emery's voice was an out-of-pitch falsetto.

The song ended and we all cheered. I sat on the pit wall and watched as the soldiers in Mike platoon discussed which song they were going to perform. I took a toke from the pipe Mack had just passed me. Emery stood in front of us, tall, skinny and smiling with a red eyed, stoned grin.

"Emery, man," I said, "you sounded terrible."

"Nah, it wasn't me," he said. "I was good."

"Good?" Moore said. "Man, Emery, you sounded like a cat that gotta stick stuck up its ass."

Emery laughed and said, "What you talking about, bro? I was cooking."

I didn't drink any whiskey but the weed really messed me up. I needed to lie down. I went to find my lean-to but when I left the circle of light around the mortar pits I was lost. The darkness fell over me like a black velvet cloth and I stumbled around, totally blind. It was so dark I had to close my eyes to make sure they had been opened. As it turned out it didn't matter if my eyes were open or shut so I kept them closed. It was better that way anyway. I could see beautiful colored lights in my mind. With both of my arms stretched out in front of me and my eyes still closed, I felt my way one step at a time. I was doing good too until I tripped over sandbags and crashed into someone's lean-to. I disentangled myself from the ponchos and made my way back, crawling the last long yards to the lights by the mortar pits. I found the sandbag wall and must have crashed there because in the morning that's where I found myself. Or should I say that's where Sergeant Bell found me.

"Gee-bart! What the hell are you doing?" he bellowed out in his best Fort Benning voice.

I opened one eye. Sergeant Bell stood over me with his hands on his hips. "I was sleeping, Sarge."

"Yeah, but why aren't you at your own foxhole instead of laying sprawled out here, like you're laying in some gutter somewhere."

I looked at him and blinked. "What was the question?"

Bell couldn't help but laugh. "Why the hell aren't you by your own foxhole?" he said, serious again.

"I couldn't find it."

"You couldn't find it? Say, do you know what happened to my hooch?"

"Huh? Your what?"

"My lean-to. I came back from the NCO club last night and found my tent a shambles. Someone knocked it down and trampled all over my stuff. Was that you Gee-bart?"

"It might possibly could have been me."

"What do you 'mean might possibly could have been'?"

"I remember crashing into something. It could have been yours, Sarge. But I wasn't the only one who couldn't see in the dark."

"No, but you're the one I'm putting on KP. Get your dumb ass up and over to the mess tent. You're on KP this morning, AND tonight too." He walked off talking to God knows who, his arms flapping at his sides. I watched him disappear into the mess tent. I figured I'd better head that way myself. I needed coffee, bad.

After drinking a pot-full and eating some biscuits I sat down amongst a pile of pots and pans outside the open flaps at the back of the mess tent. It wasn't much fun either until two of the cooks came out and lit a doobie. "You want some?" The white cook with a Roman nose asked me.

"I guess, yeah, thanks," I said. I took a hit off of the roach clip.

"I'm James Mancelli," he said. "They call me Buffalo. This is Walter Painter."

"Hey, breeze," Painter said. He was a black man and taller than Mancelli. He had a beer belly and wore a tiger's tooth on a shoelace around his neck.

"Hey," I said.

"Where you from?" Mancelli asked.

"Union, New Jersey," I said and handed him back the roach clip.

"I'm from Buffalo."

"I kinda got that," I said and Painter laughed.

"He is stupid sometimes, 'specially on this funny weed."

"It is good stuff," I said, feeling the effect of the grass. It was very good. I started to have fun. Washing the pots was like taking a bubble bath. Only problem was, I learned later when the water dried, my fatigues were covered in cooking grease. That problem was solved pretty nicely though because after chow one platoon at a time we walked down to the plantation house to take showers.

"It looks like an old Southern mansion in a movie," I said as we passed by the two-story house. It had four white pillars in front and wide wooden steps. The steps led up to a porch that encircled the entire first floor. Large tropical plants grew against the walls of the porch and tall palm trees graced the front lawn. "This was a French colony only ten years ago," I said to Delino.

"Those French people lived pretty good, huh?" he said.

"I think it was the Michelins that owned this place," I said. "It was their rubber company, I'm sure of that."

"Well, the general lives in the big house now," Delino said."

We went to the administration buildings across the road from the mansion. They were freshly painted white and had dark wood shutters at each window. We stood in line until our platoon was called in. Each of us received two new sets of fatigues, drawers and three new towels. The supply personnel pointed us towards the showers. It had been 10 weeks since I had a decent hot shower. When it was my turn, I let the water run over my head. "This is sheer bliss," I said to Emery. "Sometimes you got to get dirty to know how good it is to feel clean," I said as I soaped myself real good.

"We're clean like motherfuckers," he said with a smile through the soap lathered on his hair and face.

I stopped scrubbing. "How clean *is* a motherfucker, anyway?" I asked.

"Pretty clean, Jack. Pretty clean," Emery laughed.

Dressed in my new fatigues I walked back to the plantation house and sat on the front lawn under the shade trees with the other men in Oscar platoon. We lit up marijuana pipes and I was grooving on the scenery when I heard Charles say, "I'm tired of it. We're nothing more than second-class citizens. They send us to fight their war but at home their laws say we can't go here, can't do this, can't do that. We can't even vote and that ain't right. I'm tired of it."

"They use us to fight wars that got nothing to do with us and in return we get a crumb or two," Moore said. "We should do like Malcolm X says and leave these white people."

"Yeah? And go back to Africa?" Charles put in. "That isn't going to happen. Besides Africa isn't my home, America is."

"Yeah," Moore argued, "but if we can't get justice there, we'd better find some place where we can."

"We can't hardly get work," Charles said. "You don't think the white man is going to give us a couple of states do you?"

"Nah, they ain't gonna *give us* nothing. But if we take it..." Moore began.

"How are you going to *take it*?" Charles interrupted him.

"Well, if we had listened to Malcolm..."

"No, I don't want a separate country." Charles said.

"Me neither," Jesse agreed.

"Well, what ya gonna do then?" Moore asked. His voice had gotten high pitched.

"What do you think, Paul?" Jesse asked me.

I had known the hurt of anti-Semitism but I knew that the injustices black people had suffered in America were many times worse. I considered my words before responding. "I think it is going to get better," I said. "Change is coming."

"I don't know, man," Moore said. "Don't feel no different to me."

"Yeah it is, some," Jesse said. "Look at music and sports..."

"That doesn't count," Charles interrupted. "The same Americans who love a black star still treat other black men with contempt."

"I'm just saying it ain't like it was twenty years ago," Jesse said. "It is changing."

"Not enough and not fast enough," Charles said and we all agreed.

"I don't want to be an athlete or a singer," Charles continued. He looked down at his hands. "I want people to see my work, without regard to the color of my skin or the kind of hair I have. I want to feel proud of myself and what I do." There was silence.

"You will, Charles," I said.

He looked at me.

"You will," I repeated. "Goodness will prevail in a righteous world."

"Nah," Moore said. "Earth is hell. We all died on some other planet and came to earth to suffer."

Charles looked at Moore and shook his head, "You better quit smoking that funny stuff, Mack. I'd take a day or two off if I was you."

We all laughed and headed back to the tarmac for lunch.

The dirt in Quon Loi was a bright orange color and with the Chinooks and other choppers coming and going all day blowing it around, it wasn't long before our new fatigues and all of our gear had a layer of orange dust on them. I was sitting on top of the sandbagged bunker that night relaxing and dusting the red dirt off my fatigues when a firefight broke out in the distance. It was only five or six miles from Quon Loi on Highway 13. I recalled that they named it Thunder Road and I knew why when I heard the artillery batteries inside the fort fire round after round in support. In the distance red tracers rained down from Cobra gunships as they circled above the battle.

"It's almost Christmas," I said, feeling the irony of young men dying at the happiest time of the year.

Delino nodded, "Some of them will never see Christmas again." He crossed himself and said a short prayer for the men under fire.

I had a hard sleep that night listening to the artillery batteries banging away. Sergeant Bell woke us before dawn. We were to relieve the unit that had been hit. I got up and stood in chow line as morning stars still shown in the dark night. I could see my breath in the chill air. Cool lit a pipe of grass and offered it to Moore and then to me but we both passed on it.

After breakfast, still in the dark, the squads fixed up their webbing and checked their ammo.

"Take two canteens," Rojas told me. "It's going to be a long day. We're going to see some shit too. I can feel it." He checked my gear. "Those guys have been hit hard. They're going to be happy as hell to see us coming in."

"You know it, man," Gardner said. "We're the cavalry coming to the rescue."

I felt good about that but at the same time I recognized the fear in my gut.

We didn't have picks or shovels to carry just our combat webbing and rifles. I had one magazine locked and loaded and a second one taped to it for a fast forty rounds. Everyone had at least two hand grenades strapped to their suspenders; some diehards carried four. We each had a smoke grenade, every platoon with a different color.

The young men of Bravo Company were fully armed and ready to rumble. On the tarmac we knelt and waited. I saw men dozing off but I couldn't, my hands were sweating. As the first light of day brightened the eastern sky a pale blue, the helicopters approached. Without a signal two hundred men stood up and readied to load.

Eighteen helicopters came in single file, landed, then quickly lifted off and flew south following the red clay road. A ten minute ride in "V" formation and the choppers went back into a single file. They came in fast to the LZ. I caught a glimpse of the battlefield. The camp was in a large open field alongside Highway 13.

"Let's go! Let's go!" I heard people yelling. The chopper pilot hardly touched down when we jumped out and hit the ground running. I heard the roar of the engines behind me as they flew off at full throttle. We ran into the ditch on the side of the road but before I had time to catch my breath, Sergeant Bell shouted for us to get up and join the company patrol.

Lima walked point, then came Mike, November, Headquarters and finally Oscar. We walked outside of the camp. I looked in beyond the concertina barbed wire and saw soldiers sitting on the roofs of their foxholes. They looked tired, unshaven, and dirty. No radios played and only a few men walked around.

Our patrol crossed over the road that the choppers had just landed on. I stopped to look at two pieces of white plastic, melted into scorched black earth twenty feet wide by thirty feet long.

"Napalm made this black mark," Delino said. He stood next to me in the center of the napalm hit.

"Yeah, but what's that?" I pointed to the two pieces of melted white plastic.

Delino bent down and looked closer. "Some guy got blown right out of his sandals!"

"Dear God," I said. "And where's the rest of him?"

"They probably dragged his corpse off."

We walked on in silence. I couldn't get the picture of the melted shoes and what had happened to the man who once wore them out of my mind.

We entered the tree line south of the camp. No one was sure what remained of the NVA unit or where they might be now. Bravo Company was to mop up but we could be walking into an ambush. We patrolled cautiously through the jungle for over an hour. I saw VC corpses off to the side of the trail but we made no contact. We came out of the tree line back into the large field this time north of the camp. Oscar now had the point and the platoons behind us were in the reverse order from when we had entered the tree line. The sun blared down and Bravo Six ordered a halt and a five-minute break. I lay down and drank the last of my first canteen. Soon enough we had to move out. Emery walked point, I was behind him, Jesse and Rojas behind me. We walked parallel to the tree line and had gone to the far right of the large clearing when they ordered us to halt and make a left face. The next order was for us to walk, on line into the jungle. I heard the veterans complaining.

"Once we enter that tree line," Rojas said, "our visibility will be less than ten feet. We're going to lose sight of each other."

"What if some guys get in front of the others?" I asked.

"That's the problem with this brilliant maneuver," Emery said. "It's going to be a mess in there."

"Let's go slow," Rojas advised, "and keep the man to your left in sight, even if you have to walk next to him, then spread back out when you can."

Oscar platoon was on the far right of the company formation, Delino's squad was the farthest right. The line of 200 men walked slowly into the tree line but we had gone in only forty feet when a shot rang out and everyone hit the dirt. I lay in tall grass and I couldn't see anyone but I heard shouting fifteen yards to my left then two more shots rang out.

"I'm hit, I'm hit!" I heard Sergeant Bell yell.

Rojas could see into the small clearing to our left and he yelled to me and Emery, "Cool is down. Sergeant Bell went in to help him and he got hit too."

Because Oscar didn't have its own medic I heard them shouting for one. I saw Doc Stevens run up the line from November platoon.

"There's a sniper in the there," Delino yelled to him when he got to us. "Stay down, Doc. Don't go in there!"

"I have to," Stevens said as he knelt next to Delino. "There's wounded out there and that's my job."

"Well, stay low, man. Keep as low as you can, Doc."

Stevens, bent at the waist and unarmed went into the small clearing to attend to Cool and Sergeant Bell. Moments later another shot rang out and Delino's voice echoed through the jungle, "They've hit the doc! Stevens is dead!"

No one volunteered to go in after that. Bravo Six wanted us to open fire into the small clearing but Delino shouted into the radio receiver, "No, no, our guys are still in there!"

Nothing happened for what seemed like a long time. Next to me Rojas stirred then stood up. "I'm going in," he said.

His words shocked me.

He pointed to our right. "We have to set up a semicircle with enough firepower to hold our flank," he said. "If we get hit from there, they'll fold us up one man at a time."

I could see just what he meant. "Okay," I said. I pointed to a bush ten yards away. "That'll make the top of the semicircle."

"Paul, stay down, goddamn it." Emery was not happy about me getting up but he covered me.

When I reached the edge of the clearing, Jesse called over, "Paul, Paul! Cover me."

"Okay, go!" I hollered and Jesse belly-crawled out to a position farther to the right. I looked at Jesse then back to Emery. The three of us were only thirty feet apart but it felt like a mile. Rojas watched us set up a defense. When he was satisfied we had the right flank covered he stood up and disappeared into the thick brush to our left.

There were several minutes of silence broken by the sound of automatic weapons and then I heard Rojas yelling: "Come on in! Come on in! It's over. I got him."

I saw people running into the clearing to work on Sergeant Bell and Cool. Rojas came out of the jungle brush with an AK-47 strapped to his back. He came over and lay down next to me.

"What happened in there?" I asked him, studying his face.

"I went in and laid down next to the sarge," he said. "Bell pointed straight ahead and said, 'He's right there. He's right THERE,' but I couldn't see anything, just brown grass and trees, so I crawled out into the bushes."

"Towards the sniper?" I asked.

Rojas nodded. "I figured if I was going to protect those men, I had to be in front of them not next to them." I shook my head in disbelief.

"I crawled out about fifty feet and stopped where it opened up. There were trees but no jungle grass. Out of the corner of my eye I caught a small movement. The sniper was less than a hundred feet to my left! Our eyes met and I fired first. I was on full auto so I hit him with seven or eight rounds and he just slumped over. I expected return fire from other VC but nothing happened. It got quiet and I decided I'd better get that guy's weapon before he recovered so I went over to him but he was dead. His eyes were just staring into space."

"How come he didn't see you crawling out?"

"I actually went past him," Rojas said. "He was squatting down behind a tree facing forward, toward that little clearing. Somehow I got past him and when he did see me I was sideways to him and the tree in front of him didn't shield him from me."

"What happened next?" I asked.

"I headed back towards the clearing with his AK-47. That's when I realized all your weapons were pointed in my direction."

Just then Delino yelled, "Gebhart, you and Emery get in there and help."

"Okay, okay," I shouted back. I patted Rojas on the shoulder and went to join Emery in the small clearing. Bell and Cool had already been taken out but Doc Stevens' body still lay there. His eyes were closed and his face looked peaceful. His helmet had been knocked off but somehow his hair was still combed.

"He looks like he's sleeping," I said to Emery. "There's almost no blood on him."

"He's been shot through the neck," Emery said. He turned Stevens to inspect the wound. "Here." He pointed to the bullet hole halfway up the side of his Stevens' neck. "It didn't hit his jugular but it must have gone right through his spinal chord. He died instantly."

Emery lowered Stevens' head and we rolled his body onto a poncho. I knelt next to him and looked at the wound again. It was a clean entry on one side and a three-inch slit on the other side of his neck where it exited. I could see down into his pink neck muscles. I could imagine how bad this was for his family.

"Shit! That son of a bitch!" I shouted. Emery looked at me, not comprehending who I was yelling at.

"Come on, Paul," he said. "Take hold." He nodded toward the poncho and we lifted Stevens' body and carried him out of the jungle and laid him down in the clearing. I covered his face with a corner of the poncho when soldiers came to look at him. They asked us what had happened and Emery told them.

Headquarters sent over two soldiers to take charge of the body and we left to re-join Oscar platoon. As we headed towards the camp, Emery and I passed Sergeant Bell and Cool lying on the ground waiting for a Medevac. Nearby, two medics sat next to each other. Bell and Cool both had been given shots of morphine and the sarge lay on his back staring at the sky. Cool lay on his side. He still had his sunglasses on.

"Hey, man," Cool said when he recognized us.

"How ya doing, man?" Emery asked as we walked up.

"Shit, I'm fucking great," Cool said, half sitting up. He spoke with a slur as if he was drunk, not quite forming his words. The bandage on his right arm was soaked through with blood.

"Light me up, okay?" He pulled a joint from his fatigue pocket with his good hand and Emery lit it and passed it to him.

"Man, I'm going home," Cool said, "I'm through with this fucking place."

"Yeah, that's right man," Emery said. "You'll be home in a couple of weeks. You dog, you."

"I hope your arm's okay," I said.

"Yeah, I don't know," Cool said. "I can't feel it at all." Cool looked at me for the first time. "That white boy died trying to save me," he said looking into my eyes. "He shielded me with his body as he bandaged me up and tried to stop the bleeding. He got hit and fell on top of me. I'm never going to forget him, never."

"Emery! Gebhart!" The men from Oscar called to us to catch up.

"Well, man, you take care of yourself," Emery said to Cool.

"Yeah," I added.

"Okay," Cool said. "You guys, too." He leaned back and lay down completely.

"So how is it," I said to Emery as we walked towards the barbed wire, "that when Cool gets hit, it's the sarge that got up and went in to help him? Everyone else had pulled back."

"Yeah, I know," Emery said. "But you can never tell what you or anyone else is going to do under fire."

"Cool could figure more ways to get out of work than anyone," I said, "and Sergeant Bell was always yelling at him. Just this morning, in the chow line I heard him shouting, 'Don't you be smoking any dope in front of me goddamn it! You ever do that again, Cool, I'll have you put in jail. Yeah, you think that's a joke but you'll come out of the brig and still have your days left in Vietnam so straighten up asshole! You hear me?'"

Emery laughed at my impersonation of Bell. Across the field we saw that the patrol had resumed. Bravo Company was headed into the camp and we jogged to catch up. The men in Oscar waited for us just outside the barbed wire.

The wire was strung in three rolls, each roll three feet round, two rolls on the ground side by side and a third strand on top of these two. I noticed two makeshift ladders the VC had used to try and scale the wire with. The bodies of a dozen Vietnamese soldiers hung in the wire. One man had been shot in the head. Half of his face and skull were gone and part of his brain hung out. I glanced into his skull but it was all a little too much for me—too naked the truth, too brutal a reality. I felt nauseous.

Two soldiers from November platoon had a deck of playing cards and were putting a card into each corpse's mouth.

"The Vietnamese will be back for their dead," Emery explained. "The cards will let them know it was the First Division that got these guys."

"Hey!" I heard Rojas yell to one of the soldiers. "You're disrespecting them."

The soldier ignored him so Rojas walked over and put his foot on the soldier's hand. The rifleman pulled it out and looked up at Rojas in surprise. "They're gooks," he shouted.

"They're men," Rojas said. "Leave 'em alone."
I could tell Rojas was serious and so could the grunt. Rojas was ready to dice it out with him but the soldier left without saying another word.

The dead Vietnamese looked like rag dolls to me; torn up rag dolls. They were human beings as Rojas said but to me, I was numb towards them. If they hadn't been shot at the wire they would have killed the men inside the perimeter. I felt bad for Doc Stevens not for the attackers.

The men in Oscar platoon poked through the clothing of the dead men, looking for wallets and personal effects.

"Man," Emery said, "I ain't never seen nothing like this back in Dallas."

"Not in Jersey either," I agreed.

I noticed some small white pills in the dirt below one of the bodies hanging in the wire. "Hey," I pointed to them. "What's that?"

"That's their dope," Gardner said. "They get all fucked up before they try this shit."

Delino looked at me. "They're not feeling any pain when they make the final charge to the barbed wire."

I picked up the pills and blew the dirt off. "It must be some good shit," I said.

"Hey, Gebhart," Gardner said, "don't take that, man."

"Why not?"

"You crazy? What if it's poison?" Gardner's eyes were round in disbelief.

"What?" I laughed. "You think they had a plan to poison Americans crazy enough to take their pills after they were blown up at the wire?" I went to put them in my pocket, Moore saw me.

"Hey, Paul, don't," he said." You don't know what that shit is."

I looked at him for a minute, shook my head and tossed the pills to the ground. "Okay," I said, "but Santos would be pretty upset if he knew we were throwing away good dope like that."

The lieutenant from November Platoon called to us and we all went through the zigzag entrance opening in the rolls of barbed wire. On the other side we passed a line of foxholes and some soldiers.

"They charged that wire and we were shooting the world at them," one of the riflemen said as we went by. He was an overweight black man with his fatigue shirt hanging out of his pants. His partner was a short, muscular man; darker and with an angry mouth and hard eyes.

"They were trying to climb the wire to get to us," the shorter one added in a tired voice.

"We may not have a cause to die for like them," I said, "but Sergeant Bell went in to save Cool. Doc Stevens went in to help them and Rojas crawled in after the sniper. None of them had a cause but their people needed help."

"That's what it comes down to, man," Gardner said.

"The army doesn't care if we make it home or not," Jesse added. "All we got out here is each other."

"Amen, brother," Delino said and we all agreed.

Chapter Four
He's a Soul Man

January 1968

Bravo Company returned to Quon Loi and for the next 10 days we walked morning patrols through the rubber trees and had the afternoons off. On one of those hot afternoons I sat in the mortar pit with Emery and Moore. Our rifles were apart and our cleaning kits lay on green towels. We had our shirts off and the radio playing.

I listened as Emery sang along to Sam and Dave's *Soul Man*.

"I'm a Soul Man, I'm a Soul Man," he sang over and over.

I laughed at him. "Hey, Emery. You're out of tune."

He couldn't hear me over the music but he looked up and smiled, "Pretty good, huh?"

I nodded, "Excellent."

"I'm getting me some pussy," Moore said.

"Yeah, me too," Emery said.

"I'll go into the village with you," I said, "but I'm not looking to get laid."

As we discussed our plans three soldiers from Lima Platoon walked over. Desusa was from New York City. He looked like a choirboy with red-brown hair and freckles. Kenny Serena was from the Bronx. He was tall with black wavy hair and green eyes. He had a pencil thin mustache. I had heard people say that Serena was the best point man in the company. I also knew anywhere you saw Desusa you saw, Serena.

"Hey, anybody got any acid?" Desusa asked as he came up.

"Yeah, right," Moore answered.

Desusa laughed. "Want to drop some and see what this place is like with your mind blown?"

"You'd probably walk off into the jungle," I said.

"Yeah," Emery said, "and make peace with the Vietnamese."

"I knew two old heads who did drop some here," Desusa said.

"No way, man." I waved my hand at him.

"Yes Sir," he insisted, "when I first came into country. They were in my platoon."

"I wouldn't want to try it," I said. "It's too dangerous. Hey, man," I reached up for Desusa's M-14 rifle, "let me see that."

The barrel of the M-14 was longer than the M-16's and it had a wooden stock. He handed it to me and I stood up and felt its balance. "I used to train rotcees at the firing range with M-14s," I said. "I forgot how heavy they are."

"Yeah, but it's worth the extra hump to carry it around," Desusa said.

"Yeah?"

"Hell yeah. It's the best." Desusa made a face of assurance. "When you're out on point these M-14s are money in the bank, man. They fire every time."

"Yeah, but the AKs are shorter and lighter," I said. "More maneuverable too." I passed the rifle to Moore.

"Yeah, but I'll still take the M-14 over their AKs," Desusa said.

"Yeah," Serena agreed. He was carrying an M-14 too. "There's only seven of these in Bravo Company and we have to loan them out to whoever's walking point."

"You guys walk point every time it seems," Emery said. "How come? You don't want to loan out your rifles?"

"Hell, no! Shit, take it," Desusa answered. "Go walk point, is what I say."

"It does seem like we walk point more than most guys though," Serena said.

"Hey," Desusa said, "I knew a couple of guys who were here when I first got to 'Nam, who would walk your point for you and pay you for it."

"Get out of here!" Emery laughed.

"No, man, it's true," Desusa said. "They told me, 'Hey, they let you kill here. You do this back home and you get the chair. Here you can kill all you want.'"

"Say what?" the other soldier with them was a new guy. He tilted his head to one side and his forehead wrinkled. We all stopped and looked at him.

"What's your name?" Emery asked.

"I'm Willie Forman," he said, "but my friends call me Monk." Monk had a wide, wide mouth and a friendly smile.

"Monk?" Moore asked. "How'd you get a nickname like that?"

"When I was a kid and people asked me what I wanted to be, I'd say a monk 'cause then I wouldn't have no girls around me."

"You don't still feel that way, do you?" I asked. Monk laughed.

"Nah, but the name stuck."

"Where you from, bro?" Emery asked.

"Atlanta," Monk said with a southern drawl.

"Yeah, I been there," Emery nodded. "Got some nasty white motherfuckers down that way."

"Say what?" I tilted my head to one side and imitated Monk's voice.

"Hey, let's go into the village already," Desusa said. "I need a drink." He took back his M-14 from Moore.

"Okay, Breeze," Serena said, "don't get the tremors."

Desusa just laughed and said, "Hey, Kenny, ya got any dope on ya, man?"

"Sure," Serena answered.

"Well then share it, shithead."

We reassembled our M-16s and walked across the runway and down the hill toward the village. We had on clean fatigues and were all wearing sunglasses but a coat of orange dust covered us as it did everything in Quon Loi.

"This is the strangest damn place," I said. "Everything is orange. I feel like I'm in 'The Wizard of Oz.'"

"Well then click your heels three times and make a wish," Desusa said.

The dirt road led into the main street of the Quon Loi village. Wooden buildings with thatched roofs lined both sides of the street. The windows in the buildings were just openings in the walls, without glass. There weren't any sidewalks to walk on either so we shared the dirt street with young Vietnamese men riding little scooters that spewed grey, oily smoke into the air. Serena read one of the bar signs out loud: "Girls Here, Good Bar."

"It reminds me of the Old West," I said. "Except the signs are written in pidgin English."

"You Like, Good Times," Desusa read another one.
"Come to think of it maybe the signs in the Old West were written in pidgin English too," I said. "It sure isn't like my home town, I'll tell you that."

"Hey, check it out," Emery called to us. He was standing outside a bar with a mamasan trying to pull him inside the front door.

"You come in, good time," the mamasan said as we walked up.

We looked inside and saw a few GIs and some girls, but the place with the loud soul music down the block seemed to be the better destination.

"Later," Emery said to the mamasan and we crossed the street.

The music from the second bar blasted away as we stood at the doorway for a minute to check it out. Inside was packed with GIs. "Hey, there's Carter." I pointed to a table in the far corner. We went in and walked over to Carter's table.

"Que pasa, dude?" Carter said as he stood up and shook hands with everyone. We put some chairs and tables together and ordered drinks. Five girls came over from the bar. They laughed and would move around nice in our laps if we bought them little shots of tea which they drank from whiskey glasses.

The music played nonstop: The Four Tops' *Reach Out And I'll Be There*, Percy Sledge's *When A Man Loves A Woman*, The Capitals' *Cool Jerk*, The Temptations' *Ain't Too Proud To Beg*, Lee Dorsey's *Working In A Coal Mine*, and The Supremes' *My World Is Empty Without You*. When Wilson Pickett's *Land Of A Thousand Dances* played we got up to dance. *Soul Man* came on next and the brothers were battling it out for the title of best dancer in the battalion. Carter and Jesse had beaten everyone and were dancing solo with the rest of us forming a circle around them. We all sang along to the music as they danced. They took turns doing leaping full splits, down to the floor.

"Jesse won," I said to Moore. "He can move his arms, legs and back like he doesn't have a bone in his body."

"The original rubber band man," Moore agreed.
When the song ended we went back to the tables and ordered more drinks from the lap girls. Moore worked a deal out with the head mamasan and took one of the girls away to screw her. I saw a young Vietnamese woman sitting at the bar. Her long, dark hair grew down to the waist of her blue sequined mini dress. I guessed she was seventeen or eighteen years old. She sat on her stool expressionless.

"She's got an absolutely perfect body and the face of a movie star," I said to Emery.

"I know her," he said. "We were here in September and I saw that she doesn't like Americans," Emery warned me. "She won't be any fun. The other girls like to fuck."

"But just look at her," I said.

The mamasan who ran the place saw me and said, "You like?"

"Yeah, well..."

She grabbed my arm and walked me over and introduced us. The young woman didn't smile. Even so I paid the mamasan a hundred pees, that's about ten dollars US and I followed the girl to a large room behind the back of the bar. Paper screens partitioned the room into twelve cubicles, six on either side of the hallway down the middle of the room. Each cubicle had a narrow bed and small wooden nightstand. The girl went into one on the right and when I walked in she took her miniskirt off. I stared at her perfect bullet tits and absolutely flawless body.

I took my pants off and she washed me then lay down on the narrow bed. I tried to kiss her but she turned her head away. She lay under me like a block of ice.

"Why are you here if you don't want to be?" I asked her. She glanced into my eyes then turned her face towards the wall.

I left the bar and walked alone back up to the tarmac. On my way to Bravo Company I ran into Monk.

"How was it?" he asked.

"Depressing," I said.

"What happened?"

"We've turned their daughters into whores and their sons into pimps. They hate us and I've just become a part of it and I feel dirty."

"Well, that's just the way it is here," Monk said. "They've got to eat. Besides there's nothing you or I can do to change it."

Monk's words didn't make me feel any cleaner. I felt quilty about cheating on Mary too. "I love screwing," I said.

"But if it's going to leave me feeling this bad afterward I shouldn't do it."

"That's right," Monk agreed. "If you have feelings for a special person you should be happy about that and not screw around."

"Even when everyone else is having fun?" I asked.

"Even when everyone else is catching clap," he said.

Our orange-coated boots crunched on the gravel as we walked past the runway to the sandbagged bunkers of Bravo Company. There was a letter from Mary waiting for me. I stared at the envelope. I loved her, everything about her even her handwriting. She wrote that she was lonely and missing me every day, all day.

Charles sat down with me. He had a letter in his fatigue shirt pocket. "How you doing, Paul?" he asked me.

"I want to be home with my wife so bad," I said, "the pain of separation is like a knife in my stomach." I felt a tear roll down my cheek and I wiped it away.

"It's tough, I know," he said.

I blew my nose. "How are you doing?"

"I can't sleep anymore," Charles said.

"When do you go home?"

"I have seventeen days left."

"You are short," I said. "What's the first thing you're gonna do when you get back to the world?"

"You mean after seeing my mother and family?"

"Yeah, what are you going to do for fun?"

"Hmm, well I'll tell you. I think I'm going to go shopping in downtown Chicago. Yes, Sir, I am."

"What are you shopping for?" I asked.

"Oh, I don't know, nothing special. I just want to see it all. You know what I mean? I just want to be back in the world, seeing all the fullness of it."

I laughed with Charles at the thought of him walking through the stores like a man shipwrecked for a year.

"Yeah, we have so much," I said. "We'll appreciate it more now. Don't you think?"

"I know I will," Charles agreed. "But I'm not there yet."

The following week the battalion received its orders to move west to the hills in Trey Ninh Province by the Cambodian border.

"We were just out there in November," Emery said as he packed his gear next to me. "Loc Ninh was all I ever wanted to see of that province. Every time we're out by the border we lose men."

The veterans all knew this and I could feel the tension in the air. The joking and horseplay stopped. We left the old foxholes and waddled to the runway; burdened with our weapons and the equipment needed to convert another piece of Vietnam into a defensive position.

"We'll be in the seventh wave," Delino told us as we sat on the tarmac. He had Oscar platoon's radio on his back. "The Reconnaissance platoon will go in first. They'll let us know if it's a hot LZ or not."

"If you want to see lots of action you can volunteer for the Recon platoon," Rojas said. "You don't even have to sign up for an extra year. They don't hump all this weight like us, but they pay the price, they're the first in and the last out."

We heard the choppers approaching. There were six in each wave. When they landed men from Bravo Company boarded. As soon as one wave of helicopters rose in the air, the next wave came in to land. When the choppers were all in the air, they went into formation and flew southwest with infantrymen hanging out of the doors. I watched the treetops flash by below. "It's supposed to be quiet," Delino shouted out.

The choppers came into the landing zone quick, touched down for just several seconds and gunned it out of there. As we piled out the chopper crew shouted to us, "Hustle up! Let's Go! Let's Go!" As the last infantry man's feet touched the ground they lifted back up and were gone in seconds.

I felt tight and anticipated the worse as I looked around the clearing and into the tree line. We went to the center of the clearing and unpacked the mortar equipment as rifle platoons walked cloverleaf patrols around the perimeter. They went into the tree line then came out to the edge of the clearing then back in again. That was they covered every foot of ground around the camp.

"We have to dig foxholes for ourselves, another one for the mortar rounds and then the two mortar pits," Delino explained to me.

He pointed to the riflemen digging bunkers out by the tree line. "They set up in squads, their foxholes eight to ten yards apart. The firing ports are not in the center of their foxholes," Delino explained. "They're in the front corners, that way Viet Cong shooting straight ahead, their rounds will hit the sandbags in front. One bunker will be firing at the VC attacking the adjacent foxholes, while their own bunker will be covered by the foxholes to their right and left."

"The overlapping fields of fire are our best defense." Rojas said.

I nodded. I saw the logic of making every foxhole deliver a crossfire.

"We'll work in teams using the picks and shovels," Delino continued. "You get three minutes with the pick just like a round in a prize fight. When your three minutes are up the next guy jumps in and shovels out your work. After he cleans out the hole the third guy jumps in and starts three more minutes of picking then the first man is on the shovel. Got it?"

"Got it," I said.

The ground was as hard as cement and the digging was difficult work. As I waited my turn I watched riflemen enlarge the clearing by using hand axes to cut down bushes and trees. Other soldiers inspected the ground in front of the foxholes to make sure that their lanes of fire were unobstructed.

The afternoon wore on. Charles called me over and we wrote in grease pencil on the round board the bearings, the elevations and the charges needed to hit the clearings in the area. "This way we'll be ready to fire back if the VC mortar us," Charles explained.

"Gebhart, you're with me and Rojas," Delino called to me.

"Okay, I'm coming."

"We finished the foxholes." Delino pointed to the ammo hole next to the outline of the round mortar pit. "The Chinook brought in these steel bars," he said. "Help me put some across the top of the ammo holes. We'll fill sandbags and lay them on the bars."

When we had finished roofing the two foxholes and the ammo hole, I thought I'd take a break but Delino pointed to the partially completed mortar pit.

"You're on the pick, we rotate every three minutes."

"Okay," I nodded. "How deep are we going?"

"The pit needs to be two feet deep, fifteen feet across. Then we fill sandbags two-high around it. Okay, guy, let's get to it." He handed me the pick and I went into the depression where the mortar pit was to be dug. I swung the pick into the hard clay; the handle vibrated and stung me like I had struck concrete.

We dug all afternoon. Darkness came and we still weren't finished.

"Isn't this good enough?" I asked Delino when the pit was a foot deep. "It doesn't have to be perfect."

"No," he shook his head. "We've got to finish digging-in. No matter how tired we are, we've got to be dug-in."

I didn't say anything.

"You remember that, too," he said. "Do you hear me?"

"Yeah, of course I hear you," I said. "I'm standing right next to you, right?"

"Yeah, but sometimes things go in one ear with you and out the other. This is important, Gebhart. No matter where you are, no matter how late you get there, you dig in. You hear me?"

"Yes, I hear you."

"Don't you ever forget it either."

"How could I? You just made it a philosophy lesson or something."

"Tony's right," Rojas said seriously. "These holes will save your life one day."

I felt they were treating me like a kid so when my turn came around again I jumped in the hole and swung the pick as hard as I could. I grunted with each throw. Delino lay on his side holding the red-filtered flashlight for me.

"Boys," he called out, "I think this new guy's gonna be all right. That's how you make your reputation out here," he said to me. "People pay attention to a guy who carries his own weight." He gave me a wink of approval.

We finished about eleven o'clock and I fell asleep after eating cold C rations. About midnight it started, a soft thump... thump... thump from out in the jungle. The first men to recognize the sound shouted the alarm.

"INCOMING! INCOMING!"

I sprang to my feet and ran for one of the foxholes. There were already people inside but I pushed my way in. The men underneath me shouted, "Come on! Come on!"

The more bodies on top of them the more the shrapnel would be slowed down if any made it into the doorway. The sound of the mortar barrage made it all quite clear.

The big gunner, Eddie, tumbled in.

"Oooff!" I moaned as his two-hundred-thirty-pounds landed on me. "Hey, wait, Ed, you're crushing me."

"Sorry," Eddie said and we shifted around.

"Okay, that's better," I said as his weight lifted.

Someone's head smashed into Eddie's nose. "Ow!" he yelped.

It was madness; arms and legs and shoving—but nobody was leaving.

The last two men could only fit their heads into the hole. "Make room! Make room!" they shouted as they tried to squeeze in further.

"Ain't no more room, ain't no more," the men on the bottom of the pile shouted.

"I can't breathe. I can't breathe!" I heard a muffled yell.
I felt the foxhole's cool moist walls against my back. Outside, the enemy's mortar rounds were landing and from the sound of it, not too damn far away. We were safe in the hole, unless a mortar landed right smack in the opening, but I heard machinegun fire. What if they break through the line while we were still down here? I didn't want to get out and I didn't want to stay.

"LET'S GO! LET'S GO!" I heard Delino shout.

I scrambled out with everyone else and dove over the sandbags into the mortar pit. Eddie maneuvered the mortar tube while Emery, acting as his assistant gunner held a mortar round. The other men pulled wooden boxes out of the ammo foxhole, cracked them opened and tied canvas charges to the mortar rounds. They stacked them by the sandbag wall, sorted by the number of charges.

"We've got to knock out that enemy mortar," Charles said to me. He and I sat in the pit with our backs to the wall. He searched the map with his red-filtered flashlight. "Oh man, oh man," he muttered over and over.

I looked up from the map and saw that Charles had his helmet on backwards so that it stuck up high on his head. I noticed that he had the map upside down too.

"Charles, Charles, look," I said. I turned the map right side up for him.

He looked into my eyes. "Oh, shit!" he said. "I don't know if I can handle this. I'm shaking."

Delino saw what was going on. "Let Gebhart do it," he called out. "You just check him. Okay, Charles?"

"Yeah, yeah, okay," Charles said.

I found the clearings we had marked up earlier in the day. "Which one of these do we want to hit first?" I asked.

"They sounded pretty far out to me," Charles said, "hit the farthest one, there." He pointed to a clearing two hundred fifty yards out.

Another series of enemy mortars exploded inside the perimeter. I hurried to give Eddie the coordinates. "Heading two-four-oh degrees, elevation fifty-five."

"Heading two-four-on, elevation fifty-five." Eddie repeated it back to me as he set the mortar tube to those coordinates.

"Charge three," I said.

"Charge three," Eddie yelled, both to me and to Emery.

"Four rounds left to right," I shouted over the mayhem. "Fire when ready."

"Four rounds, left to right," Eddie repeated. "Ready?"

"Ready," Emery shouted.

"Fire!" Eddie shouted.

Just as our round went out an enemy mortar shell burst just outside the mortar pit. Shrapnel whizzed over our heads and we all kissed the dirt.

"Stay below the sandbags," Delino shouted.

Emery, tall and lanky, tried to drop the next mortar down the tube without standing straight up. He was tall and exposed when he stood up. With the enemy's mortar shrapnel whizzing in the air he hesitated to drop the rounds down the tube. Moore saw this and said, "Here let me do it." Moore was shorter and quicker for that matter. He took Emery's place and dropped the rounds down the tube as fast as they could hand them to him.

Each round fired out of our mortar tube made a loud THUMP and the tube sounded a loud RING. The ringing hurt my ears but just then I didn't mind. It felt good to be fighting back. Our rounds exploded in the jungle but within a minute there was another VC barrage. This series of shells landed right outside our pits. I looked over at Rojas. He shrugged his shoulders and said, "If one lands in here with us, we're gone."

"We'll be alright," Delino said. "Just keep low. Listen for where those mortars are coming from."

"They're calling in artillery for us," Rojas said. "We're going to be okay."

His words of confidence helped me to relax. I was able to function. I felt a strange feeling though. We were in the jungle, miles from civilization and under attack by the Vietnamese. Whoever could fire the most ordnance would win. It had to be us otherwise we all died here this night. My hands felt stiff as wood and my knees trembled but I was resolved to fight for my life.

I was able to hear the direction of the enemy's thumping mortars. I found clearings on the map in that area and called the coordinates to Eddy. We fired a second volley at one of the new clearings as Gardener in the other mortar pit went to work. Their first round was a flare that drifted slowly overhead, hanging from a white, silk parachute it burned a brilliant, phosphorous light, turning night into day.

I heard shouts from the perimeter, "Here they come! Here they come!" Trip flares went off at the tree line and I could see figures of men running around and diving for cover as our riflemen opened up. The bright light of the trip flares illuminated narrow sections of the woods in a cold, white light. A tingling sensation went through my body. People were coming to kill us.

As the riflemen let go with another volley their red tracer rounds showed me the killing fields of fire they were laying down. All around the perimeter Bravo's machine guns and M-16s opened up in sporadic, sometimes insistent firing. Whoever was coming for us would have to go through some bad dudes firing streams of bullets. The firepower of Bravo Company was awesome to behold.

"Flare round, Paul," Delino yelled to me. I looked up. The mortar flare overhead was sputtering.

"We need to keep the flares constant now," Charles said, "so the riflemen can see the VC. If it goes out before another one is burning the darkness will seem twice as black."

I calculated the charge and elevation.

"Head it into the wind," Charles told me.

I saw which way the first flare had drifted and hollered out, "Flare round, heading one-two-oh."

"Flare round, heading one-two-oh," Eddie repeated as he maneuvered the mortar tube.

"Charge three, seventy degrees."

"Charge three, seventy degrees."

"Fire when ready."

"Ready?" Eddie asked Moore.

"Ready," came the reply.

"Fire!"

It went up over our heads and burst into light. For fifteen seconds both flares burned then the first one sputtered out and ours lit the battlefield.

"Continuous light," Delino cupped his hands and shouted to the men in the foxholes, "brought to you by the Oscar Platoon Lighting Company."

The enemy mortars had stopped but the ground attack grew heavier. Both mortar pits targeted the tree line. The first round I directed landed too deep into the jungle.

"We need to put those just inside the tree line," Charles said to me.

"So I bring it up five degrees?"

"Yeah. Try it and see."

"Raise elevation five degrees," I called to Eddie. "One round, fire when ready."

"Elevation to eighty degrees, one round. What charge?" Eddie frowned angrily at me.

"Same. Charge one."

"Charge one, ready?" his deep voice shouted to Moore.

"Ready," Moore said.

"Fire!" Eddie yelled.

This time our round exploded just yards inside the woods. It knocked down trees and obliterated underbrush.

"Perfect," Delino shouted to me.

"Okay, four rounds, fire when ready," I called to Eddie.

The next four rounds tore the hell out of the jungle and the small arms fire stopped coming in from there. We saw muzzle flashes and green tracer rounds from another place and we turned our mortar on them.

Both mortar crews blasted the attacking VC with round after round and without missing a beat each pit took a turn firing a flare to keep the illumination going. Each mortar round we fired left a cloud of gunpowder smoke and now after twenty minutes of battle, there was a gray haze covering the field around us.

Finally after forty minutes the attack broke off. The jungle grew still and we recovered from our efforts.

"Medevac coming in," Delino warned us. A few moments later we heard the chopper. A blinding spotlight on its belly beamed through the dark night. The Medevac landed near our mortar pits and a tornado of wind threw our gear all over camp. After the wounded riflemen were loaded it lifted off. As the heavy sound of the rotors deafened us, whatever hadn't been blown away on its landing flew away now in the take off.

Moore and I found our air mattresses and laid them next to the pit wall.

"Shit, that was something, huh?" Moore said.

I saw that my mattress had been punctured by a piece of mortar shrapnel and I ran my fingers over the hole.

"Yeah, goddamn scary," I said. I lay down on the ground. "Shit, this doesn't get it," I said.

"Here, you can share mine." Moore moved halfway down his filled, blown-up air mattress. "We can lay head to head," he said, "our butts and legs on the dirt our backs and shoulders on the air bag."

"Thanks, Mack," I said. The top of our heads touched and one of us moving bounced the other around but for me it was better than sleeping on cold hard ground.

I put my hands behind my head and looked up into the night sky. "Damn!" I said. "I was scared when those mortars kept getting closer. It's sheer luck that one of them didn't land right in our pit. My heart is still pounding."

"Did you hear the way the shrapnel was zinging over the mortar pits?" Moore asked.

"Hell yes, I did. That goddamn 'WHISH' sound scared me good. I don't know, Mack, maybe we'd be better off in a rifle platoon. They get to stay in their foxholes while we're out here above ground."

"Yeah, maybe," Moore said, "but I don't like the idea of having to go on ambush either."

"Yeah, you're right about that," I said. "How are we going to survive ten more months of this?"

"I don't know," Moore said. "I sure as hell just don't know."

The next day Charles packed his gear and I sat with him by the mortar pit as he waited for the Chinook to come in.

"Last night," Charles said. "I was trying to read upside down numbers. They looked like strange symbols I'd never seen before. My last night in the field and I'm under fire. Man, I'm sorry but I was just too short to handle it."

"You had your helmet on backwards too," I said. I put my helmet on backwards and made a goofy face and we both laughed.

"Good luck, Paul." Charles shook my hand.

He was going home and his joy rubbed off on me. I was happy for him.

In the afternoon Rojas and I went on day LP. We took our rifles and grenades and walked down the hill and set up ten yards from the tree line. We sat, back to back, looking into the jungle.

"Can the VC sneak up on us without being seen or heard?" I asked Rojas.

"Uh-uh," he said. "They're just like us. We make noise walking through the jungle and so do they."

I still had my doubts. "They must be quieter," I said.

"Look," he said. "I'm going to walk around out there." He pointed to the trees. "Don't shoot."

"Yeah, sure," I laughed.

Rojas went into the bushes. "You can hear me, right?" he called from the jungle.

"Yeah, I can hear you."

I could hear branches moving, grass crunching, twigs snapping as he moved. I thought of Rojas crawling out to get the sniper outside of Quon Loi.

"I'm being as quiet as I can," Rojas called again. "Can you still hear me?"

"Every time you move," I said.

"I'm coming out now."

"Okay."

"Those are men we're fighting not ghosts," he said as he sat next to me.

Several days later we tore down the camp and the slicks came in to get us. The battalion flew east to Long Binh. On the flight I listened to the men talk about what they were going to get at the PX and the women they were going to see at the USO. I looked forward to sleeping on a cot under a roof. We landed on the tarmac in Long Binh and deuce and-a-half-ton trucks drove us to barracks.

"Whose barracks are these?" I asked Delino as we entered one of the buildings.

"An infantry unit based in Long Binh," he said. "While they're out in the field we'll use their barracks just like companies use ours in Di An when we aren't there."

"Seems like we never go into Di An." I said.

"No, we don't. It's a secure area, has been for more than a year. The action's out here, so here we are."

We weren't in the Long Binh barracks a half-hour when Lima's platoon leader, Lieutenant Faro called us together. He was in his late twenties. He was due to rotate home soon and his year in Vietnam seemed to have caught up with him. He had a haggard look about him. He needed a shave and to my eye, a strong drink.

Oscar Platoon needed a new lieutenant and since platoon Sergeant Bell was wounded Delino had been calling the shots. Today headquarters sent Lieutenant Faro over with our orders.

"Oscar's been put on detail to string barbed wire out on the perimeter," the lieutenant said when he had us assembled.

"What?" several soldiers cried out in unison.

"Shit!" Emery said.

"Man, this is fucked," Jesse called out.

"Long Binh already has three strands of wire around it," Delino said.

"Well, you're being sent out to make a section of it doubled," Faro said. "That is, three strands in front of three strands."

"You know you can't be too safe," Delino said, "especially when you can get some grunt unit to do the work for you." It was the first time I had seen him angry.

While the rest of Bravo company had the day off each of us picked up a pair of rawhide gloves and a wire cutter before jumping into the deuce-and-a-half trucks that had come for us. We stood at the railings and rode out to the perimeter.

Emery shouted to Delino. "Why do we have to string their frigging barbed wire?"

"These Remfs are assholes!" someone yelled out to a soldier walking along the road.

"What's a Remf?" I asked Rojas.

"Rear Echelon Mother Fucker." He took one hand off of the rail and gave the finger to another soldier walking along. The soldier looked confused for a second; then saluted Rojas back.

A young sergeant from an engineering corps rode with us. He had a plain face and blond hair. He was in charge of the detail but he didn't say a word when he heard us cursing out the engineers.

"He knows we got a raw deal," Rojas said, "and that the engineers should be stringing the wire for Long Binh."

The truck pulled up at the end of the road and we jumped out.

"Okay, let's get it up," the engineer sergeant called out. We unloaded rolls of barbed wire from the second truck. When there was enough down for that section we cut the bands that held them together and dragged a new roll across the ground. It unraveled like a slinky toy.

The sun baked the ground and there wasn't a hint of a breeze. It was hard, heavy work and we were all beat. After an hour several men drifted off to lie down in the shade. A pipe came out and I joined them. Eventually everyone except Delino and the engineer sergeant were in the shade taking a break. Delino, still wearing his shirt buttoned, collar up and sleeves down, walked over. His uniform was ringing wet. He sat next to me and took a long drink of water from his canteen as he watched the young sergeant still hard at work. Delino looked me square in the face, pointed and said, "Now THAT'S a sergeant!"

"Yeah, he sure is," I said.

Delino went out to help him and it was just the two of them for a while. They were going to do the job themselves or die trying.

"Damn it," I said. "We can't let them do it alone." I went to help and before I reached them the entire platoon was up and back into the killer sun. The cursing had stopped and the only sounds I heard were the snipping of the cutters and the wire being dragged across the ground. At 5 p.m. the young engineer sergeant told us we could call it quits and load up.

We rode back to the barracks in silence. The PX had closed and all of the hot water in the shower sheds was used up. We crashed on our bunks, exhausted. Storm clouds gathered outside and I could smell rain in the air. As evening fell the trade winds shifted the palm fronds outside. Someone turned on a radio and soft music floated across the barracks. Life stood still. It felt good just to be lying on a soft mattress with music playing. The balmy evening air lulled me to sleep.

When I woke in the morning for a moment I thought I was in my room in the house where I grew up but then I saw Delino sitting on the edge of his bunk putting his boots on.

"For a minute I forgot where I was," I said.

"You're in Vietnam, guy," he smiled at me, "so rise and shine."

The squad waited for me and when everyone was ready we walked to the mess hut together. I looked them over; Delino, Rojas, Emery, Mack Moore, Astoga, Donny Langford, Yoakum, Gardner, Eddie, Toby and the others. We were a gang. A barbed wire gang it's true, still, we all knew we were part of a team. It was us against the army, us against the entire fucked-up world for that matter.

On the way back from chow Moore touched my arm and said, "C'mon, Paul."

He walked across the road and we went into one of the engineer's barracks and stopped at a bunk with an air mattress. With an ease borne of practice he quickly but without rushing, let the air out of the mattress, folded it neatly and stuffed it under his arm and walked out.

"Here," he said when we hit the road, "now you got your own again."

"Thanks, Mack," I said.

"Yeah, take care of it will ya?"

"Fucking A, absolutely," I said.

While we were in Long Binh the battalion commander rotated home. After chow one night they put Bravo into a company formation outside the barracks. The sergeant major put us at ease and Colonel Cavasos asked us to gather around him. He was stocky with black crew-cut hair and a square jaw. I sat down with the other men in a semicircle around him. The colonel sat on the sandbags of a foxhole and looked into each face. He spoke slowly.

"I've been going to all the companies to personally say goodbye to the troops," he started out. "I wanted to thank each of you." He nodded to some of the faces he recognized then said to all of us, "It has been the highest honor for me to have been your battalion commander. We've been through quite a lot you and I. Quite a lot." He paused.

"I want you all to know that I will never forget your bravery, your loyalty and your hard work. You always did whatever was asked of you, no matter how dangerous, no matter how difficult." He paused again to look at the young faces before him. "I would choose this outfit for any fight they wanted me in."

He straightened himself up and said with feeling. "I want you to know that I did my best to get you home." His voice choked with emotion and he hesitated. His eyes glazed over and for a moment, in his mind I think he saw the bodies of the young soldiers who hadn't made it.

"I want you all to take care of yourselves," he continued. "Do your duty and go home to your families knowing that you have served your country well. Thank you, and God bless you all."

I looked Delino square in the face, pointed to the colonel and said; "Now THAT'S a Battalion Commander!"

Delino laughed, patted me on the back and put me ahead of himself in the line to shake the colonel's hand.

The new colonel came around two days later to inspect the troops. Unlike Cavasos, Colonel Deiter didn't smile. He was tall and thin. His hair was almost white and his eyes were the color of water in a drinking glass.

The men around me snickered after he left the barracks.

"Did you see the pearl-handled 45?" Emery asked.

"He looks like a cocksucker to me," Jesse put in. "We're in for it now."

Later that week the battalion went on an afternoon patrol. We flew out of Long Binh and into a clearing six clicks east of Ben Cat. It was late afternoon by the time we set off on a jungle trail towards the village. After leaving the clearing the column halted and Bravo Six gave the order for flankers to be put out.

"Every squad will send a man out fifteen feet off the trail," Delino explained to me and Moore. "Okay, Gebhart," he pointed first to me then to the jungle. "You'll walk flanker to the right."

There was no path fifteen feet off the trail. I had to walk through sticker bushes while branches slapped me in the face; but the worst part was the exposure. If the VC had an ambush up ahead, I stood a good chance of walking right into it. Sure, the patrol would be warned but I'd be stuck in no-man's land.

Not only did they expect me to walk flank but they had me carrying a stupid pick as I did it. I had my flack jacket and rucksack on too. My webbing was fully loaded with canteens, ammo and grenades and I struggled under the load.

"Shit. Goddamn it! Son of a bitch," I complained.

"We can't see you but we sure as hell can hear you," Delino called to me.

Gardner suddenly yelled, "VC! VC!" and we all hit the dirt. "I saw three or four of them, I'm tellin' ya." Gardner pointed to the jungle on the right side of the trail. "They were behind those trees about a hundred yards out. I'm not bullshitting"

No one else had seen them but when the patrol continued I felt worse than before. I walked slowly five yards off the trail, looking for the VC that Gardner swore were out here with me. I pictured the pungee pit with bamboo needles laced with human feces and walked even slower. Delino had his eye on me though and he came out from the trail.

"You've got to keep up, Gebhart," he said.

"You're going too damn fast," I said.

"Push on through, Paul. You've got to keep up," Delino said, then went back to the trail.

I began to whack my way through the underbrush.

"Motherfucker!" I shouted as a vine tangled me up.

Delino walked over again. "Here," he said when he reached me, "give me your stuff." He took the pick from my hand and said in disgust, "Now go back to the trail." He turned and walked away before I could say anything. I watched him push hard through the brush, without a grunt or moan.

I followed behind him; after a couple of minutes I caught up and he stopped to look at me. "Okay, Tony," I said, "let me have my stuff back."

He hesitated.

"Come on," I said, "let me have it back."

He handed me the pick and went back to the trail. I kept my mouth shut after that and just struggled with the load like a soldier.

When we reached Ben Cat there was only enough light left to surround the village. Alpha and Charlie companies took a position on the far side of Ben Cat; Bravo Company had the southern half of the hill. Night fell and the stars came out with a quarter moon. Looking up the hillside we could see the lights inside the huts. We ate our C rations cold, out of the can without fires. My watch time was at 10. At midnight, Rojas took over for me and I fell asleep on the damp ground until 2 a.m. when he shook me awake.

"Charlie Company's spotted a VC squad," he whispered.

I sat up and Rojas went down the line to wake the other men in our squad.

Suddenly a burst of rifle fire ripped through the dark. On the other side of the village red and green tracer rounds fired out in every direction. The tracer rounds were shooting up into the night sky and that seemed odd. I sat next to Delino and we both watched as twenty green tracer rounds fired off into the heavens.

"What the hell are the Vietnamese shooting at up there?" I asked.

"Beats me," Delino said.

Thirty red tracers shot wildly straight up into the air. "Well, whatever it is," I said, "our guys are shooting at it too." We both laughed but kept our heads down.

"You know, it's amazing," I said, "Washington and Hanoi can't agree what day of the week it is but somehow they worked it out that they would use green tracers and us red ones."

Delino laughed. "Charlie is way smarter than us. The AK-47s they use can fire our 7.62, M14 and M60 machine bullets, so if they ever get a hold of our ammo they can use it; but their bullets are a millimeter too big for us to use."

"How come we didn't think of that?" I asked.
Our conversation was interrupted by the shock of artillery shells hitting the jungle. The artillery barrage ended the night infiltration and at daybreak the battalion formed a patrol to go up the hill and into Ben Cat. Wet, cold and tired we took the steep trail that led to the dirt road that ran through the village. Dogs barked at us, chickens flew off squawking and the villagers watched from their huts as we came through their backyards. We checked some huts for weapons but there wasn't any action and in a couple of hours the choppers came in and flew us out.

That afternoon in Long Binh, Oscar platoon met its new platoon leader, a Lieutenant Truck. I heard from Delino that he was twenty-six years old and had made officer through the ROTC program at his college in New England somewhere. The lieutenant was a big man with a big butt, thin blond hair and chubby, pink face.

"We just got our orders to relocate to a firebase on Highway 13," I heard Delino telling Rojas. "Lieutenant Truck told me you're to go out with us."

"Is he crazy?" Rojas asked. "I'm down to eight days. If I go out today I'll just stay the night and get the morning Chinook back in."

"Well, that's what you'll do then," Lieutenant Truck interrupted from the doorway, "but you're going out for the night."

Rojas looked at him. "No, uh-uh," he said. "I'm not going."

"We'll see about that," the lieutenant said. He turned and walked out and down the barracks' steps.

A half-hour later I heard Delino quietly tell Rojas, "Captain Allen agreed with you. You can stay in Long Binh when we leave. The captain's an okay guy, you know?"

"Yeah, he sure is," Rojas said. "Thanks, Tony,"

That afternoon as we packed our gear, Rojas came over to me. He held out his hand and I shook it hard and held it a moment.

"Hey, you take care of yourself," Rojas stuttered.

"I will," I said. "What are you going to do when you get home?"

"I'll go see my family in Texas and California."
When I first met him, I used to finish his sentences but I waited for him to complete his thoughts without interrupting.

"Hey, Rojas," I said. "You know that was the bravest thing I ever saw." He looked at me and smiled. "It was also the *dumbest*. Crawling out to go one on one with a hidden sniper? Goddamn, man!"

Rojas chuckled. "Well, you know there's a fine line between crazy and brave."

"Yeah, right, a fine line," I smiled.

He patted me on the shoulder. "I'll write to you and send you some food." We shook hands again and I left the barracks feeling good for Rojas—and sad too knowing that it would be different without him.

We were out on Thunder Road the following week when Delino's big day came. I watched him pack his rucksack outside the mortar pit.

"Well, guy," he said to me as he slung it onto his back, "I've taught you everything I know."

"You taught me good, Tony. Thanks," I said and started to walk with him.

"You're going to make it," he said. "Don't you ever let yourself think otherwise."

"Yeah, sure," I said.

"Well, okay then. I'll be thinking of you and the guys still over here."

"I know you will."

"And quit smoking that dope; it'll make you stupid." He laughed and faked a slap at my face. I blocked it and faked a right hand back at him.

"Hey, I'm already stupid," I said. "I'm here, ain't I?"
"Yeah, but if you'd stay off that stuff you'd almost be a nice guy. So cut it out."

"Okay, Tony, just for you."

He waved his hand and made a face, "You'll be stoned an hour after I leave."

"Ten minutes you mean."

"You hippie."

"You got that right. Hey, how about sending me some love beads when you get home?"

"Yeah, I can just see you now," he grinned at me, "patrolling through the jungle with love beads on."

We reached the landing area as the Chinook came in. It landed loud and threw dirt all over the place. In the middle of the dust storm we shook hands. Delino yelled something that I couldn't hear then turned and walked up the back ramp. I turned my back and protected my eyes as the Chinook lifted up. I watched it fly away until I couldn't see or hear it anymore.

Three days later I was in my lean-to writing a letter to my parents when I heard Lieutenant Truck call for me. "Gebhart? Where's Gebhart?"

"Here," I hollered. I stuck my head out and caught the lieutenant's eye.

"You're on garbage detail," he said. "Follow me."

I picked up my M-16 and followed him across camp to the mess tent where five other men from the line platoons waited for us. A deuce and a half truck drove up and the lieutenant shouted, "Okay, let's get it done."

We loaded the camp's garbage into the truck bed and climbed on top. The lieutenant sat in the passenger seat and after a ten-minute ride the driver backed the truck up to a large hole that the engineers had dug alongside the road. Peasants from a nearby village, mostly old women and children came out to scavenge. They motioned to me to hand them the garbage bags rather than throw them into the hole. They wore ragged clothes and needed baths and I felt sorry for them so I handed them down the garbage bags to let them pick through the contents.

"They'll take any piece of food that isn't totally stinking rotten," I said to the other men on the detail.

"Gebhart," Lieutenant Truck shouted, "throw that trash into the hole." He stood on the step by the passenger door looking back into the truck bed.

"They're hungry," I said.

"I don't care. We're not here to feed them, we're here to dump the garbage."

I stared at him. "What's so bad about letting them sort through it first?"

"It doesn't look right," the lieutenant shouted. "They're eating our garbage."

I pretended to look around for the crowds of disapproving people. Hands held out to my side palms up, I searched then shrugged. "Ain't nobody here but us, Sir. And to them it ain't garbage, it's food."

"Just do as you're told!" the lieutenant yelled. "Throw the goddamn bags into the hole!"

The old women reached up for my plastic bag but I shook my head and threw it over their heads. They climbed right down into the hole and worked the pile; throwing their findings up to the kids to sack.

"Okay," the lieutenant called out when the truck was empty, "cover it up."

The other men shoveled dirt into the hole and the mamasans had to scramble to climb out. A couple of them were slow and were hit with the dirt.

"Hey, Jesus Christ!" I hollered. "Let 'em get out."

The soldiers, hot and tired, yelled at the Vietnamese, "Dee dee moi! Dee dee moi!" (Hurry up! Move it!). One grunt yelled back to me; "Listen, if we let them pick through this stuff we'll be here all day. They'll be back for more when the next truck comes out."

"Okay," I agreed, "but wait for them, they're getting out." We did wait until the women were out then filled the hole.

When we were back in camp the men on the garbage detail joked about the argument I had with the lieutenant. I realized that Lieutenant Truck could hear them and that their laughter did not make me his favorite person.

Chapter Five
Consa and Coca-Cola, So Refreshing

January 1968

Lieutenant Truck introduced two new sergeants to Oscar Platoon while we were out on Thunder Road. Sergeant Meyers would replace Delino as squad leader. He had a thin face and dark sunken eyes. He was a staff sergeant an E-6 from Alabama who'd been in the army for seven years.

The new platoon sergeant replacing Sergeant Bell was an E-7. Sergeant Rigoni was heavyset with black crew cut hair and eyebrows that met at the bridge of his nose. He was in his mid-thirties. He didn't smile when he was introduced but coldly looked each of us in the eye, determined I suppose to show us that he was in charge.

Two days after Sergeants Meyers and Rigoni arrived Bravo Company relocated to a firebase in a very large clearing thirty clicks northwest of Lai Khe, just below the central highlands and a couple of miles from the border. The first night passed quietly until just before dawn when a VC mortar crew began to drop in handfuls of 60mm mortars. Oscar platoon dove into their two pits as explosions lit up the night and showered the air with shrapnel. Sergeant Meyers sat with his back against the sandbag wall, his M-16 in his hands. He kept his mouth shut and watched us work. I thought he looked scared but at least he had come out of his foxhole which was more than could be said of Sergeant Rigoni and Lieutenant Truck. They were nowhere to be seen.

"What can I do?" Sergeant Meyers asked when he saw me looking at him.

"Let's make sure each pit has mortar rounds ready to fire," I called back to him.

Sergeant Meyers worked right alongside the enlisted men pulling mortar rounds from the ammo hole and stacking them for the assistant gunners.

The VC followed their mortar barrage with a ground attack and Captain Allen requested air support. At dawn a small propeller driven spotter plane circled overhead. Several minutes later two fighter jets made a pass at treetop level. The Vietnamese fired their machine guns at the jets as they roared by. Two black canisters dropped lazily from the jets' bellies. A moment later that stretch of jungle disappeared into a ball of orange flame. I peeked over the sandbag pit wall and the heat wave from the napalm passed across my face.

The two jets made a circle high over the area; one fell out of formation and came in and fired two rockets. The rockets screamed through the air and dug a furrow in the ground, knocking down trees before exploding. Debris from the explosions rained down on us.

"I don't know how the VC feel about it," Emery said, "but if it was me I'd Dee-Dee Moi out of there, NOW!"

"God, the sound alone is enough to scare you to death," I said to Moore.

After the second jet ran its rocket run they both came back and one at a time dove straight down firing their canons. Just above the tree line each jet pulled out of its dive in an almost V-shaped maneuver. The sound of their engines was deafening but even above the engines' roar and the canons firing, I could hear a long loud *rip* as the planes literally tore through the air column, pulling up and away.

The jets' ordnance delivery signaled the end of the action as the VC wisely retreated into the jungle.

After their last canon run the two jets flew one more circle around the area before making a last pass at treetop level. They flew wingtip to wingtip and dipped them in a salute as they roared by. We shouted and waved our arms to them.

"I think that's the best feeling out here," Gardner said. "When those boys show up we know we're gonna win, no question."

"If I ever meet one of those fighter pilots," Emery said, "I tell you what, I'm gonna thank him, even though he doesn't know me or why I'm shaking his hand."

I think we all felt the same way.

A half-hour later Sergeant Rigoni came out of his foxhole, walked over to the mortar pit, looked around and said to me, "You, soldier. Clean up those loose boxes there. Let's get them stacked up."

At first I just smiled at him but when I saw he was serious, I had to shake my head and explain, "That may have worked for you in Germany," I said. My tone was instructional, speaking to a man new to the game. "But out here it's gonna make you enemies. Nobody pulls rank on people their first week in the field."

"Soldier I'm ordering you to police up this area," Sergeant Rigoni shouted at me. "Now move it!"

"Listen," I said, louder than I intended, "this isn't maneuvers. We're in a battle zone."

"You're going on report, mister." By this time Rigoni had everyone in the platoon watching us. "Lieutenant! Lieutenant," he called to Lieutenant Truck. "I want this soldier put on report, Sir." He pointed to me and said in a serious tone, "Insubordination."

"And Lieutenant," I called out, "your report should include the fact that Sergeant Rigoni's foxhole needs to be made a bit wider. Seems he gets stuck in it until just after the fighting is over."

"That will be all, Gebhart. Sergeant," the lieutenant turned to Rigoni, "may I have a word with you?"

The lieutenant and Sergeant Rigoni walked away from the pits towards headquarters. The lieutenant stopped halfway and looked out at the tree line but Rigoni kept walking. I laughed when he did a double take and went back to the lieutenant. Truck spoke to him without looking into his face. I sat on the pit wall and tried to imagine how their conversation went;

"The situation out here is unlike anything before," Lieutenant Truck said.

"Insubordination is insubordination." Rigoni's face was flush with anger.

"Yes. You have every right to file charges."

Lieutenant Truck looked at the foxholes on the perimeter. "The captain will deny them, though."

"Discipline must be established," Rigoni said.

"They're lighting up their morning pipes of marijuana." The lieutenant pointed his chin at the riflemen at the perimeter foxholes.

"You know this and allow it to go on?" Rigoni asked with disgust.

"I know it," the lieutenant nodded. "The captain knows it. The major and the colonel know it. That's how they get through it all." The lieutenant still had not looked into the sergeant's face.

Rigoni went to say something but coughed and spit out phlegm. The lieutenant folded his arms. "The thing is with Gebhart and the others is that when the fighting starts they fight."

"High on dope?" Rigoni scoffed.

"Yes, and I'd prefer that they weren't." Now he did look at Rigoni. "But they fight hard and know exactly what to do; know it without instructions or orders. They know it instinctively and as the first bullet goes by their heads, they sober up. I've watched them. In a firefight there are none better."

"There were better soldiers in Korea, in the second. By far better," Rigoni snorted.

"There are none better because they are willing to die for each other. Nothing we do can make a man do that."

"Gebhart is a bum," Rigoni spit out the words.

"Sergeant, my life and yours are in their hands and Gebhart is a fighter. I don't like him, I don't respect him but I need him. Sergeant Rigoni had grown pale with the realization that his authority was limited. He felt lost for a moment, suddenly not knowing his role in the platoon.

"Our job is to put them into position," Lieutenant Truck said, "and let them fight. If they lose, we lose." The lieutenant turned and faced Rigoni. He noticed the sergeant's clean-shaven, pink jowls and bushy eyebrows.

"The best way to deal with the men is through their squad leaders," the lieutenant continued. "They have an understanding. The men can bitch all they want but in the end it must be done, whatever is asked of them."

A few hours after the argument the lieutenant came back to the pits and ordered Moore and me to put out a day LP. We strapped our gear on, took the radio and one rucksack filled with C rations and walked out of the perimeter and set up our LP in the clearing about fifty yards past the barbed wire. Five minutes later, the lieutenant walked out to us.

"I want you in the tree line at the bottom of the hill." The lieutenant pointed to the trees several hundred yards away.

I looked at him and half laughed. "That's ridiculous," I said. "If we got hit while we were out there, there's no way we could make it back alive; running two hundred yards uphill."

"Shut up, Gebhart," Lieutenant Truck said. "Just get your gear and follow me."

Reluctantly Moore and I followed him to the tree line. The lieutenant found a spot at the bottom of the hill. It was about ten yards into the jungle. "Okay, set up in here," he said.

I looked around and saw how far we were from the camp. "Lieutenant, you can't leave two men here alone. This is too damn far out."

"Just do what you're told, Gebhart."

"Goddamn it!" I yelled into his face.

Lieutenant Truck smiled at me, turned and walked away.

"Who does he think he is, putting us out here like this?" I spit on the ground. "I've got family that would be just as heartbroken as his, that son of a bitch."

Truck was in the clearing, walking uphill to the camp. I put the back of his head in my sights. "I ought to shoot the muthafucka."

"Paul, don't!" Moore said.

"We'll say it was a sniper," I said without losing the bead on the back of his head.

"Paul, man, don't shoot."

"Ballistics, you're right. Okay, we'll say it was an accident. I dropped my rifle and it went off."

"Hey, Paul, don't. You just had an argument with him."

I lowered my rifle and looked at Moore. "This man thinks me and you are trash," I said. "He doesn't feel any responsibility for our lives. Look where he's put us. He wouldn't have stayed out here with us. You know that."

"Yeah, he's an asshole. I know it," Moore said.

"How in God's name can he send us to do a job he wouldn't do himself? I want to kill him while I still have the chance."

"If you do they'll put you away for a long time, man. You know?"

"Yeah, yeah, you're right." I relaxed my grip. "But what if we get VC coming through here? How the hell will we get back?"

"I don't know," Moore said. "We'll either hide or fight."

"I'm going to be a father soon," I said. "If I die out here, Truck will have made my baby fatherless and then gone on with his own life. I can just hear him ten years from now, 'Oh yeah, Gebhart and Moore. They were killed on LP duty that one time.'"

"He won't even remember us in ten years," Moore said.

"I think he might," I said under my breath. "I think he just might." I looked around at our predicament. We were in open brush but just fifteen yards away I saw a stand of bamboo.

"Let's check out that big grove."

"All right," Moore said. "Let's check it out."

We walked to the narrow entrance at the base of the bamboo grove and I forced my way in. There was a little room in the middle, just five feet across but surrounded by thick stalks.

"Hey, this is cool." Moore looked up and around as he came into the natural fort.

"We'll be able to hear movement in the jungle," I said, "but we'll be hidden from view."

"The only thing is we don't have a field of fire," Moore said.

"Hell, man if VC come through here we aren't firing on them. Unless they start coming in here, we'll just stay quiet, let'em pass, and warn the camp."

"Okay," Moore said, "let's bring our stuff in."

We brought in the radio and the rucksack and fixed up our position. I took out a couple of C ration cans and Moore used the tiny P90 can opener he kept tied on his dog tags to open them up. We sat back to back, listening for movement. Birds twittered in the trees calling to one another. Although the day was humid without a breath of a breeze, we were comfortable in the shade of our little fortress. The strong scent of the earth filled my nostrils and I studied the beautiful delicate green leaves and the smooth yellow wood of the bamboo plants. The grove was mature; some of the stalks were more than twelve inches around.

"I really like the jungle," I said, breaking the silence.

"Yeah," Moore said, "me too."

"This is as far out in the wilderness as I've ever been. We're what, twenty miles from the nearest village, which is two hundred people living with no electricity. The jungle is raw but beautiful."

Moore held his index finger to his mouth. He tilted his head and listened, intent on identifying the sound he had caught. I saw him freeze refusing to make any movement that might give us away. A wave of fear swept through me. The birds had stopped singing and I held my breath. I could hear it too, a faint rustling of leaves down the trail that led through the bush.

It was a few minutes before we both breathed easier. Whatever had gone by, a deer or a lone VC, our talking that afternoon was over.

"Oscar LP, over," the radio softly called a half-hour later. I adjusted the volume down, took the hand phone and put my lips up against it. "Oscar LP, over," I said as quietly as I could.

"How you doing out there? Over."

"It's Emery," I whispered to Moore when I recognized the voice.

"We're lonely, over."

"Oscar LP, we'll check your loneliness each half hour, over."

"Oscar base, roger that. We're going to acknowledge with squelch break, over."

"Roger, Oscar LP, two breaks, you have movement, one break, all clear, repeat, over."

"Roger, Oscar base, two breaks, movement, one break, all clear, over and out."

Dragonflies darted among the bamboo and beetles plowed through the leaf litter. I watched them but never lost my concentration as I listened for any new sound. Every bird that landed on a branch nearby was duly noted and identified in my mind. In late afternoon at the regular half hour check, the radio softly squelched.

"Oscar base to Oscar LP, over."

I pushed the handset's activator one time to break the squelch sound.

"Oscar LP, roger squelch break. You can come back in now, over."

"On our way," I whispered into the handset. "Over and out." We came out of the bamboo, out of the far tree line and walked the long walk uphill to camp. When we reached the mortar pits everyone greeted us. They were happy that nothing had happened. The radio played Hendrix's version of *All Along The Watchtower*.

"Well, that fits. Said the Joker to the Thief," I said it along with the song and Moore laughed.

After that incident, we followed their orders but neither of us would speak to the lieutenant or Rigoni. There were no cordial, "Good mornings" between us.

A few days later Monk walked up from Lima Platoon and dropped his rucksack by the pit wall.

"You quit and going home?" I asked.

"No," Monk smiled, "they told me I've been transferred to Oscar."

"Get out of here. Really?"

"Yeah, no shit."

"I never heard of anyone getting transferred to the mortar platoon," Moore said. "How did you manage that?"

"I have no idea." Monk shrugged. "They just told me to go get my stuff and report over to Oscar. Man, I've just been moved off of the line, can you believe that?"

"Well, you're in our squad then." I turned and asked Sergeant Meyers, "Okay, Sarge?"

"Yeah, sure," Sergeant Meyers said.

We started a game of Bid Whist, Monk and Moore against Emery and me. We enjoyed each other's humor and I felt we had the best damn squad in Vietnam but the good feeling of having Monk aboard ended that same night as the camp came under fire. An enemy mortar attack started things off. It was a pitch-black night but still as humid as the day had been. The men jumped into the mortar pit with just their pants and boots on.

We fired on three of the four clearings shown on our map but the barrage continued so I called to Sergeant Meyers and he crawled across the pit.

"Look, Sarge," I said, "we're gonna get killed out here if we don't stop those mortars from coming in on us."

Shrapnel WHISHED over the mortar pits and we both slid as low to the ground as we could go. I turned the map around so he could read it and pointed to the clearings, "We've fired on these three clearings here, here and here. Toby's hit the fourth one, here." I had to yell into his ear to be heard over the commotion of people yelling and mortars exploding.

Sergeant Meyers shined his red-filtered flashlight on the map and studied it for a moment. "Let's hit this here big clearing to the north one more time," he said in his southern drawl.

"Okay, one more time," I said. "How about putting both tubes on it at once?" Meyers nodded. "Yeah, good. Tell Toby to turn his mortar around."

"You tell him, Sarge." I took the map back. "I'll get my gun directed."

I crawled over to the gunner, Eddie.

Sergeant Meyers called to the other pit. His voice sounded thin and nervous. "Toby! Hey, Toby!" Toby looked up.

"We're gonna fire both guns at the clearing at three-twenty-five degrees, 210 yards out," Meyers yelled.

"I'll walk mine left to right," I hollered, "you bring yours in north to south."

"Okay," Toby shouted.

"Four rounds each gun," Sergeant Meyers ordered. He watched as both tubes prepared to hit the target. "*Fire* when ready," he yelled in his southern twang.

The two mortar crews fired eight rounds into the target in a crossing pattern. We alternated each round; pit one fired the first round, pit two the second round and so on:

Thump-thump..thump-thump..thump-thump..thump-thump.

The two gunners turned their hand cranks one rotation between each round to walk the mortars across the clearing. When they exploded, it sounded like a bass drum beating in the jungle:

Boom-boom... boom-boom... boom-boom... boom-boom.

We heard the rounds explode and cheered, "YEA!"

The enemy mortars stopped and the ground attack fizzled and afterwards I sat on the pit wall with Sergeant Meyers. We were too wired-up to sleep.

"You know Sarge," I said. "your 'fire when ready' sounds exactly like '*fair* when ready.'"

Sergeant Meyers patted me on the back, "You got my drift though, right?"

I laughed with him. "Yeah, Sarge, I got your drift."

We were still in that big clearing when the Tet offensive started. We heard over the radio that the old capital, Hue, had been seized. Saigon was under heavy attack and even Di An had a ground attack. Lieutenant Truck was called to a meeting in the captain's tent. When he returned, he asked us to gather around the mortar pit.

"We're going out tomorrow morning," he said. "We'll tear it down here then patrol and set up in a new clearing due west."

I heard the boys grumbling, but the lieutenant ignored them. "Tonight we're on full alert. That means the watch teams are two hours on, two off. If anyone is caught sleeping, the captain will want to see them personally." The lieutenant paused. "We'll start to tear it down at first light. Any questions?"

"Yo," I called out.

"Gebhart?"

"What do we have to carry, Sir?"

"Everything."

"What exactly do you mean by everything, Sir?"

"Everything is everything."

"We're gonna carry the mortar tube and the mortar rounds?"

"Yes, they're coming with us."

I heard the men cursing in the dark.

"Sir," I said, "we can't shoot the mortar on patrol, not from under trees. The mortar equipment should be loaded up and flown out on the Chinook, then flown into the new camp, just like they do with the water trailer and headquarters' tents."

"Well, we're to carry the mortars," the lieutenant answered.

"And the picks and the shovels and all our own gear," I said. "Don't you see, Sir? We'll be loaded down, in the heat and humidity..."

"Those are our orders," the lieutenant shrugged.

"Well go argue for us," I said. "If they want us to patrol like the rifle platoons we should carry just what they carry. We've been through this before. After a couple of clicks we'll hardly be able to pay attention to what's around us or where we're going."

"Couple of 'clicks'?" Truck asked.

"Miles—kilometers; they're called 'clicks' here, Sir."

The lieutenant thought for a moment. "Those are the Captain's orders," he finally said.

"So go argue with him; explain it to him."

"That's not my job," the Lieutenant raised his voice.

"It sure as hell is, Sir," I answered back.

"That will be all, Gebhart. Any other questions?"

There was silence and the Lieutenant and Sergeant Rigoni walked to their foxhole.

"They are absolutely fucking nuts," I said as I packed my stuff. "We're hearing reports of NVA regiments and divisions moving around and they want us to do a company-size patrol out at the border? God damn them!"

"This little walk in the sun tomorrow is gonna be a bitch," Gardner said.

"Just a nice stroll through the woods, La Dee-Daa," Jesse said.

"Yeah," Moore put in, "then when we gets wiped out the general will shrug his shoulders and say; 'I didn't think they needed any backup out there.'"

We left camp the morning of the next day. Serena walked point with Lima platoon then came November, Headquarters, and Mike platoons. Oscar was the last to leave the clearing. Sergeant Meyers with the lieutenant's radio strapped to his back handed out our assignments. When he got to me I said, "I'll walk caboose."

He looked up from his clipboard. "Okay, Gebhart," he said and stayed with me until everyone had started off. We were the last two to go into the tree line. "You be careful," he said.

"Don't worry about me," I said, "and don't come near me again with that radio on. That's the first damn thing they shoot at. And anyone near the radioman they figure must be an officer so they shoot them next."

Meyers didn't laugh. "Listen," I said in a softer tone, "if we get hit just stay down. No matter what, just keep the fuck down." He nodded and jogged up the line to Lieutenant Truck.

I looked back into the empty campsite and realized its remoteness. I knew I'd never see the place again or ever forget it.

As we patrolled I walked sideways or backwards, keeping an eye on the trail behind us. Walking caboose was as dangerous as walking point that's what they said anyway but I'd rather be here than alongside Serena at the front of the parade.

Despite the turmoil engulfing the rest of the country Bravo Company out at the border alone didn't run into a single Vietnamese soldier.

"They must have gone by us on their way into the cities," I said to Moore at a rest stop. "We're probably in the safest place in Vietnam; wandering around out in the jungle."

"Colonel Dieter must have felt that way too," Emery said. "Word just came down the line that our orders have changed. We're to be picked up and flown into Saigon."

When we arrived at the new clearing we waited for the choppers and in less than an hour four waves of Hueys came in. Bravo Company loaded up and flew down to Saigon in one large V formation.

"This is the first paved road I've seen in three months," I shouted into Moore's ear as we looked down on Saigon.

Moore yelled back into my ear to be heard over the sound of the Huey's engine, "There's supposed to be a big fight going on at the racetrack."

All of us searched the landscape.

"There it is, there," Emery yelled, pointing.

"Yep, that's it!" Moore pointed with him.

I couldn't see movement from that distance but the rising column of smoke and the Cobra gunships circling above the racetrack battle verified the firefight.

"Alpha, Charlie, and the Recon platoon are all in it," Emery shouted.

"I hope they leave us out," Moore said.

"Yeah, but where are they sending us alone?" I asked. My question ended the conversation.

Fifteen minutes later the choppers landed us on a paved road in what looked to be about six miles north of the center of Saigon. South Vietnamese soldiers sat on top of armored personnel carriers guarding the highway that led into downtown. There was no civilian traffic but throngs of Vietnamese kids ran over to watch the helicopters land. As Bravo Company disembarked from the choppers and patrolled down the highway the children came up to us. To them it was still a Tet holiday and they laughed and shouted to each other. They asked us for money and cigarettes which we gave them. I saw admiration in their eyes and it made me feel good.

Our patrol walked into a clearing behind a water treatment plant across the highway from a Vietnamese mechanized unit. *Thu Duc,* the black lettered sign at the front of the building read.

We dropped our stuff and started to dig in. At the first opportunity, Moore and I stole inside the building to explore. We found hot water showers and quickly stripped off our dirty fatigues and jumped in.

"It's gotta be four weeks since we've had a hot shower," he said.

"This sure beats the hell out of being out in the jungle," I laughed and we toweled off with our fatigue shirts.

"Goddamn right it does," Moore said. He lit a yellow joint and we smoked it sitting in the cool of a tiled hallway.

Bravo Company had lucked out. We hadn't fired one shot the first day of Tet; not on patrol in the morning out by the border not at the racetrack with the rest of the battalion and not at the power plant. Just lucky and to boot Tet got us out of the jungle.

In my letters home I had described my friends and their ways and the living conditions but never mentioned the firefights. I wrote them now that our unit had missed all of the action on Tet. I was safer than I had been all year. Which was true enough but I knew it would be hard for them to believe. As they read my letters I know they wondered where I was at that very moment. And of course as they watched the nightly news they couldn't help but worry.

The showers soon were off limits to everyone but the officers. There was nothing to do except play cards and listen to the radio unless you were put on detail. Every day Bravo Company sent eight men to the roof of the power plant. Their guns had a commanding view of the area but the roof was broiling hot and despite shade from tents made from our ponchos, it was hard duty. The other daily chore assigned to Bravo was to guard a bridge on the outskirts of Saigon. Every morning a detail loaded up a truck and drove north on the blacktop road. At the bridge after unloading the guards walked down an embankment to a shack underneath the span. Vietnamese refugees lived along the riverbank in huts with roofs made of flattened beer cans. Some of the refugee women sold sex, others dealt consa Vietnamese grass. During the daylight hours there hadn't been any trouble at the bridge and the soldiers away from officers and sergeants, made it something like a clubhouse. When it was Oscar Platoon's turn to send a detail I quickly volunteered. We loaded up the truck and I rode shotgun has Gardner was already behind the wheel. The rest of the guys jumped into the back and Gardner drove out to the bridge and parked along the highway. As the other men unloaded the gear he and I went down the embankment. We stopped in front of the dilapidated old shack and laughed. It didn't have a foundation and the walls leaned at an angle. Gardner opened the flimsy front door and we looked in. A wooden telephone cable spool lay on its side in the middle of the shack. Wooden milk crates were used for chairs. I sat on one and started to roll a joint. Gardner looked out the hole in the wall that was the window.

"These new recruits are as nervous as whores in church," I said as I concentrated on constructing the joint. "Coming into country during the Tet offensive shook 'em up."

"I don't like these gook women and children so close by," a new recruit said. He was short and fat. Shorter than me even and a good thirty pounds heavier. He had a large square head with bright red hair and a bushy red mustache. "I was told that the women and children are used by the VC to kill GIs," he bellowed. His voice was louder than was necessary. "They better not come around here," he said in a deep voice. "I'll shoot the sons of bitches."

"You can't just open up," I said to him as I rolled another joint. "What's your name, anyway?"

"I'm, Max," he said.

"Wa-well, wa-wa-what if they're-a, there're-a VC?" another new soldier named Gerald asked. Gerald was a mulatto and a good foot and a half taller than Max.

"If you see them with arms or grenades then, hey, you blow 'em away," Gardner explained, "but you gotta see weapons first."

"That means they could get off the first shot," Max said.

"Or a, be-be hiding their gren-grenades," Gerald said quietly.

"Yeah, it's a bitch," Gardner agreed, "but that's how it is here. We don't kill kids or women. That's not what we're about."

"Yeah?" Max said. "Well if I think a kid's got a weapon I'm shooting him first and checking later."

"Hey, listen good now," Gardner spoke slowly. "You shoot an unarmed kid or unarmed woman. You won't make it home. Understand? You'll be hit in the next firefight." He paused to let it sink in. "You won't make it home, man. I'm telling you straight."

I stopped to look Max in the eye. "Guaranteed," I said. "I wasn't raised to be in the goddamn German Gestapo. We're Americans. The good guys, see? That's how I was brought up."

"Me too," Gardner agreed. "Even over here we aren't going to throw that away."

Max fell silent and walked outside. Gerald followed him and they sat under the bridge together. I could see them through the open door, talking and laughing.

"It's funny," I said, "those two guys are as opposite as day and night, yet they're best friends."

"Not only that," Gardner agreed, "but that redheaded big mouth is the only person Gerald will talk to at all. He's so shy that when I asked him something this morning he couldn't even answer me."

"I wish Max was as shy," I said.

"Yeah, they're a strange couple, okay." Emery had overheard us. "But they fit right into this strange war."

"Yeah, I guess," I said. "He sure has a big mouth though. Listen to him. He's not even shouting and his voice is LOUD." I imitated Max's voice.

"I talked to him for a couple of minutes this morning," Moore said. "Whew, that white boy is real lifer material. He's been in the army four years and re-enlisted for four more while he was in Germany."

"Oh, Lord have mercy," Gardner groaned.

"Shit, man, just what we need," Emery cursed.

"Yeah," Moore said. "Max says the maneuvers back in Germany were like the real thing and he's ready."

"Oh, man, shit. MAN-EU-VERS!" Emery yelled and we laughed.

We were playing cards when Max and Gerald came back into the shack. "Y'all smoking dope?" Max asked.

I went to offer him a hit, figuring he wanted some but Moore spoke before I could say anything. "Yeah, man," Moore said. "What's it to you?"

"I'm going to have to report this to the CO," Max said.

Moore put his cards down, placed both of his hands on the table top and laughed, "Oh yeah? Listen, you pumpkin-headed asshole, you keep your mouth shut. You understand?"

A big "Oohh" went up from the soldiers in the shack. Max didn't say anything. I thought he was searching for a comeback when Emery jumped in.

"Look here, muthafucka,"—Emery sounded stoned, "you're gonna end up with your head busted open if you say anything to anyone about what we do. So cool it. And try to fit in why don't-ja."

"That's good advice he's giving you," I nodded.

Max went to answer, thought better of it and went back outside. Gerald got up and went with him.

Later that afternoon, I needed some air so I walked down to the riverbank and stood at the end of a cement dock. A few Vietnamese boats floated slowly down the green river. On the other side, across the way, I saw huts peeking out behind the lush jungle vegetation. A large grey powerboat with a crew of three men came around the bend to my left. Two of the soldiers waved to me as they passed by and I toasted them with my beer can. The boat made a tight circle and came full speed right at me. Just before ramming the cement dock, the driver pulled back on the throttle and the hull flattened out. The speedboat floated smoothly into the rubber tires, its big inboard engines rumbling. Their wake rolled in behind them and splashed up on the dock. I hadn't moved an inch, which is what they were looking to see.

The powerboat had dual 30-caliber machineguns mounted on its front deck and a fifty-caliber on the stern deck. The three crewmen all wore black berets.

"Hey," I said, "this is a great boat you got here."

"Yeah? You like her?" a short black soldier asked me.

"Fucking-A I do. What kind of horsepower?"

"Horsepower, shit, she runs on booze and dope just like us." A blond guy with a heavy metal cross hanging down his chest came out from behind the wheel. They tied the bow to the dock.

Another black soldier, wearing sunglasses taped together with a Band-Aid said, "She'll crank about 475 horse at 4,000 rpm."

"That'll get it done," I said as I watched him tie the stern to the dock. The words "Mary Jane" were painted in fancy scroll across the front of the bow and from inside the cabin Aretha's "Chain of Fools" was thumping loud.

"You want to trade some C rations for some grass?" the short brother asked.

"We already have C rations," I said. "What else have you got to eat?"

"Shit," the blond guy said, "we got all kinds of stuff. You got any smoke though?"

I pulled out my waterproof canvas stash bag and threw it to him. "Help yourself," I said. "If you like it there's more in the shack up there with my buddies."

"Hoo yeah!" they yelled in unison.

The soldier with the broken sunglasses went into the boat's cabin and handed me three bananas and half a dozen Tasty-Cakes. "I'm Smitty," he said. "That there's Donald." He pointed to the white guy. He pointed his chin towards the shorter black soldier and said, "That's Michael."

"Tasty-Cakes! Man, this is great," I said. "Come on over and meet the boys."

With the music left on and playing loud we walked up to the guard shack. I introduced them around and Donald and Smitty sat in at the poker game. Smitty threw a handful of Vietnamese dollars on the table. "These pees have got to be spent, damn Monopoly money."

"They sure do look like Monopoly money," Gardner laughed.

A while later a mamasan came over from the huts and made a deal to bring five young women to the guard shack. Everyone but me and a couple of others took turns with them; some men were going at it with them in the guardhouse a couple others went back to the boat with two women. Music blared from the speakers on the boat and from the radio in the shack and the poker game went on non-stop.

"I'd like to have your job," I said to the white guy, Donald as he looked at his cards and threw in 20 pee.

"It'll cost you a two-year tour of duty," he said.

"No, I couldn't do that," I said.

Donald shrugged, "Everything's got a price, man."

"Yeah," I nodded, "you're right about that."

While we were partying at the bridge, the rifle platoons walked a patrol through the neighborhoods around the power plant. When we came back from the bridge just before dark I heard that someone had been killed by sniper fire. I walked across the camp to Lima Platoon to find Serena. From a distance, I saw him sitting on the sandbags of his foxhole. He held his head in both hands, bent over. Was he crying?

"What's wrong?" I asked him when I got closer.

"Martinez was killed," he said without looking at me.

"What?"

"The scumbags could have saved him," Serena said. "He was hit in the leg, but there was some confusion over the coordinates, and while the Medevac flew around looking for us, he bled to death."

I was shocked. Romero Martinez was from Miami; Cuban born with a medium build and straight black hair. He had a handsome face and carried himself tall and upright, like a matador.

"Martinez was at the mortar pits just yesterday," I said. "We had a Polaroid and he kept pulling out joints and waving them around for the camera. He sent the photos to his girlfriend to show her how we partied."

"Martinez was a trooper," a Puerto Rican with dark wavy hair and gray eyes named Francisco said. "Man, he seen a lot of action and he always distinguished himself."

"When the VC attacked the perimeter where Martinez was," Serena got his voice back, "we knew that they were going to have some trouble because he could fight. He always held up his part of the load. We're really gonna miss him." He started to cry again and nobody said anything.

I hadn't seen the body and it was hard for me to grasp his death. I would feel it for a moment, the finality of a life gone forever, but then it seemed impossible. How could he be dead when just hours before I had heard his voice and seen him laughing?

The next morning all of Bravo Company went back to patrol the neighborhood where Martinez was shot. We walked along the highway for a half-mile before moving over to a dirt path that ran parallel to the roadbed. Around the first bend the bodies of two Vietnamese men lay sprawled across the ground. They both wore white silk shirts and dark shorts. One of them had on a dirty, white linen jacket. Their faces were frozen in a frightening death stare. Black flies drank the fluid from their eyes and mouths. They lay in the middle of a circle of red where their blood had soaked into the brown dirt road overnight.

"Hey," I said, "they don't have any weapons."

"Their buddies must have taken them," Emery said.

"They would have taken their bodies too," I said. "No, I don't think these guys were VC."

"Well, maybe not," Emery said. "It might have been the VC who took them out here and executed them."

"None of the officers are making anything of it." Moore pointed down the road to the platoons walking away. "They're counting them as two dead VC."

"That's two for Martinez," I heard one of the riflemen say as he walked by.

"Life is too damn cheap here," I said.

"Well, that's the way it goes." Monk nudged me with his shoulder to move on. I walked next to him as we caught up with the rest of the company.

A few miles further, on the street where Martinez had been hit, the platoons went door to door looking for weapons. Oscar walked to the end of the block and went into the backyard of a large property. I sat on the cement wall of a fishpond in the middle of the garden.

"This is some place," I said to Monk. "I haven't seen a house this nice since I drove through Short Hills."

"This is something," Monk nodded. "I didn't know there were any rich Vietnamese."

The lieutenant called to us from the back of the house and we walked over and joined the rest of the platoon on the back porch. Grandfather papasan sat in a rocking chair with his two little granddaughters standing on either side of him. He was a distinguished old man with silver white hair and beard. He looked to me like Ho Chi Minh just a little heavier. There were deep character lines etched into his brown face and he had an air of wisdom about him.

Lieutenant Truck said "Good morning," to the grandfather, but it was the woman of the house, a lady in her twenties, who responded. She bowed to the lieutenant and asked him in English what we wanted. Lieutenant Truck explained that he was sending us in to search their home. She made a face and said, "No, that isn't possible. Not in our house."

"I'm sorry, we have orders," the lieutenant explained.

She continued to argue but Lieutenant Truck signaled for us to go inside.

"Check all the rooms and closets," he said as we filed past the young woman.

The porch door led into the living room. Mamasan followed us from room to room. She was worried that we would steal something and I could understand her concern. The living room had fine mahogany furniture; porcelain and jade statues. Beautiful vases were displayed on the tables and bookcases. There was a painted screen separating the living room and dining room. Ink landscape drawings hung on the walls.

We went up the wide carpeted stairway from the living room to the second floor. The bedrooms up there were all large and shaded from the sun's rays by wooden awnings and shutters. The bedroom furniture like the living room furniture, was hand-carved dark mahogany.

Red silk oriental rugs on the floor contrasted the yellow flowered wallpaper.

We searched the closets and looked under the beds but found no arms and under mamasan's watchful eye we went back downstairs and out to the porch.

"I guess papasan isn't a communist after all," I said.

"Okay," Lieutenant Truck said, ignoring my remark, "let's move out."

I bowed to the lady of the house but she didn't smile. Papasan did though and I waved to the little girls as I passed them. They giggled with their hands over their mouths.

When we returned to the power plant I had a letter and a package from Rojas. We all shared packages from home so I took one of the two bottles of hot sauce from the wrapping and threw the other one to Moore.

"Hey," I said to Moore as I read the note, "Rojas has been awarded the Bronze Star."

"Yeah? He deserved more than that," Moore said.

"Yeah, you're right about that," I said.

"And I got a letter from Cool," Moore said. He came over and sat with me on the pit wall and read the letter to himself.

"How is he?" I asked.

"He's in an army hospital in Virginia. A candy-stripper wrote for him. He's lost his right arm at the elbow but he's happy to be out of Vietnam with his life."

"That's a heavy price to pay," I said, "but he'll be getting disability now for the rest of his life. That'll make him happy. The only work he was ever good at was getting out of work." I meant it as a joke but Moore answered me seriously.

"Man's got to have his work," he said. "If they take that from you, they've really won. A man has got to come home at night knowing his work paid for the food and rent. If you're living on welfare and hustling unemployment or disability, well you may get by but then they'll have robbed you of your manhood."

"I see what you mean," I said.

A few mornings later the lieutenant called us together. He put us into formation and called us to attention. "It seems the captain has had reports that individuals from this platoon have been drinking and smoking dope while on duty at the bridge."

"Damn," I said, "now who would say a thing like that?"

"Yeah," Emery said, "this is a bad rumor, Sir."

"Can it, both of you." The lieutenant was not laughing. "Because of these fuck-offs we've been ordered out on a platoon-size patrol."

"Well that's one way to get rid of us," I said. "Send us out alone into the jungle."

"Gebhart, goddamn it, I said shut up!" The lieutenant's face turned red.

"Come on, Gebhart!" Toby said. "You'll get us all hung." Toby's backing the lieutenant took me by surprise and I shut up. We ate breakfast then came back to the mortar pits to get ready for the patrol.

"This is not very smart," I said as I put my webbing on. "A platoon on patrol will be a tempting target for snipers or an ambush."

"Hey, Gebhart," Toby called out, "how come they don't ever listen to you?"

"Beats me," I said. "If they did, we wouldn't have half the problems."

"Yeah, right," Toby said. "So when are you going to officer's school?"

"Right after you re-enlist, Toby." The boys laughed and Toby shut up.

Twenty-two of us walked out of camp and into the jungle. After a quarter mile the trail ended at a wide stream. I stopped to look into the brackish water.

"It's yellow," I said.

"Looks like turtle's piss," Emery agreed.

"Okay, we're going across," the lieutenant said. He waved his arm to signal us to follow him. He stepped into the stream but I hesitated.

The sound of insects filled the dead humid air and sunlight reflected off of the stagnant yellow water. Something in my soul recognized this piss-poor spot...

"In the tropical heat the insects don't fly, they crawl to the feast," I said to the guys around me.

The polluted yellow water expressed to me the suffering of the Vietnamese people. "Always the suffering of the poor," I said, but nobody understood me.

"Life is so much larger than the history books; bigger than all of the books and all of the things people try to tell you about it." Still nobody listened to me. "I never wanted to see this side of life," I said, "now I'm going to swim in it."

"C'mon, Paul." Moore coaxed me from behind and I stepped into the still water. The stench of rotting decayed life filled my nostrils. At the deepest part the water was waist high. I held my rifle up and waded across. "If we get hit now," I said, "we'll be wiped out."

"Shut up, Gebhart," Toby yelled from up ahead. "I'm tired of your bitching."

"Oh, yeah? Well, fuck off, Toby. I'm tired of your ass-kissing." As I said it, Toby turned around in the water and came at me. Emery and Moore jumped in between us.

"You guys nuts?" Emery said as he held Toby. "You're in the water, in the middle of the jungle."

"Come on, settle this later." Moore held me back.

"Gebhart! Toby!" Lieutenant Truck yelled from the far bank. "Get moving!"

We went up the muddy bank and through a narrow strip of jungle.

"Shit, I got leeches," Moore called out.

"Me too," Sergeant Meyers said.

"Okay, let's keep alert while these men get help," the lieutenant said. The patrol sat down on the trail and while most of the men kept watch, Moore stripped off his shirt and I lit a cigarette.

"Don't pull at them," I said to Moore. "I got to put some heat on their heads to make them let go."

"Don't burn me, Paul." He looked over his shoulder to try and see how many were on his back.

"It's just two of them," I said. "Let me get 'em." I slowly brought the red end of my Marlboro closer and closer to his skin. I had to hold the cigarette pretty close for thirty seconds before the first one let go. Moore stomped on the mother before I could go get the next one.

After the leech operation Lieutenant Truck waved his arm and the patrol continued down the trail until it led us into a field of rice paddies. We came out of the tree line and I could see a couple of huts on the far side of the field. A herd of water buffalo grazed near the huts and as our patrol walked across the top of the dike wall the bull in the herd looked up and eyed us. We had gone halfway across the dike when he charged. He trotted through the shallow water in a straight line and there was no question he was coming for us. He tossed his horns in anger and bellowed like he intended to knock us into the next rice paddy. We all hit the dirt as if we had been shot at. The kid who was tending the herd halfway between us and the bull, ran in front of us, splashing through the water screaming and yelling at the bull.

"Hold your fire," Sergeant Meyers shouted.

The boy intercepted the bull's charge and whacked him in the head with a long, thin sapling stick. The bull pulled up, still eyeing us. He bellowed one more time but the fury had gone out of him and the kid turned him back to the herd with another whack on the butt.

"I tell you what," Sergeant Meyers said as we resumed the patrol. "That kid did one hell of brave thing, running in front of our guns like that. He must be only twelve years old."

"I guess he was afraid of what his Dad would have done to him," I said, "if the bull had gotten blown away while he was supposed to be watching it. I can just imagine my father if it was me. 'Hey, where's the bull?'" I impersonated my father's voice. "'What do you *mean* he got shot?' My father has this way of biting the inside corner of his bottom lip when he gets upset and he always yells the same thing: 'Jesus CHRIST! GOD DAMN IT! What the HELL'S the matter with you?'"

I laughed, but I would have given anything to be home with him, yelling or not.

Our fatigues and boots never dried from the stream crossing and my foot blistered. By the time we made it back to Bravo Company I was limping. While we sat around the mortar pit and laughed about The Charge Of The Water Buffalo, Desusa, Serena, and a dozen brothers from the rifle platoons came over to hang around.

"We all curse too much," I said as I listened to my friends' talk.

"You're the worst one of us, Gebhart," Gardner said. "What the hell does 'Fucking A' mean anyway?"

"Fucking-A? Why, it's Italian for 'That's absolutely correct, my good fellow.' Besides my 'Fucking-A' isn't as bad as all the 'muthafuckas' you hear around here all day."

I peeled off my wet socks and laid the piece of blistered skin back across the open flesh. "I think every sentence I've heard for one entire year—no, two—has had 'motherfucker' in it."

"That could be due to the overall dissatisfaction everyone has with the army," Desusa said.

"Hey, you gonna go stand in chow line?" I mimicked Emery's voice. "Fucking A, let's go," I said in my own. Jesse laughed so I imitated him; I bobbed my head up and down as I spoke. "Hey, that muthafucking sergeant put me on latrine duty again!"

"Fuck you, Gebhart," Jesse said.

I laughed. "Hey, you want a hit off this roach?" I half shut my eyes like Desusa when he's stoned. "You're fucking-A I do, muthafucka," I said in my own vernacular. "Heck of a way for a nice Jewish boy like me to talk, huh?"

Jesse called to me, "Hey, Gebhart would you lick pussy?"

"This is his favorite subject," I said to the guys near me. "Yeah, fucking-A I would," I called back to him. "I love to hear them moan with delight."

The black soldiers all scoffed at me. Jesse's head bopped up and down as he laughed. Pointing to me he said, "You lick dick."

"Fuck you, Jesse."

"Well, there's been a dick in that pussy and you're licking it." Jesse laughed.

The black guys let out an "Ooh."

"You know it's black men that got what it takes to make them moan with delight," Jesse said.

"Yeah?" I said. "Well, Jewish men have the *widest* dicks, so we aren't jealous of anybody."

"Yeah, but you still suck dick," Jesse mocked me.
"Okay," Desusa called out. "All black guys who suspect someone of sucking cock please step forward."

"Hey man, fuck you," they yelled back to him.

"Okay," Desusa unbuttoned his fly, "everyone take out your dick and let's all wave them to the big cocksucker in the sky."

"Oh, man, fuck up," one of the brothers yelled.

"Desusa, you're gonna burn in hell for saying that," Gardner said seriously.

"You mean I'm not in hell now?" Desusa laughed. "Besides, I want to go to there—that's where all the fun girls are."

"Nah, it's probably like the army," Monk said. "It's all guys and you get put into different platoons."

"Oh yeah?" I said. "Well, next time I'm gonna stay at Division Headquarters, definitely."

A week after the buffalo incident Bravo Company flew out to a village called Cu Chi. The choppers landed us in a clearing and we ran to the tree line and hit the dirt. We expected to draw fire but instead out of the jungle came an old mamasan in black pajamas. She was wearing a woven reed hat and chewing black beetle nut. Behind her were three teenage girls and two young boys. The boys struggled with a metal cooler. I heard the mamasan ask one of the riflemen, "You want Coca-Cola? You want? Cold, you like." The two young boys opened the metal box and pulled out a few cold bottles.

"Consa? Good consa. You-like? Good price for you, 200 pees," mamasan said when the cokes didn't move as expected.

"She must have heard our choppers coming in," I said to Moore as we lay in the grass. "She gathered her work force and came out of the village to sell us consa, cunt, and Coca-Colas—everything a GI needs."

The riflemen didn't buy anything so she led her staff farther down the tree line to where November platoon lay prone in the grass covering the tree line. She walked up behind them with her entourage and I heard Carter yelling at her, "Not NOW, lady! Deedee moi! Dee-dee moi!"

Mamasan ignored him and led the young girls around to each squad, offering them to the troops. The two young boys followed behind, plenty tired of carrying the metal box. I laughed when I saw them making faces at each other.

"She's gonna make a sale no matter what," Moore laughed.

"She better hurry up, before those two boys fall down," I said.

It wasn't until a couple of men put their weapons on her that mamasan stopped. November men searched them for grenades then made them sit in one spot. They had to keep a guard on the old woman too. She couldn't believe that they would interfere with her business like this. She squatted under a tree, her teeth black from beetle nut speaking in rapid Vietnamese to November's platoon leader.

"Time is money. Time is money, she's trying to tell him," I said, "but the lieutenant, he doesn't get it."

Later, back in camp we were around the mortar pit and Carter told the story for the men who hadn't seen it. "What the hell kind of war is this anyway?" he asked.

"Did stuff like this happen during the Crusades?" I asked Desusa.

"Beats the shit out of me," Desusa said as he pulled on the roach he was hogging.

"Consa, cunt, and Coca-Cola," I said. "That's how this war should go down in history."

"Yeah, but it's so refreshing," Emery said and we all laughed.

* * *

By the end of February it seemed that every whore in Saigon knew there was an American army unit at the water plant. They arrived by bus, bicycle, moped or on foot to stand outside the barbed wire of our company perimeter hoping to do some business. We were playing cards one day when a girl about nineteen walked up to the barbed wire and began to take her clothes off.

"What's she doing?" I asked.

"Ooo wee!" Gardner yelled. "Look at this! Look at this!" he shouted to Emery.

The young woman called to us, "I good fuck. I give you plenty. Me number one."

"She's pretty cute," I said.

"Damn right," Moore agreed.

She danced naked, a little bump and grind as she ran her fingers over her breasts and crouch. "Ooh, me so hot," she said. "You like? Me like. Ooh me like."

"I'm getting a hard-on just watching her," I said.

It was Gardner who showed her where the opening in the wire was. She came through and he took her to the guard shed by the road. Some of the men peeked in to watch the action but I turned away. Ten minutes later I heard the girl scream and saw her run out of the shed; naked and crying. Gardner was right after her. He had on his green undershorts and was barefoot. He cursed her while he tried to load his M-16. I jumped up and grabbed his arm. Emery and Jesse grabbed his other arm and the M-16. Gardner struggled with us, intent on getting his rifle free.

"I'm gonna kill this son of a bitch," Gardner shouted. "I'm gonna kill her I'm telling you!"

When she saw we had him, the girl stopped and turned around. She stood ten feet away and yelled back,

"He cheat me. He big cheat."

"Shut up!" Emery shouted at her.

"What happened?" Jesse asked Gardner.

"She called me a nigger," Gardner yelled. "I'm not going to take that from anyone, especially some gook, motherfucking whore."

"He pay me only ten dalla," the girl shouted back at him.

"Shut up, goddamn it," I yelled at her.

"She wanted twenty bucks," Gardner said. "I paid her a hundred pee, just like all the rest. Ain't no fucking gook whore worth no twenty bucks."

"Relax man. Take it easy," Emery said.

"Yeah, be cool bro," Jesse said. "Be cool, now."

Emery managed to get the rifle out of Gardner's hands and he stopped struggling with us. We relaxed our grips when we saw he had regained his composure.

"I paid her ten dollars just like all the others..." Gardner went to explain.

"He make me suck him. That ten more," the girl said.

"She ain't shy, I'll give her that," I said. "Will someone get her out of here?"

"I number one," she said. "He number ten thousand." She yelled this over and over as she put her pants and shirt on. Toby finally led her to the barbed wire and we all watched her go before we resumed the card game to get Gardner's mind off it. As I played my hand, I realized that it was the first time I heard the word "nigger" since being in Nam.

The next day, after a tough day pulling guard duty on the roof because I wasn't allowed to go to the shack anymore, I was in my lean-to writing a letter to Mary when Monk came back from guard duty at the bridge. He poked his head in and said, "Hey, Paul another boat came by today."

"Oh yeah," I said. "Same kind of dudes as on the Mary Jane?"

"The Mary Jane's been blown up," Monk said in a low voice.

"What?" I sat up.

"Yeah, man. The Vietcong hit it last night with an RPG round from an ambush along the shoreline. The boat was blown to pieces. They were all killed."

"No," I said. I was shocked.

"They were some fun-loving guys," I muttered after a bit.

"They're gone now, man," Monk said. "It's all over for them."

I sat at the opening of my lean-to and stared out at the camp. It was a hot late afternoon, only a few men walked around. The camp was a makeshift affair: sandbags used for tables, wooden milk crates used as cabinets, tents made from plastic ponchos tied with rope.

"They had fixed up their boat nice," I said, "to make it like home. But it wasn't home; everything a soldier has is temporary."

Monk sat down and handed me a cigarette.

"If I was just back in the States; driving my car or mowing the front lawn," I said. "But the odds are against us making it back."

"You can't calculate them," Monk said. "It's a crap shoot, who gets hit, who doesn't; pure luck, bad luck or out of luck."

"Every day is precious," I said, "but we're wasting our lives in this goddamn war. Yesterday was the Mary Jane's crew's last day on earth. Can you believe it?"

"I want to make the most of my days," I continued when Monk didn't answer. "But how? Getting high so I can groove? I'm tired of getting high. Smoking weed is just a habit now, a way to fight the boredom and avoid the fear I've got in my gut. I want to stop getting high but who am I kidding? I'm not going to change. I'll go on doing what I've been doing and counting the days."

"Isn't much else we can do," Monk said. "Listen, I'm going to chow. You want to come along?"

"Nah, I'm not hungry," I said.

I laid back and listened to The Lemon Pipers' *Green Tambourine* over and over again on the cassette player.

It was dark when Moore got me up to play cards. We sat at a card table made from a piece of board on sandbag legs.

"This is Lionel." Moore introduced me to a black man from Baltimore. "He's just in country."

"What platoon?" I asked.

"Mike," Lionel said.

We smoked some weed and had a few beers as we played a round robin Bid Whist tournament. Lionel was friendly enough and he seemed to like Moore but in repose his face was somber, almost sullen. He was well spoken though and I had the feeling from listening to him that he was only tolerating me, the lone white man. Eventually the others turned in until it was just Lionel and me awake both of us pretty stoned.

"Hey, guy," I said on impulse. "Something's eating you up. What is it?"

"What makes you think that?" he asked.

"I don't know. It just seems like you're waiting for somebody to say the wrong thing or something. Seems like you're on guard."

"You want to know what's eating me?" A jeer came into his voice.

"Yeah," I said. "I wanna know."

"This, man." Lionel pulled the skin of his cheek. "This black skin is what's eating me." He was full of cold fury and I was sorry I had asked, but I felt I had to stay with it.

"That doesn't count for anything out here, man. We're all in this together."

"Like hell we are," Lionel said. "You're here because you're stupid. I'm here because my life doesn't count. You make it through and go back and get a job. If I make it through, I go back to this," he pinched the skin on his forearm. "You don't know what it feels like to live in America with the wrong color skin."

"We're going to change things," I said. "This war is changing things."

"Nothing's going to change racism," Lionel said. "Not in our lifctimc."

Chapter Six
I Wish It Would Rain

April 1968

Monday or Sunday our routines hardly varied. Everyday felt the same. I wanted to be home on a Saturday morning mowing the lawn with the sweet smell of wet, cut grass filling my lungs. Later I would go to the ball field. I could smell my leather mitt and feel the bat crunching a fastball. I looked up from out of my lean-to and saw a tall black soldier named James Randolph walk by. He owed me money. I forgot about Saturdays and followed him to the shed at the entrance to the camp.

"You heard we're moving out, right?" Randolph asked. He sat with his legs up on a crate. We both looked out the door to the barbed wire and dirt road that ran from the paved highway to the rear of the water plant.

"No, really? I didn't know." I said.

"Yeah, I overheard the captain making plans on the radio. We're going to join up with the battalion out at the border."

"Really?"

"Yeah, no kidding," Randolph said. "Say, you wouldn't have twenty you could lend me, would you?"

"Shit, you still owe me twenty. That's why I came by."

"I owe you? Well, loan me another twenty and we'll make it an even forty, okay? I'll pay you right back."

"Pay me right back the first twenty."

"How 'bout some grass? You got any?"

"What am I, the Red Cross?"

"Well, you ain't gonna need money or weed out by the border," Randolph laughed.

"But you will, right? Next payday, man. I want my twenty back."

"Yeah, yeah," he said.

Outside the barbed wire a South Vietnamese soldier named Thanh walked by. His face always broke into an instant smile whenever he saw me. I waved to him and he stopped. We talked across the barbed wire strands.

"You look sad," he said in a thick Vietnamese accent.

"Missing my wife," I said.

"It's hard for you, so far from home."

"It is, Thanh."

"I understand," he said. "Sometime we go way for two-three months. I missing my wife and children."

I felt bad for him; he'd have to fight this thing out to the end. What chance did he have, did any of them have, year after year in this rotten war.

Thanh went across the highway to the South Vietnamese camp and I walked to the mortar pit and passed the word around.

"There it is," Emery said. "The party's over."

"At least when we're moving around time goes faster," I said.

"Not for me," Moore said. "We got pussy here. We got weed here. We're not going to have it this good again, you'll see."

While we talked the word came down through Lieutenant Truck. Tear it down and be on the highway in two hours. I went into my lean-to and brought out my rucksack and a cardboard box that was filled with the extra things I had accumulated over the past three months. I laid everything out on the ground and looked them over.

"Not all this stuff is going to make it to the border," I said. "I'll keep the extra stationery but the aluminum eating utensils will have to go. It's back to bamboo chopsticks. I don't think I'll need the carved walking stick, either, do you?"

"Nah, you should keep it," Moore said. "I don't think the Vietnamese would shoot a guy walking down the trail with a walking stick."

"They probably wouldn't but I'm not humping it around."

I carried an armful of things to the perimeter and called to Thanh. He waved and trotted across the street to meet me at the barbed wire.

"Here you go, man." I handed him my extra stuff. Thanh bowed several times before he noticed that I wanted to shake his hand.

As I finished packing I watched Moore stuff things into his pack and the pockets of his fatigue pants. "Hey, Mack," I said, "even if you manage to get it all in, I give you two, maybe three clicks then you'll be throwing that stuff all over the jungle."

Moore looked a long time at his things. I imagine he pictured himself, like I said, out on patrol carrying this and that and everything else they put on us. After a thorough analysis he picked half of it up and brought it to the perimeter to give to another South Vietnamese soldier. By now there was a group of them waiting at the wire to get the discards from the men in Bravo. The only difference was there were no more giveaways. The items were being sold—I should say exchanged. Moore came back with a half bag of good grass. Emery had a bunch of green bananas and Monk got weed and a deck of nude playing cards.

In the afternoon we put our gear on and waddled to the road. An hour later the choppers came in and airlifted us out into a narrow clearing along the border. We humped in three kilometers to a defensive position along the Ho Chi Minh Trail. The battalion was already setting up in a large clearing. One squad from each company patrolled the tree line as the rest of us dug in.

It was an uneventful night, and the next day, as soon as everyone had eaten, we went on patrol. Recon had point with Alpha Company, Bravo Company and Headquarters behind. Charlie Company brought up the rear. An hour from base camp Lieutenant Truck signaled us to stop and we knelt down and covered the trail.

"Reconnaissance has just captured four North Vietnamese soldiers," Sergeant Meyers spread the word. "Three of them were lying in their hammocks smoking grass. The fourth one was cooking rice."

"He must have had the munchies," Emery said.

"They had to be pretty stoned for Recon to just walk right in on them like that," I said. "What are we doing now?"

"They're interrogating them," Sergeant Meyers said.

A half-hour later based on what Intelligence had learned, we changed direction. Recon led us up a trail due north. Fifteen minutes later we halted again.

"They just found some North Vietnamese bunkers," Meyers said.

"Shit," I said as I felt fear grip my stomach.

The patrol resumed and the trail meandered through a meadow of waist high grass. As we walked across it, with the sun beating on our heads like a hammer, the far side of the meadow seemed to invite us into the shade. But I had a bad feeling about entering the tree line. As we went into the canopied forest I had to blink to adjust my eyes. The sunlight filtered through the tall trees leaving the ground in deep shade. It was hot and steamy and I picked up the scent of covered-up latrines. I had walked in just a few feet when I saw the bunkers and froze. I felt nauseous. My stomach gurgled and I needed to pee. Every leaf that flickered got my attention. Everywhere I looked there were camouflaged bunkers.

"Someone's going to die in here," I whispered. "Maybe all of us. This is a huge complex."

"A regiment at least," Emery whispered back.

As we went further in we passed Alpha Company pulling bicycles out of a large bunker. "There's a hundred more down there," one of the soldiers said.

Thirty yards away another crew from Alpha stacked medical supplies. "They have a complete underground operating room," their lieutenant told Truck.

My eyes met Lieutenant Truck's. The color had gone out of his face. "We should get the hell out of here before the three bears come home," I said. The lieutenant nodded his head in agreement.

Time seemed to stop. Our rifles at the ready, safeties off, we walked further in. I could see row after row of the camouflaged bunkers.

Lieutenant Truck held up his arm and we got down. He conferred with brass on the radio then stood up and signaled for us to backtrack out.

We made it all the way home to the mortar pits without a shot being fired but I felt my hands tremble and a palpable tension hung over the camp. The lieutenant returned from the captain's tent with orders for a battalion-size Mad Minute.

An hour later ,just before dusk, we anticipated the signal. Alpha Company opened up first—ten seconds of full-bore firing. Charlie Company went next, letting go for another ten seconds.

We waited our turn. Moore held the first mortar round in the mouth of the tube. The lieutenant had one ear to the radio and his right arm raised in the air. When the captain gave the order, Lieutenant Truck dropped his right arm and yelled, "Fire!"

All the guns in Bravo Company blasted the tree line. Our two mortars sent up four rounds each. I bet Toby that Moore could fire his four rounds faster than Jesse and I was right. Moore moved without any wasted motion and his fourth round came out of the tube a second before Jesse's. We all cheered as the eight rounds exploded into the tree line.

Recon had brought out a fifty-caliber machinegun and one of their squads shot it from a bunker near us. The gunner fired with a rhythm, squeezing off rounds like he was playing a bass drum: boom boom boom de boom-boom de boom boom boom de boom boom. The fifty had a deep sound and I could feel the concussion from each shot. I watched as its red tracers cut trees in half.

"Cease fire!" the captain yelled.

The roar from the Mad Minute echoed through the woods.

"We've got beaucoup fire power," I said before anyone had moved, "and we're dug in. We're gonna kick ass if they try to storm us."

"Six hundred against two or three thousand?" Moore said. "Man, I'd hate to see it."

"Only so many can come out of the trees at one time," I said. "As long as we have artillery and air support, we'll be all right."

Lieutenant Truck called us to the other mortar pit.

"Mike platoon will have ambush tonight." He read from his notes. "Each line platoon in each company will send out a two man LP in front of its part of the perimeter."

"What about us?" Jesse asked.

"No, we won't supply any LPs tonight," Lieutenant Truck said, "but we'll send a detail of men to man several bunkers on the line. Before anyone goes out, they're going to have artillery zero in the tree line."

"Good idea," I said.

"We'll need to schedule our watches and plot the h and i fire," the lieutenant continued. He looked at me. "There's Special Forces men over by battalion headquarters getting ready to go out."

"We're going to need to know their location," I said.

"Right," the lieutenant said. "You'd better go get it."

I took my map and M-16 and walked to where Battalion had set up in the middle of the camp. I went past the colonel's tent to the foxhole where the four Green Berets sat. They were three white guys and a black man. Two of the white soldiers looked like the Marine Corps' recruiting poster: perfectly square jaws, blond hair, blue eyes, six feet tall, a hundred and ninety-five pounds. Except for his color the black soldier was their twin. I stared at the fourth man; a tall white kid who looked just eighteen or nineteen years old. As I came up to them I heard them laugh at a joke, or at me. I didn't know which.

"I'm from Bravo Company's mortar platoon," I said. I tapped the map with my pencil. "I'm plotting the ambushes and need for you to show me where yours will be so we don't hit you." I directed the question to the three older soldiers but to my surprise it was the skinny young one that answered.

"We're not setting up an ambush," he said.
It looked like he didn't need to shave yet—at least not every day.
"What do you mean?" I asked.

"We're going on night patrol," he said.

"Okay, then I'll need to know the trails you're going to use going out and coming back."

"We're not coming back." He smiled.

"You're not coming back?" I smiled too and waited for the punch line.

"No, uh-uh," he said.

"So you're going out but you're not coming back?"

"We're going out about twelve clicks," he explained, "then we'll get picked up tomorrow morning by our own people."

I still wasn't sure if he was joking or not.

"We're preparing for an attack by a North Vietnamese regiment and you're going to walk around at night, just the four of you?"

On Thunder Road

"That's right," he said. I saw that all of them had a gleam in their eyes. They were looking forward to it.

"Well, okay, good luck to you guys," I said.

"Thanks, man. You too," the young one said and the other three nodded to me.

Just before dark I watched the Green Berets clear the perimeter and disappear down a jungle trail. I told the lieutenant about their mission.

"They're not even wearing helmets," I added.

"Those are some crazy motherfuckers," Gardner said.

"I wouldn't do that for a million bucks," Emery said and everyone agreed, except Moore and Jesse who said that for a million dollars they would give it a try.

"Yeah, right," Emery said.

"Yeah right, muthafucker," Moore said.

"Shit," Emery said and it went back and forth like that until they got tired of it and opened up some C rations. We cooked the rations over a small fire and the flames lit up the mortar pit as the jungle disappeared and darkness took hold of the land.

"Better put this fire out, now," Sergeant Rigoni said and we all agreed. We didn't need to be the only figures visible from the tree line.

Every thirty minutes all night long our mortars fired a round in h and i. We hit the trails or the tree line beyond the LPs. The mortar platoons in the other companies did the same in front of their sections of the perimeter.

I sat with Moore and Eddie for my four hours of watch. It was a pretty evening, full of stars and the air was clean and cool. Except for the men on watch everyone was tucked inside their poncho liners. The moon hadn't risen yet and we sat on the pit wall smoking cigarettes in our cupped hands. I looked out across the dark ground barely able to make out the outline of the bunkers on the perimeter.

"The jungle is quiet tonight," I said.

"This place gives me the creeps," Eddie said.

"Me too," Moore agreed.

"Where do you think that NVA unit is?" I asked.

"Man, I don't know," Eddie said, "but I hope they're not anywhere around here."

"Well, let's lay one out there," I said, "just in case they're coming up on us right now."

Eddie looked at his timepiece. "Yeah, okay. A couple of minutes more, then we can put one on that trail about a hundred and fifty yards out."

Every fifteen minutes for the next four hours Eddie and I had the same exact conversation. When our watch was over I lay down and tried to sleep as the men on the next watch talked and smoked in the dark. About five in the morning Sergeant Meyers and Sergeant Rigoni came around.

"Prepare for a dawn attack," I heard Rigoni whisper. I sat up and wrapped my poncho liner around my shoulders. I nodded and he went to the next sleeping body.

I stretched, picked up my M-16 and walked to the pit where I sat down on the sandbags next to Moore and watched the sunrise melt the darkness. The morning was clear, warm and peaceful.

At 9 a.m. the ground started to rumble and word came down to us that the Air Force was flying B-52 strikes on the Vietnamese bunkers.

"B-52s fly at 50,000 feet," Toby said as we searched the skies. "That's why we can't see or hear them."

"Sure as hell can feel them under my feet." I put one palm on the ground. "Man, they're bringing the world down on that place."

"Can you really feel it?" Monk asked me.

"Shit yeah," I said. "Try it. It isn't as far away as I thought."

The B-52 strike went on for another fifteen minutes and in late morning we returned to the NVA bunkers. On our approach we had to go around a bomb crater; thirty feet deep and sixty feet across.

"What size bomb can make a hole that big?" I asked Sergeant Meyers. "A two-thousand pounder? Three thousand?"

"I don't know," Sergeant Meyers said. He stopped with me to gaze into the hole. Exposed red clay inside the crater stood out vividly in contrast to the green jungle vegetation outside the crater. Tree roots, rocks, and rubble littered the sides and floor of the crater and for twenty yards around the big hole trees were knocked flat to the ground.

"How can soldiers take this kind of pounding and keep on fighting?" I asked.

"They don't seem to know *how* to quit," Meyers said in his southern drawl.

"Someone should have explained that to us before we got into a war with them," I said.

We went around the bomb crater and into the canopied forest. Bravo Company was between Alpha and Charlie, Recon had the point and Headquarters walked last. Ten minutes in I heard a shout, "Chew Hoy! Chew Hoy!" then a burst from an M-16 and we all hit the dirt. A minute later I saw Lionel coming down the trail.

"I got them," he said. His face was alive with excitement. He held a pistol in his hand and had another one tucked into his belt. "What happened?" Lieutenant Truck asked.

"They just walked up on me," Lionel said. "They were on the trail that crosses this one and they threw up their hands when they saw me but I shot 'em."

The lieutenant interrupted Lionel to take a call on the radio. The colonel wanted to know why the NVA officers had been killed instead of captured.

"They went for their weapons, Sir," Lieutenant Truck said. I was surprised. His lie had saved Lionel from a court martial. The lieutenant and Lionel both waited intently for the colonel's response.

"Yes, Sir," Lieutenant Truck said. "We'll search them for maps."

We searched the bunkers for more Vietnamese as well but found none. In the afternoon we headed back for our camp but halfway home shots rang out and we hit the dirt again. I lay prone and looked for movement in the jungle brush. Suddenly a Puerto Rican named Ramon Diaz ran by me screaming at the top of his lungs, "Yiiiiiii!"

"Get down, GET DOWN!" everyone yelled to him but he ran for another twenty yards before he dove into the dirt next to a couple of his buddies.

I knew Ramon to be a soft spoken and calm man so I turned to Moore and asked, "What the hell was that all about?"

"I don't know," Moore shrugged. "I think he just freaked out."

Later in camp Diaz walked by and I called him over.

"Hey, Diaz, man, what were you doing out there today?"

"Oh man," he grinned, "when I heard that shot I hit the ground." He spoke in a heavy accent, "But I'm laying there and I feel something moving so I look. Oh mamma, it's a snake! I get up and run."

"You probably scared the shit out of the snake too," I said and Ramon laughed.

Lionel sat at the mortar pit cleaning his Vietnamese trophy pistols and I heard him laugh at my joke.

"Hey, Lionel, man," I said. "Why did you shoot 'em?"

"Why not shoot them?" he answered.

"They were trying to surrender," I said.

"Fuck them," Lionel said. "If they found a wounded American soldier they'd shoot him in the head without blinking an eye." He slammed the ammo clip into the pistol.

"You're right about that," Moore said, "but I don't think I could have killed them with their hands up in the air."

"Yeah, well I could," Lionel said and we left it at that.

We had a mad minute each of the next three nights, but were never attacked and on the fifth day the slicks came in to pick us up. Bravo Company flew to Highway 13 while the rest of the battalion went into Long Binh. On Thunder Road we unloaded from the choppers and began to dig in. Riflemen strung barbed wire at the perimeter and I helped fill sandbags. We were there about an hour when the radio fell silent. The announcer came on and read a news release: Reverend King had been murdered. We listened to the details of the assassination but when the music started again the men turned off their radios and the camp fell silent.

"Damn!" Emery said. "You knew it was coming. *He* knew it was coming. It was just a matter of time before those sons of a bitches got him."

"Those stupid assholes," Jesse said. "They killed the one who was calling for peace; the one who didn't want revenge."

"Yeah, well that's over," Moore said. "Gonna be some payback on this one, goddamn it. They've taught us how to make booby traps, how to set up ambushes. Well okay, we're gonna use that someday to get those motherfuckers."

"We should be in the south fighting the KKK bastards," I said, "rather than these peasants here. These patrols should be in Mississippi, Alabama, and Louisiana. How can things get so upside down?" I said. "It's easy to see what's right and what's wrong but wrong seems to be winning everywhere I look."

"It gets to the point where it's easy to hate all you white people," Jesse said.

"I can't blame you," I said, "but if you do then they'll have won. That's what they want: separate nations within the nation. All blacks here, all whites there and don't get caught where you're not allowed."

"Gebhart's right," Emery said. "Living like this, out in the boonies with no walls. We share everything and us knowing each other the way we do, we've gotten to a place where we're just people. If we let ourselves hate someone because of their color then we're as bad as they are."

"You know," I said, "I think the way Dr. King stood up to those brutal racists was about as brave as you get. The way he did it people couldn't help but see that this wasn't the America we'd been told about in school. He showed us through his bravery that the Bill of Rights and the Constitution didn't mean a thing if people could act that way. He was the greatest man of our time. I mean that."

"Here we are," Gardner said, "in Vietnam fighting for our country when at home our leaders fighting for our rights, they're being murdered. It ain't right."

"It's worse than ain't right," Moore shouted in a high pitch voice. "Damn these white people."

"I feel the same way," I said. "I'm pissed too."

"That's how great Reverend King was," Monk put in. "He must have felt the same anger when those little children were blown up in Sunday school," Monk continued. "He's human too but he controlled those emotions and worked for peace."

"He could have made it happen too," I said. "All he needed to do was call out for armed resistance and guerilla warfare would have broken out all across the country."

We were all depressed by the assassination but I don't think any of us could foretell just how much it would change the race relations in Vietnam. Nor how it would call for each of us, blacks and whites to have to confront our own prejudices.

Several weeks after Dr. King's death, Bravo Company joined the battalion in a move back to the Ho Chi Minh trail. I looked down from the assault helicopter and saw the rolling hills turn into jungle covered mountains. We were going farther north than I had ever been before. I saw a waterfall and a bank of fog caught in the green valleys but Vietnam's natural beauty didn't ease my fear. The Hueys landed us in one of the fog-covered valleys where a troop from the Fourth Cavalry already had a perimeter set up. Their campsite was in a clearing on the crown of a hill. As we dug foxholes in between their armored vehicles we talked to the men in the Fourth Cav. I looked into one of the personnel carriers and saw that it was fixed up like a tiny apartment.

"It beats humping," a black Fourth Cav man said from on top of his PC.

"Yeah, but I wouldn't trade places with you," I said. The soldier looked surprised. "Your vehicles are too damn loud," I said. "The Vietnamese can hear you coming from miles away, then they set up ambushes and fire anti-tank rockets at you. No, uh-uh, I'd rather be on my feet where I can be as quiet as I want and can hit the dirt when the rounds start coming in."

"Shit, I told you these grunts were stupid," a tall, black Fourth Cav soldier said from the adjoining PC. "Man, see all that steel?" He tapped on the side of his personnel carrier. "That's safety and comfort. Yes, Sir, safety and comfort."

"Shit," Emery said. "All it needs is a bulls-eye to make it a little easier to hit."

"You a fool, man. We ain't afraid of no rockets."

"You ain't?" Emery came back. "Shit, then you the fool, bro."

Jesse laughed his comic-book "ah-hee, ah-hee, ah-hee" laugh, his head bopping up and down in glee and I could see that we had managed to put a little doubt into their minds.

The sun burned the fog off and the afternoon turned hot and humid. We had a tape player with us and as we dug in we listened to The Temptations' *I Wish It Would Rain*. Gardner sang the lead part and the rest of us sang the chorus.

"It might sound strange," I said to Mack, "but I really do wish it would rain."

He laughed and sang in falsetto, "Rain, rain, rain."

The Fourth Cav men sat on top of their vehicles and covered the tree line with their machineguns. After the first verse they joined in and our combined voices could be heard across the camp.

About twenty minutes later I saw dark monsoon clouds approaching. I pointed to them and said, "You ask for rain, you get rain."

Our laughter stopped when the sky opened up and a heavy downpour pelted the ground. Within minutes we were drenched and cold and our foxholes filled with water. The ground became ankle deep in mud. The cavalry soldier who had argued with me, dry as bone in his vehicle, stuck his head out of his PC. "Hey," he shouted, "sure is wet out there, huh?"

"Up yours, mutha," we shouted back at him.

One of the tank drivers saw our misery and started his engine. He revved the big diesel and six of us huddled behind it. We stood in front of the exhaust grill, sopping wet, towels wrapped over our mouths and noses as the warm fumes blew by us.

"Ain't this a mutha," Emery shouted over the engine.

"Yeah, well it's better than standing out here cold and wet," Jesse yelled back at him.

"Yeah, right! We're lucky to have a tank here so we can stand in the diesel fumes to get dry," Emery said.

We had to leave the warmth of the tank fumes to finish digging in and by nightfall we put up our poncho tents; I was with Emery, Moore, and Monk. We tied our ponchos together, secured them to sandbags and dug trenches to keep the rivulets of water out. We sealed the door closed from the inside and tried to get some sleep as the rain beat against the plastic ponchos.

Sometime after midnight I heard someone sloshing through the mud. The stranger went to the tent next to ours and I heard muffled voices. I followed his footsteps as he squished to our tent. A young soldier put a flashlight in and asked, "Gebhart? Is Gebhart in here?"

I sat up and looked at him. His poncho covered him from neck to foot but rainwater dripped down his face.

"Yeah," I said. "I'm here. Why?"

"Captain wants to see you."

"Okay," I said, "I'll be right over."

"What ja do?" Emery asked me as I put my boots on.

"It's Mary," I said. "She's had the baby." I laced up my jungle boots and outside, secured the tent's flap. I had to use my red filtered flashlight to pick a path through the ankle-deep mud. Slipping and sliding all the way I found the captain's tent.

"Gebhart reporting as ordered, Sir," I said to get his attention.

Captain Dennis opened the flap. He had replaced Captain Allen just two weeks before. He was a West Pointer, tall with blond hair balding at the front. He had a ruddy complexion but his blue eyes were clear and his face was honest and open.

"Gebhart?" he asked with a smile.

"Yes, Sir."

"You're the proud father of a baby girl."

"Really!"

"She was born on April 17th." The captain read from a piece of paper and I stuck my head in the tent and tried to read it upside down. "Six pounds, nine ounces," Captain Dennis continued. "Mother and baby are doing fine. The Red Cross just called me a half-hour ago."

"This is the twenty-first," I said. "We must be pretty far out for them to take four days to find me."

"Congratulations," the captain said. He reached out and shook my hand.

"Thank you, Sir."

I walked through the mud and light drizzle back to the hooch but I had to stop as tears mixed with the raindrops. I wanted to be with Mary so much it hurt.

"Hey, man, what's happening?" Moore asked as I came into the tent.

"Mary's had a baby girl," I said.

"Paul, that's great!" Monk said.

"All right! Congratulations," Emery said.

Moore lit a pipe of marijuana and Monk took out peaches and pound cake, my favorite, and we had a little party. A half-hour later we lay back down to sleep.

I was cold and wet and miserable; nothing was right. The joy of knowing I had a daughter washed small against the fact that I couldn't see or talk to Mary. I ached to hold them both but could hold nothing. I rocked back and forth to ease my pain.

The next morning, I took a black felt pen and wrote "Nadine" in balloon letters across my helmet cover. It was the name I had picked if it was a girl. I noticed that Cloud Six had almost faded away.

Later that morning we boarded the armored personnel carriers and went down the hill and out of the clearing into the jungle. It was very thick jungle on either side of a narrow trail and before we had gone three-hundred yards the VC blew an ambush on us. I jumped off and hit the dirt. The tracks turned to face the Vietnamese guns and we had to watch that we didn't get run over by them. The Fourth Cav opened up with their machineguns and the incoming fire stopped but the situation was so chaotic along the downhill trail that command ordered a retreat by foot back to base camp. They told us later that the bodies they found were North Vietnamese Regulars. We had two killed and twelve wounded.

We tried the same maneuver the next morning and even though we used a different trail it went just about as the first day; an ambush and the chaos of men and machines too close together. I never got the body count but we lost another 6 men none fatal.

"We're getting our asses beat out here," I said back in camp as we cooked up C rations. "We've never lost people like this. Bravo's gone from two hundred men just the beginning of the month down to a hundred and thirty. How long will they keep us out here?"

"No question they need to re-think this," Emery put in.

The third morning was overcast, cold and dismal. The air was heavy with diesel fumes and the sound of big engines rumbling. I looked up from my breakfast to see Rucker, a black soldier from St. Louis walking across the dew-laden grass. He was just six feet tall but as strong as any man in Bravo Company. I had seen him in two fistfights in Long Binh; both times he had beaten up bigger men who had started a fight with him. They had made a mistake; no one who knew him ever messed with Rucker.

"Hey, bro, how's it going?" I asked.

"Oh, man, I'm not doing too good." He sat down next to me on the sandbags. His face had a smooth complexion the color of dark chocolate. When I looked at his expression I could see his kindness and just under the surface the fierce intense energy that was his soul.

"What's up?" I asked.

"I've got two days left in the field and I got the feeling... I'm gonna get hit."

"Easy, Rucker, you've got to think positive."
"I can't help it. I can feel my death. It's coming for me." He looked at me but I didn't know what to say.

"I can feel it, man. It's waiting for me out there." He looked at the tree line then back to me. "Do you understand what I'm saying?"

"Yeah, sure," I said.

"You do, don't you?"

I thought of the times he and I had gotten really stoned. We pointed to the vibes coming from the radio and said to each other; "You see that, man? That's cool. Did ya see it?"

"Yeah, well, I don't know if it's your death," I said, "but there's that darkness vibe out there, I can feel that."

"It's mine, man. I'm gonna die today."

"Listen," I said, "let's just say it is out there waiting for you. That doesn't mean it has to win. You've got to fight it, Rucker. You've got to picture yourself on the bird going home. You hear me? You're sitting in the plane going home."

"Yeah, yeah, sure."

"Hey, Rucker, if the shit hits the fan out there today, you shout it back. Do you understand? You shout it back. Don't let it take you."

Rucker hung his head.

"Why don't you go get some breakfast?" I asked.

"Nah, I tried. I just threw it up." He looked at his hands and said, "God, I'm too short to die now. I went through a whole fucking year out here. I ain't gonna die now." Rucker looked up at me.

"That's right," I said.

"I'm going the fuck home!"

"Fuckin-A," I said. "You're just short, that's all."

"Yeah, man." He blew his nose and smiled, embarrassed at his emotional display.

Later that morning, still under dismal skies the tracks tore through the mud and the infantrymen lined up to board them. I saw Rucker on top of one of the peecees as it went by. He had his collar turned up, his rifle between his knees and his hands stuffed into his pockets. He saw me and pulled a hand out to flash me the peace sign. I gave him a thumbs up.

Within the hour our patrol drove into yet another ambush and command called in fighter jets and artillery. The fighting lasted a couple of hours and when it was over I heard that Medevacs were coming in to get sixteen casualties. One of them was Rucker. He had been shot through the shoulder. I tell you no lie, I bent my head and prayed that he'd be all right.

It was late afternoon when we came back into camp. The cooks had already dished out a hot supper. Oscar, the last platoon to come in, cold and hungry, walked directly to the mess where a cook stood behind a row of large green Thermoses. All of the Thermoses had their lids off, a sign they were empty. "Sorry, guys," he said, "there's nothing left."

"How come, man?" Emery asked. "Why didn't you bring enough for everyone?"

"The colonel had us take some off so we could bring him another tent and some fresh uniforms."

"That asshole!" Moore said.

"We're out of C rations too, so it looks like we're just plain screwed," Emery said.

"Don't you have anything left?" I asked.

"Well, there are some cold mashed potatoes," the cook said, "but they got covered with dirt when the Chinook took off."

"Let's see 'em," I said.

He pointed to one of the open Thermoses and I looked in and handed him a paper plate. "Let me have some."

"Man they're pretty dirty." He took my paper plate but made a face at me.

"That's okay," I said.

He shoveled out a mound of potatoes and I cleaned off a layer of dust with the side of my fork. They were cold and the dirt crunched in my mouth.

"Got any salt?" I asked.

He handed me a saltshaker. I sprinkled it on heavy and dug in.

"As hungry as I am this isn't so bad," I said to the guys around me. They studied me to see if I was decoying them but when I went to get seconds they jumped in front of me and scraped the Thermos clean.

"Hey, man," a black cavalry soldier with a round face and a bit of a belly called to us from the back ramp of his PC, "we've got some C rations. Y'all are welcome to them." He went into his PC and came out with a case. Other cavalry soldiers brought a few of their cases over and we sat on top of their vehicles, eating and joking with them. We sang along to the soul music from their tape player.

Jimmy Mack came on and our voices rose:

"Jimmy Mack, when are you coming back?"

I saw Mack Moore at the front of the PC and our eyes met. I smiled and he nodded back to me. Moore's girlfriend had been writing him those very words.

The next day our patrol managed to get three clicks into the hills. We were halfway across a scrub brush clearing, seventy yards wide and three hundred yards long, when an anti-tank rocket whistled through the air. It hit the side of the lead carrier and glanced off but not before melting a chunk of steel. Another rocket hit the carrier in front of the one I was on. Those were all the orders I needed. We all abandoned ship. The drivers turned and followed us into the lower tree line as bullets bounced off their vehicles.

The North Vietnamese had the advantage of firing downhill at us and their ordnance sizzled over our heads. We were pinned down until one of the personnel carriers to my right broke out of the tree line and charged up the hill. I was astonished to see that Gerald was on top manning the machinegun and Max's red head peeked out from the driver's port.

Gerald fired the machinegun as he bounced around on top. He was erratic at first then better as he learned to wait until his butt wasn't in mid-air. An RPG round went *Shoosh* over their carrier and out into the jungle. Gerald kept firing at a machinegun emplacement. The other cavalry crews, psyched by the one PC attacking the enemy charged out of the tree line to join them. With Max at the front the armored vehicles blasted the Vietnamese ambush with their automatic weapons.

After the firefight, we walked the three clicks back to camp.

Max and Gerald came into the mortar pits right after us.

"Hey, congratulations!" Sergeant Meyers shook Max's hand.

"It was Gerald," Max said with a broad smile. "He did all the shooting. All I did was drive the damn thing."

"How'd you get control of the personnel carrier anyway?" I asked him. To my surprise, it was Gerald who answered.

"The peecee's crew were stunned from that first RPG round," he said. "We took them out, then Max said, 'C'mon let's go.' He got in to drive and I took over the M-60."

Gerald spoke without stuttering and Max listened without interrupting.

"You just decided to charge them?" Emery asked Max.

"Well, just like Gerald said..."

I noticed a humility about Max that had not been there before. He had faced the enemy and to his great relief he had been brave. The experience changed him. His macho bullshit was gone and we got to know Max the man. He was different than Max the boy acting like he thought men should.

We left the highlands at the end of the second week. Our casualties brought us to half strength—just over a hundred men. The company was demoralized and subdued as we dug in on Thunder Road.

Lieutenant Truck came to one of the half-finished holes and motioned for me. "Captain Dennis just signed a four-day pass for you." He handed me the paper.

"Four-day pass?" I looked at it, not understanding.

"To go back Long Binh to call your wife."

"I didn't know it was possible to call home," I said.

"Go to the Red Cross at Division Headquarters; they'll get you through."

"Thank you, Sir. I appreciate it."

"Congratulations." The lieutenant reached out and I shook his hand.

I took the morning Chinook to Long Binh but I was told to wait until 10 p.m. to go to Division. I found the Red Cross Quonset Hut in the dark that night and the radio operator made a connection to a ham operator in Oregon who telephoned Mary in New Jersey.

"Hello?" she answered. Her voice sounded down but I felt a rush of elation.

"Hi, it's me!"

"Oh, Paul! Where are you? Are you okay?"

"Yeah, I'm fine. God, I miss you. How's Nadine?"

Mary started to cry. "She's fine, Paul. She's such a good baby and beautiful. Oh, I want you home with us so bad."

"I know, me too."

There was a moment of silence.

"Where are you?" she asked.

"I'm in Long Binh. They let me come back here to call you. Who does she look like?"

"I sent pictures," Mary said.

"I haven't gotten them yet."

"She's got your eyes."

"Not my nose I hope."

"It's just a little button nose," Mary laughed. "She's adorable, with little fingers and toes."

We talked for five minutes before the operator signaled that I had to get off so the next soldier could call home. "I've got to go now," I said. Tears came to my eyes.

"Okay," Mary said.

"I love you," I whispered.

"I love you so much, Paul. Please be safe."

"I promise I will. Tell my folks I called and that I'm okay."

"I will, right after we hang up."

"Okay, good-by, Mary."

"Good-bye," she mumbled.

I couldn't talk to thank the radio operator. Alone on the dark road on the way back to headquarters, I pictured Mary. I had to make it home to her. I had to.

The next day I was road on my way to the PX when I saw Mack Moore coming the other way.

"How'd you get out of the field?" I asked him.

"Medical pass for the clap," he said. "I just got my first shot."

"I called Mary," I said.

"She okay?"

"Yeah, she's fine. The baby's healthy but the father's having a tough time. I want to be with them."

"C'mon," Moore said, "let's go to the PX and get some hamburgers."

"That sounds pretty good," I said. "Where are you staying?"

"Just down the road," Mack answered. "Come on."

We walked back the way Mack had come. The road was dabbled in shade from the coconut and banana trees and a light morning breeze made the walk comfortable. Barracks lined both sides of the lane. Mack found the one he had been staying in and I followed him up the steps. His bunk was by the door and I dropped my rucksack and rifle on the one next to his.

"Anyone else here?" I asked.

"Just two rednecks," Mack answered, "but they keep to themselves at the other end so no sweat."

"Alright, let's go get those hamburgers and shakes," I said.

We walked to the PX and I shopped for stationery and socks. We got haircuts and had hamburgers with fries.

"Let's go get something to drink," Moore said when we went back outside.

"Okay," I said. "Want to hang out at the USO?"

"Yeah, c'mon. Let's see who's around."

We went across the street to the USO club and ordered tequilas.

"That's Willie McDaniels," Moore said to me as four soldiers came over to our table. McDaniels was a tall good looking black man with high cheekbones and light brown eyes.

"Who's he?" I asked.

"He's in Recon," Moore said.

"Hey, que pasa, breeze," McDaniels smiled and shook Moore's hand. As his group came up to our table.

"This is a buddy of mine, Paul Gebhart," Moore said.

"Nice to meet you," I said.

We shook hands and McDaniels introduced his three friends. Each of them shook Moore's hand in the newest soul shake, slapping front and back of one hand then the other then sliding palms with the other man's. It was all in rhythm and with style. When they shook my hand, I didn't try anything fancy. I just shook the old brother's way.

After a couple of drinks McDaniels asked Mack, "How long since you been home?"

"I came over in November," Moore said.

"You don't know then."

"Know what?"

"Well, it's just that... he's the only white guy sitting with blacks."

"What does that mean?" I asked.

"The old days are over," McDaniels said. "It's Black Power now and that means not needing white people for anything."

Moore and I didn't say anything.

"Look," McDaniels said, "in the boonies it doesn't matter what color your buddy is but back in the rear it's like the States now. There's Uncle Toms and black men who aren't going to take it anymore. What I'm saying is that you're not helping Moore by hanging out with him."

"I'll go anytime he says he doesn't want to drink with me," I said.

"I know you would," McDaniels said. "I'm not saying it's you. This is part of the shit that comes down from all the crap at home; the murders and lynchings."

"Look, man," I said, "we've just got a couple of days out of the field. We came here to get fucked up and relax. What's the problem?"

"There's no problem, Paul," Moore said. "Willie is just telling me I have to understand where I am, that's all." He looked at McDaniels for a moment, thinking. "There's no problem," he repeated to break the silence. "Let's have another couple of shots. I'm buying."

Six hours later, totally shit-faced, Moore and I sat on the front steps of the USO as Marvin Gaye's *Trouble Man* played on the jukebox inside. Moore sang along in a high falsetto. He sounded good too, drunk enough to sing it with heart.

"I don't think I can make it," I said when we stood up. "The whole world is spinning. I'm gonna puke."

"C'mon, let's try walking," Moore said.

He supported me for a few yards until he stumbled and I had to keep him from falling.

"Say, who's holding who up?" I asked. He laughed and we both went to our hands and knees. I rolled on my back and looked up at the star-filled night. "Sure is a pretty evening," I said.

Moore started to heave; "Oh God, oh, oh God," he moaned with each wave.

"Christ, what a wasted life," I said. "Lying on the ground, drunk in Vietnam." Moore was talking to God and didn't object to my take on the situation. "I wish I was with Mary," I said as I looked at the beautiful stars. "I'd give anything to have her in my arms."

When we reached the barracks I crashed heavy. The next day I woke with the hard, tropical sun beaming through the open windows. Moore was in the bunk next to mine.

I sat up and rubbed my temples to dull the throbbing. "Jesus, that tequila got me good," I said. "How come I don't ever remember that?"

"My heads hurts too," Moore said.

He fell back to sleep but I put my boots on and went out to shower. The cold water from the fifty-gallon steel drums in the shower shed sobered me up. I washed the drunk out of my hair and toweled off. I put on fresh fatigues and was lacing up my boots when two white soldiers came into the room.

"Hey, boy," one of them said in a thick, southern twang. He had deep acne scars on his cheeks. The other one was short but muscular. He smiled at me. I didn't respond and the first one poked me on the shoulder with his finger. "Hey, I'm talking to you," he drawled. I left my boot unlaced and stood up.

"We don't take to no white man hanging out with niggers. Ya hear me?"

I backed away. I felt my face flush with a wave of depression and fear.

"You and that black boy got an hour to clear out," Acne man said. "If you don't, we're going to crack your heads open like melons. You 'stand, Jew?"

I nodded, "Okay" and casually reached down for my M-16 as if to go. I chambered a round with one quick pull and release of the bolt. They just stared at me but when I clicked the safety off a look of concern swept across their faces and they both backed off. I could see the wheels turn inside their heads. *This white boy wouldn't really shoot us. Shit, I don't like his eyes.*

"Excuse me," I said and motioned with the barrel toward the door. They stepped aside and I walked out without turning my back on them, my shoelace dragging on the ground.

Mack was still in his bunk when I came in. He looked over at me as I finished lacing my boot and began to pack my rucksack.

"Where are you going?" he asked.

I stopped to look him in the eye. "It seems you've picked le Hotel KKK to stay in. I met our two roommates and didn't get a good vibe. Know what I mean?"

"What did they say?" Mack propped himself up on an elbow.

"Nothing too pleasant," I said and resumed packing. "Listen, you and me have got to go back out to the field. Let's catch the morning Chinook."

"I got two days left on my medical pass," Moore said. "So do you."

"I understand," I said, "but Long Binh has got too many bad going on. Bravo Company's just out on Highway 13. There's card g going on and they haven't been hit."

"I'm not afraid of those assholes," Moore said. "I'll kill 'em if they s anything."

"Exactly," I nodded and looked him in the eye. "And I'm going to hel you. And that ain't gonna get us home."

I paused and just like I would on patrol I lowered my chin for emphasis and said slowly; "We need to get out of here."

It was probably from force of habit, knowing that your buddy only you a look like that when he's spotted movement but Mack, cursing u his breath, slowly rose and began to pack.

We shouldered our rucksacks and carried our M-16s to the airfie make the morning Chinook. When it landed us on Highway 1 dumped my gear at the mortar pits and went to the perimete visit Serena. At Lima's foxholes the radio played next to a p game. I took a toke from the pipe that was being passed aro Lima had gotten in new men. One of them was a white with dark hair had a tattoo of a Black Panther climbing up right forearm. Lines of red ink suggested the cat's claws scratched him held on.

"Hey, that's a great tattoo," I said. "It's neat, where'd you get it?

"Pittsburgh."

"Yeah? You from Pennsylvania?"

"Yeah. How about you?" he asked.

"Jersey. What part of Pennsylvania?"

"A little town outside of Allentown," he said.

"Oh yeah? I went to Penn State for a year. I'm Paul Gebhart." I reached out and we shook hands.

"Jeffrey Collins," he said. He had black wavy hair and his nose was bent where it had been broken.

"How about you?" I asked.

"Nah, no college. I worked at a motorcycle shop after high school." He sat down next to me and lit up a Lucky Strike.

"Oh yeah? What kind of motorcycles?" I asked.

"Triumphs and Nortons."

"Yeah? I have a five hundred Ariel sitting at home."

"A single cylinder five hundred?" he asked.

"Yeah, that's right."

"Yeah, they're pretty sweet bikes, good torque. But I'd take my seven-fifty Norton over it."

"Well sure," I agreed.

"I got the Ariel for fifteen hundred. The Norton's what, twenty-five hundred bucks?"

"Depends. A new one goes for four thousand."

"See, so it should be a better bike. Say, what's happening at home?"

"Man, it's all fucked up." He made a face.

"Yeah?"

"Yeah," he said. "The blacks hate the whites. The whites are tired of all of the complaining. The Black Panthers are calling for revolution; everyone's tired of the fucking government. People are smoking dope in the streets. There's peace marches and guys burning their draft cards; all kinds of shit happening."

"The whole thing is falling apart," I said.

"The changing is hard to take but the changes are the right ones," Collins said.

"You're right about that. How do they say it's going over here?"

"Like we're getting our butts kicked."

"Yeah?" I said. "Well, except for our last mission it was us who were doing the ass-kicking. A couple of more Tets and this war be over."

Collins showed me photographs of his parents and two younger sisters, one ten years old and the other fourteen.

"That's a nice family you got there," I said as I handed him back the photos. "Is there fish in that pond in the back?"

"There's some small bass and perch but a few miles away there are some real good lakes."

"Maybe someday you'll show them to me," I said.

"Yeah, that would be fun," Collins said and we both drifted off into memories of home and fishing trips we'd been on.

The next morning, after the Chinook came in from Long Binh, I saw McDaniels walking to our mortar pits.

"What's he doing here?" I asked Moore.

"Beats me." Mack shrugged and we both watched McDaniels cross the camp. When he reached the pits he shook both our hands.

"You're not going to believe this," he said, "but Long Binh was rocketed last night and that barracks you two were in…"

"Yeah?" I said when he hesitated.

"It was hit, flattened!" McDaniels said. He looked to Mack then back to me. "It's gone now, blown to shit."

Mack whistled and shook his head in disbelief.

"Really?" I asked. "Was anyone hurt?"

"Couple of white guys were killed," McDaniels said, "blown up as they slept. You two weren't around and I came out to see if you were still alive."

"It's unbelievable," I said.

"No, uh-uh. It's no lie, man," McDaniels said.

Mack turned to me. "Man, if you hadn't made us leave, we'd be dead."

"Man, we were lucky," I said.

I thought about the two redneck boys. I hated them but I felt bad for them too. I kept thinking they were too young to die.

In the days that followed I took the time to visit Collins on the perimeter and he hung out at the mortar pits with me. Like everyone else when they first come into country he didn't know what to expect in the field; whether he'd fit in or if he were tough enough. He saw it was like everywhere young men gathered; we were all toughs but we were all fallible. There was no use trying to hide it, not when you live together as we did without walls. We were all weak sometimes but sometimes brave and always ready for fun.

It was that same week that Oscar Platoon received in a few new men too. One of them, Peter, was from California. He was an easygoing surfer with blond hair and blue eyes. He had a year of junior college so Sergeant Meyers asked me to teach him how to compute. I brought him to the mortar pit and showed him how to use the mortar manuals and the maps just as Charles had shown me.

"You lucked out being chosen to be my backup," I told him at the end once I saw he could do the math.

"How's that?" he asked.

"The Fire Director is crucial. I have to be around the mortar pits, especially at night so I'm exempt from LP duty. That's how it will be with you too, once you take my place. First of course you'll have to show the sarge that you can compute under fire. Otherwise he's got to find someone who can."

"What's el-pee duty?" he asked.

"Right, you don't know. Well it stands for listening post," I said, "but we call it the lone patrol."

The following week orders came down for Bravo to move to Phouc Vinh, 50 kilometers due north of Bien Hoa. We tore down camp and walked to the road to wait for the choppers.

"First assault ride?" I asked Peter.

"Yeah," he said.

"When the slicks come in you'll be in the middle next to me and Moore," I said.

The choppers landed and we waddled over and loaded up. Once airborne the pilot made a hard right bank and Peter screamed as he started to slide out.

"Don't worry," I yelled into his ear, "no one's ever fallen out."

"I might be the first!" he hollered. Moore and I laughed and hauled him in.

The company made camp in a clearing so narrow that the rifle platoons' foxholes were in the trees.

"They won't be able to string barbed wire in the jungle," Emery said.

"The riflemen don't have any fields of fire either," I said. "We can't even see them and there's no tree line to wire in for our mortars to hit."

"On top of everything else," Moore said, "they didn't bring out the sandbags. We can't dig in."

"Yeah, well Delino taught me better," I said. I took a shovel and started to scratch out two shallow mortar pits. The other men joined me and we dug a hole for the boxes of mortar rounds as well.

Tall brown grass grew waist high across the clearing.

"A VC crawling up on us wouldn't be seen from just five yards away," I said as I took a breather.

"Looks like Captain Dennis has decided to place headquarters with one of the line platoons," Sergeant Meyers said. He pointed with his chin to where the men from

Headquarters were going off into the tree line. "That leaves just us in the clearing."

I had a bad feeling about this set up but there was nothing to do except find a good place to spend the night. I walked around until I found a small indentation in the ground some thirty feet from the mortars and I laid my air mattress there.

At 2 a.m. I went to the mortar pit for my watch and sat with Emery and Moore. We smoked cigarettes and listened to the ambush and LPs on the radio. About 4:30 November's LP reported movement. Before we could wake everyone the LP's stopped whispering and in one chaotic eruption of action we heard grenades explode and automatic weapons firing. We heard them screaming in the dark too. "Don't shoot! We're coming in! We're coming in! Don't shoot!"

Once the two LPs cleared their own line the riflemen opened up. There was a racket of firing and a general confusion over where the North Vietnamese were. The radio crackled with orders as Bravo Six brought the other three LPs in through the lines just as the VC began their ground attack. I felt the adrenaline pumping through my veins as I heard them shouting in the dark.

Luckily the North Vietnamese seemed as disorganized as we were. Apparently not all of them had been in place when they started and they attacked in bits and pieces; now on this side, now on the other. There was a stillness in the night between each new assault and during those brief lulls, with the biting sharp smell of gun powder in the air, I shivered—not from the night, it was a balmy evening—but from the sheer terror of it. I had no doubt that someone was going to get hit; someone was going to die. Would it be me this time or you?

"Dear God, Almighty God," I said under my breath. "please God, please don't let us be overrun."

Under the bright white light of the phosphorous flares the trees, ground and sandbags were all silver gray without any color. Every shadow was deep black and everything flickered as the flares sputtered overhead. Maybe it was the limited view—I could only see thirty or forty yards—or the stage lighting effect of the flares but I heard every sound, every spoken word as if I were on a stage on Broadway. Or off Broadway I should say. Yeah, we were *off* Broadway all right, less than 200 men alone out in the jungle!

I was too frightened to laugh at my good wit. I looked around at Mack Moore and the others in the pit. Every face had wide-eyed terror written on it. Some men had withdrawn into themselves while others, also wide-eyed, shouted as we fired the mortar rounds. These active soldiers had a look so focused, so intense that I felt their gaze pierce my skin. Our collected fear hung in the air as thick as the grey cloud of gunpowder smoke that hung over the mortar pits.

We had all seen this before and here we were again. With death close by the beauty of the starry night and wilderness landscape evaporated and it felt like the Angel of Death was our audience.

By daylight the assault had petered out and a Medevac came in and flew out three dead and four wounded. The atmosphere was somber as we hung around the mortar pits with a few men from the rifle platoons. The soldier who had done most of the hollering last night was a new black guy named Davis. I had seen him before over by November platoon. He was six foot three with wide shoulders and huge biceps. A lifetime of hurt showed in his eyes. He stayed to himself and if you looked at him for more than a second he'd get aggressive. "What the fuck you looking at punk?" was his favorite expression. As far as I could tell he hadn't made any friends in the two weeks he'd been in the field but this morning he came over to the mortar pits with some of the November riflemen.

"What happened last night?" Emery asked him.

"There were VC crawling up on us in the dark," he said. "I was talking to headquarters on the radio but then we didn't have time to wait for permission. We had to do something. 'Fuck the Captain!' I yelled and tossed my grenades. I was throwing them hard, too, so they would penetrate the brush. I threw them like you'd pitch a fast ball." Davis demonstrated and made his eyes as big as half dollars to show how scared he had been. "I'm laughing about it now," he said, "but I'm a lucky motherfucker to be here to make fun of myself."

"We heard you yelling too," Monk said.

"Yeah, you got that right," Davis said. "I was scared shitless. Those bastards were crawling up wanting to slit our throats."

I laughed at his impersonation of himself. Our eyes met and Davis smiled. I think he realized we were the only ones who knew what had happened to him and like us or not we were family now.

The rest of the night was without incident but at dawn the next morning we came under mortar attack. As the first rounds exploded in the clearing I held my head with both hands and hugged the dirt. I was in the little ditch near the mortar pits and after the first four rounds, I got up and ran.

"Let's go! LET'S GO! Come on!" I shouted. "Oscar Platoon, let's GO!"

The Vietnamese had our clearing wired in. Their first rounds had landed smack in the middle of camp, just where the captain's tent should have been. A second set of mortars exploded and I heard shrapnel *whish* by my head.

"We have to hit them back," I yelled as I jumped into the pit.

The squad dove in behind me. Eddie and Moore worked the mortar tube to the left where I was sure the VC mortar crew was firing from. "There's a clearing just a hundred yards out," I shouted. I yelled the heading, elevation and charge to them. Monk set the charge and handed the round to Moore. He dropped it down the tube but before Monk handed him the second one he called to me,

"Paul! Paul! Di-did you say 'Charge None'?"

"No!" I shouted. "Charge ONE!" His mouth dropped open.

"What was that round?" Eddie asked him.

"No charges," Monk stammered.

"It's gonna be short," I said.

We couldn't see it but we heard the BOOM of the explosion.

"That sounded awfully close," I said. "We might have hit our guys." I felt sick. "Man," I turned to Monk, "I never say charge none. I'll say zero charge. God damn it, we may have killed someone."

"Okay," Monk said without looking me in the face.

There was a ground attack but the Vietnamese were beaten back and as soon as the last shot was fired a rifleman came out of the tree line from where that short had landed. He walked towards us and we all watched him approach across the field. None of us wanted to know who we had hit.

"Hey, you know that first mortar round you fired?" the rifleman hollered as he got closer to the mortar pits.

"Yeah," Eddie answered.

"Man, it was fucking GREAT! It landed just thirty yards in front of OUR foxhole. Shit, we knew nothing was coming for us from out there, not after that round! I wanted to come right over to thank you."

"Yeah, well," I said, "we thought we'd get that first one in real close then pan them out."

"Yeah," Eddie said, "we had that shot wired, man."

"First Sergeant! First Sergeant!" Lieutenant Truck's shouts interrupted our laughter. I looked up to see he was halfway across the clearing. "You've got a man here in the grass." The lieutenant yelled. He stood in tall yellow grass up to his waist.

"Medic! Medic!" Emery called out as we ran towards the lieutenant.

When I reached them I saw Collins on the ground. The lieutenant knelt next to him and supported his head and shoulders.

"He's been hit by mortar shrapnel," Truck said to us. Collins' fatigues were soaked in dark blood and he moaned with pain.

"Am I going to die?" he asked the lieutenant.

"No, you're going to be okay, just hang on," Lieutenant Truck said.

A medic cut open Collins' shirt. He looked at Lieutenant Truck and shook his head.

"How is it?" Collins asked weakly.

The medic busied himself preparing a morphine syrette.

"Am I going to die?" Jeffrey asked again in a hoarse voice.

"It's okay," Truck told him. "You're going to make it. He's giving you a shot. Just hang on."

"Medevac! Call a Medevac!" Emery yelled.

"They're on their way," men shouted to us from headquarters.

"Mom..." Collins moaned in a low voice like he had seen her standing in front of him. His body relaxed and his eyes stared into nothingness. The lieutenant laid him on the ground and shielded his own face from us by putting his hand across his brow.

Emery laid a momentary hand on Lieutenant Truck's shoulder then he and Monk put the body on a poncho and covered it. I watched in silence.

All that day and off and on for the next few days I saw Collins' face; I heard his laughter and saw the black panther tattoo.

He would never see his family again. No more Christmas mornings, no chance to get married and have kids, no more motorcycle rides on backcountry roads. I imagined his parents and sisters getting the news in the house in the Pennsylvania countryside. Their lives would never be the same.

A tear came to my eye but nothing came out. I felt empty inside.

Chapter Seven
Trouble Man

June 1968

In May and most of June the First Division had us join up with several other units for some operation or another. The fancy names they put on these maneuvers never really mattered to us. The only thing we wanted to know was where they were sending us and how much support we could count on.

After two weeks on the border taking part in the operation, we were back out on Thunder Road. I sat at a makeshift card table by the mortar pit. I had on dark sunglasses and wore leather sandals without socks. My fatigue pants were rolled up into cuffs and a cigarette dangled from my mouth.

"Four low," my partner Emery bid.

"Four high," Mack overbid him.

"Four No," I said.

"No trump?" Jesse said. "Don't start that shit."

I laughed at him. "What's the matter, Jesse?" I said, "No trump too complicated for ya?"

"Gebhart," Lieutenant Truck called me from the mortar pit.

"Yes, Sir." I played a card from my hand without looking up.

"Your name's at the top of the R 'n R list." The lieutenant almost sang the words.

"All right!" I hollered and laid my hand down.

"You have a choice of only three," Lieutenant Truck said as I approached the mortar pit. He was clean-shaven and had his crew cut, blond hair slicked straight up.

"Why only three?" I asked.

"They're overbooked at the other sites."

"Everyone wants to go to Bangkok," Emery said from the card table.

Lieutenant Truck looked at his clipboard. "You can go to Camron Bay…"

"Thanks, but I want out of Vietnam."

"Or," the lieutenant continued, "Taipei or Sydney." I took a long drag from my cigarette and weighed my options.

"If you choose Sydney," the lieutenant said, "you'll get ten days leave, Taipei is seven."

"Really? Well, Sydney then."

"The girls are better in Taipei," Jesse called out. "I was there in April and fucked good every day."

"Yeah? But an extra three days out of 'Nam," I said.

Lieutenant Truck handed me the clipboard and I signed the papers requesting Sydney. I finished the card game, took a joint and went into my lean-to. Maybe Mary would meet me with the baby? Probably too expensive and too far but I could ask her.

Moore came in and laid down on his air mattress. "Sure is hot out. You excited about your R 'n R?"

"I am. I've never been out of the States, except this little holiday here. I think Australia will be interesting."

"I'm going to Bangkok or Taipei when I get my turn," he said. "The girls are waiting for the GIs from Vietnam."

"Yeah, but Australia is English. It will be like going back to the World."

"I don't know anyone who's ever chosen it," Moore said.

"That's true," I said, "but I don't want to be with whores anyway and it's three extra days out of Vietnam."

"Yeah, I understand." He took the roach from me and I lay back and put both hands behind my head and stared at the ceiling. I wanted to see Mary. There had to be a way.

Four days later I was back in Di An and as I walked across Bravo's compound, across the dirt quadrangle from the headquarters' Quonset hut to the barracks, I saw images from the mortar barrages and ground attacks I had been fought in. I had made it through those firefights by sheer luck. I had made some great friends too. "Always work hard and do your best, no matter what." That was my father's motto and a good one I admit. He wouldn't be proud of what I was thinking but I had to get out of the field. I was going to get hit if I didn't. I could feel it. I took a long shower and put on clean fatigues. A Puerto Rican named LaPonte came into the toweling-off room. He had a pencil thin mustache and tight, wavy hair. He was a rifleman from Lima platoon but I hadn't seen him in the field for a few weeks.

"Want to smoke some weed?" he asked.

"Sure, LaPonte," I said. "How you been, man?"

"Nice. I've been nice," he said. "I got out of the field with a hernia so I just hang around here partying."

"How do you go about getting a hernia?" I asked.

"Shit if I know." LaPonte smiled a sheepish grin. "I just picked up my pack one day and busted my gut."

I took the joint from his hand. "A hernia huh? Hard to give myself one of those." Stoned, I went back to the barracks. I hadn't been in a cot in weeks and I slept for the rest of the day and through the night.

The next morning, I got a ride to Bien Hoa and walked to the mess hut by the processing center with my plane tickets proudly sticking out of my shirt pocket. I sat by myself and drank a warm soda. A light breeze blew in through the screened windows. Outside soldiers walked around the compound. I could tell by the color of their skin who were the veterans leaving for home or R 'n R and who were the new recruits just coming into country. Sergeants barked out orders to the new soldiers but no one messed with me or the other veterans. I felt like I was on vacation.

My thoughts ran to Mary and the baby. If I could just go see them. What if I had money wired from home? I could take a boat to Europe. Mary and the baby could join me. Why not? It was better even than getting out of the field. I would just never come back! I decided I would have Mary wire me the money as soon as I got to Sydney.

That afternoon I boarded a commercial jetliner at the airfield. I felt exuberant. As we cleared the coastline I watched the green jungle fade into the horizon. My plan was going to work. I would talk my way aboard a freighter to India then trains or boats to Europe. I felt giddy with happiness. We would move to Paris. I could paint and write and Mary would cook meals for our artist friends. I fell asleep with visions of living in a studio on the Left Bank.

I woke several hours later and looked out the window. The plane cruised over the open South China Sea. Each minute, every mile took me further from Vietnam. If I went AWOL I'd have to figure a way to get us home to the States someday. I'd find a way. Something could be done but right now just having us all together was the main thing.

When I arrived in Sydney I carried my duffel bag outside the terminal and shivered in the cool evening air. Life in the tropics had thinned my blood. Something felt strange too. I felt like I had forgotten something. I thought for a minute then realized it was my rifle. For seven months that had been my main concern: where should I put my M-16 when I ate? When I slept? Everywhere, every moment my rifle hadn't been more than an arm's length away; now I felt naked without it.

I walked to the front of the taxi line where a young Australian wearing a red plaid shirt leaned against a cab. When he saw me approach he opened his trunk up. "Cab, mate?" he asked.

"Okay," I said. "How much to town?"

"Just ten dollars."

"Okay, good."

"On holiday from the war?" he asked as he hoisted my bag into the trunk.

"Yeah, that's right," I said.

"Well, welcome to Sydney, mate. I hope you have a good time. You deserve it." The cabbie reached out and shook my hand.

"Thanks, appreciate it," I said. "Got any ideas about a good hotel?"

"How much you plan to spend a night?"

"Forty bucks or so. Can I get anything decent for that?"

"Try the Excelsior first. If you don't like it there are other hotels along the same street."

"The Excelsior it is then." I slid into the back seat and stared out the window. There weren't any huts along the highway, or mopeds, or peasants loaded down with possessions. White lines neatly divided the paved highway. The buildings and shops along the road were freshly painted and well maintained. Grass medians separated the traffic. It all looked so rich and well done. I felt a rush of euphoria. I had made it out alive now it was time to calculate my next move, getting money wired from home. Would Mary leave her family and America? Maybe she wouldn't want to go. How could we live in another country? How could the baby grow up without knowing her grandparents?

No, Mary would go. She'd always talked about getting out of New Jersey. Still, it would be better to call Stephen for the money. Once that was arranged I would surprise her with my plans.

"Friend of mine just got back from Vietnam himself," the Aussie driver said as he weaved through traffic.

"That right?" I said. "Good for him. I heard there was a unit of Australians in the Mekong Delta, right?" I looked at his eyes in the rearview mirror.

"Right, mate. Bloody hell of a place me friend says."

"It's no bloody Excelsior Hotel, I'll tell you that." I mimicked his Australian accent and he looked into the mirror for a long moment then laughed.

"It must feel good to be out of there," he said.

"It feels good not having to worry about an ambush along this road as a matter of fact."

The driver looked a second time in the rearview mirror and studied me for a moment. "I suppose it will take some time to adjust back to civilian life," he said.

"I hadn't thought about that," I said. "I suppose it will." The cab stopped in front of a large hotel.

"Enjoy our city, mate and good luck," he said.

"Thanks, guy." I paid him the fare as the hotel's doorman opened the cab door for me.

"Afternoon, Sir." The doorman played it well, touching two fingers to the hard brim of his red cap.

"Good-day, mate," I said. "Have I arrived at the world-famous Excelsior?"

"That you have, Sir." He carried my duffel bag and led the way through the red-carpeted lobby to the front desk. A middle-aged man with a bad hairpiece stood behind the reservations counter. "How much for a nice room for nine nights?" I asked.

"Vietnam vets get half price here, thirty-five a night."

"I'll take it," I said. I took my wallet out and counted out the fare. The twenties felt good in my hand. "American greenbacks," I said, "real money."

"It certainly is, Sir. Enjoy your stay with us."

I followed the bellman to the elevator and we got off on the seventh floor. The nice carpet in the hallway brought a smile to my face. The bellman unlocked a room and held the door for me and I went past him into a large room. Sunlight filtered through two curtained windows. A blue and white pinstriped chair was in one corner; a mahogany desk and small television set were in the other. The king-sized bed sat opposite the windows.

I tipped the bellman and ran the water for a bath. While the tub filled I tested the john by flushing it a few times. When the bath was ready I stepped into the steaming water and lay my head back and closed my eyes. All the hot water I could ever want. I remembered standing under the port-a-shower bag of cold water out in the jungle. No more of that; I was back in the World. Hot baths, clean sheets and indoor plumbing; I would never take them for granted again.

I changed into civilian clothes and left the hotel to enjoy an early evening in Sydney. Two blocks down I went into a nice restaurant and a blond older woman sat me at a table along the light paneled walls.

"Get you something from the bar, deary?" she asked.

"I'd like a Scotch on the rocks with a splash of water, please. And then a thick steak."

"Right-tow, be back in a flash."

While I waited for my drink, I thought about having to go back to Vietnam. "But I'm not going back," I murmured. "I'm going to get out. I'll make it work."

The waitress brought my drink and as the warmth of the Scotch spread across my chest, I sighed, "Only thing missing is Mary."

After dinner, thinking about my plans to go AWOL, I walked back to the hotel. My mind was busy with dreams of the future, but seven months of hard ground and the good meal melted my body into the soft mattress.

The alarm woke me at 6 a.m. and I had the hotel operator make the telephone connection to New Jersey.

"Hi, it's me," I said. I heard "Hi, it's me," echo four times across twelve thousand miles of cable.

"Paul!" Mary shouted. "Oh, it's so good to hear your voice. Where are you?"

"I'm in Sydney on my R and R."

"For how long?"

We had to time when we spoke to allow for the echo.

"Ten days. How's Nadine?"

"She's wonderful. Paul. She's the best baby. She sleeps through the night already. She's so happy, she almost never cries."

"That's great. Can she say mama yet?" I teased her.

"No, but she gurgles and makes noises. Here, I'm going to put her on, listen."

Mary put the telephone near Nadine.

"Hello, darling," I said. "Are you a good girl?" To my surprise, Nadine greeted me in baby talk.

"What talent!" I said when Mary came back on the line.

"Oh, Paul, I miss you so much. Are you okay?"

"I'm fine and I miss you too. I think of you, Mary, all day, every day."

"I miss you, Paul," Mary said. "I love you and I'm happy you're out of Vietnam, even for just a few days."

I wanted to tell her of my plans but thought better of it. We spoke about family and Mary's daily routines.

"I'll call you again tomorrow," I said. "Is this a good time?" I asked.

"What time is it in there?" she asked.

"Let's see." I looked at the clock on the desk. "It's six-twenty."

"In the morning?"

"Yeah," I chuckled, "in the morning."

"You can call me four hours later."

"Are you sure?"

"Yes, honey. I can't wait to hear your voice again."

"Okay, I love you," I said. "I don't want to hang up but I have to. I'll talk to you tomorrow."

"I don't want to say goodbye either," Mary started to cry, "but we must, goodbye, Paul."

I lit a cigarette and walked around the room thinking of my daughter and Mary. I longed to be with them; to have Mary in bed. I'd give anything to be with her. But how?

I called my parents next. They were so excited to hear my voice that they both talked at once. I laughed at my mother when she couldn't figure out the echo.

"Everything is fine," I said then paused to allow my words to bounce across the earth. "I'm safe and you shouldn't worry."

"Only seeing you again is going to stop our worrying," my mother said, beginning to figure out that she had to speak slowly and wait to hear her own words repeat before she could say more.

I called my younger brother Stephen at Memphis State.

"How are you, hippie," I said when I recognized his hello.

"Paul! God! How are you?" He sounded jubilant.

"I'm in Sydney on my R 'n R," I said. "How's school?"

"It's okay. I'm having fun with my friends, dropping acid and smoking dope but failing everything. It must feel great being out of Vietnam."

"Yeah, it does. It feels funny to be in civilian clothes too. I haven't worn anything with colors in a while. I feel like when we were kids and wore pajamas on Sunday nights after our baths, remember?"

"Sure, I remember. We had to call who was going to take their bath before Lassie or before The Ed Sullivan Show."

"So how long is your hair now?" I asked.

"Down to my shoulders."

"Yeah? What does Dad say about that?"

"He freaks out. I'm going home for the summer and he said I can't stay in his house unless I get a haircut."

I laughed. "Bummer. You'd better get the grades up though or you'll end up in Vietnam."

"I'd go to Canada first."

"Funny you should say that, Steve. I don't think I'm going back."

"What do you mean?"

"I can't take it anymore. I just want to be with Mary and the baby."

"How can you do that?"

"I want you to send me a couple thousand bucks. I'll get a boat out of Australia and meet up with Mary in Europe."

"Paul, how could you do that?"

"I don't know. I'll go down to the docks and ask around about a freighter."

"No, I mean not go back. They'll send you to prison."

"Only if they find me."

"But you'll never be able to come back to America. Where would you live? How would you support them?"

"I don't know, but I can't go back, Steve. I've had it. You've got to help me."

He hesitated, "Okay, I'll try. Where do I get the money?"

"From Dad or Grandpa. Tell them you need it."

"They'll want to know why and both of them are slow with money. I have to beg each semester as it is."

"Okay, borrow it from your friends. I'll pay them back. You can call some of my buddies too."

"All right, I'll try."

"Stephen, I have to get out of here."

"Okay," he said, "I'm going to try."

After the calls home, I fell back to sleep. I dreamt of fishing with my father and brother in a powerboat on a quiet lake, early in the morning; the water as smooth as glass. There was a mist on the water in my dream and when I woke, I could still smell the aroma of the clean lake water.

I dressed and went downstairs and sat in the lobby on a plush chair. I put my pad and pen on a fine coffee table and called a freighter company from the hotel phone. The fare to South Africa was $493 dollars. I only had my military ID; could I travel without the proper papers? I didn't ask. I'd work out all those problems once I had the money.

It was only 11a.m. but there wasn't anything to do so I went to the corner pub. It was filled with smoke and packed with men. I took a stool at the far end of the bar and ordered a beer. A soccer match played on a television above the bar. Australian men seemed to prefer bars that excluded women. They liked their beer warm and they went nuts over guys kicking a ball up and down the field, only scoring once every two hours.

"What's yours, Mate?" the bartender asked.

"I'll have a warm dark one," I said with sarcasm.

"American?" he asked.

"Yeah."

"What do you think of Robert Kennedy's assassination?"

"Robert? You mean John Kennedy."

"No, it was just shown on the morning news, Robert was shot in Los Angeles last night."

"What? I can't believe it. What happened? Who did it?"

"An Arab," the barkeep said as he studied the anger on my face.

"An Arab? That doesn't make any sense. Why?" I asked.

The bartender's face had turned somber. "Bloody strange" he agreed with a nod of his head. "Sure, I guess it was for money." He slid the tall brown draft to me and I paid him.

"Bloody strange is right," I said and finished half the glass in a slug.

I drank three of those ales trying to shake the depression I felt over a world gone mad. It didn't work but I had to stumble back to my room late in the afternoon and crashed heavy; not waking until the next morning's bright sunlight filtered through the white curtains. I was still depressed. My mind wandered through the days ahead and the days behind, all of my thoughts coming back to the one constant: Vietnam. Stephen had to get me the money. I could make it to Europe if I had enough cash.

I went to the harbor and bought a ticket for a boat ride across the bay. On the ferry's second deck as the ship pulled out, I cupped my hands against the salty breeze and lit a joint. As soon as the marijuana took hold I threw the roach overboard, disgusted with myself. I had a daughter now; I couldn't get stoned *every day*. Seagulls glided lazily behind the boat. I watched their effortless flight while I drifted off into thoughts of Mary and Vietnam.

On the other side of the bay, I found a sandy beach tucked into a rocky cove. My bathing suit already on underneath my clothes, I spread out the hotel towel and undressed. Children made sand castles and romped in the gentle surf. I watched them play as I fell into a dreamless black sleep. Hours later I woke up alone on the beach. My towel flapped in a steady breeze and sand stung my face. I walked back to the dock to catch the last boat back.

That evening I called Stephen.

"Hi, it's me," I said when he answered. "How are you?"

"Okay." Stephen sounded hung over.

"I made a few calls here," I said. "I think I can get a freighter from Sydney to South Africa, then to Europe."

"Paul, you can't do it. You'll ruin your life. You'll be running forever."

"Look, I'd rather run forever then be buried forever. I'll make it work, just get me the money and help Mary with her parents."

"No, Paul. I can't do it. I tried to get it for you but couldn't, besides one of my friends told me about a cousin of his that went AWOL in Texas. He's serving time now in Leavenworth."

"Dumb bastard got caught is all," I said. "I'll be smart, you'll see."

"Someone else told me they trace money wired to soldiers."

"Bullshit," I laughed. "How could they do that? And even if they did so what? I'll be long gone."

"I'm sorry, Paul," Stephen said in a quiet voice, "but I'm not going to be a part of you ruining your life. I can't do it. Dad would kill me." He choked up and I waited for him to clear his throat.

"Stevie..." I went to tell him about Vietnam, but stopped and took a deep breath instead. "You're right," I said. "I know that but I've had enough. I miss Mary. I want to be with her and the baby."

Stephen didn't say anything but I knew what he was thinking; I had to go back and take my chances. I had to come home with an honorable discharge and get a job and support my family. I felt the bubble of hope burst inside my chest. My plan was crazy; there was no way out, I was going back. I heard a rumble of discontent in my stomach and what else was I feeling? Fear, yes fear underneath all my feelings and thoughts.

"Stevie, promise me one thing," I said, breaking the silence.

"Sure, Paul, what?"

"If something happens to me, you'll take care of Mary and Nadine."

"Absolutely," Stephen's relief was palpable. "You got it. I swear to you I'll be there for them."

"Okay, thanks. I'll see you."

"Write me, okay?"

"Sure, Steve. I will. You take care."

I sat on the bed with my head in my hands. What was I going to do? I could take off for Australia's backcountry? No, uh-uh. I was going back to Vietnam.

I showered and dressed and went out feeling lonely and horny. I wanted to touch a woman. Without trying to I found the red light district. A group of hookers stood on the corner but I went past them. Halfway down the block a pretty redhead sat on a chair in front of a four-story brick apartment building. She turned towards me and I saw her bare, smooth legs and a flash of white panties under her short skirt.

"Got a light?" she asked.

I lit her cigarette and she smiled. "Thirty bucks for a date. What do you say?"

I answered with my eyes and she led the way up two flights of stairs to her flat. A light in the bedroom and a small lamp on an end table dimly lit the living room. A nicked-up wooden coffee table held a stack of paperback books and an empty coffee cup. The carpet was old and dingy. The green walls needed paint. Incense burned in a brass pot and Picasso prints hung on the wall between two curtained windows. All in all the apartment was pretty cool and I could see that she really lived there. I sat down on the couch as the redhead locked the door.

"You got the thirty?" she asked.

"Yeah, sure." I paid her and followed her into the bedroom. She was pretty enough and she didn't rush through it. Afterwards she lit a cigarette for me.

"How long you been in Vietnam," she asked.

"Seven months." I took a wet washcloth from a white bowl on the night table. As I wiped myself, I felt a wave of shame and guilt flash through me.

"Where are you from," she asked.

"New Jersey. Ever been there?"

"No, not quite," she laughed. "I've never been out of Australia. I'd love to travel someday though. It's the best education; travel that is."

"So I've heard," I said.

"You wear a wedding ring."

"Because I'm married," I said.

"You look too young to be married."

I looked at her closer. She had beautiful green eyes and a shadow of a blond mustache. I put her in her late twenties.

"I have a baby daughter," I said. "She's just two months old."

"Really, that's great. I bet you can't wait to see her."

"No, I can't."

"Do you want a drink?"

She was nice, not like the cold hookers I had known in the States but I didn't trust her.

"No, thanks," I said, "I should be going."

"What's it like in Vietnam?" she asked as I dressed.

"It sucks," I said. I sat on the edge of the bed and put my shoes on.

"Have you ever been shot at?" she asked.

I turned and looked at her. "Well, yeah, of course."

"And you're not scared?"

"Of course I'm scared," I said. "I'm scared to death. It's just a matter of time before I get hit."

"Why is that?"

"The odds start to pile up against you," I said. "It's just a matter of luck, who gets hit and who doesn't."

"I was in a car accident once," she said. "I saw my death coming to me. It was a black dot that came from out of the sky and tried to take me. I imagine it must be the same thing you go through." I looked at her again.

"Death is a darkness in the woods," I nodded my head. "I've seen—no not seen but felt—that black dot hovering in the tree line. I think, if you get hit the darkness rushes in and overwhelms you."

"I felt peaceful when I started to lose consciousness," she said. "I saw a white light. The light from God's presence. That's what Jesus promises us, that we'll be with him in peace and glory."

"I hope," I said, "but not right now. I want to make it home to love my wife and to raise my daughter."

"Of course, but death is a part of life. Think of all the people before us. They all went through death. To be alive means we must die."

"Yeah," I said, "but not right now."

She laughed. "Just one more day in the Garden of Eden."

"Or in Vietnam," I said.

"Are you sure you don't want a drink?" she asked.

"No... no thanks," I said. I looked into her face. She wanted me to stay but I knew only being with Mary would cure my blues. "I've got to go," I said. "Take care of yourself."

"You too, good luck." She put her dress on and showed me to the door.

I lit a fresh cigarette outside and walked to the corner pub. I found an empty booth and ordered a beer and thought about Stephen and my father. I recalled my father's ways and his expressions. I laughed out loud. Stephen was right, if I had gone AWOL, Dad would have killed him.

In the morning I walked for hours through the streets of Sydney. The temptation to return to the comfort of the redlight district was strong but I shopped instead. I bought Nadine a soft koala bear and Mary a gold ankle bracelet. After I arranged the shipping, I went back to the hotel and called Mary. We talked about Robert Kennedy's assassination and made plans for me to return to college when I got home.

I called Mary every day and my parents one last time the day I left for the airport. We, all of us were pretty quiet on the phone.

Twelve hours after leaving the hotel, I processed back through Bien Hoa, got a ride back to Di An and returned to Bravo Company's barracks. I found an empty cot and threw my duffle bag down.

"Hey, Gebhart!" Carter called to me from a bunk down the aisle as I unpacked.

"Yo, Carter. You going home?" I called back to him. He walked over to my cot. "Yeah, man," he smiled. "I made it."

We shook hands. "Hey, all right. Congratulations!"

"How you doing?" he asked. "You look like you lost some weight."

"I might have," I said. "Truth is I'm more scared now than when I first came into country."

"Getting short is all about being scared," Carter said. "Knowing you're going back out and thinking about the shit you're going to be in."

"Yeah, that's me all right," I said. "There has to be a way out."

"No way out, man." Carter shook his head. "You got to do your time."

"Well at least we can go get drunk. You want to party tonight?"

"Hell yes," Carter said. "It wouldn't be right for me to leave here without a hangover."

I changed into clean fatigues and sunglasses and we walked to the USO. Inside, the music played sweet soul music and we were able to find an empty table and order drinks. Three black soldiers sat at the table to our right. Two of the men smiled and said "Hi" to Carter. The third guy stared at me.

He was slim with light brown skin and a thin face. He was wearing sunglasses: small square, green lenses in a thin brass frame—granny glasses. The second man had reddish hair, brown skin, and freckles. The third one was short, stocky and dark skinned.

"What are you doing hanging out with this whitey?" the soldier in granny glasses asked Carter.

"Hey, man," Carter said, "don't start no trouble."

"Educate yourself, farm boy. These white devils got you and your race over here getting killed so they can make their millions."

"If you say so," Carter said.

"Don't be ignorant, man. These people ain't your friends."

"You call me ignorant again," Carter said, "and I'm gonna educate *your* ass right here." They stared at each other.

"No one's insulting you, brother," the redhead said.

"Yeah, man," granny glasses continued. "What's insulting is you hanging around with this white Jew devil."

"Ah-shit," I said. "Listen, hating me isn't going to make anything better."

"You got something to say to me?" Granny glasses spit out his words.

"I would just like to state for the record," I said, "that I haven't made any money on the war, at least not up to this point."

Carter laughed but the other three kept their hard looks.

"You fucking, Jew," granny glasses said.

I put my drink on the table and studied his face. Hatred shot like shafts of light from his eyes.

"You know what?" I said.

"What?" he asked.

"Fuck you."

"You're as sick as the white crackers down in Mississippi," Carter added.

"You're brainwashed, farm boy," granny glasses snapped at him. "These white people are the devils and the worst ones are the ones who act like they're your friends. Back in the States this boy wouldn't be seen with you."

"Oh, man, shit," I said. "What the fuck do you know about me?"

"Fuck up, white punk," granny glasses raised his voice.

"Hey," Carter stood up. "I don't want you to say another word. If you do I'm gonna pound the shit out of you, got it? And as far as my buddy is concerned, I'm going to judge him by the content of his character. Just like I'm gonna judge you. You dig?"

Granny glasses leaned back in his chair, balancing his weight on the back legs. He folded his arms across his chest and looked Carter in the eye. His two buddies stood up and I did too.

I figured my best play was to dive head first into granny glasses and knock him over backwards but I hesitated.

"The poison just seems to spread," I said. "This isn't the way we should be treating each other."

"Sometimes you got to knock sense into assholes like these," Carter said.

"Easy, man." The short one reached out to Carter.

"Take your hands off me." Carter pushed his arm away.

"All right, okay, easy, brother," the soldier said.

"I'm gonna go, Carter," I said.

"Okay," Carter said, "let's get out of here."

"Come on, man, stick around," the redhead said. "There's gonna be some dancing in a little bit."

"Yeah, come on, brother. No hard feelings," the short one said.

"Where you going, man?" granny glasses said when Carter turned to leave.

"I'll tell you where I'm going," Carter stopped and said. "I'm going with my friend to a place where the color of your skin and your religion don't matter. Maybe you brothers will join us there someday?"

We left the USO and walked back to the barracks. The familiar odor of the damp Vietnamese earth hung heavy in the air. In the moonless night only the lights from inside the barracks lit the road. The richness of the sensory experience of Vietnam juxtaposed against its difficulties.

Carter turned to me, "I'm sorry they called you those names."

"They're angry," I said, "I can't blame them."

"I can," Carter said. "You want justice? You have to *be* just. You want equality? You don't get it by being a bigot your own self. Man, they're stupid. They have no idea what we've been through out there. Shit, Paul, you're more a brother to me than some stranger with black skin. Besides," he added, "I don't let anyone talk to my friends like that."

"Thanks, Carter," I said.

"I was surprised too," Carter said. "I thought you'd hit him over the head with a chair or something."

"Six months ago, I would have," I said. "Now I don't want to fight anyone over anything."

"I know what you mean, man. I know what you mean."

We walked in silence until I said, "This is like being in two wars at once."

"It sure is," Carter agreed.

"The racism we've all grown up with in America, it's created a distance between us," I said, "and when we try to bridge it, to meet another human being and enter into their world, it's like I'm crossing through a field of fire. You see what I mean?"

"Exactly, I do," Carter nodded, "but we gotta keep trying, even if we get shot at once in a while."

We spent the night on the steps of the barracks drinking beer and telling war stories to some new recruits. In the morning I watched as Carter climbed into a two-and-half-ton truck. He saluted me from the rail and I came to attention and threw him my best military salute. He held up his hand in the peace sign as the truck drove out of sight down the dirt road.

"I may not have a hernia," I said that evening to Juan LaPonte, "but I have an addiction." I passed him the pipe. "I start each day determined not to get stoned but by nightfall I'm tokin' away."

We sat outside on the barrack's steps and LaPonte swatted at a mosquito. "No sweat," he said.

"Sure, no sweat, except I don't want to get high. The army should help me with this."

"Yeah, right." He blew out the yellow smoke he had held deep in his lungs.

"I'm burnt out on dope," I said.

"You going to tell them you're a head?" he laughed. "That'll get you 30 days in the Long Binh jail. You'll quit then."

"Are you kidding? There's as much dope in the stockade as you want. No, I'm going to tell them they have to help me."

"Good luck, man." LaPonte passed me back the pipe. I waved off the offer. "Nah," I said, "I'm done."

The next morning, I waited in the shade of a tree outside the chaplain's Quonset hut until a clerk called me in and led the way to an office next to the chapel.

"Why did you want to see me?" the chaplain, a captain, asked from behind his desk.

235

"I'm having problems with drugs, Sir." I stood, holding my baseball cap in both hands.

The chaplain's face turned scornful. He tapped his pencil on the desk and leaned back in his chair. "What drugs?"

"Marijuana mostly."

"Why are you smoking that stuff?"

"I don't know," I said. "I started when I first got here and now I can't stop."

"Why not?" His tone was abrupt.

"I don't know. I want to but every day I'm smoking something, even after I tell myself that I'm not going to get high. I haven't been sober for months, Sir."

"You'd better stop it," the chaplain said.

"I need help, Sir. I was hoping, maybe I could get transferred to Di An for a few weeks and get counseling."

The chaplain studied me. I felt his eyes linger on the sunglasses in my fatigue pocket. He shook his head. "I'm sorry," he said, "there's nothing I can do."

I looked into his eyes. "I have a wife and baby daughter," I said. "I don't want to go home to them all screwed up. You could make some calls."

"No, that's impossible. You need to discipline yourself like everyone else."

"Like everyone else?" I almost laughed at him. "Everyone else is as screwed up as I am."

"There's nothing I can do for you." The captain tapped his pencil again.

Despite his disguise I could see that he was a lifer like the others.

"You have no idea how bad I feel about Jesus getting killed," I said on impulse.

"What are you talking about?" The chaplain looked puzzled.

"No idea, I'm telling you, because two thousand years later people hate me for it. *I didn't do it!*"

"This discussion is over." The chaplain rose from his chair.

"If I had been there," I said, "I would have gotten him the hell out. Believe me, Jesus is a friend of mine and I didn't kill him."

"You're dismissed, soldier!" he shouted at me and the orderly came into his office. He walked in and stood between me and the chaplain. He motioned to the door and I turned and walked out.

On the dusty road in the blazing afternoon sun, I finished the conversation. "I think you killed Christ," I said out loud. "Yeah, you and people like you."

Juan LaPonte stood in the barracks' doorway as I approached. He grinned at me through bloodshot eyes. "Hey, man," he said, "we got some righteous stuff. You wan' some?"

I looked into his happy face. These were the men who understood me and what I was going through. Getting high was a part of what united us. I took the pipe from his hand and pulled on the lit embers. I felt the marijuana kick in. The sunlight striking the barracks door took on a peaceful, holy light. "It *is* righteous stuff," I said handing him back the pipe.

"I told you." LaPonte smiled.

"You were right," I said. My buddies knew more about Christ's compassion too.

On my way to rejoin Bravo Company the next day, I learned that the VC had fired rockets into Long Binh every night for a week and that Bravo Company had been called in from the field. "It's not just the rocketing either," a grunt with a pock-marked complexion told me as we waited for the Chinook. "Twice in the past month sapper teams have gotten *into* Long Binh. They've blown up a couple of helicopters and a barracks. Seventeen servicemen have been killed."

"You finally make it back to base camp then get blown up," I said and the grunt agreed; there wasn't any safe place except maybe Camron Bay.

The night I returned to Long Binh Oscar Platoon had night watch. Just before sundown I put my gear on and walked with the others out to the tarmac. We patrolled around sixteen helicopters parked inside roofless, green sandbagged bunkers. The sky was clear and full of stars but I was bored. I tried to come up with an excuse to sit down but Lieutenant Truck was right there with us. We walked around, up and down the tarmac until just after midnight when a rocket whistled over our heads. Red sparkles fizzled in the black sky as it streaked over the base. It exploded barely a hundred yards away and we ran for the foxholes off the runway. I found myself in a bunker with six people including the lieutenant. The bunker was built above ground and as we stood huddled together looking out the doorway a second rocket exploded with an orange and red flash just fifty yards away. We knelt down and held our hands over our helmets waiting for the next one.

"They're getting closer," someone said.

"That door's too wide," I hollered, "one of those rockets could land right inside here."

"Remind me to report this to maintenance," Lieutenant Truck said. He spoke without looking up or taking his hands off his helmet and we laughed at him. The lieutenant looked up and smiled a sheepish grin.

It was just those two rockets but they caused heavy damage to several barracks and we heard that a half dozen engineers had been killed.

The next morning I was outside behind our barracks washing my fatigues when Moore came out to see me.

"Emery said that some good grass just came in. Want to go? with me to get some?"

"Yeah, sure, I'll go with you. Let me hang this stuff up first." I draped the wet fatigues over the side of the wooden shower wall. The moment the tropical sun struck them, steam from the evaporating water rose into the air. I took my M-16 and walked with him across the open field to the next line of wooden buildings.

"Give me ten bucks," he said outside the first barracks. I handed him a few Vietnamese bills and he went inside.

"Hey, Victor. Victor, man." I heard him call to his friend. Moore wasn't gone five minutes before he came back down the steps in a hurry.

"Keep going," he said under his breath.

We ducked behind the wall of the next barracks. "Their lieutenant came in just as I got the stuff," Mack explained.

He brought out two one-ounce bags of grass. "Five bucks each," he said. He handed me one of the bags and five hundred pees. I opened the bag and sniffed the sweet weed.

"Mmm, nice aroma," I said. "Rich with a hint of wildflowers."

Moore checked around the corner of the wall and signaled with his head for me to follow him. We crossed the open field and went into our own barracks. The men in Oscar Platoon were putting their gear on and looked up at us.

"Que pasa?" Moore asked Emery.

"They got Bravo Company going out to patrol the area where they think those rockets were launched from last night."

"What, in the afternoon?" I asked.

"Gebhart! Moore!" Lieutenant Truck yelled. "Get your shit together. Let's go!"

On the dirt road outside the barracks, a column of two-and-a-half-ton trucks pulled in and Bravo Company loaded up. The trucks drove us to the edge of Long Binh where we waited under the trees for an hour before moving out in single file. I followed Moore and Emery down the slope into the jungle. Bravo patrolled through the jungle in a large arch west of Long Binh. It was stifling hot and I wanted to sit down but it was two hours before the captain called a rest halt. We kneeled down on the trail and looked out into thick undergrowth with no more than ten feet of visibility in any direction.

I figured we were safe. The VC hadn't fired rockets during the daytime. The Vietnamese had more sense than us anyway; they wouldn't be walking around in the heat of the afternoon. This was just a little walk in the sun so I lit a pipe of the new grass and inhaled the thick smoke.

"This smells great," I said. I took another toke and handed the pipe to Moore. A buzz went through my body.

"I mean this is some kick-ass stuff. I'm tripping," I said.

I took the pipe back for another long pull. Before I let out the yellow smoke, I was smashed. The sounds of the jungle insects reverberated in the humid air. I watched a colony of red ants go by my feet. I followed them as they crawled up a rubber tree, took white juice from a gash in the trunk, went across the ground, climbed up a plant stalk and used the rubber ooze to cement three large leaves together to make a nest.

"These guys are doing one hell of a job," I said to Moore. "Look at the perfect seams they've made."

Moore didn't pay any attention but I watched intently. "I swear I can hear them walking over the leaf litter." I looked over to Moore and smiled. Suddenly shots from automatic weapons rang out.

Ditditdit-ditdit-ditditdit.

"Stay DOWN!" Moore motioned with one hand, palm down. "Just where you are."

I heard shouting from up the trail: "C'mon, let's go, let's go!"

The men ahead of us rose and ran towards the firefight but I froze. "Mack, Mack," I whispered hoarsely, "I can't move. I'm stoned."

"C'mon, right by me," Moore yelled.
He was crouched over and looking up the trail. When I didn't get up he turned and looked at me through bloodshot eyes.

"Ya got to, c'mon!" he yelled and punched me on the shoulder to unfreeze me.

I ran behind him up the trail. We could hear the firefight grow in intensity.

"Oh, Jesus," I said.

"You okay?" Moore turned to check me out.

"No!" I shouted over the commotion.

"Okay, stay cool, stay cool."

We pushed our way through the brush along the narrow trail. My head pounded and my field of vision narrowed. All I could see were my boots and the ground going by underneath. Everything else was out of focus.

"This is it," I whispered to myself. "This is where you die, you stupid fuckin' jerk."

We drew closer to the fighting. The trail widened where it opened up into a clearing. At the edge of the clearing Oscar platoon hit the dirt. One at a time the squads on the trail rushed out into the open field but before Moore and I had to join them the shooting stopped. The men in Oscar got up and walked into the clearing but Moore and I both hesitated.

"They got 'em," Emery called to us. "C'mon."

"What do ya mean?" Moore asked.

"It's over," Emery said. "They're all killed."

We got up and I followed Moore out into the clearing where men in Mike platoon combed the far tree line. Serena and the men from Lima stood in tall brown grass in the middle of the meadow. Six Vietnamese bodies lay strewn around a large rocket launcher.

"What the hell is that?" I asked. "That's no RPG rocket."

"I'm not sure," Sergeant Meyers answered.

"It looks like a goddamn baby missile," I said. "Imagine them wheeling this bad boy through the jungle?"

"Yeah, well this crew is done wheeling anything," Emery said.

"These aren't kids." Gardener motioned with his chin. "Looks like Lima's taken out some valuable people."

They had and a week later a special formation was held in Long Binh to present Kenny Serena with the Silver Star. He showed it to us as we sat around in the shade outside the barracks after the ceremony. In the background the radio played *Time Has Come Today* by The Chambers Brothers.

"I was walking point," Serena explained, "when I came out of the tree line and into the clearing. The Vietcong were just about to launch the rocket when I shot and killed the gunner."

"I remember that," Desusa said.

"Four of the others shot back at me. One had his gun jam, the other three all missed. I heard the bullets hit the ground and some go right by my head."

"Damn!" I said. "That wouldn't happen again in a hundred years; four automatic weapons missing from fifty yards!"

"I know," Serena shook his head. "Before they could adjust their fire I hit the ground and the other guys from Lima joined in, drawing their fire away from me."

"We didn't have any casualties and all six of them were put down," Desusa said.

Serena took the medal out of its case and looked at it. "I've seen a whole lot braver shit than that," he said. "I just walked into it."

On Thunder Road

We had been drinking and smoking grass and Serena's emotions showed. "Look at all the shit we've been through," he said. "All the friends we lost and they give you a fucking piece of metal." He had tears in his eyes and his voice choked.

"Well, that's the way it goes." Monk shrugged, nudged him with his shoulder and passed him the joint.

"Yeah, right." Serena took a hit off of it and passed it to me.

I took a toke but felt my hands start to tremble. My legs and fingers became stiff as wood.

"Shit, this feels awful," I said. "This weed is bringing back the paranoia I felt on that patrol."

"Here, try some of this." Moore took a small piece of opium Thai stick from his shirt pocket, put it into a pipe and lit it then passed it to me.

I pulled in on the black tar smoke; I exhaled and felt a strong buzz. My fingers felt supple. I felt peaceful and relaxed. I was released from the fear that had gripped me. It was the best feeling I had had in a long time but I needed to lie down.

I went into the barracks and lay down on my cot. I fell into dreams both strange and magical. When I woke up I went with Emery to the mess hut. In the middle of a conversation with him, eating lunch, I woke up again and I was still on the cot in the barracks. I'd talk to some other soldiers, think I was awake, and damn I'd wake up again! Dreams within dreams within dreams; all as real as real life.

"This is some good dope," Moore said when I woke yet another time. "Let's go smoke some more out by the showers."

I wasn't certain if I was in another dream or not. I figured it didn't matter much anyway. Just go with the flow.

"We could get hooked on this stuff," I said.

"Yeah, and we could get killed tonight, too," Moore answered. "I'm gonna go smoke me some more."

He searched through his rucksack for the black sticks. I wanted to stop getting high. I was sick of the dope routine but Moore was right, I may not have another day and I didn't want to feel that fear anymore. That was the worst. I followed him out to an empty field behind the barracks where he ceremoniously lit the opium pipe.

* * *

At the end of August, the word came down that we were moving out. "We'll be in the fourth wave." Lieutenant Truck stood in front of our formation outside the barracks in Long Binh. "They'll chopper us to the Vam Co Tay River south of Saigon," he said. "The battalion is to guard an engineering corps as they build a bridge across the river." The lieutenant glanced back at his notes. "After we land, Alpha, Charlie, Headquarters and Recon will be deployed on one side of the river. Bravo will be on the other side with two troops from a Fourth Cav unit. Let's get squared away. Anything you leave behind has to be burned."

At noon we loaded onto trucks. At the runway helicopters with their engines idling waited for us. After a twenty-minute air lift I could see the LZ.

"Hey, look." I pointed to personnel carriers inside the perimeter. "Cavalry."

"Oh shit," Emery said, "not those guys again."

After we landed, our backs to the river, we set up a perimeter facing west. The rifle platoons dug foxholes less than thirty yards from the jungle tree line. Two cavalry tanks were on the perimeter and six personnel carriers were inside behind the foxholes. Also inside the perimeter the engineers' had three bulldozers, a crane and a gasoline tractor-trailer.

The ground was a hard red clay and night fell before we had finished digging in. I held the flashlight for Eddie as he shoveled out a foxhole.

"Hey, Eddie," I said, "wait. Look at that." I aimed my flashlight at something moving on the wall. Eddie turned around and came face to face with a large black scorpion. It was seven inches long with black leathery scales. The scorpion froze in the light and held its stinger over its head.

"Yo!" Eddie yelled and jumped straight up and out of the hole.

"I swear," I said to the men who heard him yell, "he didn't touch the sides. Just *zoom,* and he was out of there."

"I always said that man's farts were strong enough to lift him off the ground," Monk said.

"Go fuck yourselves," Eddie growled. He took his shovel and brought the scorpion out of the hole where he cut it in half and squashed it with his boot.

"I wonder if there's any more of them around?" Monk said.

"Good question," I said, and we all searched the ground with our red-filtered flashlights. We didn't see any more but I couldn't sleep thinking about those black scales and that stinger.

I walked to the riverbank the next morning to watch the engineers work. Their heavy crane and dozer engines rumbled as the men assembled a prefabricated bridge across a narrow part of the river.

"Gebhart," Lieutenant Truck called me from the trail, "next time tell someone before you walk off."

"I just wanted to see what they were doing," I said. "It's pretty interesting. That crane lifts those sections like they were…"

"Never mind that," Lieutenant Truck said. "You and Moore are on day LP along the riverbank. Get back to the mortar pits and get your gear."

I followed the lieutenant back into the clearing. Moore was already packed and had his rucksack on. I grabbed the radio and we walked out of the camp and onto a trail lined with banana trees and ferns. At the riverbank downriver from the bridge construction we set up on a little crest of land ten feet above the water. Both sides of the river were thick with vegetation; the big-leaf kind they call elephant plants. The forest drowned out the engineers' construction noise around the bend and the dark-green river flowed peacefully by. Moore opened up cans of C rations with his miniature can opener and I used a pinch of C-4 to start a fire to cook an early lunch. Before we had finished eating, Emery, Jesse, and Monk came out to join us and we sat around the small fire and held the C ration cans over the flames with branches.

"Man, Emery," Moore said, "you're getting pretty short now, ain't you?"

"That's right, mutha." Emery grinned.

"Me too," Jesse said. "Emery and me will be back in the World in just a couple of weeks."

"And you boys will still be eating C rations." Emery pointed to the can of beans Moore stirred over the fire. "What year were those beans canned in anyway?"

"Same year you first licked pussy," Moore said.

Emery laughed, "Shit, them is some old beans, bro."

"The river looks good, doesn't it?" I said.

"Yeah, it does," Monk answered.

"If you guys want to go in for a swim me and Moore will cover you."

"Yeah?" Emery said.

"Yeah, sure," Moore said. "It'll be okay."

They talked it over and decided to try it. They took their rifles and walked down the slope to the riverbank. Emery striped to his shorts and jumped in. "Hey, the water's great!" he called to

Monk and Jesse. He floated on his back and treaded water against the river's slow current as they stripped.

Monk jumped in and swam out ten yards, turned and floated on his back too. "It's deep and clean," he hollered, his wet face shone like black polished marble in the sunlight.

"Okay, I'm gonna try it," Jesse said. He checked the temperature with his foot, gathered his courage and cautiously jumped in feet first. He arched his back to keep his head above water. When he bobbed to the surface, he doggie-paddled around near the riverbank while Monk and Emery swam farther out.

When they came out of the water they dressed and went back to the perimeter. Not long after, a call came in on the radio.

"Bravo Six to Oscar LP, over."

"It's the captain," I said. "You talk to him." I handed Moore the radio receiver.

"I can't," he mumbled, pointing to his mouth. "I goth foodth in my mouff."

"You what?"

"I GOTH FOODTH IN MY MOUFF!"

I picked up the handset, "Oscar LP, over."

"Gebhart, are you swimming? Over."

"No, Sir. Over."

"Well I heard men were swimming out by you, over."

"A couple of men were swimming but we were guarding them, over."

"So you didn't go into the water? Over."

"No, Sir. Over."

"Okay, I'm going to let some more men go swimming but someone has to stay on guard, over."

"Yes, Sir. We will, over and out." I hung up the handset.

Fifteen minutes later six soldiers walked down the jungle path and into the narrow clearing along the riverbank. They were carrying their air mattresses and I saw them look around to see if it was safe. Moore pointed his M-16 to the jungle on both sides of the river, showing them that it was okay, we would cover them.

"Where's the best place to go in?" one rifleman called to me.

"Right there," I hollered back. "Over by that tree is where they dove in." I pointed down to the riverbank.

They went down the steep bank and we watched them strip naked and jump in.

"This is like a pool party," I said.

"'Cept we gotta keep watch with our M-16s," Moore said.

"'Cept we gotta keep watch with our M-16s," I agreed. "But they're having fun and their minds are free. It's just like a Saturday afternoon back home."

In the late afternoon, the sun sank slowly over the vast Mekong Delta. There was a golden glow on the leaves of the vegetation as Moore and I packed our gear and walked back on the narrow path. The leaves cast shadows that grew deeper until by the time we got back inside the perimeter it was almost dark.

The long tube of a 160mm mortar stuck out of the top of a personnel carrier parked next to our pit. After supper I talked with the First Cav mortar crew. Carl, their squad leader, was a black man from Kansas City. He had smooth, black skin and prominent eyes.

"It doesn't make sense to me," I said. "You've got a whole battalion out here. Why put two-thirds on one side and have just our one company on this side all by itself?"

"That's probably because the clearing on this side of the river is so much smaller." Toby joined our conversation.

"That's true," I agreed, "but you have all of these engineers here. Make this clearing bigger; knock down some jungle with those bulldozers and tanks."

"Yeah, they could do that," Carl said. "I guess they're behind schedule on the bridge and don't have the time."

"Yeah, right," I said. "They should take the time to be safe."

"Well, you've got the Fourth Cav here too," Toby said.

"That equals it out some," I allowed. "It seems strange though; seems you'd want to equal out your infantry too."

"I'll tell you another problem," Carl said. "If we get hit, our mortar will be useless in this small of a clearing."

"Yeah?" I said.

"Uh-uh," Carl shook his head. "That 160 mortar, the closest it can fire is 150 yards." "Really?" I said.

"Yeah. The damn tree line is only what, thirty or forty yards away?"

I looked to where he pointed. "Yeah, we're pretty tight in here," I said.

"And our tanks out on the perimeter," Carl went on, "they're too close to that tree line too. Their canons will be firing point blank but hitting the trees about six feet up. I don't suppose the VC will come in standing up. Do you?"

"No," I said, "not really. That and the fact there isn't any wire strung means they can crawl right up to the riflemen's foxholes. Not good. Not good at all."

The subject changed to talk about home. We were all tired and the conversations trailed off and we turned in early. I held up the air mattress I had stolen in Long Binh and called to Moore on the other side of the pit wall.

"I've got my own bag."

"How'd you get that?" he asked.

"Just like you showed me, I requisitioned it from a REMF."

"Well, okay. I see your training out here is finally starting to pay off for you."

"Yeah, right." I waved him off and set up my air mattress in between Emery's and Jesse's.

I dozed off and had a dream I was with Mary. We sat on a bench by a large pond as two white swans swam by. The ripples from their wakes traveled out in a calm "V" on the smooth water. Mary and I held hands in the shade of a weeping willow tree. Then I heard it, from out in the jungle, a soft thump... thump... thump. "Even sleeping," I said to her, "I can recognize that thumping sound."

She frowned.

"Incoming! INCOMING!" I sat up screaming.

I scrambled for the foxhole, Emery and Jesse right behind me. Mortar rounds exploded across the camp. After the initial barrage, Sergeant Meyers yelled for us to get out. The men around me charged up and through the hole but I was frozen scared and couldn't move.

"Gebhart? Gebhart?" I heard Sergeant Meyers call me but I lay in the foxhole, alone, rolled up in the fetal position.

Toby stuck his head in and yelled, "Gebhart! C'mon. Let's go!"

I still didn't move.

"Get out, goddamn it!" he yelled. "We need you. Let's GO!"

"Okay, all right," I said. I pulled myself out of the damp, earthen hole into the fresh night air. Toby moved over to give me room and we leaned shoulder to shoulder against the roof of the foxhole. Hundreds of red tracers shot out of the riflemen's bunkers at the perimeter. An equal number of green tracers streaked into camp from the tree line. I heard bullets tearing the air above our heads. There was a flash of white light and a loud explosion to our right. An RPG rocket hit the turret of the one of the tanks on the line. Another RPG round hit the gas trailer to our left. In a huge explosion, the trailer disappeared inside a bright, orange fireball.

"Damn!" I said, instinctively pulling back.

"Holy shit!" Toby's face was orange in the light of the explosion.

I had an image of my mother and father crying as they received my body bag at the airport. In a second, the heat wave passed my face as the orange fireball billowed up several hundred feet into the night sky. For a few moments the entire camp was lit up bright as day. The flames turned to thick black smoke and my attention went to the Vietnamese soldiers in the tree line. Trip flares at the edge of the tree line illuminated them as they charged into the clearing.

The light from the gasoline explosion faded, the trip flares sputtered out and it became pitch black. Toby dove over the sandbags into the other mortar pit.

"We need flare rounds!" Sergeant Meyers yelled to me.

"We need to hit the tree line," I shouted back. I tried to compute the elevation and charge needed to bring our mortars to bear on the VC.

"A flare round first," Sergeant Meyers yelled again. All the while bullets zinged over the mortar pit and thudded into the sandbags.

"Stay down! Stay down!" Emery shouted to Eddie and Moore.

The fighting at the perimeter had grown fierce; soldiers on both sides screamed as they fired their weapons. The riflemen's full throttle response put a stymie on the VC. They hugged the dirt. Eddie and Moore could stand up in the pit now. I called out the numbers and they threw up a flare round. The bright phosphorous light shone on a large group of VC coming out of the tree line towards the disabled tank. The foxhole to the tank's right couldn't cover the front of it with rifle fire. The foxhole on the tank's left was out of position too.

"They're gonna break through!" Sergeant Meyers shouted to get everyone's attention. We lined up inside the pits, ready with M-16s to fire on the VC when they passed the tank.

I knelt next to Sergeant Meyers. "We'll be firing towards our own people," I said.

"If those Vietnamese break through," he said, "we won't have any choice." Sergeant Meyers clicked his safety off. Strangely, in all that commotion that tiny sound reverberated through my mind. I had the depressing realization that we were going to be killed. As we watched, one of the men in the tank popped out of the top of the turretless tank and surprised the Vietnamese with a clip full from his M-16. He ducked back inside and a second tanker came up and emptied his magazine into the approaching Vietnamese.

"Look at those guys!" Moore yelled.

"Goddamn it!" I said. "Let's get some mortars out in front of them. Hey, Sarge, can you get Charlie and Alpha to fire the flares for us?"

"I'll try to get through to battalion," Sergeant Meyers said.

He grabbed the radio as Eddie and Moore rotated and aligned the tube. We managed to send out a mortar or two and our work was acknowledged by a dozen tracer rounds aimed at Moore's head. He hit the ground, swearing. I tried to adjust the rounds to land in front of the disabled tank.

"They're still landing too far into the woods!" Eddie hollered at me.

"Okay, zero charge," I shouted, "elevation eighty-seven degrees." Eddie and Moore both looked at me.

"Straight up?" Eddie asked.

"It's the only way to get them close." I still had to shout to be heard over the ordinance being fired by both sides. "Look at those tankers fight." I pointed to the tank and Eddie nodded.

"Eighty-seven degrees, zero charge, one round," Eddie called to Moore and Monk.

"*Fair* when ready," I yelled.

The round exploded right at the tree line. "That's it," I shouted to Eddie. "You're kicking ass now."

On the far left of the perimeter VC charged out of the tree line shouting at the top of their lungs. Their war cries scared me but it did something else too. It pissed me off. "Let's get those motherfuckers!" I screamed.

Toby's crew had thrown out two or three rounds when a new recruit named Goodwin was hit in the neck. He collapsed in the pit and several men tried to work on him, but the life had gone instantly out of him. He had only been in the field a week and a half.

To my left I noticed a brother fast crawling from November's foxholes across the compound to the rifle platoon's ammo bunker. "It's Tony," I said, recognizing him. He was built like a linebacker and loved to sing the blues. He was from Florida and had only been in country a couple of months. I recalled that Carter had shown him the ropes before he went home.

At the ammo bunker Tony pulled out two long wooden boxes each filled with cans of ammunition. He lay on his right side, his M-16 strapped across his chest and he pulled the two heavy wooden ammo boxes behind him. His legs churned with effort. Green tracers threw up clods of dirt as he crossed the open ground but Tony kept moving. He reached the perimeter and went from foxhole to foxhole until all the bunkers were re-supplied.

The Fourth Cav men fired their M-60 machine guns non-stop from on top of their personnel carriers. The two tanks that hadn't been hit fired round after round from their canons. Carl was right, their ordnance did hit the trees too high up but the violent flashes from their cannon barrels and the horrible noise their rounds made had to have put terror into the hearts of the Vietnamese; not to mention the carnage it was doing to the trees. For his part Carl and the other men in the mortar carrier, safe inside their armored vehicle, abandoned it to come help us. They belly-crawled to our pit wall then rolled in over the sandbags.

Time has a way of acting funny when you're in something like this. The heavy fighting that seemed to last for hours had only been forty minutes. Bravo Company and the Fourth Cav beat back the VC's initial attempt to overrun us. There was another half hour of sporadic small arms fire after that. After each sniper shot everyone who had a field of fire unloaded on that part of the jungle and simply blew the hell out it. At some point, I don't think we even knew quite when the jungle fell silent. The riflemen on the perimeter stumbled out of their holes for air. Less than a minute later, a sudden burst of light and the loud crack of an artillery shell smacked into the tree line. The exposed riflemen hit the dirt. A loud "BOO" went up across the camp.

"Not NOW, you fucking assholes!" one rifleman yelled.

"It's OVER now, goddamn it!" someone else screamed.

I laughed.

"Yeah, it's funny," Emery said, "but it's not funny. You know what I mean?"

"Exactly, I do," I said.

We chose up watches and people lay down almost where they stood. I was exhausted too but I couldn't fall asleep. I rested in the pit sitting with my back against the sandbags until just before dawn when I got up and half stumbled to my bedroll outside the pit wall. Jesse and Emery came up behind me. My air mattress was as flat as a pancake next to their two, fat mattresses.

"Oh shit," I said. "I can't believe it, not again!"

"Hey, Paul! Look at this, man." Emery leaned over and pointed to a piece of mortar shrapnel sticking up through the middle of my mattress. "That was right where your heart was, man."

"Yeah. Goddamn, you were lucky." Jesse pulled the four inches of sharp, twisted steel out of the ground.

"Lucky?" I took the shrapnel from Jesse and looked at it. "I just got that air mattress. Another three weeks of hard ground! Fuck, fuck, FUCK!"

The jungle vegetation shimmered green in the first light of dawn. The men from Oscar walked out to the disabled tank to our right. Two soldiers sat on top of it with their poncho liners wrapped tightly around their shoulders. They had their eyes on the tree line. Both of them were white; one had black hair, the other brown. They were unshaven and their hair uncombed. Corpses of a dozen Vietnamese lay in the grass around the tank. The body of the third tanker lay under a poncho next to the left side track.

"They're in shock," I said.

"Jesus, look at this." Monk pointed to the turret lying on the ground behind the tank.

"Yeah, that first round hit us bad," the dark-haired tanker said. "It killed Terry. He was from Iowa City and a hell of a nice guy too." His voice wavered as he spoke.

"We'd been together almost seven months and through a lot of shit," the other one continued. "Terry called to us just before the RPG round exploded. He didn't know what hit him."

"You guys did a great job holding this position," Moore said.

"Yeah, that was some fight you were in," I agreed. "We tried our best to back you up but there were times when you were in it on your own."

"We don't know what made you stay and fight it out but we all appreciate it," Toby said. "They would have broken through if it wasn't for you two."

"Yeah, shit" the brown haired one said. "I think if it had crossed our minds that we could get out and run away, we probably would have."

"I'm glad you didn't think of it then," Monk said.

"What're your names?" Emery asked.

"I'm Freddy, this is John."

"Glad to meet you, Freddy. You too, John." I reached up and shook hands with both of them. The other men from Oscar all did the same. Without saying anything else to the two tankers, we walked to the burned-out metal frame of the gas tanker.

Several Fourth Cav soldiers stood with five engineers next to the smoldering wreck.

"The driver usually slept across the front seat," one of the engineers said as we walked up. "We can't find anything of him."

"No dog tags even?" Emery asked.

"Nothing. Everything's been melted down. We think there were two more of our engineers over here with him too. Anyway, two guys are missing. They had to have been over here, talking to him."

"It will be tough on their families," I muttered, "not even to get their bodies back."

We examined the burnt-out cab in silence. The inside was torched. The naked seat springs were visible and the plastic steering wheel had evaporated. Just the steering wheel column came up out of the floorboard.

"Come on." I stepped down from the truck. "Let's go find Tony." We made our way to the foxholes to the left of the gas truck. The troops at those positions were out in front of their bunkers standing over two bodies wrapped in ponchos.

"Our LPs were killed right off," one of the men said as we came up.

"Who was on LP?" Emery asked him.

"Two new guys: a brother, Floyd, from Dallas and a white kid, Roger, from Nashville."

"They never had a chance," one of the other riflemen said.

Twenty feet away other soldiers went through the pockets of thirty Vietnamese corpses.

"They got awfully close," one of the riflemen said. "They were just yards away from us."

I looked at the bodies of the VC. They were young: sixteen or seventeen years old.

The riflemen pulled out valuables and keepsakes from the young men's pockets and passed them around. I handed a wallet to Moore without looking through it.

"They must be pretty hard up," I said, "sending kids out to die like this."

"They're pretty young, okay," a rifleman from November said, "but they're tough and had no fear."

"They were probably scared to death just like us," I said. "But they are tough. They fought hard for their cause." No one argued the point.

"Hey, where's Tony?" I asked.

"Don't know." One rifleman looked around. "He was here a few minutes ago."

"I'm going to chow," Monk said.

"Yeah, me too," Emery said.

We all walked to the mess tent. The morning dew in the short grass had soaked our fatigue pants.

"I need coffee." Emery said and rubbed his hands together as we stood in chow line. No one else said a word.

We brought our paper plates and coffee cups back to the mortar pits and I sipped the good, black brew and let the new sun warm me. Then I saw Tony walking across the compound.

"Hey, Tony! Tony," I called to him. "Come here, man."
When he came over I got up and shook his hand. "That was great what you did last night," I said.

Tony sat down on the sandbags.

"Yeah," Monk said. "I can't believe how fast you were moving, crawling on your side like that."

"I can't believe I even did it!" Tony sounded disgusted with himself. "What will I do next? Charge the fucking tree line?" He shook his head and looked down at his hands.

"No, man, it doesn't happen like that," I told him.

"No?" Tony looked up.

"Nah, uh-uh," Emery said. "You'll know what you're doing. Last night you did what you had to do."

"Honest, I don't know what happened." Tony shook his head again. "We needed ammo, I jumped out of the foxhole and went and got some. Stupid, huh?"

"Stupid? Shit, that held that side of the perimeter for us," Moore said.

"The camp would have been overrun if you hadn't done what you did," Emery agreed.

I reached over and patted him on the back. "Thanks, guy."

The other men toasted him with their coffee cups.

Later that morning, Medevacs came in to take the dead and wounded. More choppers approached after the Medevacs left.

"They're bringing Recon Platoon over from the other side," Sergeant Meyers told us as we watched from the mortar pits.

The Reconnaissance soldiers walked a cloverleaf pattern through the edge of the woods. Then came back into the perimeter and dug foxholes, strengthening our defense.

The engineers pulled the wrecked tank off the line and two bulldozers knocked down trees to make the clearing 40 yards wider. I went out and sat on a foxhole and shot the breeze with several of the Recon men as they dug in. The soldiers I spoke to were as sick of the army as I was.

The afternoon turned to dusk and night began to close in. I sat on the sandbag wall of the mortar pit and watched the tree line. My hands trembled and I fumbled with my matches to light a cigarette.

"You're short is all," Monk said when he saw me looking at my hands.

I pulled the cigarette smoke into my lungs.

"I want to get out of this place," I said. "I want to get out of Vietnam."

"You and me both, bro." Monk wrinkled up his forehead and nodded. "You and me both."

Chapter Eight
Within You and Without You

August to October 1968

The last week of August the battalion moved from a camp near the village of Lai Khe to the woods five clicks from Phouc Vinh. It was our third new camp in four weeks. The weather was hot and humid and the sun's rays beat down like a steel press. I finished my turn with the shovel and went into my poncho lean-to and sat looking out to the men in Oscar Platoon. In the three weeks since the attack at the river, Emery, Jesse and Gardner had gone home; Carter in June, Desusa and Serena in July, and Delino and Rojas were old memories now. The new replacements were all good guys but things didn't feel the same to me. I had ten weeks left in country— but of Vietnam time.

I watched as Lieutenant Truck and Sergeant Rigoni stepped over fallen trees on their way across the littered field.

"These ponchos have got to come down," Sergeant Rigoni said as he came up to the mortar pits.

"Huh?" Toby popped his head out of his lean-to.

"The major's orders; no shade until all of the foxholes are finished," the lieutenant explained.

"You've got to be kidding," I said.

"No," Rigoni said. "Let's get them down and finish the holes."

The new men in the platoon began to tear down their shade without protest. I called to Lieutenant Truck from inside my leanto. "What the hell is he trying to do? Does he want to make it as *hard* as possible?"

"The major said it took too long to dig in at the last Night Defensive Position," Lieutenant Truck explained. "He thinks if there weren't any shelters the perimeter will go up faster."

"That son of a bitch."

"That will be all, Gebhart," the lieutenant said.

I came out of my lean-to and stood next to him and watched the men tear down their shade.

"You know, Sir," I said, "the major's been here for three months and in all that time he's never come around to meet us, not once. I think he might act differently if he spent some time with his men on the line."

"He has a lot to do," Lieutenant Truck said without looking at me.

"Wouldn't you want to know who was doing the fighting for you?" I asked. "Maybe he'd even see himself in some of us. People will fight for you if they know that you respect them and that you care whether or not they live or die. How come they didn't teach him that at West Point?"

If Lieutenant Truck was listening to me he didn't care to answer.

I walked to the half-finished mortar pit.

"Here, give me that pick," I said to a rookie. He handed it to me and I stepped into the shallow crater and went at it full bore. I swung with all my might to burn my anger off. After a three-minute non-stop round, I stepped out of the pit to rest. As I watched them shovel out my work funny little black dots danced in front of my eyes. My periphery vision closed in, I got double vision and waves of nausea overcame me. I lost my balance and fell forward onto my knees and vomited.

Sergeant Meyers came over and knelt next to me. He put a hand on my shoulder. "Are you okay, Paul?"

"I don't know," I said. "My head hurts. It feels like a hundred little needles are being stuck in me."

"Here, drink some water." Sergeant Meyers handed me his canteen and I rinsed out my mouth. He soaked a towel and hung it over my head and shoulders. I sat in a stupor, half asleep; the movement and noise around me made a dull, droning that sounded miles away. I nodded off but a cheer from across the perimeter woke me.

"Hey!" Toby shouted. He put the radio headset down and broadcast to everyone, "the major's been killed."

"YEA!" the men in Oscar shouted a cheer.

"What happened to him?" I asked. My head pounded with each word.

"His two-man chopper was hit with fifty-caliber ground fire," Toby said. "One round went through the floor board and got him in the leg. He bled to death before the pilot could reach the rear."

"They've got fifty-caliber machine guns out here?" I said. "Oh, Lord."

I was weak and had a constant headache for the next two days. On the third morning Lieutenant Truck sent me to headquarters for a checkup. Outside the battalion CQ tent a young white medic examined my eyes, nose, and throat.

"I have to get the duty officer to sign the papers to send you to the rear for a full exam," he said. "I'll be right back."

"Okay, sure, thanks," I said.

He brought back the papers and handed me one copy. "These are your orders to go into Bien Hoa for a medical."

"Okay," I said. I put them in my fatigue shirt and went to get my gear. I told the lieutenant and Sergeant Meyers that I'd be gone for three days then loaded my rucksack and went on the morning Chinook into Long Bihn. From there I rode in a truck down to Bien Hoa. The driver let me out in front of the medical center. I thanked him and walked up the path towards two dozen round roofed Quonset buildings laid out in neat rows; each building had a red cross painted above their double front doors. I walked between the buildings looking for the reception office. There were flowerbeds and palm trees growing in between the buildings and the landscaping made the facilities seem pleasant but I sensed a heavy vibe. Through the screened windows I saw bandaged GIs in hospital beds. A few of them watched me walk by. The faint odor of blood and antiseptic made me realize that the vibe I picked up was of death and mutilation.

A nurse in her thirties sat at a desk inside the front office. She had short hair, almost like a guy's. She had a plain face and didn't smile when I handed her my orders. She read them and had me sit in an empty examination room for forty minutes before a young doctor came in. He was a captain, tall and skinny with dark, curly hair. He felt my spleen and liver, took my temperature and listened to my heart.

"You're dehydrated," he said as he put away his stethoscope. "You may have had a sunstroke." He paused to look at me. "I want you to drink eight glasses of water a day."

"Glasses? We don't have glasses out in the field," I said.

"Then two canteens a day."

"Some days we run out of water," I said.

"For more than twenty-four hours?" he asked.

"No. No, the most we might go without water is eight or ten hours."

"Well, do the best you can."

"Yes, Sir." I buttoned my fatigue shirt.

"Are you smoking dope?" he asked.

I was taken back by his directness. "No, Sir," I stammered. I could be court-martialed and sent to jail for admitting to an officer I was getting high.

"Well, if you are, I recommend that you stop."

"Yes, Sir." I said.

"Well, okay, good luck, soldier," he said and shook my hand.

I finished dressing and went outside and waited on the road by the front gate until a supply truck stopped. I told him I was headed to Di An and he opened the door and I hopped on board.

At Bravo Company's front office the same old floor fan stood in the corner its blades spinning slowly in a hopeless effort to cool the room. There was a new clerk sitting at the desk underneath it. He was young with a medium build, blond hair, brown eyes and a thin face. His skin was very pale and I wondered how he could possibly stay so white in the tropics.

"It feels like years ago that I first stepped into this office," I said.

"I bet it does," he said. "It's Specialist, Gebhart, isn't it?"

"That's me," I said. "I've just been to the medical center in Bien Hoa. Here's my pass." I took the humidity-worn papers and laid them on his desk.

"Yes, I know," he said without looking at them. "You were on the morning report. What did the doctor say?"

"He said I should probably go home." The clerk just smiled. "He said I had some kind of heatstroke and I shouldn't be out in the sun."

"Did he sign any orders for you to give me?"

"No," I said, wishing now I had asked the doc for orders.

"He's got to give me written orders before I can pull you out of the field," the clerk said.

"Yeah?" I shrugged. I knew I had screwed up an opportunity. "Well, maybe he didn't know that," I finally said.

"I don't think so," the clerk said. He stopped to write a note to himself. "I'll call over there and find out what he wants to do."

"Okay," I said, "sure."

I left the office and dropped my gear off in the old barracks then walked across the dirt road to battalion headquarters. As I came through their quadrangle, a black man called to me from the steps of a barracks, "Hey, Gebhart!"

I had to stare for a moment before I recognized McDaniels, the reconnaissance soldier Moore had introduced me to in the USO club in Long Binh.

"What's happening?" I asked.

"Que pasa, Breeze," he greeted me. "Where's Moore?" We shook a white man's handshake.

"Mack's in the field," I said. "I'm on a three-day medical pass. How have you been?"

"Good," he smiled. "I'm on my way to Kuala Lumpur for my R 'n R."

"Oh yeah? Cool."

"You want to smoke some opium?" McDaniels asked.

"Fuckin' A. You got some?"

"Fuckin' A," he mocked my Jersey accent. "You just happened to have found the best opium den in Vietnam. Come on in and let me introduce you around."

It was stifling hot inside the barracks and thick blue smoke from the opium pipes hung in the air. A dozen soldiers lay crashed on cots. A black soldier with dark glasses and slick hair handed me a pipe with a Thai stick smoldering in the bowl. I got high while the Beatles song *Within You And Without You* played on the tape player.

Listening to the sitar music in the tropical humid atmosphere hypnotized me. I felt it too, peace that is, seeing myself from the outside. I was just one of a billion stories and life goes on without me. My realizations were interrupted by an agitated voice.

"It was hell," a white guy said. He was sitting on the floor, his back against the cot next to mine. "We walked right into it," he mumbled. "They let go with homemade claymores, huge things made from washtubs filled with nails and scrap iron. I think half the guys were lost in the first explosions."

I sat up. He was talking to McDaniels and four brothers. I noticed that his eyes were sunken inside dark circles and his blond hair was uncombed and dirty. His wrinkled fatigues and haggard look made me think he'd been on an opium jag for a couple of days.

"When was this?" I asked him.

He looked over to me. "Last month," he said.

"Which outfit?"

"Twenty fifth Infantry," he said.

I could see that he had a hard time focusing in on my face. Every time he started to, he'd blink and look down, gather himself and try again.

"I didn't hear anything about it," I said to McDaniels. "We should have heard. Where did it happen?" I asked the soldier.

"Out by the border," the trooper continued. "We had fifty-eight killed and twenty-nine wounded. There was only a hundred-fifty of us on the patrol to start out with."

"Jesus," I said, "that's a massacre!"

"Fucking right it was," he said. I could see the trauma's impact on him by the tightness around his mouth. He spoke, but hardly moved his lips.

"This is the third time you're telling us this story," McDaniels said. "Don't you remember? It was just an hour ago."

"Wait," I said. "I want to hear this," I said. "How did you get out of it?" I asked him.

"They called the artillery right in on top of us," he said. "I was in the rear of the column. The gooks came up the trail shooting our wounded and taking their steel helmets and flak jackets and putting them on as the artillery shells landed around them. We could hear our friends calling for them not to shoot them but then we heard the shots. There was no mercy, no mercy; a living hell, I'm telling ya." He started to cry.

"Yeah, man, okay," I said. I patted him on the shoulder. I couldn't think of anything else to say so I wrapped his fingers around the stem of the opium pipe.

Men lay sprawled on the cots, dreaming opium dreams away from the realities of Vietnam for a few hours. I lay down and dreamt about Mary and the baby. I was with them at her parents' house eating lunch on a summer day. A soldier shook my arm and woke me up. I talked to him about being home and all the things I missed. Someone shook my leg and I woke again. The first soldier I had talked to was a dream. It was a dream within a dream and it startled me and made me laugh. Then I woke again!

It was quiet in the barracks. I realized I had dreamt all of it. Was I awake now or still in a heavy opium dream? I had no way of knowing; the other times I thought I woke up were no different than this.

"Well, dream or real?" I asked myself.

"What are you talking about?" McDaniels asked.

"Oh nothing, nothing," I said.

"C'mon, time to get out of here," he said.

We walked back to Bravo Company together in the heat of the late afternoon.

"He lost a lot of friends in that ambush," I said as we moved off the dirt road to let an earthmover go by. "He'll have their faces and voices inside of him forever," I yelled to be heard over the sound of the diesel engine.

"That was a hell of a beating they took." McDaniels nodded. We turned our backs to let the dust drift by. The earthmover passed and the silence settled around us like the dust that settled back to earth. Mirror heat waves shimmered up from the road and we walked toward them.

"I'm thinking of transferring to Recon," I said.

"What?" McDaniels stopped and looked at me. "Are you nuts?"

"Man, I can't take this humping anymore," I said. "I'm sick of Lieutenant Truck and Rigoni. I'm tired of being a pack mule. You guys don't have to carry mortar rounds and picks and shovels."

"No, but Gebhart you should see the places they drop us into. They put us out there on our own, trying to get Charlie to fire on us so they can bring in the battalion. Listen, last week a buddy of mine got his thumb blown off in a firefight. You know he was the happiest guy I ever saw. I'm serious. He lay there waiting for the Medevac, laughing and telling us; 'I'm going home, man. I'm goin' home.' And we all thought he *was* lucky! I've been thinking of shooting myself in the foot for Christ sake. Volunteering for Recon was the worse fucking mistake I ever made in my life. Don't you do it, man."

We walked in silence after that. He was right of course, still a part of me wanted to see some action. The days went faster out in the boonies but it was more than that. There was an intense awareness that comes during a firefight. A rush of excitement as your body and mind go on automatic and your instincts take over.

It was nuts to think this way. Here I was scared to death of getting hit but wanting to test my luck. No, it was really stupid. I didn't have a magic shield around me and I better not forget it.

At the barracks I started a letter to Mary but was interrupted a little while later by the company clerk standing at the foot of my cot.

"The doc said he never ordered you out of the field," he said.

"Really? Well, that's what I thought he meant."

"Sure," the clerk answered with a smirk.

"Look." I sat up, "I don't mind being on the line; I've been out there all year. It's the damn humping. I'm down to a hundred twenty pounds, I can't carry a hundred pounds around in that damn sun."

"I understand," he said.

When he didn't argue I paused. After a moment I continued in a softer voice. "Send me back out but tell them I can't carry anything; just my rifle and my backpack, no more shovels and shit."

"I can't do that," the clerk said. He was a little pudgy and wore his hair combed straight forward but I liked him. His manner was respectful.

"No. No, I guess you can't," I said.

"I can't," the clerk repeated, "but let me see what I can do. In the mean time you can stay here in Di An for a couple of more days."

"Okay, great. Thanks. What's your name anyway?"

"I'm Nicholas Page."

"Thanks for your help, Nick." I stood up and shook his hand.

"You want to get a coke?" he asked.

"Sure," I said.

We went outside and up to the headquarters Quonset hut and he went in and came out with two cold coca-colas. We sat on the steps outside the front doors and talked about home and the men in Bravo Company. For every man he named, I told him a story about what I had seen him do in combat. Reminiscing, I realized I was now an old head.

"You guys get close out there," Nicholas said. "It's the only thing about being in the rear that I regret."

"Yeah we get close," I said. "It comes from going out on patrols. You have to be silent, just a glance with our eyes does the talking. To know a man's facial muscles and their meaning, that's how close we get."

"You were at the river battle?" he asked.

"Yeah, of course," I said. "But as bad as the river fight was, the most frightening place I've ever been was the empty NVA bunker town on the Ho Chi Minh trail. Ever since that week I've known that I'm living on borrowed time. It was just pure luck they weren't there. If they had been most of the men on that patrol would have gone home in body bags."

"A lot of the guys who were out there feel the same way," he said.

We finished our sodas and hung out until it was time for chow.

A couple of days later I was still in Di An and getting bored with the rear but I figured if they weren't going to come find me then I'd just sit tight. At the end of the week though I got a message that Nicholas wanted to see me. I walked across the quadrangle in the morning's fresh tropical air. I went up the steps and into the headquarters office figuring that my R n' R was over and I was headed to the field.

"Gebhart," Nicholas called out when I came in the door.

"Yeah?"

"I got you transferred. You are now a cook."

"A cook?" The news surprised me. "Well, sure. Hell, yes." I said. "I haven't cooked six meals in my entire life but that's the army for you. I'm happy as hell about it too, thanks." I reached over the desk and shook his hand.

Although cooks belonged to battalion headquarters each company had its own mess so I was still a part of Bravo. I slept in the company barracks in Di An and went to battalion to be trained. A week later I helped pack the food and equipment into a Chinook and flew out with three regular cooks. We landed inside the perimeter of a night defensive position on Thunder Road. With the help of a detail of soldiers we unloaded the mess equipment and got ready to serve breakfast. I started the stove and cooked 40 pounds of bacon. Using the bacon fat to grease the pans I began to fry the eggs.

"Okay, let 'em in," I hollered and the men waiting outside the tent began to file through.

"Hey, Gebhart! You a cook now?" someone down the line called out.

"Looks that way," I said without looking up.

"How did you get this job?" the rifleman asked, loud enough for everyone to hear.

"Through correspondence school," I said.

"Very funny. You faking some kind of injury or something?" I ignored him but when it was his turn and I asked him how he wanted his eggs. He sneered at me and and said;

"Over easy, REMF motherfucker." The other men "Ooh"ed and waited for my response.

I cracked a couple of eggs into the frying pan and watched them for a moment before reaching down and picking up a handful of dirt. "You want some sand on them eggs?" I asked. "It'll give 'em that Vietnam kind of flavor."

"Hey, man, c'mon, don't do that," he pleaded. The chow line laughed and I asked the next grunt how he wanted his eggs.

"Scrambled," he said. "Hold the dirt on mine too."

A little while later Oscar Platoon came down the line. I saw question lines form on Monk's forehead when he saw me. He tilted his head to one side and asked, "Say, Paul, you a *cook?*"

"Yeah, Monk. I made it out."

"Say what?" He laughed and we shook hands.

"Go and figure," I said as I flipped his egg. "I've never cooked in my life but they taught me." I put an extra egg in the frying pan for him. "I'm best at making mashed potatoes," I said. "The powdered kind. I make 'em so you'd think you were eating fresh-peeled mashed potatoes. The only thing is I only know how to mix a batch to feed two hundred, so I figure it won't help me out much later on in life."

"Maybe not, but maybe you'll open a restaurant," Monk said. "Yeah, right, a mashed potato place," I said. "I know just the spot in Jersey City."

Bravo was on Highway 13 for ten days before the battalion moved west. The company cooks had been ordered to travel with them and I helped load the morning Chinook in Di An with a lifer mess sergeant.

"All the cooks I knew slept in the rear on cots," I said as I carried a green Thermos past the sergeant and up the Chinook's back ramp. "They had pillows and mattresses," I said as I passed him on the way down the ramp. On the way back up with another load, I added. "Now I'm a cook and they change the policy?"

The mess sergeant smiled at my complaint. He heaved a heavy stove onto his back. "They say the landing zone is okay," he said as we passed each other on the ramp, "but they were hit last night with mortars."

I watched the sergeant come out and go back up, this time he carryied two propane tanks. He was in his late thirties and had been in the army since he was 18. He carried his load and filled out his paperwork. Whatever they asked him to do he did the best he could and with a grace that came from acceptance. His years in the army had taught him that he wasn't headed any particular place. He did his work day by day taking pleasure in doing what needed to be done and relaxing afterward with a cold beer. The army was home to him and he was comfortable in its predictable way of life.

I was different. I felt I should be somewhere else, anywhere else. The army was a waste of my time. I couldn't handle the privilege of rank either, especially when it seemed everyone outranked me. And then there were all the army's rules. It drove me crazy to trade my freedom for three meals a day and the promise of a good retirement. I admired the mess sergeant though. He was comfortable with where he was and what he did.

I loaded my personal gear on the Chinook and sat inside with the other cooks for the ride out. After landing we set up the mess tent inside the battalion's perimeter. We were in a clearing in the foothills below the Central Highlands, west of Song Be.

When I finished my work and had a chance I went around visiting my friends. There were a lot of new men in Bravo Company but still old heads to meet and talk with. Towards evening I sat with Sergeant Meyers and Toby on the pit wall.

"If anything breaks out while I'm out here," I said, "I'm coming over to help, okay?"

"Yeah, sure," Sergeant Meyers said. He had lost weight. His face was thinner and the dark circles around his eyes had puffy bags under them.

"Hey, where's Mack Moore at?" I asked Toby.

"Don't really know," he said. "The last time we saw him, a week ago, he was in Long Binh."

"He out on medical?" I asked.

"He had a three-day medical pass," Sergeant Meyers said, "but that was up four days ago. He's headed for trouble so if you see him in the rear, you tell him to get his ass out here."

"I will," I said.

I went back to the mess tent and finished my work then played poker with the other cooks until turning in. We were all startled awake at 4 a.m. when mortar rounds began walking their way across the camp. The other cooks ran for the foxhole but I grabbed my helmet and M-16 and sprinted across the clearing. I dove into the mortar pit just as an enemy round exploded outside the pit wall. We all hugged the dirt. I saw

Peter, the California surfer who had replaced me as the fire director sitting with his back against the sandbags. I crawled over to him.

"Got your clearings marked?" I asked him. He looked at me without responding. "Which clearing are you going to fire on?" I asked again.

"I don't know," he stammered. He was curled up and rigid. "I'm scared," he said.

"You're supposed to be," I said. "We're all scared. The thing is if we don't fight back, they'll kill us with their mortars."

He didn't move.

I pointed to his squad. "Those guys are counting on you."

Peter looked to his buddies and slowly sat up. With the computer board on his lap, he focused on the numbers. "I'm not sure where to fire," he said.

"Me neither," I said. "Ask Sergeant Meyers."

"Sarge, Sarge, which target?" Peter called out.

"Hit the large clearing at three hundred yards first," Sergeant Meyers yelled back.

"Double check your coordinates and get them going," I said.

Another set of VC mortar rounds walked across the camp. We lay prone, concerned that our helmets stayed below the two rows of sandbags that lined the mortar pit. When the last mortar exploded, Peter called out the numbers and the crew fired four rounds. After that he loosened up and soon was working with his gunner in an even rhythm.

A ground attack began at dawn but it quickly turned into sniper fire as artillery shells wrecked the Vietcong's enthusiasm. By 8 a.m. the firefight was over and I had to get back to the mess tent.

"Thanks for the help," Sergeant Meyers said as I started to walk away.

"Gebhart," Toby called over, "you take care."

"You guys too," I said. "I'll see you at chow."

"Hey, Paul." Peter called me from the pit and I walked over to him.

"Yeah?" I asked.

"Thanks, man." He reached out to shake hands.

"Listen," I said, shaking his hand slowly, "there were times I was so frozen I couldn't get out of my foxhole. My friends had to scream at me to get me moving. We've all been there and you'll be there again. You're going to make it home, don't you ever think otherwise. Got it?"

"Yeah, I understand, thanks," he said.

The following week the battalion flew into Di An. It was the first time in my tour of duty that we had all been there together. While new recruits processed in and replenished our ranks it turned into a week of in-country R 'n R for us.

I was relaxing on my cot in the old barracks one morning after a night of drinking. I looked out the open the window by my bunk. The sun baked the dirt quadrangle into pools of heat waves. I turned on the radio and lay back down. The other cots were all but empty; most of the guys had gone shopping at the PX or were trying to make their way into Saigon without passes. I tried to ignore the heat and catch up on some sleep.

Lionel, the soldier who had shot the two North Vietnamese officers who had tried to surrender to him, came into the barracks with another brother named Ralph.

"Hey, Gebhart," Lionel called to me as he walked to my bunk.

I looked up from my bunk. "Hey, what's happening?"

"Just this," Lionel said and took a swing at me. His punch grazed the top of my head and I rolled on my back and flailed out with both feet. I caught him once in the face with my boot and he backed off. His lip was split. I got up and Lionel came at me. Instead of boxing, I took him down with a double-leg drop. Lionel's face hit the wood floor. I smelled whiskey on his breath as I got off him and stepped away.

"What the hell's the matter with you?" I asked.

Lionel wiped his bloodied lip and his bleeding nose. "You're white," he said looking up.

"No shit. So what?"

"All you white people are the devil."

"What are you talking about, Lionel? Me and you... we've been friends for six months." I went to shake hands with him. "Come on, let's just be friends."

Ralph jumped in between us, "No, uh-uh," he said. "Lionel don't need no white friends."

I looked at them not understanding. How could people change for no reason? Well, that was it; they felt there was a reason.

"As bad as things are at home," I said, "you can't take it out on everyone just because they're white."

"Why not?" Ralph said. "You take it out on us because we're black."

"I haven't," I said. "Doesn't that mean anything?"

"All you white people are bad. You devils," Ralph said.

"Okay, Ralph, whatever you say." I was disgusted with them and with America for putting this hate into them.

The fight with Lionel depressed me. I hadn't seen Mack Moore in over a week and I hoped when he showed up that he could smooth things out.

The next day while I was in the toweling-off room in the shower shed I saw him go up the barracks steps and called to him. "Hey, Mack, how ya doin'?" I shouted.

He walked over and stood in the doorway. He was quiet and didn't smile. I sensed things had changed between us. I sat down on the wooden bench and put my fatigue pants on and was buttoning up my shirt. "What's going on?" I asked.

"Well, Paul, I'm through with it," he said.

"Huh? What do you mean?"

"I ain't going back no more."

"How's that?" I asked.

"I'm going AWOL," he said in a hushed voice.

"Nah," I laughed.

"What do you mean 'nah'? I *am*, I'm tellin' ya." His voice rose to a falsetto.

I stopped working the laces of my boots and looked up.

"Okay, sure," I said. "I'm just thinking, you only have six weeks left; when they catch you, you'll go to the Long Binh stockade for 30 days, when you get out they'll send you back to the field and you'll have the same friggin' six weeks left."

"They ain't gonna catch me," he said coldly.

I stood up and tucked my fatigue shirt into my pants. "No? Where you headed?"

He hesitated, thought something through, then said "I can't tell ya."

"Why not?" I asked.

He looked me straight in the eye and said, "Because you might tell them."

"Don't be ridiculous," I said. "You really think I'd do that?"

"I can't trust anyone anymore," he said.

I didn't know how to respond. After a moment's thought I said, "You and me, we've been through some shit together, Mack. We're partners."

"I guess that's all over," he said. "You're in the rear and I'm getting out of here with some other brothers I met."

"Okay," I said. "I wish you the best, we're still friends though, right?"

"I guess, yeah, but you're white and all you white people got the devil in you."

"Oh, Good Lord have mercy!" I moaned in disgust. "Listen, man, if it's one thing I'm NOT, it's the goddamn devil."

He laughed at my exaggeration but didn't answer. My mind flashed through the past year; that first day we met, the shared air mattresses, the firefights and patrols. I couldn't let our friendship end this way.

"This doesn't have anything at all to do with me," I said. "We both want out of Vietnam. You're getting out of the field the best way you know how, just like I did. I don't think you're going to be able to escape from Vietnam is all I'm saying. There's rumors about guys who tried to stow away on ships and shit like that but I never heard of anyone making it out." I paused. "But, hey, maybe you can. Yeah, if anyone can escape from Vietnam it's you, Mack Moore."

He looked me in the face but didn't say anything.

"And as far as this white devil thing," I said. "Shit, man, we've been through too much for me to think you really believe that crap. But I understand, you got pressure on you and they'll be calling you Uncle Tom if you don't agree with them."

Moore smiled.

"Hey," I said, feeding off his smile, "remember the time we stole the C rations? We were out by the border. Remember? There was only one Chinook a day, sometimes not even that because of the ground fire. The entire battalion was running low on C rations and we were down to the stuff that nobody wanted, like ham from 1945 and shit like that. Remember?"

"Yeah, sure," Moore said. "That was out past Lei Khe."

"You looked up and saw the Chinook coming in. 'Come on, Paul,' you said. 'We're gonna get us some of them C rations.' We walked up just as the Chinook's back door dropped down. A detail went into the cargo bay and you got in line and followed the last guy in and I followed you. Remember?"

"Yeah, yeah, I remember, sure." Moore smiled now.

"We each hoisted three cases on our shoulders and while the other guys dropped their boxes in a stack and went back in to get more we just kept right on across the camp. The Chinook was blowing dirt all over the place. Between that and just doing it no one noticed us or said a word. At the mortar pits we threw the cases into the ammo hole and I went down and started opening the boxes. It was like a little deli down there. I called off the contents of the different cans and you passed them out to the guys. We laughed our asses off about it too. 'In broad daylight,' I kept saying. 'In broad daylight.'"

"Yeah, that was funny." Moore flashed a smile of straight white teeth.

"Well," he said, "look, I've got to go now."

"Yeah, okay, man. You take care of yourself, Mack."

"Yeah, you too, Paul."

We shook hands, one last soul shake. The blue sky shown through the open beam roof and the two black fifty-gallon water drums overhead dripped water onto the wood floor. The smell of the water-soaked wood and mildew brought back the memory of smoking grass with Santos and Moore here in this same shower shed almost 11 months before. Moore and I had been through a lot since then but I could see his point. When we got home I was headed back to college and Moore to the inner city. We'd probably never see each other again. Moore smiled and nodded his head like he had read my thoughts. He turned and walked out of the shower shed and went into the barracks to get his stuff. After he was gone, I went for a walk alone around the compound. I thought about his life and wondered how things would go for him. Despite how it ended, Moore's friendship was one of the best I ever shared.

I decided to go to the USO club and while I was walking there I ran into Monk. I told him about the fight with Lionel and about Moore going AWOL.

"In the end Mack made sure to say goodbye," I said. "I appreciated that. If I was a betting man, I'd give you odds that he was headed to Saigon."

"Yeah, probably," Monk said.

"I've heard about grunts holing up down there," I said. "They crash in the old hotels downtown or in an apartment with a Vietnamese woman. I know Moore will have himself one hell of an adventure too."

Monk laughed. "Say what?"

"Oh, you know it. He'll be partying every day, and screwing 'til his money's all gone."

"That's him, for sure," Monk said.

"After he's broke," I said, "you know he's going to find some sweet young mamasan to take him in."

"Yes, he will." Monk laughed.

"I can just see him in Saigon with his Wayfarers on, smoking a doobie at one of the outdoor cafes. He'll be cool too. You know how he just looks at people and smiles when he's messed up; like he knows something nobody else does."

Monk laughed, "Yeah, that's him. He'll be cool until they catch up with him."

"Makes me jealous of what I'm missing," I said.

"It'll be an interesting R 'n R okay," Monk said.

"Say, we're in the rear," I said. "Why don't we just go get drunk? C'mon, I'm buying the first round."

Two mornings later, recovering from what had turned into two days and nights of drinking, Bravo received orders to relocate to Highway 13. I came in from the showers and saw Monk carrying his gear outside to wait for the trucks.

"Good old Thunder Road, huh?"

"Yeah, we're headed out again," Monk said.

"You take care of yourself," I said.

Monk shouldered his rucksack and picked up his rifle.

"Yeah, see you at dinner tonight," he said. "Hey, bring me some ice-cold milk, okay?"

"Okay, sure, you got it," I called to him.

Lieutenant Truck came up behind me.

"Gebhart," he said, "I've decided to put you in for the Bronze Star."

"Huh? Really?"

He laughed at my surprised face. "I'm serious," he said. "As soon as I have some time, I'll do the paperwork."

I didn't say anything but the lieutenant saw my disbelief.

"I got to thinking about what I've seen you do these last ten months. Even when you were a cook, you ran over from the mess tent through a mortar barrage to help out. You fought at the river you fought every place we ever were hit. I think you deserve the recognition."

"Thank you, Sir," I said.

He reached out and I shook his hand.

"Good luck, Gebhart."

"Thank you, Sir. Good luck to you too."

I watched them load into the trucks and pull out of the quadrangle and when they left I began a letter to my father. I stopped short of mentioning the Bronze Star. My grandmother taught me never to talk about something until you had it. "Don't divide up the bear meat until the bear's been killed," is how she put it.

After the letter home I went to the mess hut for lunch. When I came back an hour later, it was hot enough to fry eggs on the hood of a Jeep. I double-timed across the dirt quadrangle to get into the shade. La Ponte called to me from the barracks steps.

"Hey, Gebhart! Bravo Company got hit this morning."

I stopped short in my tracks. "No, where? On Thunder Road?"

"Yeah, out west of An Loc. Oscar platoon took casualties."

"Really?"

"Yeah," he said. "Lieutenant Truck and a couple of guys were shot coming out of their chopper."

"The lieutenant, really?"

"Yeah."

"Who else?" I asked.

"A guy named, Toby."

"Toby? How bad?"

"Pretty bad. Him and the lieutenant are on their way to Japan."

"Shit. Anyone else?"

"Yeah, Gebhart... Monk was killed."

"What!" I felt sick to my stomach. "What happened?"

"He took a round right in the face," LaPonte said.

"Oh, God, no. Not, Monk."

"Sorry," LaPonte said.

I looked at him but saw Monk's face in my mind.

I walked away and without realizing it made my way to the large foxholes on the perimeter across the street. I saw the one where I had pulled guard duty with Emery, Toby and the termites long ago. I sat on its sandbag roof and looked out towards the tree line. I could see their faces: the lieutenant, Toby, Monk.

What a funny person you were, Monk. You would listen to us bullshit and you'd drop in your little observations that would crack us up, but you always did it without hurting anyone. You would carry anything you were given too and not complain even when the load took your breath away.

I saw his face and heard his laughter. "Oh, Monk, man," I said out loud, "you deserved to live. We were all motherfuckers, but you deserved to live."

I felt bad for the lieutenant and Toby too. I should have been there with them. I don't know what difference it would have made but I hadn't held up my part of the load and I felt guilty.

I sat at the foxhole until they called me from the barracks. I walked over. LaPonte and several other rear echelon boys sat on the barracks' steps. Word had it that the battalion was pinned down. The cooks would go out tomorrow as soon as a Chinook could land.

I sat with my back against the wall and listened to LaPonte's jokes and watched the horseplay but it didn't seem funny. I felt something move inside my soul, it was a feeling I never had before. It took me a few moments to recognize that my boyhood had just ended. The childish joy that had been a part of how I looked out at the world was gone. The sun still shined but the light, the light around me, had changed.

* * *

In the beginning of October I had only three weeks left. I could do that easy I thought, except each day became longer than the one before. Time seemed to stop. I needed an early ride out so every night that I could, I hitchhiked to division headquarters to try and meet someone who could cut me orders home. The First Division compound was similar to Bravo's but larger with six long buildings and several quadrangles of barracks. I found the nightly opium party and smoked with a dozen rear echelon clerks. I told them my story and listened to theirs. After three visits I connected with a few people and the first afternoon I could get away, I walked to the division offices and waited to get in to see one of them.

I sat outside on a bench in a dirt courtyard and watched as new recruits just coming in from Bien Hoa, processed in. Seeing them, knowing that they had a year ahead of them, frightened me. I had this thought that they would change the rules and I would have to stay too. I shook the nightmare from my head and got up and walked behind headquarters to go to the head. Two soldiers were on latrine duty there. They were cleaning the four fly-infested latrine shacks. They were both privates: one white, one black. Three fifty-gallon rusted steel drums cut down to a third of their height burned at their feet. The smell of gasoline and flame was only slightly better than the stench of feces and urine. I nodded to the unhappy soldiers and went into the only shed still in use. On the way back I smelled the sweet scent of burning marijuana.

"How come John Wayne never got latrine duty?" the white guy asked as I walked by. He had pale blue eyes and blond hair.

"This is Vietnam, too." I pointed to the burning can at their feet.

"It's a smell I'll never forget, I'll tell you that," the black guy said.

He handed me the joint.

"It's a smell we're all going to remember." I waved off the offer. "No thanks, guy."

Sometime after lunch, a middle-aged sergeant called my name and I followed him into the office complex. He motioned for me to wait in the busy hallway. Clerks walked in and out of private offices and I had the sense that I was near the source of my prayers.

"Specialist Gebhart." A soldier I had met at the opium party the night before called my name.

His name was Troy Knight. Troy was tall and blond. He looked like a Mormon preacher but his looks were deceiving. Troy stayed stoned, day and night, as I had seen at the nightly parties. He led me into a small office with filing cabinets and two metal desks piled high with papers.

"Your journey leads you here," he said. "Have you learned much?" he asked in a clear voice.

"I've come through some strange times with crazy people," I said.

"Consa, cunt and Coca-Cola?" Troy remembered my description of Vietnam from the night before.

"Exactly," I said.

He sat at his desk and I stood with perspiration starting to color my fatigue shirt. I waited quietly while he opened my file and read to himself.

"You're pretty short, Gebhart," he said. "You're due to rotate home in two weeks." He put his index finger to his forehead and thought for a minute. "Hmm, I think it won't hurt the war effort much if we put your name on the top of the list." He typed my orders in triplicate and left the room to get them signed. I was soaked in perspiration now. What if no one would sign them? And we got busted for trying? And I went to the brig for 60 days?

Troy came back in the room and handed me two copies of my orders home. "No sweat," he said, noticing, I'm sure, that my fatigue shirt was now a wet dark green.

"Yeah, right, no sweat," I said.

Troy laughed.

"Thanks, man," I said and put out my hand. He shook it hard.

"Have a safe trip my friend." He smiled and patted me on the shoulder.

I left headquarters with orders from the First Division's Personnel Commanding Officer directing me to be on the morning flight October 10th and to report into Travis Air Base, Oakland, California, October 12th. They were the most precious papers I had ever carried. I folded them neatly and put them into my fatigue shirt pocket and walked back to Bravo Company. I was happy and excited at the thought of being with Mary.

After breakfast on October 9th I packed my gear and carried it outside to the dirt quad. A truck came by and I threw my duffel bag up and climbed on. As the truck pulled away I looked back at Bravo Company's buildings. I saw Santos popping his fingers and Cool's slow shuffle walk. Memories of all of my friends flashed through my mind; I saw Sergeant Bell, Rojas, Delino, Mack Moore, Emery, and Jesse. I saw Doc Steven's face as he lay in the small clearing and Jeffrey Collins as Lieutenant Truck held him. I saw Carter carrying the M-60 machine gun out on patrol. I heard their laughter and remembered Serena crying for Martinez. It was a time that would never be again, and the best part of it all was this feeling now: I'm headed home.

I showed my travel orders to the processing clerk in Bien Hoa. Despite my efforts to keep them dry the humidity had turned the paper soggy. The clerk typed new documents and pointed out the window to the barracks I was assigned to. I carried my duffel bag into a barracks then unpacked at an empty bunk and went out the back door. A dozen soldiers smoked cigarettes around a sandbag bunker. I sat down with them and listened as the conversations centered around what it would be like to be home. I noticed a soldier with dark hair staring at me. He had a square jaw and a dark tan.

"Hey, Fuqua," I called to him.

Fuqua was a French Canadian from Maine. He had volunteered for the draft with a couple of his high school buddies and they were all in my squad in basic training at Fort Carson.

"Hey, did you hear about O'Donnell?" Fuqua asked me after we shook hands.

"No, what?" I felt the hair on the back of my neck stand up.

"He was killed back in May."

"No," I said, "come on."

"Yeah, Gebhart, he was." Fuqua brought out an obituary list from his wallet. It was an article cut out of an old "Stars and Stripes" showing that week's casualties.

I scanned down the two columns of Killed In Action until I saw *O'Donnell, George—503rd Infantry Brigade.*

"Oh, my god, I can't believe it." I sat stunned. "How did he die, do you know?"

"I heard they were overrun one night," Fuqua said.

"Damn it!" I shouted. I hung my head and stared at the ground.

"Were was that?" I asked after a moment.

"I don't know, man," Fuqua shrugged.

I smoked a cigarette and tried to keep up my end of the conversation with him but in my mind I saw O'Donnell's face, his smile, his way of talking—but I didn't cry. How could I not cry? O'Donnell, I loved the guy. I was screwed up inside. I could see that now. I couldn't cry for anyone but myself.

Fuqua shook my hand, "I've got to go," he said. "Take care of yourself, Gebhart."

I sat dumbly looking out at the Bien Hoa buildings and fields, quietly grieving for O'Donnell.

The next morning I rose early, shaved, put on my khaki dress uniform, had breakfast and returned to the barracks to get my duffel bag. I put it among a pile of others outside then lit a cigarette and waited inside the barracks. At 9 o'clock, with sixty other excited men, I boarded a green army bus and rode to the airstrip. We waited in an empty Quonset hut right off the runway.

Other soldiers came on other buses and joined us; about eleven o'clock a commercial jet flew in and the Quonset hut shook as it roared by. The plane turned at the end of the runway and taxied back. Stairs were rolled over to let the passengers off and I stood in the open doorway and watched the new recruits experience their first blast of heat and the smell of Vietnam. Their eyes were wide open, taking in everything at once. This was the first day of their tour; some wouldn't go home and they knew it.

"Welcome to Vietnam," I said under my breath, "and good luck to each of you."

We boarded the plane and I found a seat halfway back. The plane was humid and smelled from the body odor of nervous men who hadn't showered in two days. The doors closed and we taxied away from the Quonset hut. The last man in hadn't found a seat yet when the pilot accelerated around the corner onto the straightaway. The plane lifted off and we all cheered.

We cheered again eighteen hours later when the tires touched the ground at Travis Air Force Base in California. It was the middle of the night and floodlights lit up the airfield. I walked down the stairs and across the cement tarmac to the single-story terminal building. I wanted to kiss the ground just like the GIs did when they arrived back in the States after World War II. Oh My Lord, it felt *good* to be home. "The Stars and Stripes Forever" played over the public address system and a few Travis personnel stopped their work to watch us walk through the building.

We loaded onto buses and drove on empty freeways to Treasure Island. Paved highways and streetlights, it all looked solid and rich.

Half past midnight we arrived at Treasure Island and a young lieutenant read roll call then gave us a choice: we could go to sleep and process out later in the day or process out right then. We formed a line, not one man chose to delay his freedom.

We went as a group through medical examinations, equipment paperwork, orders paperwork; paperwork, paperwork and more paperwork. Most of the men would have to report to a stateside base after thirty days leave. I had spent a year stateside already before my year in Nam so I was processing out of the army and each station brought me closer to the freedom I longed for.

It was 4 a.m. when I reached the last clerk. He had a crew cut and polished boots but needed a shave. He looked through my file; everything seemed to be in order and he began to type my discharge papers then stopped after just two entries. "I've run out of ribbon," he looked up and said.

"Well, go get another one," I said.

"I can't," he said, holding both palms up. "Supply is closed until oh-eight-hundred."

I studied him. His eyes told me he wasn't messing with me. "Try running the ribbon back," I said.

"I've been doing that all night," he said. He pulled the form out of the typewriter and handed it to me. "Here, look. This is how it comes out."

He was right. I could hardly read the two words he had typed. "Looks fine to me," I said handing it back. "Keep on typing."

The clerk did too, hitting each key HARD so something would show on the form.

I took the discharge papers and my duffel bag to the payphones. It was just after 7 a.m. in New Jersey. The phone rang a dozen times but I didn't care if I woke her.

"Hello?" she said quietly.

"Hi, it's me!"

"Paul!" Mary shouted. "Where are you?"

"I'm home, honey, in Oakland. I'm out. I mean O-U-T, OUT. I'm a civilian!"

She screamed with delight and started to cry. She put the baby on the phone and Nadine made noises for me. Tears came to my eyes.

"Why don't you and the baby meet me in San Francisco?" I said after I got my voice back. "Then we'll fly to New Jersey together after a week in California."

"That's a great idea," she said. "I'll make the reservations. Call me from your hotel."

"Okay, I will. I want to call my parents now."

"Good, I'll talk to you in a little while. I love you." I heard Mary kissing into the phone.

"I love you too," I said.

Both my parents were home and both cried when they heard my voice. I told them of our plans and they agreed it was a good idea. After a quick shower and shave, I put on a new dress uniform and went outside to get a cab into San Francisco. I walked up the line of yellow taxis outside of headquarters. The cab driver in the first cab came out to help me with my duffel bag. He had light brown skin and an honest smile.

"Congratulations, man and welcome home," he said.

"Thanks," I said. "How are you doing?"

"Doing good, doing good. Where to, the airport?"

"No, I'd like to go into the city and find a decent hotel."

"Sure, we can do that." He swung my duffel bag into the trunk.

Sitting in the back of the cab, I pulled my discharge papers out of my shirt pocket and began to read them as we made our way off Treasure Island and into the Bay Bridge traffic. I noticed that the clerk had listed my military occupation as a Forward Observer.

"They can't get anything right," I said.

"Huh," the cab driver said.

"They have me down as a forward observer in the artillery," I said. "I never did that. How the hell did he come up with that?"

The cabby looked at me in the rearview mirror.

"You're infantry, right?" he asked.

He had recognized my infantry combat badge and Vietnam ribbon.

"Yeah," I said.

"Well, maybe you were observing."

I thought for a moment, got his point and looked at him in the mirror.

"Yeah, maybe I was," I said.

I checked into a downtown hotel and went up to a room with a good view of the city. I turned on the television and lay down on the bed and laughed. "I'm back in the World! Thank You, Lord. Thank You, THANK YOU!"

The next day I went to the airport to meet Mary and my six-month old baby daughter. I was early and waited at the gate. I saw dozens of soldiers in dress uniform; tanned faces, headed home after a year in Vietnam.

"United Flight 907 nonstop from Newark," the public address announced, "arriving at gate 35."

My heart beat wildly as I watched the runway. In a few minutes I saw their jet taxi to the gate. A couple of minutes more and people began to come into the terminal. First Class, then coach and Mary holding the baby. I ran over and put my arms around them. We both cried and kissed and held each other tight. I looked into the baby's eyes as Nadine watched us quietly. I smiled at her and she laughed a baby's laugh from deep inside her belly. Mary and I both laughed to hear it. I carried Nadine and Mary took her carry-on bag and we walked slowly to baggage claim, stopping several times to kiss and hold each other.

We spent a week of shopping and sightseeing in San Francisco before we flew as a family to New Jersey. My parents were at the airport to meet us. Mary held the baby as I hugged my mother and father. My dad asked me something but I couldn't talk because of the lump in my throat. His hair had turned completely white and he looked ten years older.

"He hasn't had a full night's sleep for the entire year," my mother said when she saw me look at him. "He'd wake up in the middle of the night and sit in his reading chair in the living room with the lights off thinking about you until dawn." I hugged my father again.

He drove us back to their house and loaned me the car and I took Mary and the baby to her parent's home. Being together again was different than what I had expected. There was a strangeness between us. I couldn't put my finger on it; Mary looked wonderful, her body as tight and firm as ever. She wore just enough makeup to look sophisticated but not so much that you really noticed it. She had cut her long hair into a short, pixie style and she carried herself with quiet dignity. I could see she was a woman now, not the young girl I had left a year ago.

We adored each other but on another level there was a distance between us. Both of us had been through a lot in the past year. We had both had to negotiate difficult times on our own and we each had grown from in but not in the same way.

I loved her and the baby but I felt the pressure of having to provide for them. I didn't want a nine-to-five job. I wanted to go to California and drop out. There was a struggle inside me; I should be responsible and do the right thing but that wasn't what I really wanted.

It was Mary who broached the subject on our second night home together.

"You've changed," she said as we lay in her bedroom with just the dresser light on.

"How?" I asked.

She turned and lay on her side facing me. "You're quiet. You used to joke about everything."

"I still joke," I said.

"Not like before. There's a space between us that wasn't there."

I felt it too, like I said; she was right, I had changed. The truth was I didn't want to get a job and join the rat race. I needed time for me. I didn't know how to explain it to her or where to begin. It was easier whenever the subject came up, to just deny it.

It was months before the newness of being back in civilian life wore off. It took even longer to re-establish my relationship with Mary. Loving each other kept us going but a part of me was empty inside, not even her love touched me there and she felt it. I started to get high again too. I couldn't find opium and smoking marijuana brought back the terror I went through on the patrol outside of Long Binh; I bought heroin instead. Heroin is a love drug; they don't describe it that way but it was for me. Mary and I used it to make the passion last all night long.

We moved to Northern California and I went back to college on the GI bill and worked part time but my occupation was getting high and playing music. Mary surprised me. She turned into a hippie as well and we had a lot of fun but there was a price to pay for my drug problem.

"Everything's got a price," the crewman from the Mary Jane had said in the guard shack at the bridge. He was right.

EPILOGUE
He's My Brother

January 1993

It's twenty-five years since I came home from Vietnam. I'm divorced now. I live by myself in a Spanish style home in the foothills of the San Gabriel Mountains. My house has a panoramic view across eleven canyons and beyond to the Angeles National Forest.

I was enjoying the view from a lounge chair by the pool as my brother Stephen floated on an air mattress. He had a joint in one hand and a can of beer in the other. Stevie Ray Vaughan's, *May I Have A Little Talk With You* played on the radio.

"It's a perfect southern California day," the radio announcer's voice came on. "Seventy-six degrees and clear blue skies. On the horizon I can see the mountains they're still edged in snow from the storm that passed through two days ago. It's Saturday, January 23rd, 1993, and the beaches are packed. It's fiesta time, Amigos!"

The portable telephone rang and I reached for it. "Hey Steve, Stevie!" I called to my brother. "Lower the radio."

Stephen balanced the joint and beer in one hand and paddled to the radio with the other. "This is Paul," I said.

"Paul, this is Train."

"Hey, Train. How was New Orleans?"

"Nor-lins, brother."

"Yeah, right, Nor-lins. It was a good gig?"

"Yeah, very cool, but the money should have been better."

"I got you a third more than what they opened with," I said.

"Paul, man, listen. I need you to find me a hotel in Miami."

"I'm your agent, Train, not your travel agent. Why don't you just call yourself?"

295

"I don't know any places there." His hoarse voice groveled over the phone.

"Come on, man," I said. "I thought we agreed you wouldn't ever ask me again."

"Unless it was an emergency."

"This isn't an emergency, Train."

"It is. I don't know any place there. I'll book myself into a third world smuggler's den. I need you to do this for me."

I laughed. "Even if there was a shootout, it wouldn't wake you. I know how you sleep. Listen, call me next week at the office. I think that Seattle concert is going to happen and for the price we wanted. I've got to go now, okay? I have company."

I hung up. "He thinks for my ten percent I should do everything for him."

"That Train Bickers?" Stephen asked.

"Yeah."

"He can play a sax though."

"He plays as easily as you and I talk, sure, but still, he never says, 'Thanks, you did a good job.'"

The telephone rang again. I picked it up with an attitude. "Yeah?"

"Hi, Paul, this is Rojas."

"Hey, hey, Rojas!"

"Paul, you're not going to believe it but I think I found Delino." Rojas spoke with a slight stutter.

"Really?" I said. "How?"

I listened as he told me a story of a chance meeting with a friend of a friend who had worked with Delino.

"Man, this is great," I said. "You found him!"

"Well, I'm not sure," Rojas said, "but I think so. I gave them my number to give to him."

"What do you mean you don't know? This guy's name is Tony Delino, right?"

"Yeah."

"Okay, and this Tony Delino was in Vietnam, right?"

"Yeah."

"So how many Tony Delinos do you think were over there anyway? I'm telling you, you found him. Listen, after you talk to him give him my number, or get his telephone number for me, okay?"

"Yeah, of course."

"Okay, you take care, Rojas. I'll talk to you soon." I clicked off the remote phone and called to my brother. "Steve, it could be that we finally found my old squad leader."

"That would be great." Stephen floated on the air mattress soaking in the sun like a seal on a rock. "You haven't heard from him in twenty years?"

"That's right," I said. "January 1968. Can you believe it's been that long? It seems like yesterday. Remember when I called from Sydney and asked you to get me money so I could go to Paris?"

"Yeah, I remember. I still feel bad..."

"Nah, don't. You did the right thing," I said.

"But if you would have died," Stephen said, "I would have been crazy the rest of my life thinking I should have gotten you the money and helped you go AWOL. Nobody—I mean nobody—wanted you home more than me after that."

I laughed. "Well, there was one person."

We barbecued chicken, then Stephen left and I sat at the table outside and watched the colors change on the mountains. I thought about Tony Delino. Rojas and I had searched for him for years. I had thumbed through telephone books in Colorado and Arizona while Rojas did the same thing when he was in New Mexico and Texas, but we never found a trace of him.

I waited by the phone. Eight o'clock came, then eight-thirty, then nine o'clock; finally it rang.

"Hey, hey," Rojas said. I could tell by his voice that he had spoken to Delino.

"It was him, wasn't it?" I said.

"Yeah, it really was."

"How is he?"

"He's good, same old Tony. He lives outside of Albuquerque. He's a foreman for a construction company."

"I'll bet he's a hell of a foreman too."

"You know that guy that is a friend of my friend?" Rojas asked.

"Yeah."

"The day after I spoke with him he drove an hour to go to the construction site where Tony worked."

"That was nice of him."

"Yeah. So, he sees him walking across the yard and says, 'Hey Tony, there's a guy named Rafael...' and before he could finish the sentence Delino says, 'Rojas, here give me that.' And he took the paper from the guy's hand."

"He was happy?"

"Oh yeah, he was so excited he could hardly talk."

"Him? I haven't heard you sound this happy since Emanuel was born."

I wrote down Delino's number but after I hung up with Rojas, I paced the floor thinking of what to say, then I laughed. It didn't matter what we talked about; just knowing he was okay was enough.

"Hello?" Delino answered.

"This is Cloud Six calling Oscar base."

"Gebhart, goddamn! How are you, guy?"

"I'm good, man. How's the world been treating you?"

"Terrific, I can hardly believe it. It feels like I've just found two brothers after twenty-five years."

"You're right," I said. "It feels exactly like that."

"Whenever Rojas and me were together," I said, "there was always an empty spot because you weren't with us. I'd lift my glass and say, 'This one's for Tony' and we'd toast the empty chair."

"I thought a lot about you too," Delino said. "Wondering where you guys were and how you were doing. When I first got home, I wanted to go back to Vietnam to get my boys."

"You nuts?" I said. "Man, I never wanted to go back."

"Yeah, but I left just when Tet started, I was in Bien Hoa when the shit hit the fan and I felt like I should go back out to the field to help you guys out."

"You missed some shit, I said, "but it wasn't as bad as Loc Ninh.

You had what, seven-hundred body count in three days of fighting?"

"Yeah, something like that. Well, we're not going to lose each other this time," he said. "You guys are my brothers. I want you to know that anytime you need something, you come to me."

"Thanks, Tony."

"So tell me, are you married? Got any kids?"

"I'm divorced," I said. "I have a boy and a girl. How about you?"

"I'm divorced too," Delino said. "We have three girls and a boy."

"Really, that's great. How old are they?"

"My oldest daughter, Jean, is 26, then Sharon, she's 24, then Christine is 18, and Tony Junior is 15. How old are yours?"

"Nadine is 24 and Joshua is 20."

"You living with anyone?" Delino asked.

"I did up until a couple of months ago," I said.

"I've been living with a lady named Peggy for five years," Delino said. "We own a house together."

"The kids live with your ex?" I asked.

"No, no, after the divorce all the kids stayed with me."

"Really, how come?"

"They wanted to. She left and the kids wanted to stay home." Delino paused. "So how have you been? Rojas tells me you're a famous agent."

"No, no. I'm a music agent, mostly jazz musicians but I'm not famous or anything. I get by and I don't punch a time clock."

"You got home okay?" Delino asked. "What have you been through? How come you got divorced?"

"I came home unscratched except for a bad problem with drugs. That's what messed my marriage up."

"You're clean now though?"

"Oh yeah. I lost my home, my kids and my wife over that stuff. I hit bottom and I couldn't blame anyone but myself. I went and got help. It's been years since I've gotten high."

"Good. I knew you would be okay," Delino said. "If you could make it through Vietnam you can pull through anything."

After the call I watched television and paid my bills but my mind was in Vietnam. Later that evening while I showered I saw Doc Stevens lying on the poncho in the small clearing. I saw the bullet wound in his neck and remembered the waxy death stare. The pink of his muscles showing in the sun. In my mind I heard him explain why he wouldn't carry a weapon. I began to cry. I saw Jeffrey Collins laying against Lieutenant Truck's shoulder and Monk's face and O'Donnell's and all the sadness I felt deep down flowed out of me. I sobbed so hard I had to lean against the shower wall to support myself. The release of these long-held-back tears opened something up inside my mind too. I began to have a lot of Vietnam flashbacks so I put a tape recorder in my car and recorded the memories that flooded into my consciousness. From those recordings, I began to write about my experience.

One evening, I called Delino from my office and read some of it to him.

"Selma Alabama, Saigon—Bien Hoa,
Dr. Martin Luther King—The Ku Klux Klan,
Napalm—Vietnam,
They choppered us in but we had to hump out again.
Sit-Ins, Love-Ins, digging in,
Mekon Delta, Monsoon Rain,
Sergeant Pepper, Otis Redding,
Green Berets,
Teagirls, gunships, Catching clap.
I've six months in and it's getting old.
Bid Whist, Tet, five-card poker
Mortar rounds! Ground Attack!
Soaking wet, Tropical Heat—cold hard ground
Hand grenades, smoky-haze Vietnam.
The brother didn't make it but I've got to get me back from Vietnam."

"I know it sounds crazy but that's how it is inside me, memories and remembering the frustration I felt because wrong seemed to be winning everywhere I looked. Still, I'm proud of my generation. We changed the world. Yeah, even the guys who went to 'Nam. Maybe especially them. We were on the line and lived together without walls, in the jungle, camping out. We shared everything and all of us afraid of dying. We got to a place where the color of your skin or your religion just didn't matter. We pulled together as Americans. What did that mean to us? For the guys I was with it meant doing the right thing and treating people the way you wanted to be treated. We knew the war was wrong; you could see that pretty easy. The Vietnamese had a cause and they fought bravely to win their freedom. Our cause was making it back home so if Charlie came to kill us, we matched his bravery

with our own but winning our freedom would have to wait until we got back to America."

"That's good, stuff, Paul," Delino said. "You really got it right."

"Thanks, Tony. I'd like to write a book so people would understand that it wasn't like they see in the movies."

"They can't make it real," Delino said.

"But people think those films are the way it was and it wasn't like that. We weren't baby killers. *Apocalypse Now* is a jerk-off fantasy and *Platoon* is all Hollywood bullshit. How many guys do you think had running gun battles with men in their squad?"

"All bullshit," Delino agreed, "but they've got to sell tickets."

"Yeah," I said, "but they make it like the American soldiers were all baby killers and rapists. Shit, Vietnam's economy half ran on providing sex to GIs. How many guys raped anyone? We never burned any villages either. Did you ever burn down a village before I came over?"

"No," Delino said. "I think that stuff happened up north."

"But people think we *all* burned villages. I tell you I never saw a Vietnamese kid crying. Everywhere we went, the kids ran up to us laughing and asking for money, food or cigarettes and we gave it to them."

"That's true," Delino said.

"We had our share of tragedy," I said. "I'm not saying the war was a good thing. It wasn't, but I think for the most part at least the men I knew tried to keep the American GI tradition. We tried to make our fathers proud of us."

"It was the wrong war for that," Delino said.

"Yeah, it sucked, but nothing except the Civil War has changed this country as much and for the better too. The government just can't do business like it did before Vietnam."

"But it was wrong," Delino said. "That's why nothing about the war will ever be considered good or helpful. It just won't ever happen."

As we spoke I saw the two dead Vietnamese men on the bloodstained road in Saigon. I thought of Jeffrey Collins and pictured his parents and little sisters getting the news and how hard it must have been for them living in the house after that. I stood up from my desk and looked out my office window. Through my tears, I saw the bleary red and white lights from the evening traffic. I had a lump in my throat and couldn't speak. For his part, Delino stayed on the line and let me gather myself. We both listened to the silence.

"Over twenty years later and I'm just now crying over their deaths," I said when I got my voice back.

"That's how we got through it, man," Delino said. "We bottled it up."

"Yeah," I said. "I'm just realizing how full of tears I've been."

"When are you coming out to see me?" Delino asked.

"Rojas has his Albuquerque seminar confirmed for March," I said. "I'll make arrangements and meet you both there."

"Okay, that's great. You take care, guy, and remember you're my brother. If you need to talk, you call me, right?"

"Yeah, Tony, thanks."

"I'll see you soon then."

"Yeah, I can't wait," I said and I really meant it.

On a Friday five weeks later I flew out of Burbank to reach Albuquerque at 4:30 in the afternoon. I walked into the terminal and recognized Delino despite the fact that his hair was past his shoulders. His face was ruddier and he moved slower too but he talked the same way and he still had that funny ear-to-ear grin. We shook hands then awkwardly hugged.

On the way to the baggage claim Delino said, "I've been hardly able to sleep just thinking about seeing you again. I'm worried that I'll say the wrong thing or that you won't like me."

"Nah, Tony, it's great seeing you," I said. "C'mon, let's get my bag."

I tried to laugh it off but I realized he was right. I felt the same way. People change; what if we didn't like each other? What if I said something out of place? I felt tight and was weighing my words.

On the drive out to the suburbs of Albuquerque there were long pauses that neither of us tried to fill. Delino pulled into a Best Western hotel and we went into the bar to wait for Rojas. I ordered two beers from the cocktail waitress and we sat at a table and drank them slowly. I reminded Delino about Emery and Mack Moore, Gardner and Charles.

"Don't you remember Yokum and Donny Langford?" he asked.

"Why yes I do," I said, "now that you mention it. Of course. Yokum was that small guy from Oklahoma. He was a funny dude too and always laughing at people."

"You do remember. Yeah, Yokum was small but he never backed down. He was always there when we were getting hit too. You didn't have to go find him."

"Yeah, I remember, and Donny Langford too. I can picture him, good-looking guy about our size. Sure, I remember. He was from Tennessee, right?"

"No, but close. Kentucky."
"That's right, that's right, Donny Langford. He was an old head when I came into country. All those guys left about when you did."

"That's right. We all came over together."

At 6pm I saw Rojas come into the bar. He excused himself from his associates and walked to our table. I gave him a bear hug and Tony did the same.

In the seven months since I had last seen him, Rojas had let his hair grow long.

"Hey, you two guys look like the hippies now," I said, "and here I am the one with the short hair!" It struck me that Rojas, his long black hair streaked with gray, looked more like an Apache warrior than ever.

"I'm buying you guys a drink. Three tequilas," I called to the waitress, "and three beer chasers, Millers."

When she brought the drinks, I lifted mine and said, "Well, here's to Delino's Squad." We clinked glasses and drank the shots down then sipped our beers as we talked about Loc Ninh and the people in Bravo Company.

"Look at us," Delino said. "This is great. We always imagined that someday we would be back in the World enjoying a simple drink together out of harm's way."

"Twenty-six years, can you believe it?" I said. "We all thought that after 'Nam nothing could get us down but we've all had marriages that ended up as battles. I'm divorced and alone. Rojas is working on wife number two and you too, Tony."

"Must be a Vietnam syndrome," Delino said.

"I blame mine on the drugs," I said, "but what happened to your marriages?"

"Like you say," Rojas said, "they turned into battles."

After two more rounds we left the hotel and Delino drove us to a steak and ribs place where we ordered dinner and drinks.

"What do you do around here for fun?" I asked.

"There's plenty to do," Delino said. "I know a good country western dance hall. There'll be a hundred cowgirls two-stepping."

"Okay, I'm for giving it a try," I said.

"What? Two stepping?" Delino looked surprised.

"No. Hell-no. Going to see the girls," I said.

"Okay, we'll go right after dinner," Rojas said.

During dinner all three of us were back in the jungles opening C rations as we savored the good cut of steak on the table before us. After dinner we drove to the big dance hall and stood at the rail with tequila shots in hand.

"Hey, that one just smiled at you." Delino tapped me on the arm as we watched them go around and round.

"Yeah?" I said.

"I don't know how it is in California," he said, "but out here when they smile, it means they're interested."

I laughed, "Yeah, same in California."

We had two more tequilas and three more beers but no luck with the cowgirls so we decided to go back to the hotel and call it a night. Delino pulled his white Chevy pickup out of the parking lot and Rojas told him, "Turn left."

Delino said, "No" and went right. After a couple of hundred yards he admitted he was wrong, pulled over to the side of the road and did a U-turn. A police car immediately came up behind us with its lights flashing.

"Oh shit," I said.

A big cop with a blond crew cut came up to the driver's door. His partner covered Rojas and me from the right fender. Delino rolled down the window.

"Let me see your license and registration, please," the officer said.

Delino handed him the papers.

"You been drinking tonight, Mr. Delino?"

"They just saw us leave the bar," I whispered to Rojas. "He knows damn well Mr. Delino has been drinking."

"Yeah, I had a few beers," Delino said.

"A few beers," the cop repeated. "Step out of the car, please."

Delino went behind the truck and the cop tested him: finger to nose, walk the straight line and finally a breath test. I heard the officer say, "Okay, turn around and put your hands behind your back."

"Christ, Jesus," I said.

"This isn't good," Rojas agreed.

"That's what I like about you, Rojas," I said, "the way you size up a situation."

We laughed but stopped when the police officer came back. He leaned against the car door and put his head through the window and asked, "Have you both been drinking too?"

"Well, yeah," I said, "but I'm okay, I can drive. Where are you taking Delino?"

"Where can we bail him out?" Rojas asked.

"Let's see if you're legal first," the officer said and handed Rojas the breathalyzer. He blew into it and the cop read it and shook his head, "Point oh nine. That's no good. You can't drive."

He handed it to me. The officer shook his head again, "No, you're point oh eight, I can't let you either of you drive."

"How do we get the truck home then?" I asked.

"We'll get it towed for you."

"Our hotel's just there." Rojas pointed across the street. The officer looked across the highway then back at us.

"Why did you guys drive in the first place?" he asked.

"We went out to eat first, but you're right," Rojas said, "we should have dropped off the truck and walked to the night club."

"I can't let you drive," he repeated. "We'll have you towed to the hotel."

"Where can we find our friend?" I asked again.

"Which precinct?" Rojas asked.

"We're going to take him to a detox center instead of jail. He's lucky, this way he won't be booked. We're doing him a favor, keeping it off his record. He'll stay in detox until he's point zero-zero then you can get him."

"Which detox center?" Rojas asked.

"Here." He handed Rojas a sheet of paper with addresses and telephone numbers. "You can call this central number and find out where he is and when he'll be ready to be released. There's a detox place just a few miles from here. He'll probably be there."

"Thanks," Rojas said.

The officers waited until the tow truck showed up. A big, Afro-American man hooked up Delino's truck.

"We're just going over there," Rojas said to him.

"Huh? You guys got busted across the street from your hotel?"

"Yeah," I said. "Not much we can do about it now, but Tony's in cuffs and he's getting locked up."

"Just look at it as a new memory," Rojas said.

"This one's gonna cost Tony cash," I said. "He'll have DUI charges and attorney fees to fight it."

"We'll chip in," Rojas said.

"Absolutely," I agreed. "We'll split it three ways."

The tow operator towed us across the street and unhooked us.

"It's still sixty-five dollars," he said, "because that's the minimum."

Rojas and I split the bill and walked across the parking lot to a Denny's to have breakfast. It was 2 a.m. when we made it to the hotel.

"Let's get some sleep and call for Tony in the morning," Rojas said.

"Okay," I said. "Whoever gets up first calls the other guy."

I got out on the ninth floor; Rojas went up to eleven.

Eight the next morning I rang Rojas' room. "Good morning," I said.

"Morning, Paul. How do you feel?"

"Hung over. Did you find out where he's being held?"

"Yeah," Rojas said, "somehow he ended up at a center in downtown Albuquerque."

"Aren't we on the outskirts of Albuquerque?"

"Yeah, maybe twenty miles from downtown," Rojas said.

"Why would they take him downtown? I thought he said there was a detox place a couple of miles away."

"Yeah, that's right," Rojas said. "I don't know why they put him downtown."

"Did you talk to him?"

"They won't let him come to the phone. They told me he can call out and get released when he's point oh-oh."

"Listen," I said, "I'm still seeing colors when I close my eyes. That tequila got us good. Tony's not going to be point oh-oh until tonight!"

"Let's just go back to bed then," Rojas said, "I'm not feeling too good myself."

"Okay, we'll talk in the afternoon."

Sometime after 1 p.m. I showered and shaved and called Rojas' room. "Well, can he get out yet?" I asked.

"No," Rojas said, "they said he's not point oh-oh yet. Let's go get something to eat."

"Okay, I'll come up."

I grabbed my carry-on suitcase and took the elevator and knocked on Rojas' door. He let me in and I sat on the bed and watched the sports news on television while he shaved.

Rojas stuck his head out of the bathroom, "I think we should just go down there and break him out."

"Yeah, right," I said. "Brilliant idea."

There was a knock at the door.

"Who the heck is that?" I asked.

Rojas opened the door and Delino and a woman in her late thirties with short black hair came into the room.

"Hey, hey," Rojas greeted them.

"Hey, Tony!" I called.

"Hey," Delino said with a sheepish grin. "This is my lady, Peggy. Peggy, Rafael Rojas and Paul Gebhart."

I waved to Peggy and asked Delino, "When did you get out? They kept telling Rojas you couldn't be released."

"I just called," Rojas said. "They said you were still there but couldn't come to the phone."

"Those idiots," Delino said. "I got out an hour ago. I called Peggy and she came and picked me up."

"How did you end up downtown anyway?" Rojas asked.

"Those bastards put me in a van and rode me all over Albuquerque while they collected other drunks. They didn't check me into the detox center until five-thirty this morning."

"But they busted you about twelve-thirty!" I said.

"I know," Delino said. "Hell, after riding in the back of that cold van for five hours by the time they put me in the center downtown I was cold sober!"

"Well, at least they didn't book you. Look at the bright side," I said.

"Shit," Delino said, "I would have been better off."

"Huh? What do you mean?" I asked.

"That detox center charged me $300 and they still have me on a DUI. If I had gone to jail, I wouldn't have had to pay rent on the place."

"Shit," I said, "I see your point. "They got you good, the bastards. They told us they were doing you a favor."

"Some favor," Delino said, "but I don't care. I've been in the jungles; this is child's play. Still, that place stunk."

"Huh? What are you talking about?" I asked.

"Man, detox is filled with all of these drunks with puke all over them and breath that can knock down insects."

"That's what they said about you," I joked. "Glad that smelly mutha-ffer is gone. Excuse my French," I said to Peggy.

"You getting hungry?" Rojas asked.

"We can go to lunch," Delino said, "but Peggy's got to get to work."

"Where do you work?" Rojas asked her.

"I'm a nurse at the county hospital."

"I called her this morning," Delino said, "to tell her where I was and to come and get me. When we got to her car she had a brown paper bag and she said to me, `I brought you coffee, orange juice and a beer.'"

"Now that's a good woman," I said.

"Hell yes," Rojas agreed.

"So which one did you drink first?" I was curious.

"The coffee, then the juice and then the beer."

I nodded. "Yeah, that's how I would have done it too."

Peggy excused herself and left to go to work. I grabbed my black carry-on bag and followed her into the hallway.

"Peggy," I called to her. She turned and I took out a rolled up plastic banner and handed it to her. "I had this made up," I said. "Can you hang it in the house so he'll see it when we get there?"

"Sure." Peggy smiled. "I won't be home until nine tonight but I'll make sure the kids put it up."

I went back into Rojas' room. He and Delino were laughing.

"They assigned me a bed in the dry-out room," Delino said, "but I stayed in the recreation room the whole time."

"They have one big room full of beds?" I asked.

Delino looked puzzled. "Yeah," he said, "it's one big room and it smells bad, Paul. People are puking and yelling and burping and farting..."

"Okay," I held up my hand, "I get the picture."

"I put four folding chairs in the corner of the rec room," he said, "and watched TV all morning. But don't you know every ten minutes some drunk comes over and wants to take one of my chairs. There are fifty other empty chairs but they won't leave me alone. I told this one guy, 'Listen motherfucker, these are my goddamn chairs—yeah, all fucking four of them—so get the fuck out of my face.'"

We laughed.

"I was worried about you, man," I said. "I really was. But Rojas, he says, 'It's just a new memory.'"

Delino laughed. "Yeah, my night at the exclusive Hotel D' Tox."

"Hey," Rojas said, "we stay at the Best Western and this guy goes to a three-hundred-a-night place."

"Speaking about living high," Delino said, "let's go get something to eat. I'm starved."

After I checked out of the hotel, Delino drove us to a good Mexican restaurant. We found a table by the window and after the waitress took our orders I showed them photographs I had in my carry-on bag. "We didn't take many pictures," I said as they looked through them. "Seems now I should have taken a lot more."

"We didn't want to hump the camera stuff around," Delino said.

"Sergeant Bell gave me his camera the day they medevaced him out," Rojas said. "A lot of these pictures that Gebhart has are ones that I took with his camera."

"Yeah?" I said. "They must be because I didn't have a camera. I didn't take any pictures except these here." I showed Delino old, yellowed Polaroids. "That's down by the water plant near Saigon," I said. "We were there after you two went home. I remember the day we shot these." I tapped on one of the Polaroids. The photograph showed a group of us hanging out while soul music played on the radio. Mack Moore took the photo, I remembered. I looked closer to see the faces. There was Serena and Desusa, Toby and another rifleman from Mike. I couldn't remember his name but I recognized Martinez. He stood like a matador, tall and proud. He held a joint in each hand and had a smile on his handsome face. "Remember Romero Martinez?" I asked. "He was killed just days after these were taken."

"I do remember Martinez," Delino said. "He was in Lima. A hell of a soldier too."

"Yes he was," I said. There was an awkward silence as Rojas and Delino pictured Martinez in their minds.

"Nowadays," I said, "they have all kinds of cameras with them when they go to war. Like in the Gulf, one guy would say to his buddy, 'Okay you fight and I'll take the video.'"

Delino laughed, "That's right."

"And how come we didn't get everyone's address," I asked, "so we could all stay in touch? I'd love to see Emery and Mack Moore. And remember Carter? Wouldn't it be cool to get everyone together?"

"Hell, yes," Delino agreed, "and how about Captain Allen? Gebhart's right, we should have tried to stay in touch."

"I really feel bad about that," I said. "How come I didn't think of it? I came home and went on with my life and here I had just made some of the closest friends I'll ever have."

"It was the times, Paul," Rojas said. "Vietnam, you came home and nobody wanted to hear about what you'd been through. You weren't a hero like in the Gulf war. When those men came home everybody was proud of them and what they did."

"Yeah, you're right," I said.

"We all just wanted to go on with our lives and forget it," Rojas said. "We were all young too. Young guys don't think about stuff like that. We didn't think about how we'd feel when we got to middle age."

"That's it too," I agreed. "Still, it hurts to think I've lost such great friends."

"That's right," Delino said. "When I heard your voices, I mean, man, I started to cry. It was like brothers dead twenty years had been brought back to me. Maybe we can find some more guys. Have you tried information?"

"Yeah, they even have these programs now with the national white pages and I did call every Earl Emery in the damn country but he isn't listed. Same thing with Mack Moore. Shit, same as you, Tony. Your number isn't listed either. How come Vietnam vets all have unlisted numbers?"

"We're concerned that the North Vietnamese are going to come over and look us up," Delino laughed.

After lunch, he drove us to a little town north of Albuquerque. He parked in front of a single-family brick home. Flowerbeds lined the cement walk to the front door. A boxer puppy jumped up and down behind a chain link fence in the backyard, barking his hello.

"Nice place you got here, Tony," I said.

"Peggy and I do what we can."

The air was crisp and a light snow began to fall. "I haven't been in snow," I said, "in... in, well... it's got to be three years."

"This is a late storm." Delino stopped to look west across the flat landscape to the dark storm clouds moving in.

I shivered in my light jacket. "Let's get inside," I said. Delino opened the glass storm door, unlocked the front door, and held it open for us. The entrance way had a white iron banister overlooking the sunken living room on the left, past the banister were two carpeted steps into the living room. Straight ahead, above the kitchen door, a six-foot long plastic banner with foot-high black letters spelled out:

Delino's Squad, Bravo Company, 1st Bn, 10th Inf, 1st Div

"Hey, how did that get there?" Delino asked.

"I gave it to Peggy this morning," I said.

"This is great, just great," Delino laughed as a young woman came from the right hallway into the living room. Her hair was teased and she wore dark lipstick and eye shadow.

"Christine, these are my friends, my brothers." Delino introduced us to his youngest daughter. She smiled and said hi as she went to the living room window.

"It's snowing," I said.

"She's not worried about the weather," Delino said. "She's looking for her new boyfriend."

"He's not my boyfriend," Christine said from the window.

"Yeah, well whoever he is, he'd better stop cruising the neighborhood. I'm getting tired of him peeling rubber. Tell him to come to the front door and ask for you like a man."

Christine didn't answer, but Rojas and I laughed.

"Say, Papa, daughters will keep you on your toes, huh?" Rojas said.

"Yeah." Delino smiled. "She's in season."

We hung up our coats and Rojas and I sat on the long couch by the front windows while Delino went to the kitchen for beers.

"Where are those pictures you said you had," I asked him when he came back and handed me a Bud.

Delino dug into a drawer in the stereo cabinet and pulled out two photo albums. I put one on my lap and slowly turned the pages.

"That's Joan," Delino pointed to a picture of his first wife. "She's the mother of my four children. God bless her, I love her, but we just couldn't live together anymore."

"These pictures of the grandchildren?" I asked.

"Yeah, I have two. That's my oldest daughter, Jean. She has a five-year-old daughter. The next oldest, Connie, is married with a three-year-old little girl. The two youngest, Christine and Tony Junior, live at home with me and Peggy."

"Where is Tony Junior?" I asked.

"He went on a fishing trip to Nebraska with one of his buddies," Delino answered.

"Gonna be cold there," I said.

"They don't care about stuff like that," Delino said.

"What? Like being warm and dry?" I asked.

"They'll get a fifth of bourbon and stand out there with all of their rain gear on fishing in the freezing rain."

"God bless young men," I said. "We used to be tough too, remember?"

I turned the pages in the album, stopping to read a citation from the Department of the Army dated November 1967. It was to Sergeant Antonio Delino, a certificate for a Bronze Star. It read: "For conspicuous and continuous bravery in the face of the enemy during the three-day battle in Loc Ninh, Republic of South Vietnam."

"I didn't know you had a Bronze Star," I said. "You must have gotten it just before I came out to the field."

Delino shrugged. "Probably."

"Hey, look!" Rojas pointed to a group of soldiers sitting by sandbags drinking milk from orange and white milk cartons. "There's Charles, Gardner, Jesse and Emery."

"The crew," I said. "I loved them all; great guys. And Emery, now there was a funny man," I said. "Wouldn't it be great to see them again?"

"Yeah," Rojas said. He leaned over to show us more photographs.

"Do you remember Monk?" I asked.

"Yeah, of course," Delino said. "He was the new guy who came into country when we were up in Quon Loi."

"That's right," I said. "You know he got killed just before I came home."

"Sorry to hear that," Delino said.

"It's nice to know someone else remembers these things besides just me." I looked at Rojas.

"I remember when you talk about them," Rojas said.

"That's good," I said.

Delino handed me a second beer. "You haven't changed at all, Gebhart," he said. He patted me on the shoulder and turned to Rojas. "You know I never met anyone else who would tell you just what he thought of you and the situation, not like Gebhart does. And you know what? I think back at all the complaining this young man did, always telling the sergeants and officers why their plans were all screwed up."

Rojas laughed at Delino's description. "But you know what? Heck if he wasn't right most of the time."

"Most of the time?" I said. "Shit, you just needed common sense and that's the one goddamn thing they lacked. In fact, the higher up they go, the less common sense they're required to have."

We spent the afternoon reminiscing about Bravo Company. At six o'clock Delino's two older daughters, Jean and Connie, arrived with their husbands, Richard and Sandival. Both of them were in their mid-twenties. Richard was tall with short black hair and fine facial features. Sandival was short and stocky with large shoulders and arms. The two grandchildren played in the hallway, eyeing the strangers in the sunken living room, while the women went into the kitchen. Rojas and I shook hands with the sons-in-law.

"Hard workers," Delino said. "Both of my girls married hardworking men."

Jean came out of the kitchen and sat with us in the living room. "I remember those army pictures from when I was a little girl," she said. "Now Dad's friends are here looking at them with him."

Her husband Richard looked at the old photographs over my shoulder. "Here," I handed him two pictures. "This is what Tony was like, exactly how I remember him." I pointed to a picture of Delino carrying his M-16; the lieutenant's radio strapped to his back and an ear-to-ear grin on his face. His fatigue shirt buttoned all the way up to his collar.

The other daughters and Sandival joined us in the living room.

"I like this one." Richard showed the women a picture of Delino holding an M-60 machine gun.

Delino nodded his head. "That was a good gun."

"This is you." Richard pointed to a picture, orange from age, of me standing near a personnel carrier in a jungle clearing.

"Look at that muscular, hairless chest," Delino said.

"You were in good shape," Richard said.

"We all were," I said. "We were young men in good shape. That was not a good spot by the way." I tapped the picture. "It was out at the border."

"I remember the day I went home, Gebhart. Do you?" Delino asked.

"Sure I do," I said.

"It was the only time I ever saw you cry." Delino turned to Richard and his daughters. "He walked me to the Chinook and I saw tears in his eyes."

"I got dust in my eye from the chopper," I said.

The girls laughed.

"Was it hard for you to forget Vietnam when you came home?" Jean asked me.

I thought for a moment before answering. "I used to have a recurring nightmare," I said. "I was back in Di An. I was supposed to be on my way home but instead I had re-enlisted for another year. I was on my way back out to the field but I couldn't find my M-16. I was looking for my rifle and feeling that there was no way I could go another year without finally being killed. In the dream I'm standing in Bravo Company's headquarters office and a sergeant is telling me, 'I'm sorry, but you can't change your mind. No, I'm sorry. There's nothing that can be done about it now. You're on the next chopper out. One year with Recon, that's what you signed up for and that's what you're gonna do.'

"I would wake up screaming, pulling myself into consciousness. Sometimes my wife, Mary had to change the sheets because they were wringing wet from my perspiration."

"Now that's a nightmare!" Delino said.

"How about you, Dad? Nightmares too?" Jean asked.

"A couple," Delino said. "I remember we had a sergeant, Sergeant May. The first day at Loc Ninh a Vietnamese grenade was tossed near his foxhole and he dove on it. It blew him up but he saved the other men around him. I dream of that sometimes."

We waited for Rojas to say something. He shrugged. "Nightmares? No, I sleep good every night."

Christine put on *Boot Scootin' Boogie* and danced back to the window to look out through the curtains.

"So, Christine," I called to her, "where's the action around here? Where do you go for fun?"

"Not around here," she said. "You've got to drive down to Juarez."

"Juarez?" I said. "What, you mean down in Mexico?"

"Yeah, that's where it's going on."

"God, Juarez has to be what, a day's drive from here?"

"You can do it in ten hours or so if you take the shortcuts," Richard put in. "Juarez on Friday and Saturday nights? It's party time."

"They get stewed, screwed and tattooed," Delino said and we all laughed.

Peggy came home later and the women cooked a big dinner. The grandkids ran around the house and we drank beer with the sons-in-law and talked war stories. After dinner we decided to go to what Delino called the "lawn-jay."

"Fine French dining?" I asked.

"Neighborhood corner lounge," Christine answered for him.

The baby-sitter came over and we packed into three cars and the entire crew minus two grandchildren went off to Eddie and Al's. It was dark inside the lounge when we walked in. Behind the long wooden bar a large man with a full mountain beard was doing the pouring.

"Hi, Al." Delino waved as our entourage came through the door. Al grinned and said hello to each of us. There were a dozen people sitting at the bar, a few more scattered around at tables and a couple of guys playing eight ball. We put two tables together and ordered beers. Christine asked Delino for five dollars and went over to the jukebox. I watched her reading the menu of CDs. The colored lights illuminated her face and something in her expression put me in mind of Mary.

The beers came and the jukebox played old soul songs mixed in with country western tunes. Every few minutes a friend of Delino's came over to visit. They introduced themselves and shook our hands, happy to meet Delino's Vietnam buddies.

I danced with Christine to Arthea's *Respect*. On our way back to the table, I was startled by a loud crash. An old man with long gray hair tied in a ponytail had fallen off of his barstool. Four or five people dusted him off.

"Man," I said as we got to the table, "that had to hurt."

"That's just Dan," Delino said. "He does that now and then."

"Oh, I see. A practiced flop."

"When he's loaded, he forgets he's sitting on a stool and leans back, like he's at home on the couch," Delino said.

"Somebody should take him home." Jean looked embarrassed.

I settled back down to my own beer just in time for a drunken, middle-aged fellow wearing a red plaid shirt to come over, put his arm around my shoulders, and say in a loud voice meant as a whisper, "You got any dope, brother?"

"No, man..." I began.

"Hey, go away." Delino broke in.

"I was just..."

"You were just disrespecting me and my family," Delino said. "If you come back over, I'm going to lay you out." The drunk backed off. He tried to apologize but Delino motioned with his thumb and said, "Just go."

There was a moment of silence. "Hey, Pop," I said. "Give Christine another five so we can get the music going again."

The party ended at one-thirty. Delino had reserved a room for Rojas and me at the town's only motel. When we were in the room and undressing, Rojas said, "I told him we were going to split the DUI costs but he said no way, he didn't want any money from us."

"We have to find a way to pay our share," I said from the second bed. "It was $300 for the detox center, then it's going to be, what, $500 bucks more for an attorney to fight the DUI, right?"

Rojas nodded, spit out mouthwash into the sink in the bathroom, and said, "That's about right."

"We should put in $250 each and give it to him."

"Well I know one thing." Rojas stuck his head out of the bathroom and smiled.

"What's that?" I asked.

"We can't leave it with Christine!"

"Hell no," I said. "Monday morning she'll stick a ten in Tony's shirt pocket, pat him on the shoulder and say, 'Here, Pop, your buddies left you this. Beer money.'"

Rojas laughed. "Then off to Juarez!"

The next morning Delino picked us up and brought us to the house for Sunday breakfast. I played with his boxer puppy in the backyard while he made eggs, Mexican style with ranchero sauce and tortillas from scratch. Christine and Peggy were there and the two married daughters came over with their families. The breakfast table overflowed with dishes of food.

"This is a feast," I said.

Delino grinned at me as he dished out potatoes and eggs. "You look good in an apron," I said. He laughed. "They love my cooking."

"Me too."

"Well, anytime," Delino said. "You've got a home here now."

After breakfast, Christine went back to bed to sleep until noon; the other daughters left to visit friends and Peggy read a book.

"Hey, let's play some cards," I said.

"Okay," Rojas said.

"We don't have a fourth for whist," I said, "but we can play poker."

"Okay," Delino agreed. "I like poker better anyway. I'll get the cards."

"Do you have chips?" I asked.

Delino stopped and turned around. "No."

"That's okay," I said, "we'll use change."

"That I have."

He came back with a large jar filled with coins.

"Okay, ten dollar buy in," I said. I reached into the jar and counted out quarters, dimes, and nickels.

I had a four o'clock flight so about one-thirty I asked Delino, "How far is it to the airport?"

"What, from here?" he answered without looking up from his hand.

"No," I said, "from New Jersey. Of course, from here. We're here, aren't we?"

"Well from here," Delino laughed, "we're about forty minutes to the airport."

"Okay," I said, "then I think we should leave by two-fifteen or so. I want to be there by three."

"No problem, guy," Delino said. He threw two quarters into the pot and said, "Raise you fifty."

"You draw four then raise me fifty?" I asked.

"Yeah," he said, "you filled me in."

"You wouldn't be bluffing me now, would ya?" I looked back at my two pair.

We finished the last hand at two o'clock and Delino went for his truck keys. Rojas took the opportunity to whisper to me, "I'm going to put the envelope into his pocket when I leave and tell him to open it tonight, that it's from us."

"Okay, that sounds good," I said. "What did you write on it?"

"Nothing," he said.

I took the white envelope Rojas had put on the table and wrote, *You know you're having a bad day when you hear them say, Turn around and put your hands behind your back. Bad-Boy, Bad-Boy.*

Rojas put the envelope in his jacket pocket as Delino came into the room. We brought my bags out to the truck and rode together to the airport.

"I'll park and we'll meet you at the gate," Delino said as I got out at the curb in front of the terminal.

"Nah," I said, "I'm gonna read a book. You guys go enjoy the day." Delino put the truck in Park and he and Rojas got out.

"You take care of yourself," Delino said, "and remember, you have family here. Anytime you need anything, you call me, you hear?"

I shook his hand and hugged him tight then turned to Rojas who hugged me tight.

"Let's plan to meet up this summer," I said.

"San Francisco, my place," Rojas said.

Delino nodded, "Sounds good."

I picked up my bags and headed into the crowd of people moving though the automatic doors. A bit over an hour later I was on the flight back to Burbank. I gazed out at the Albuquerque landscape as the plane taxied down the runway. We rose into the thin New Mexico desert air and I recalled the plane taking off from the Sydney airport on my way back to Vietnam. I wondered how different my life and Mary's would have been if I had deserted and gone to Europe. It was a silly question. Once you pick a path, what could have been doesn't matter.

It was a two-hour flight and an easy ride home on the empty Sunday night freeways. The Malibu lights along my driveway looked inviting but inside, the house was dark and quiet. Without thinking why, I switched on lights in four different rooms and then turned on the television. I tried watching a show but couldn't take all the hard-sell advertising and canned laughter, not after being with real people. I turned off the television and looked out to the lights in the valley below. The silence in the house echoed in my ears.

"No family, no woman," I said to the person people alone sometimes talk to. "Just myself and living by myself is getting harder and harder."

Despite the loneliness, I felt satisfied. God had saved me to write about the men and times from that year's tour of duty. I had fulfilled my destiny and in my heart, I felt a quiet peace, like a balmy Vietnamese evening.

www.ingramcontent.com/pod-product-compliance
Lightning Source LLC
Chambersburg PA
CBHW071200100726
47908CB00002B/455